WHITE CHURCH BLACK MOUNTAIN

THOMAS PAUL BURGESS

LIBRARY WITHDRAWN

D0313983

Copyright © 2015 Thomas Paul Burgess

The moral right of the author has been asserted.

Apart from any fair dealing for the purposes of research or private study,
or criticism or review, as permitted under the Copyright, Designs and Patents
Act 1988, this publication may only be reproduced, stored or transmitted, in
any form or by any means, with the prior permission in writing of the
publishers, or in the case of reprographic reproduction in accordance with
the terms of licences issued by the Copyright Licensing Agency. Enquiries
concerning reproduction outside those terms should be sent to the publishers.

All characters in this publication are fictitious and any resemblance to
real persons, living or dead, is purely coincidental.

Matador
9 Priory Business Park,
Wistow Road, Kibworth Beauchamp,
Leicestershire. LE8 0RX
Tel: (+44) 116 279 2299
Fax: (+44) 116 279 2277
Email: books@troubador.co.uk
Web: www.troubador.co.uk/matador

ISBN 978 1784621 612

British Library Cataloguing in Publication Data.
A catalogue record for this book is available from the British Library.

Printed and bound by CPI Group (UK) Ltd, Croydon, CR0 4YY
Typeset in 11pt Aldine401 BT Roman by Troubador Publishing Ltd, Leicester, UK

Matador is an imprint of Troubador Publishing Ltd

For Mary.

As constant as the Southern Star.

And for my brother.

If anyone saith, "I love God," and hates his brother,
he is a liar; for he who does not love his brother
whom he has seen, cannot love God whom he has
not seen.

1 John 4:20 English Standard Version (ESV)

So we beat on, boats against the current, borne back
ceaselessly into the past.

F. Scott Fitzgerald, *The Great Gatsby*

I was born at the crossing of the white church*
In the shadow of the black mountain.

Where the walls bleed broken bottles
And the barbed-wire binds the fountain.

I grew up with the promise of the chosen,
Shouldered the banners of the certain,

Was cut down by the falseness of prophets,
Abandoned by the truth everlasting.

Laughed in the faces of the fallen,
Was banished to the valley of not knowing.

Mad dogs, King Rats, Butchers,
Sheebeens of wickedness and of self-loathing.

I was born at the crossing of the white church
In the shadow of the black mountain

Where the wild things burn their young
And the sparks rise up to heaven.

---

* Shankill ('Old Church') was otherwise formally 'the church of the white crossing'
(Ecclesia alba de vado).

1

When the smiling anaesthetist leaned over Eban's scrubbed and prepped body, he asked him to count backwards from ten. The anaesthetic pressed down upon him in what felt like a relentless wave of shimmering, chemical subjugation.

A calm voice in his head told him that he was about to die for some short while.

But unlike Elvis, he would never leave the building.

Momentarily, a brief eddy of recent and long passed memories bled together.

But no corridor of light.

No celestial waiting room for him.

Just the clunk and hiss of pumps and tubes.

Pushing thin red lines down drip, up catheter.

Nothingness.

Not fear.

Nor regret.

Nor suffering.

Nor loss

Just void.

Until returning, dulled and sore, perhaps to touch her hand and see her face again.

10
9
8
7

2

The red brick back-yard wall of McGrew's Pub looked daunting to such a small boy.

Looming above him and bristling with broken shards and slivers from the multi-coloured glass of bleach bottles and jam jars.

Cemented deep in there.

Jagging up like shark fins and crooked crocodile teeth.

To repel intruders and ten-year-old misfits in pursuit of lost footballs.

Eban Winston Barnard was eleven.

And fully possessed of his reasons to climb.

3

BELFAST, NORTHERN IRELAND
JANUARY 2014

It was a pattern he had imperceptibly drifted into.

Sitting up alone into the early hours.

Able to do so thanks to the power naps he took in the afternoons in Interview Room C. Left well alone by the junior officers who had noted his routine. If Detective Inspector Dan Watson missed his snooze for some reason, they agreed he was like a zombie with a grudge.

Channel-hopping at 1.30am with the sound down low.

Settling momentarily on *Family Guy*, *Come Dine With Me* or *Amsterdam Nights*, before flicking on. On to God knows what.

Fingering the ice cubes into the tumbler to prevent the telltale clinking in these silent early hours.

Splashing the Bushmills liberally from his hidden cache.

The good stuff.

The bottle 'for guests' still virgin and pristine in the drinks cabinet.

Then up at 5.30am again as usual.

Shave… shit… shower.

Making the effort not to wake Elaine, although both were now used to the futility of this.

Exaggerated sighs of annoyance and duvet-shifting.

A practised choreography of gestures.

The small of his back ached.

Had done for months now.

Not exactly muscular.

At fifty-one years of age, it could simply be his sedentary lifestyle.

Or it could be something much more sinister.

His last routine check-up from Dr Bryant the police GP revealed type 2 diabetes.

He was not alone.

A minor epidemic amongst unfit coppers with fat-roll waistlines and takeaway lifestyles had solicited an avalanche of preventive, self-help pamphlets from Human Resources.

Wankers! More concerned about sick leave than officer welfare, he thought. *Wire-necked pen-pushing middle-management wankers! Creating a little empire for themselves.*

Now he had to attend a diabetes clinic where the nurse asked him to close his eyes and say when he could feel a pinprick on his toes.

The toes were the most vulnerable apparently.

Then the feet themselves.

And perhaps ultimately the leg.

Christ!

Still, he knew that tomorrow he would still have his fried bacon and egg soda farl as usual.

And his massage.

His full body massage.

All above board.

No happy endings here.

He'd been going to Nicola, his regular massage therapist at the Sports Injury Clinic, for years now. He suspected she was a dyke but nevertheless prided himself on his ability to avoid an erection when she brushed against his inner thigh.

Mind over matter.

Even when his back wasn't bothering him, he never missed a session.

He realised that — even if it wasn't sexual — it was the only intimate touching, the only human contact from a woman that he'd had in a very long time.

It depressed the hell out of him so he chose not to think about it in those terms.

A gust of winter gale whistled down the chimney and into the dark, empty fireplace.

The curtains moved a little.

The central heating had long since clicked off.

On TV, two Dutch cops were arresting a punter who refused to pay.

The hooker complained – in subtitles – that his inability to get a hard-on wasn't her fault.

He drained the glass and wondered – was it time?

The tentative climb.

The creaking stairs.

The spare room.

4

"Eban… can I have a quick word please?"

He had been moving stealthily along the landing, head down, damp towel balled under his arm. He had already passed the open bathroom door when she called him back.

Inside Rosemary stood with her hands on her hips, looking down at the toilet bowl disapprovingly.

Emily stood beside her, arms folded across her chest, gnawing on a broken nail. She moved uncomfortably from foot to foot.

"Eban…"

Rosemary's tone as always was that of a boarding school matron; this late-forties career academic without a job. She had begun her thesis at Queen's University on the Apartheid regime in South Africa as a bright young bluestocking and been totally absorbed ever since by the self-righteous liberal authority it seemed to afford her amongst her peers.

Prominent in boycott and fundraising groups, her Arran sweaters, rosy chipmunk cheeks and pageboy haircut rendered Rosemary popular with her immediate circle if somewhat asexual in the eyes of potential suitors.

It was a look that did not improve with age or weight gain.

It seemed to Eban that she resembled nothing less than a demonic Russian doll.

And South African society had a habit of bloody changing,

didn't it, and then wouldn't you know it? – Mandela is released and a democratic election is held and...

It all played merry hell with her conclusions chapter.

Submission dates came and went, and came and went again.

Fees were due.

College and university memberships evaporated.

But still Rosemary beavered away on her magnum opus in the largest bedroom at the rear of the old Victorian detached house in South Belfast.

The corners piled high with dusty folders of newspaper clippings and photocopied journal chapters. All now largely obsolete.

She prosecuted the role of senior tenant – by dint of her longevity in the property – with an unstinting authority and in complete denial of the growing suite of eccentricities that were apparent to all but her.

Now she was pushing the pink toilet rug around the cracking linoleum with the toe of her tartan carpet slipper, a look of disgust on her face.

"Eban, if I've asked you once I've asked you a hundred times. If you insist on shaking, then please wipe the toilet seat after you!"

She looked across at Emily, inviting her to join in the admonishment. "I mean, *really*..."

Emily looked uncomfortable. She bit her nail more earnestly.

A familiar power play in the subtle dynamic of the household's relations was unfolding.

Emily knew that Rosemary was well aware of the on-off dalliances she had enjoyed with Eban over the last two years.

She understood how the other woman, perhaps due to her own frustrations, liked to humiliate them both – individually or better yet, together – when the opportunity arose.

Eban understood this also. "It might have been Pascal!" he blurted out, awkward, embarrassed and defensive.

Emily seemed momentarily emboldened. "Yes, Rosemary – how do you know it wasn't Pascal?"

Rosemary turned slowly to face them both. Her indignation was operatic. "Pascal would *never* do such a thing! Pascal is a *gentleman*."

Pascal Loncle was a PhD History of Art student from Rennes in France who had arrived at Queen's University, Belfast via Trinity College, Dublin. Along with the others he completed the ensemble of 15 Donnybrook Avenue, Belfast 9.

There was no common social area in the house – save for the kitchen – as the entire downstairs floor was partitioned off and owned by a German Lutheran congregation who met twice a week for prayers and hymns.

This meant that the upper house was effectively divided into four bedsits, a kitchen and a bathroom.

Pascal had the room to the front of the house that overlooked the tree-lined thoroughfare and caught all of the splendid afternoon and evening sunshine.

It was always immaculately maintained, the perfect venue for entertaining guests from the many societies he belonged to. Soirées would always feature superior wines, snacks and nibbles whilst the host – an accomplished pianist – for want of a piano, played passable Bach on the viola.

Rosemary – who was from the south of England – adored Pascal, believing ardently that he offered an oasis of culture amongst these 'Hibernio-heathens'.

She pandered to every Gallic shrug, every request he made, often running his bath at weekends and preparing cold suppers for him should he return late from the library.

Rosemary also felt a duty of care toward Emily.

The daughter of schoolteachers – now a schoolteacher

herself – and a fellow Englishwoman from Wolverhampton, Emily's petty bourgeois pretentions played right into the older woman's hands.

Rosemary reserved all her spleen for Eban Barnard, however.

What was a man in his fifties doing living in a communal arrangement such as this?

Surely his civil servant's position could have secured him accommodation amongst his own 'tribe'?

Where was his family?

His home?

What did he have to hide, fraudulently living here amongst the bohemian set and those of a higher intellectual calling?

She was particularly disapproving of his 'arrangement' with Emily and would listen for movement on the stairs as they passed between each other's rooms.

Now she saw yet another opportunity to drive a wedge.

"Thank goodness Pascal is not at home. Frankly Emily, I'm disappointed that you should even consider him…" – she paused, looking for the right word – "…*complicit* in such a thing. And he speaks so highly of you too – and your recorder-playing."

Pascal and Rosemary had been encouraging Emily to pursue an interest in playing madrigals on the recorder.

Pascal – whose strong equine features were not unattractive – naturally practised a well-developed Gallic facility with amorous ambiguity, thus allowing both of the women in the house to perceive subtle advances where none had been made, and to entertain daydreams of accidental sexual encounters, pressed up against his cologned, hard, sinewy firmness on the landing.

"Well…" Emily trailed off, pulling at her lank hair, breaking away from Rosemary's gaze and staring at the ground like an admonished child.

"And just look at state of that lino. Sodden!"

Eban turned on his heel and marched away, closing the door of his room behind him and locking it. He sat on the edge of his unmade bed, detecting a faint whiff of pee from the sheets.

Maybe they were right.

The curse of the uncircumcised.

At fifty-two he had the depressing thought that his room smelled of 'old man'.

Pathetic.

He was not entirely disappointed by Emily's capitulation.

His expectations of her support when challenged by Rosemary were realistically tempered. He knew that he possessed no actual currency that the other three housemates valued.

And that he had made no real attempt to seek their approval through the obsequiousness they expected. He did not speak of his life, his family, his hopes and fears to these people.

Or to anyone else for that matter.

It was not that he had nothing to say.

Quite the contrary.

If he spoke at all, he feared that it would be of his past and his memories. His nightmares. Of things left unresolved. Of images held fast, far behind his tired grey eyes.

On a loop.

Repeating.

And if he started, he knew full well that he would not be able to stop.

5

Jim Bell made you fight your best friend.

That's what he did.

That was his *thing*.

Stealing your dinner money or flicking your left testicle to leave you doubled over in agony weren't enough for Jim.

Oh no.

He wasn't much to look at. Just a stringy lad, like the rest of them, in regulation grey jumper, shorts and crooked school tie.

But Jim was different. He had a capacity for an inventive cruelty beyond his years. A devious nature. An animal cunning that screwed up his face when he smiled and turned his eyes into slits. The kind of child who did bad things to insects and small birds for the benefit of an audience. He had authority amongst the other boys, because something of that malevolence had chillingly communicated itself. The implication that he would go further – might go all the way if it came to it – until he did something *very* wrong indeed. The children didn't fully understand it, but they were afraid of it just the same.

So when it was your turn, 'Dinger' Bell made you fight your best friend.

In front of what seemed like the whole school. Up a back

11

alley, after lessons. It was either that or fight *him*. And no-one wanted to do that.

In the days running up to your ordeal, elaborate and clandestine choreography ensued. Best friends met secretly and practised.

Eban and his best mate, Stevie Burns, rehearsed their most plausible moves: half-kicks; feigned punches; full-body grappling; hair-tugging. Until they were adept and proficient in the art of pseudo-violence.

All had to appear utterly authentic.

Dinger knew when you were faking it.

They had been friends since Primary Class 2.

Batman and Robin, with duffle coats for capes.

Hannibal Heyes and 'Kid' Curry on bikes for horses.

Stevie was a strong lad, who had filled out early.

He could have beaten Eban in a fight any day of the week. Come to that, he could probably have taken Dinger Bell as well.

But as the boys were learning, in Belfast these days, it was no longer about how hard you were. But rather, how 'mental'.

So here they now were, circling each other menacingly.

As their peers screamed for blood and Dinger looked on.

Tight-closed lips stretched like an old hag's smile.

They rolled around on the ground, perspiring with mock malice, grunting with real effort, whilst trying to avoid the stools and pellets of dog faeces that littered the back alley.

It usually finished in the same way.

One or other of the combatants sat astride their adversary, pinning his arms down and dangling gob precariously over his face.

If you were lucky, an adult might happen upon the ruction and all would flee, whooping and laughing. Or sometimes one of the girls would insist that it should stop or they'd tell.

But only if they liked you.

As Eban lay on his back panting, helplessly defeated, staring at the ribbon of sky above him, his mind turned to McGrew's burned-out shell of a pub.

To an imagined land of solitude, seclusion and sanctuary.

Wiping his face with the back of his sleeve, he silently resolved to find a way in there.

6

In truth he was flabbergasted. And it took him all of his poise under pressure not to show it.

She sat across the desk from him like this was the most natural thing in the world for her.

Young people today. It just popped into his mind. He hated himself for his Puritanism and felt ancient, but was desperately struggling to appear blasé.

Officer Helen Totton uncrossed and re-crossed her legs, leaned back and cupped her linked fingers behind her neck, massaging it. It made her breasts strain against the buttons of her regulation white polyester shirt. She pushed the chair back on two legs and flicked her blonde ponytail to one side.

"Anyway, it's something to think about. You can let me know."

"Sure… right…" He was still affecting an unconvincing nonchalance.

She stood up to go, smoothing down the creases of her black pencil skirt. He stood as well, half-tempted to come around the desk and seize the moment. His pulse was racing, but he simply didn't know how to react appropriately.

His phone rang. They looked at each other.

"I better take that."

"Of course… you're a busy man."

She moved toward the door. He was looking at her in a wholly different way now.

The curve of her back, her bra-strap visible through the material of her shirt, her buttocks, smooth, round and elevated, split by the zipper of her skirt. He wondered if she was wearing black tights or stockings.

And how she would walk in stilettos and not the flats required as standard uniform wear.

"See ya." She threw it back over her shoulder as she left.

It was Sam Coulter, the team sergeant.

"Monday morning blues, chief," he said cheerily. "You asked me to let you know about any change in the frequency of requests from punters."

He paused for effect. "Up 35%!"

Coulter was referring to the response from the public following a revamping of the Historical Enquiries Team website.

Normally Dan Watson would have groaned audibly and made some cryptic quip about being careful what you wish for. Instead he wanted to share with Coulter what had just happened.

How Officer Helen Totton –newly assigned to the team, blonde, twenty-something, divorced – had propositioned him. There was no other word for it.

She must be half my age, he wanted to brag to Coulter. *Asked to see me… came right out with it.*

"*I just wanted to say, sir, if you are… well… attending any overnighters; conferences; whatever… I'd be happy to go along with you. No strings… just a bit of fun.*"

He almost laughed out loud at the thought of it.

"Dan? Sir…?"

Watson roused himself.

"Right Sam… right… drop the new applications in to me when you get a chance and we'll go over them."

"Will do."

He felt giddy.

Like a schoolboy.

He wanted to call her back in. To close the blinds. Press her hard up against the filing cabinets. To let his hands and his tongue give her his answer.

Instead he found himself looking at the graduation photos of his son and daughter on his desk: Alison in Bristol, Roddy in Hull. It calmed him.

But the box was now open.

She obviously knew he was married and her superior.

How ballsy was that? he thought.

When he saw Officer Totton again; in the canteen, at briefings, in the car park. The frisson of their both knowing. Even if nothing happened. The opportunity was there now. The unobserved electricity that would now fly between them. His ego couldn't help but be stroked.

He'd been a largely faithful husband across the thirty-years-plus span of his marriage.

Indiscretions declining proportionally with his libido, his rubric was that he would never intentionally stray, never go looking for other women. It was the deal he made with himself.

However, in the unlikely event that other women should go looking for him… well…

He knew this was a dubious qualification. A moral salve. A flag of convenience. Women were hit on all the time by men and they were expected to rise above it.

Elaine, his wife was still an attractive woman for her age. What if she applied the same code? How would *he* feel? He pushed these thoughts away.

Christ, it's a different generation… I could have her up on disciplinary charges for fuck sake, and how stupid would that make me look?

He would have to try to put it out of his mind or he would quite possibly spend the rest of the day thinking about getting away with it. Or more. His imagination was racing again.

Leaving Elaine. Starting a new life with a younger woman. The oldest dad at the school parents' meetings. The sex... couldn't keep up with her. The whispers. Career suicide. And Elaine... it would crush her. All that work building a life together; thrown away for a bit of skirt.

No fool like an old fool.

He could do with a drink.

Maybe he would pull Helen Totton's file over lunch. Get some background on her. Was she a loose cannon? Could she really be trusted to be discreet?

That would be the logical thing to do.

He opened his briefcase and removed a memory stick. He had to give a presentation at the city hall to some visiting American politicians on Friday, regarding the work of the HET. That was all fairly rudimentary. But they'd asked him to write an introduction to the event to be delivered by the top brass, and that could be tricky. As could the fact that local politicians would be in attendance, and they had got a sniff of potential funding from the Yanks.

He plugged in the device and punched up the PowerPoint.

The first slide appeared on screen and he crossed the room to turn on the projector. Returning, he moved through the proposed presentation.

The Historical Enquiries Team: Policing the Past
Introduction by the Chief Constable

Many people still have questions relating to violent deaths over a period of thirty years. These impact on the lives of many hundreds, if not thousands of people.

There are many reasons why it is important to seek answers to these questions, not least of which is the pain and hurt of those who live with them every day. I have met fathers and mothers, brothers and sisters, sons and daughters – people from all sides who struggle with questions about the deaths of their relatives. Often they just ask how or why, believing that these details will bring, if not some level of comfort, at least a measure of knowledge and understanding. Indeed, many have accepted that prosecutions may never be possible. They are simply looking for someone to tell them the story of how their relative died.

This is why we sought to devise a way of dealing with the past; to formalise and fund a special unit – the Historical Enquiries Team – to review old cases. It is a unique policing initiative and it will re-examine all deaths which can be attributed to the security situation here between 1968 and 1998.

Families will sit at the heart of all of our enquiries. We have a simple message: we do care, and we will work in a determined and genuine way to achieve our objective of bringing closure for as many people as possible.

Gerald Hanley, Chief Constable, Police Service of Northern Ireland.

He was happy with it. And anyway, he knew that the CC would be out the door the minute the tough questions began.

"Unfortunately I have a prior engagement. Just let me hand you over to my colleague Detective Inspector Watson for clarification. I'm sure he can handle any questions you might have."

He thought of Helen Totton standing at the back of the hall, clipboard in hand, all frosted pink lipstick and big blue eyes. His hands went deeper into his trouser pockets.

7

The Leisure and Tourism Department of the council offices housed the Good Relations section, and was Eban's place of gainful employment.

On the ostentatious grounds of an old Georgian manor house, the department appeared to offer a pleasant enough working environment when viewed from the road which ran by the security-gated entrance.

It was in this building that Eban had originally attended for interview many years ago, and it was here where he (not unreasonably) assumed would be the location of his future employ. But he was soon to learn that the old building was the exclusive domain of the senior council apparatchiks and jealously guarded as such.

The bus dropped him at the security hut where daily he would exchange innocent inanities regarding the fortunes of Manchester United with Frank, the retiree who opened and closed the gates all day. He walked by the 'big house', down the service slip road and around to the rear of the building.

Here stood the stone outhouses, previous artisan workshops and former stables that now contained park and cemetery maintenance equipment. A number of prefabricated huts stood raised off the ground on stilt-like constructions. The impression of impermanence they offered was in marked incongruence to the historical splendour of the old house in whose shadow they stood.

Eban splashed through the puddles and potholes filled

with overnight rain and squeezed between a number of sensible economy vehicles belonging to his workmates.

Mounting the aluminium steps up to the grey nondescript door with frosted glass panel, he glanced back over his shoulder at the bank of ornate leaded windows which looked down on the huts from their splendid, vine-tangled setting.

As expected, he noticed an indistinct figure – most likely from Human Resources – perform an elaborate charade of adjusting the blinds. The formality of this 'clock-in-clock out' mentality irritated him intensely.

Eban pulled a wide, cheesy grin and looked exaggeratedly at his wristwatch, arm outstretched and sleeve drawn back.

One minute to nine.

Bastards, he thought. *I wouldn't give you the pleasure.*

The office reception area was a monument to bland conformity.

A standard issue beige-and-grey paint job seemed designed to sap and drain away any splash of creative thought or original action. Grey metal filing cabinets and worn fabric furniture were fringed with over-watered pot plants.

Passing through the small public holding area, Eban braced himself for his regular early morning encounter with the defenders of the faith.

Blu-tacked magazine pictures of Prince William and Kate Middleton, Michael Bublé and Justin Timberlake hung beside images of cute kittens and a sunset proclaiming some nonsense about today being the first day of the rest of your life.

A plaque told anyone interested that they didn't have to be crazy to work here… but it helped.

This was the undisputed domain of Agnes Curran and Liz McDonald. Senior office secretaries, impromptu and uninvited judges of character, and self-appointed ethics police.

Liz – the younger of the two by some way – was a plump

girl with a tight corkscrew hairdo. Her fat neck and freckled arms strained the collar and sleeves of a patterned blouse that bulged into rolls around the middle and at the sides. Already – even on this nippy morning – the white nylon was darkening beneath her arms with sweat.

Animated and eager to make some point or other regarding some weekend hen party, she did not see Eban arrive at first. She was affecting the air of the disgruntled consumer seeking peer approval and sympathy.

"Honestly Agnes, they were billed to make an appearance for at least half an hour and they only did about ten minutes at best… Sandra Pringle from Accounts was just *raging*… well, we all were. Mary Higgins was covered in baby oil… she'll never get it out of that outfit. What? No, they stopped at the loincloth… I was at the front, but there was no way you could tell if he was…"

Agnes, middle-aged and soured with bitterness for reasons Eban did not wish to know or care about, jangled her gold charm bracelet and picked at a thread on her garish floral two-piece ensemble. She looked like a woman who had collapsed in on herself.

Imploded.

Yellow-brown skin stretched tight across angular bone. Try as he might, Eban could not shake the feeling that cancer was sucking her dry. Would suck her to a husk.

She just didn't know it yet.

Furrowing her brow behind heavily tinted, thick-rimmed glasses, she tried to appear supportive and mutually outraged.

Her distinctive Scots-Irish brogue identified her origins as East Antrim.

Paisley country.

"The best of the lot of them was that Johnny Hot-Rocks," she offered sagely. "He comes right into the audience and sits on your lap. Sandra Pringle was mortified at Joan's hen night… she's all talk, that one."

21

Then, as a bitter afterthought, so typical of her, "I think she's frustrated cuz she can't get herself a man."

He heard it all clearly.

Heard variations of the same virtually every day.

How could he do otherwise?

Marooned in this prefab hell, year after year. Another little bit of himself diminished.

Not wishing to acknowledge them and thus necessitate the necessary blandishments, Eban deliberately banged his rucksack against the side of a filing cabinet, announcing his presence.

With all the false bonhomie he could muster, he spoke. "Morning all… Archie in yet?"

In the silence he imagined the air crackling and freezing over in an instant.

Agnes immediately made a half-turn away from him whilst adjusting her glasses in pretence of reading one of the files on her desk.

Liz, keen to impress the older woman, haughtily replied, without looking up at him, "I really couldn't say."

Eban knew well enough that no-one could enter the office – in or out – without passing by these two hellhounds, and bubbling up as always was the almost irresistible temptation to wither them – scourge them with a verbal, looking-glass reflection of their own grotesque horror. But a public and damaging challenge to the unassailable self-importance of these two harridans was simply not worth it. He prided himself on his daily self-control in this regard and continued down the corridor toward the office he shared with the man of a thousand faces.

The great thing about working with Archie Adams was the uncertainty of who you might find across the desk from you every morning. It was a mild liberation from the awful, slow, acid-drip predictability of a career in local government in Northern Ireland.

Eban covertly celebrated Archie's eccentricities and embraced his unpredictability as the sanest reference point in an increasingly insane post-conflict normality.

Still.

He couldn't let those bitches win entirely, and so called back over his shoulder, "Just saw *The Sun*; that was a turn-up about Michael Bublé, eh: bent as a nine-bob note. And AIDS to boot... who'd have thought? It's the wife I feel sorry for... and the fans of course."

Both women looked at each other in confusion, then up to the glossy, autographed promo shot of the star, resplendent in white tuxedo and whiter teeth.

Passing by the tourism office, Eban caught sight of Gerry Ramsey and his young assistant Fiona through the open door.

Their heads were close together, looking at some document or other and laughing. Perhaps too close for a man only married some three weeks ago. A definite mutual attraction between these two had been evident from the beginning.

Gerry was a cocky, young, self-confident career civil servant. One of the new breed who wore colour co-ordinated shirt and tie combos and always carried his mobile phone in an elaborate holster device on his belt.

On seeing Eban they pulled apart rather theatrically, Fiona stretching exaggeratedly and Gerry spilling his coffee in the process.

"Morning Gerry, how's the missus? Oh, morning Fiona... didn't see you there."

He couldn't resist it.

"Oh... fine, Eban – she's gone to Dublin for a few days; volleyball trip."

Eban wondered about the Ramseys.

Were they swingers, taking separate holidays in an open relationship? A volleyball trip? He didn't think so. Poor newlywed Mrs Ramsey. Something about Gerry suggested that this was a one-way arrangement.

He'd had three different assistants in fourteen months. All of them young women, all of them let go at the end of their short-term contracts.

Some in tears.

The little fucker was a serial harasser.

"Still… you're surviving without her then?" *Turn the screw*, he thought.

Fiona flushed and dived into her bottom drawer, muttering something.

Gerry forced a grin. "Well, you struggle on… you know how it is."

Eban became aware of the wide grin splitting his own face. He was enjoying the young man's discomfort far too much.

He heard Archie's voice, unmistakable, come through the thin partition wall. It was a bizarre fusion of Ulster officiousness and bar-room banter.

"…Ya know the correct and proper council procedure for the requestin' of heatin' to be turned on in a community centre. Well madam, yes, I sympathise with the fact that yez are senior citizens… have yez considered some woollen or insulated garments in that eventuality? Well now madam, I don't think… I don't have to take… that's fine by me. Have a nice day."

Eban entered, waiting patiently until Archie removed his cowboy boots from the other man's seat.

By most people's reckoning Archie Adams was an unpredictable quantity.

Eban suspected that as he stood looking into the bathroom mirror every morning – running a steel comb through thinning, pomaded, dyed jet-black hair – Archie Adams saw someone entirely different to the middle-aged misanthrope looking back at him.

Someone younger, sexier, more vital. A young Johnny Cash maybe.

It indirectly led to what could only be described as an inflated sense of his own importance, and it simply rubbed people up the wrong way.

A devoted Country and Western fan, Archie's desk was a monument to 'the Man in Black' – mouse mat, coffee mug, bureau organiser and a variety of stationery gimmicks.

He did not hold with electronic organisation. Was evangelical about this. *"What-cha gonna do when the computers take over?"*

Pushing himself up straight in the chair and pulling down on his waistcoat, he adjusted his bootlace tie and spoke out of the side of his mouth.

"Sure, start anytime why doncha?" he said sarcastically, looking at the clock over Eban's head.

"Fine Archie, fine… may the circle stay unbroken."

"By-and-by, Lord, by-and-by!"

His expression changed. "Are you takin' the piss?"

"No way Archie… no way," objected Eban.

Archie gestured at the phone.

When he became agitated, the civil servant's alter ego briefly disappeared. It caused a dent, a momentary fracture which was filled by broad Belfast bile.

"What do these fuckin' people take me for? Do them a favour once and they'll torture ye forever."

Eban had heard it all before. "These people are paying our wages."

"Oh, here we go…" said Archie derisively.

Christ, thought Eban. *Five past nine: we've stared early today.*

He watched Archie and waited.

Usually he came back with either a defensive response, quoting a potted history of his unstinting service to this community over many years, or a pithy one-liner harvested from a Country and Western song lyric, full of pseudo-down-home philosophy designed to put Eban in his place.

"The boss man wants to see you; nobody's available to do that Ballysillan public meeting tonight."

The joke was over.

"See, there he goes again: confusing me for somebody who actually gives a fuck," said Eban.

Archie's expression was inscrutable.

"Archie, if I wanted to work I'd have got a proper job."

"Don't shoot the messenger!"

Eban pointed his thumb to a photocopied sheet he'd taped to the side of a filing cabinet. *Clerical Assistant Grade 1 Status. Job Description.*

He pulled himself up to the keyboard and switched on the computer. He rattled the keys for a few minutes; then paused and his expression became clouded with anxiety.

He reached over and took some files from his rucksack.

"*I fell into a burning ring of fire…*" he mumbled to himself.

8

Emily Atkins liked very much that she was able to cycle back and forth to work.

The small primary school in Stranmillis was perfect for her needs.

She freewheeled into the gravel driveway before dismounting and removing her brown leather briefcase and a Marks and Spencer's carrier bag from the wicker basket on the front of the bicycle.

The weather was cold, but fortunately sunny and dry.

A tallish woman, she wore her lank fair hair pulled back, away from her face and tied in a maroon velvet band. Her 'Harry Potter glasses' (as the kids called them), silk patterned scarf, cashmere cardigan and lack of jewellery cast her as a somewhat prim and proper individual.

She hailed from a middle-class housing estate in West Wolverhampton and despite her upwardly mobile mother's intentions to ingratiate her as a young girl with the horse-and-hounds set of the neighbouring Home Counties, Emily had hated all of that and had admirably refused to play the game where she might have profitably done otherwise.

This (and her student politics) led some of her former university friends to suggest that her history with men indicated a penchant for 'a bit of rough'.

What they really meant was 'losers'.

However, this implied a degree of self-confidence and design when plotting the trajectory of her own relationships that she simply did not possess.

Undeniably though, there did seem to be a pattern emerging.

Of note there had been the crusty Ed, who lived in a caravan in Wales and kept a dog on a string; Alfie, the alcoholic landscape gardener from Cheshire who had the liver of a sixty-year-old; and Gavin, a chain-smoking scrap metal sculptor and former shipyard worker from Govan.

And now Eban.

Confused, mysterious, vulnerable Eban from Belfast.

Eban, who had begged her not to return to England. To stay. To help rebuild something new and important now that the war was over. He would get drunk and go off on flights of rambling explanation.

"A potted history of the Troubles, for those only used to seeing it on the *Channel 4 News*," he explained.

Eban, who had somehow managed to convincingly fuse her own personal future happiness and prospects with those of *all* of the people of Northern Ireland.

How mad was that? she thought. *Another disaster waiting to happen.*

It wasn't a relationship per se, in the manner of the others.

He was her senior by some years and there had been no conventional courtship, no meeting of minds or souls to speak of.

They had met when he moved into the room downstairs three years ago. And prosaic as that was, having just turned forty, Emily was painfully aware that – short of the internet – opportunities to meet single men were fast diminishing.

For a while, having another man in the house certainly caused her and Rosemary to 'up their game' somewhat.

Initially the serious scholar of African Studies had laid on the foundation and blusher in industrial amounts and giggled and shrieked like a schoolgirl whenever Eban attempted something approaching humour. But finding he had clearly set his sights on the younger woman, Rosemary quickly reverted to type and snobbishly denounced the interloper variously as 'common' 'damaged goods' and 'anti-intellectual'.

Pascal Loncle's pedestal got a little higher.

Her glasses perched on her nose, and balancing her briefcase and carrier bag, Emily pushed open the door with her shoulder and scooped up the mail in the hall with one movement. It had probably lain there all day from the early morning onward.

Whilst both Rosemary and Pascal had no set routine and were possibly at home, it was likely that they had both walked over the letters on their way in and out during the day.

Sometimes she could discern a footprint on the envelopes.

It bloody annoyed her.

She gathered them up in the fingerless mittens Rosemary had knitted for her. Emily had stayed on late to talk to some parents, and to arrange the playroom and generally prepare for tomorrow.

Eban hadn't been down to her room for some months now. Nor she to his. *He's seemed more preoccupied than usual. Could he be seeing someone else?*

Eban?! That's just too ridiculous, she thought.

He was a presentable enough guy when scrubbed up. But for some time now he had let himself go in the little things. The tufts of hair protruding from his ears and nostrils; the eyebrows that met in the middle and gave him a wolf-man's scowl; the missed patches on his throat when he shaved; the occasional food stain down his front that he'd overlooked.

She didn't expect him to be a metrosexual.

She could fix all this easily.

If only he'd let her.

No. It was more likely that the daily grind and need to veg out after a hard day's work would explain a lot. She didn't miss the sex, which in all honesty had become somewhat perfunctory. Just the affection. The physical contact.

Warm air hit her in a wave.

The newly upgraded central heating was working a treat. God bless those Lutherans.

She smiled to herself and thought, *A hot bath, a glass of wine with dinner and an early night will restore the much-needed balance.*

The lights were lit on the landing and a glow seeped out from under Rosemary and Pascal's doors. But Eban's room remained in darkness. He sometimes worked flexitime, a system by which civil servants could build up leave of absence. When he availed of this however, he rarely did anything with it. Staying in his room and 'researching' on his laptop.

What, he didn't say.

She was kept at arm's length in this and in most things.

The prolonged duration of the working day was leaving a residue of weariness. It felt like the start of sniffles and a sore throat.

She popped the film on her tagliatelle carton a few times with a fork and slid it into the microwave. Returning to the kitchen table where she had dropped the mail, she quickly flicked through the letters.

"Bill... bill... Pascal... Rosemary... bill... Rosemary... junk... E...b...a...n..." She said it haltingly, out loud; turning over in her mind the information on the envelopes.

What gave her pause for thought was the Police Service of Northern Ireland crest on the top left corner of the envelope. Under this was a logo and the words *Historical Enquiries Team.* A second letter said, *Royal Victoria Hospital, Outpatients Appointments.*

The microwave pinged.

She went to Eban's door and knocked.

No answer.

"E.B?" It was her pet name for him. (Despite endless requests from him to stop using it.)

Nothing.

She felt worried by the official quality of the correspondence, and dejected by his unwillingness to share anything of a personal nature with her.

Christ, could the man be any more infuriating? she thought.

In her customary fashion, she slid the mail under the gap at the bottom of his door and sought out some kitchen roll on which to blow her nose.

9

Being Alex Barnard's little brother didn't help in the ways that it should have done.

Being the only sibling of the captain of the first 11 and the deputy head boy should have counted for something.

It didn't.

When he arrived at his new school, PE staff would invariably ask two questions:

ONE, are you Alex Barnard's wee brother?

TWO, do you play football?

In trials, when they found that he did not possess the sporting prowess of his brother, he was unceremoniously dumped. Relegated on Wednesday afternoons to the windswept playing fields of the talentless non-selectees.

The shame of always being passed over when the teams were picked. The last boy to be called out. Shivering. Humiliated.

Following a disappointing showing in his 11+ examinations, he was deemed unfit for the elite grammar stream classes within the secondary school that he and Alex attended. His brother had aced his exams, of course, and gone straight into the top stream.

Because of the age gap between them – some six years – Alex always seemed to be leaving a school as Eban was arriving.

32

If their terms did overlap, the older boy was much too concerned with the preoccupations and plaudits of a successful senior.

All he left behind for Eban was a monkey for his prematurely stooping back.

Eban stared up from his bunk bed at the bulge of his brother's shape overhead. He could not sleep and in the dark his mind raced.

Failure and success. Friendship and betrayal. Acceptance and rejection.

Dinger Bell.

Tonight they'd had to leave the house at short notice.

Always a sure sign of a domestic row brewing about money, gambling, drink or all three.

Alex, Eban and their cousin Jennifer had been despatched to the local fleapit, The Carlton. Showing there was a retro-bill, including *On the Waterfront*.

When Brando pleaded, "It was you, Charlie, it was you… you wuz my brother… you should have looked out for me a little," Eban had looked at Alex's face in the darkness.

He looked for a hint of recognition, of irony, of guilt or regret.

Nothing registered.

Such was his deep unhappiness at school that now in the mornings, Eban would deliberately 'misplace' the Yale front door key that he wore on a piece of string around his neck. He prayed that his parents would let him stay home rather than have to leave their jobs early at the local clothing factory to let him in.

With the string seemingly not fit for purpose, Eban would stage an elaborate show of hooking the front door key onto the metal S of his yellow-and-black elastic snake belt.

Then, somehow, the belt would go missing.

He would feign illness, fall downstairs and show no

appetite. If it was a cry for help or attention, no-one seemed to be listening.

It couldn't go on.

Things came to a head on a bright, sunny summer's morning when Eban embraced the unthinkable.

Informed that he had been selected to fight once again after school, the boy amazed himself by punching Jim Bell full in the gut.

Never thought about it.

He just balled his fist and... *boom!*

Right in the solar plexus.

He didn't know where it had come from.

It hadn't really hurt Dinger, who had been frisking Eban for dinner money at the time. But the surprise – the sheer audacity – engendered by such a show of insolence sent him sprawling backward onto his arse.

Eban bolted.

He was carried away on a momentary wave of adrenaline rush and never looked back.

But he was dead meat and he knew it.

10

It was as Archie had said.

Eban was required to attend an evening meeting in North Belfast.

It was an unusual last-minute request from his boss, and something that Eban had assiduously worked to avoid for the entire duration of his time in the Department of Leisure and Tourism.

He had very bad memories of the last time he'd helped them out of a jam under similar circumstances.

But tonight it would be necessary because Brian Kelly had been in a car accident. His natural successor for this gig was Colin Foy, but he was at the City Hospital maternity department with a heavily pregnant wife.

So even for Eban, it would have seemed somewhat unreasonably disingenuous to decline.

And it was for these and for no other reasons that he agreed. But it sat badly with him.

Certainly he had no fear of censure or redress should he refuse.

For Eban had single-mindedly worked hard at remaining on the lowest grade point available to him within the Civil Service employment structure. Internal promotions initiatives and in-service training came and went. Transfers to different departments carrying higher-grade status were offered to him. Even length-of-service increments were proffered. Eban turned them all down, fighting tooth and nail to maintain his coveted, lowly Clerical Assistant Grade 1 status.

He printed out his job description and displayed it proudly and perversely on the filing cabinet next to his desk:

Performs simple, routine or repetitive tasks which require little or no subject-matter knowledge. Work is closely observed, controlled and checked; few guides or instructions apply.

He did all this in anticipation of moments just like these.

And precisely so as he could tell Philip Walters, his line manager – in the nicest possible terms – to go fuck himself.

However, circumstances and happenstance seemed to get the better of him this evening and a date with the good citizens of Ballysillan Community Development Project lay ahead.

He dreaded it.

It had been a similar situation all those years ago.

A goodwill errand with unimaginable consequences.

His brief tonight was to say something encouraging about the possibility of funding and hand out grant forms for cross-community Good Relations projects.

He thought about phoning Emily in case she were wondering where he might be, but didn't.

Something about that smacked of a shared domesticity that simply didn't exist between them.

Above all, he was pissed that his 'project' would be put on hold for the evening.

Just when he was bringing it to fruition.

As the Silverstream bus rattled and rolled, Eban laid his head against the vibrations on the cool window pane and considered how long it had been since he was last in this neck of the woods.

When he was very young, North Belfast had been a much sought-after residential area. And for all intents and purposes, it still appeared to be so. But the leafy thoroughfares of the

North Circular Road and the tidy privets of Cavehill hid darker truths, and during the Troubles had come to be known to journalists and punters alike as 'The Killing Fields'.

The buildings were old, solid, semi-detached, red-brick feel-goods. A nice garden front and back. Built for the bourgeoisie who filed dutifully home from their management tasks in the linen mills and shipyards.

The Unionist merchant class who had seen their civil legacy go up in flames, but whose love of property and capital meant that a scorched earth policy was out of the question.

And so, resignedly, they abandoned these places of science, reason and commerce for comfortable homes in East and South Belfast, or maybe even further afield in Bournemouth or Torquay.

They sold them originally to the skilled labourers over whom they had for so long affected a smug superiority. Then to the new-money Loyalist trailer trash of the sink estates. And finally – unthinkably – to the rebel hordes of professionally educated 'Fenians'.

Because now apparently there was peace.

Everyone said so, so it must be true.

Despite still-volatile interfaces and dividing walls suggesting something to the contrary.

The demographics and geography of the place meant that Catholic and Protestant areas interfaced and merged in ways that determined local knowledge as a prerequisite for survival. In the bad old days, random drive-by shootings and abductions were the norm.

Driving along now, Eban could see dark housing estates – lit up by piss-orange streetlamps – ominously fringing those affluent leafy avenues. Loyalist Glenbryn bordered the Republican Ardoyne, which stretched to the better-off Cliftonville. Catholic Ligoniel edged Protestant Ballysillan, which met the prosperous North Circular Road.

The whole territory was a bewildering maze of sectarian football supporters' clubs, bookie shops, bowling teams, gardening centres and bridge fraternities.

All a mish-mash of poverty-fuelled resentment, swirled in along with affluent, palatial monuments to an acceptable level of violence.

Whether things were good or bad, the streets pretty much emptied after dark up here.

In the past that just led to the death squads phoning up taxi cabs and pizza deliveries from companies located across the sectarian dividing line.

Let your fingers do the walking.

Shit! Poor bastards!

Walking unwittingly up garden paths – pepperoni deep pan in one hand, garlic bread in the other – *Crack! Crack! Crack!*

Christ, he felt depressed.

It was all coming back to him again. In similar circumstances, the *favour* he had done so many years ago.

And what *that* had led to.

He should never have said he would do this.

He should never have come up here again.

11

Across town, on a cold, crystal-clear winter evening, the ornate exterior of City Hall twinkled in the lower south-western corner of its marbled white façade.

The city burghers were working late.

More cars than usual filled the parking area and the general services staff had been informed that due to the rescheduled address by the Historical Enquiries Team, Committee Room 2A would be in use until later than normal.

Anne Breslin – a harassed-looking woman in her late thirties, with troubled green eyes, alabaster skin and long, fiercely tamed jet-black hair – crossed the thick pile carpet of the mayoral reception area and began to climb the long winding staircase.

Her style of dress was perhaps a little old-fashioned for her age.

She rarely smiled.

Had she done so, her colleagues would have seen a face transformed.

The sleeves of her lilac cardigan were rolled up to the elbows and she furrowed her brow slightly in concentration, summoning up all of her hand -to-eye co-ordination. She carried a large tray overloaded with crockery, silver teaspoons, shortbread and a huge, bulbous teapot.

The crockery rattled with each footfall.

Every fourth step on the stairs brought the woman into eye contact with the portrait of a different first citizen.

Incumbents from the 30s to the present day looked down on her in their finery.

Pomposity and artifice were everywhere.

The elaborate chains of office; a fixed reference point in a changing, sartorial history.

Men with great Romanov beards.

Men with 70s sideburns, patterned shirts and flared trousers.

Men with tight perms and wispy moustaches.

Frail men, solid men, old men, all framed in a welter of brass and mahogany.

Everywhere, marble and brass and mahogany and deep pile carpet.

More like a museum, a library, a funeral parlour, than a place of civil business.

Here doors swished open and closed, staff whispered reverentially and volume ringtones on telephones were muted.

The deep *tick-tock* of the grandfather clock in the vestibule, neither dragging nor hurrying, offered a constant measure of things.

For some twenty years now, the woman had felt that the building, like its inhabitants, harboured an inflated sense of its own importance.

Across the span of that period, that feeling had grown from mild irritation to profound, silent loathing.

Her people.

The wounded.

The forgotten.

Her sainted mother.

Her poor crippled brother.

Still on the outside, still looking in.

Since she was a young girl, she had seen most of them come and go.

And as she reached the apex of the carpeted incline, it occurred to her, for the hundred thousandth time, that the bovine countenances peering down on her now all looked the same.

On reaching the top she paused momentarily outside the door of the committee room.

The muffled sound of voices, oaths, laughter and discord rose and fell.

Taking a deep breath, the woman turned 180 degrees and pushed against the door with her backside; the tray now wedged into her midriff.

The door gave way and she was immediately enveloped in the cacophony.

The committee room was sober and ostentatious all at once.

Important-looking green leather-bound, gold-leafed tomes stood piled high in bookcases against three of the walls. The fourth framed a large, ornate leaded window on which were depicted key events from the city's mercantile past.

It looked out upon the perfectly manicured grounds.

The high ceiling amplified the acoustics.

Several men and one woman sat around a long, semi-circular conference table covered with papers and files. The room seemed dimly lit in comparison to the stairway and the air was filled with babble and expectation.

Anne Breslin paused at the shoulder of one of the men, hoping that someone would see her and clear a space on the table for the tray of refreshments she had brought to them.

She stood and stood… *and stood.*

Jackets hung on the backs of seats and ties were loosened.

She could see that the smell of money and influence that the American visitors exuded had excited the pack.

Eventually, it was the only other woman in the room who looked up and accommodated her.

The Mayor's PA, a young woman, thanked 'Anne from Catering', as she was known, with a brief half-nod-half-smile.

Their eyes passed a succinct glance – pity perhaps – from one to the other.

The older women laid down the tray and turned to go.

The PA thought the look had said, *Rather you than me, luv.*

One small rotund man rose to his feet, hands raised in an attempt to garner order and credibility above the din.

"Gentlemen… gentlemen… *please*! Can we *please* keep sight of the business in hand? I'd remind the chair that this meeting was convened to address issues arising from…" – he looked quickly at his order of business – "…item seven on the agenda. Now, forgive me if I'm mistaken, but nowhere is there mention that we have to sit here and listen to the apologists for Republican murder gangs lecturing us – *us* – on our duties as elected councillors of this great city!"

His last words were swallowed up by a great wave of audible indignation from the bottom end of the room. When it subsided somewhat, a dark-looking, moustachioed fellow stood up, in an unhurried, gradual manner.

"Our right to be around this table as representatives of the Nationalist community is one which the British war machine in Ireland will never again deprive us of."

Again, a confusion of noise and catcalling as the barracking recommenced across the table and around the room.

This time it was the Mayor himself who rose to his feet.

Councillor Ronnie Simpson of the Democratic Unionist Party was a dapper man, who was not easily fazed by the cut and thrust of local government power-sharing.

He basically opposed it.

No ifs or buts. Simple as.

With his high forehead, sharp nose, pointed silver goatee and centre parting, he might have passed for an Elizabethan courtier if decked out in doublet and hose.

He cleared his throat and pushed out his chest, hooking a thumb in his waistcoat pocket as was his style.

It had the desired effect.

The noise level fell considerably.

Ronnie Simpson was a man who had built a small commercial empire from nothing. He was a man who, in dealings with all and sundry, demanded respect; one of the reasons ensuring that he got this deference from the chamber sat beside him now.

Arms folded.

Scowling, self-contained, seemingly indifferent to Ronnie Simpson's preamble.

Above all else, Simpson was a businessman. And he had business to conclude here this evening.

"I would remind members of last month's meeting, when this chamber had to be cleared and the police called in to restore order. I will have *no* hesitation in resorting to the same measure if necessary."

He tucked his thumbs in his trouser loops. It signified an 'I'll take on all comers' bravado.

Audible rancour petered out.

"Furthermore, I have instructed Councillor Herringshaw…"

He gestured lazily with his head toward a rural bull of a man who sat beside him.

For all the world like some cattle baron who had just hired in muscle for a range war.

"… to act in his capacity as a former RUC sergeant… should the need arise."

The big man was gazing down at the table.

He lifted his head slowly, like some carved stone grotesque. So low, he almost seemed to have been resting it there amongst the reports and minutes.

He appeared to be noticing the hubbub for the first time, and with the hint of a smile playing around his lips, theatrically pulled back the front of his tweed sports coat, ostensibly to replace a biro in the inside pocket.

There, in full view, the councillors could all see the large, legally held shoulder-holstered service revolver as he had intended.

Cecil Herringshaw, aka The Loyaliser, could hold an audience.

The discord had stopped completely now.

The Mayor, happy that he'd made his point, proceeded. Tapping a pen on the side of his water glass and clearing his throat, he went on.

"Now, the sooner we get through this business, the sooner we can all get home." He replaced his glasses and read from a document he held in front of him.

"Ahem... Item seven: as part of this council's continuing commitment to the principles, aims and objectives of a Good Relations policy..."

There was a good-natured, ironic ripple of derisive laughter from all around the chamber.

Simpson carried on regardless.

"... we are here to welcome our friends and colleagues from the US Special Presidential committee on Northern Ireland..."

An impromptu round of applause broke out. He adjusted his glasses for effect, appeared just a little unconvinced, and paused. Ronnie Simpson liked playing to the gallery.

"... to discuss the work of the Police Service of Northern Ireland's Historical Enquiries Team."

The Mayor waited for the expected gale of battle-hardened, cynical ridicule.

It didn't come.

Instead, the creaking of chair-backs filled the moment, as elected representatives seemed to physically push themselves away from the table at the prospect.

Ken Strain, a colleague of Simpson's, was the first to contribute. Wide-eyed, he slowly blew out his puffed cheeks in the manner of practised incredulity and world-weariness. Others rubbed their faces with their hands and looked like they needed something like *this* as much as they needed cranial ventilation. Some looked imploringly at Simpson, who shrugged his shoulders as if to disassociate himself from the idea.

"And of course, we're also here to discuss with our esteemed American colleagues the allocation of future funds for such an initiative, as they are related to an increase in the Good Relations Budget…"

At the mention of unallocated revenue, pandemonium was reinstated.

Mobile phones were activated, red-faced men formed conspiratorial huddles, and the chamber resembled the trading floor of a stock exchange or perhaps a bookie's shop. Peace money from the EU; peace money from the UK; peace money from America.

Cross-party bidding had begun.

"… *as members… will have… clearly… gathered,*" Simpson wearily concluded.

All the while Chief Inspector Dan Watson sat on the sidelines, patiently awaiting his invitation to present.

The level of professional discourtesy and disrespect shown to him was appalling.

He could only imagine how it looked to the Yanks.

The Chief Constable had got wind of the general mood and as predicted, absented himself, leaving the entire presentation to Dan.

Later that evening, as councillors pulled on their car coats and tweed caps, the usual clandestine clump of connivers hugged the periphery of the walls around the room and the sanctuary of the gents' toilets.

Ken Strain was worried and suspicious.

He screwed up his face into a map of creased, yellowing lines.

The cloying scent of wall-mounted air freshener was choking him and his bladder burned.

"What do we actually *know* about this fella Watson?" he hissed, searching deep in his open fly for a tug on flaccid skin.

His sometime election agent, Geoffrey Barnes, was eager to please.

"Well, I checked with personnel. Something of a career cop by all accounts. Lifer. Pretty dreary really. Wife... two grown-up kids... bit of a know-it-all by all accounts."

"No... no... never mind all that. The name: Dan Watson. He's one of *ours*, right?"

The lavatory door swished open and Leo Price, the Sinn Féin member, joined the other two at the piss trough.

Barnes and Strain fell quiet.

"Is this where all the big lads hang out?" he said cheerily.

"Aye... this is for the members' members," offered Strain with false bonhomie.

All laughed, but the echo off the tiled walls and the tinkling urine made the subsequent silence linger. It was all the weightier for that. At last Strain spoke, affecting good nature.

"You'll see *your* ones do alright out of this Good Relations lark, Leo."

He turned to Barnes whilst shaking and zipping.

"See these Fenians, Barnsey, they're not too fond 'o the crown... but they'll not say no to the *half-crown!*"

All the men laughed self-consciously. Price couldn't let that go.

"Word is Ronnie Simpson's already earmarked three hundred grand for OAPs and summer schemes. Keeping the rates down and buying in the votes, eh lads?"

"Sure, it's money from America, Leo."

"And from Europe," corrected Barnes punctiliously.

"It has to be spent... *and we're the boys to spend it!*"

All nodded and laughed again. Strain thought he'd push it.

"What's the craic with this Historical Crimes Enquiries then? Your boys won't want anything to do with it... digging up the past and that." He paused. *"Will they?"*

Price smiled conspiratorially. "A Truth Commission is what this country's being crying out for. It's about time we shone some light on state collusion with Loyalist murderers."

Both Strain and Barnes looked like they had been filleted. They stared at Price, incredulous.

He smiled. "Don't worry. It's cross-community isn't it? How do you propose to do it without us?"

In a moment, Strain and Barnes realised he was right. If the government wanted to throw money at this, then both recipients were bound at the hip pocket.

A chain gang arrangement.

It was business.

Just business.

Mayor Simpson had seen that right away, and unbeknown to his colleagues, had already promised monies for the GAA and the Irish Language to the Nationalists.

Price shook his hands under the dryer and moved to the door.

"Leo," called Strain, "if you're still interested in those deep fat fryers, give me a shout next week."

"Right Ken... sure I'll see you upstairs later for a wee drink," Price said and left.

"He's not the worst," ventured Barnes.

"Fenian bastard!" spat Strain back at him. *"Ya couldn't trust 'em. They're all the same."*

12

It was around now that Eban's serious truanting began in earnest.

It started innocently enough.

Walking aimlessly around the town, through Smithfield market. Over to the Waterworks.

He figured that he would be caught within days.

Welcomed and feared it in equal measure.

But after three weeks of absence, and with his classmates reporting that no apparent interest one way or the other had been shown by Mr Gilchrist his form teacher, it dawned on him that he was now in chaotic free-fall.

Amazingly for him, no-one seemed to mind.

So with things getting out of hand, and without consciously knowing it, Eban Barnard found himself an *out*.

A way back through the maze. A break in the loop.

It would have to be extreme, but desperation was now where it was at.

Teaming up with Sandy Courtney, an older boy of correction facility infamy, Eban embarked on an attention-seeking whirlwind of petty crime and altogether forbidden activities that made his head spin.

The Belfast of the late 60s and early 70s was an intoxicating playground for a degenerate, where redevelopment and civil turmoil invited recklessness, abandon and adventure.

A mere bagatelle got them off and running.

Climbing into Belfast Zoo without paying was a relatively straightforward affair.

Dropping in over the outside perimeter fence, they landed directly in the chimpanzee enclosure.

Hairy little men ran screaming and shrieking in all directions for cover.

Sandy had chased a few and flapped his arms, gibbering in idiot imitation.

Eban began to see why people said that Sandy had '*a wee want in him*'.

Clambering over a low wall without any apparent sign of detection, they strolled cockily past the brown bear enclosure and by the snake house.

It only took a matter of moments for them to be apprehended, the zoo, unbeknownst to them, being completely closed to the public during renovation works.

Three keepers with brooms and disbelieving indignation rushed them.

"What if you'd dropped over the wall and into the lion's cage, eh? What *then...* eh?" yelled the man.

"Frank, call the police."

A woman in blue overalls and wellingtons arrived on the scene, carrying a hose. Eban saw his chance.

"Missus," he said tearfully, pointing, "the big boy made me do it."

He knew from experience that puppy-dog eyes and hot tears would carry some weight in these matters.

Sandy looked hurt. He whimpered; then tried to run, but was held.

Reprieve.

They were turned loose with firm admonishments.

Sandy's momentary ire was dismantled adroitly with blandishments and promises of new and better schemes. Eban Barnard was discovering a penchant for manipulation.

Soon they'd moved on to frequenting the little secondhand shop in Derry Street. The owner was always glad to see them, for they invariably produced the goods.

Fagin-like, he made them tea and biscuits whilst surveying the spirit levels, power drills, socket sets and wood planes the boys would deliver him. Building sites within a three-mile radius were fair game.

When Fagin expressed an interest in cigarette coupons (exchangeable for gifts or cash), Mrs Barnard's five-year stash of Embassy Regal slips disappeared.

Alex copped the blame for that one.

Result.

The money and what it brought made everything worthwhile.

A fortune to him, it bought fake blood and plastic vampire fangs, ice cream, American comic books and boiled sweets.

But that wasn't the real reason for *any* of it.

Quite simply, Eban ached to be noticed.

Once, when lifting copper sheeting from the roof of a light engineering factory that they assumed was unoccupied, Eban found himself gazing down on a busy workshop floor.

All at once the workmen – in blue dungarees, cigarette butts behind their ears – stopped their lathes and were gazing up at him.

For one incredible moment it was as if time stood still.

He looking down on them and they staring back up at him.

It couldn't go on of course.

He ended it, poetically, in a blaze of self-destructive performance art.

The Rogers lived just three doors up from the Barnards. They had been family friends for years before moving to one of the new housing estates appearing around the fringes of the city for the first time.

Eban knew that their coin gas meter had yet to be emptied. Just three doors up.

Beautiful.

They climbed over the back yard wall in broad daylight, and failing to gain entry to the house, kicked their way through the panels of the back parlour door.

The racket was enough to start every dog in the street to barking and howling.

Emptying the coins, they returned to the back yard and found some paint-pots on the shelves there.

Immediately they set about hurling canary yellow and aquamarine in all directions, and at each other. They poured the rest down into the outside toilet cistern and flushed and splashed until the bowl and whitewashed walls were splattered in psychedelic pastels.

Stealth had never been a consideration, so when the din brought old Mrs McGiven to place her one good eye against a hole in the outer door, the party was over.

"*I see ye Eban Barnard... I see ye wee lad... wait-'til-I-tell-yer-Da!*"

Dripping paint and still smiling, the mention of his father made Eban turn from his endeavours.

For a solitary moment he considered dropping his trousers and sticking his arse up at where the voice had come from.

But that seemed like something Sandy might do.

Not *his* style at all.

The laughter stopped.

In that moment, it was all over and done with.

Frogmarched back to his own house. Voices raised, his mother in theatrical floods of tears, his father's slow footfall

51

on the stairs to the bedroom. His belt slapping through his trouser hoops as it was withdrawn and doubled. The indispensable crack-lash and smarting ache, denoting a line drawn in the sand.

And a chance perhaps to start again.

Redemption presented itself in the most unexpected of opportunities.

It was only two weeks hence and the Belfast Primary Schools Choir and Orchestra were about to have their moment.

Stage lights fashioned from one hundred watt bulbs burned bright in hollowed-out aluminium cake tins.

The schools ensemble of seventy massed recorders had taken *In the Silver Moonlight* just about as far as it could go.

It was time for the huddled ranks of pubescent musical excellence to take stage centre.

Brass and wind orchestras gathered for the massed denouement to the evening.

Hundreds of expectant parents packed the auditorium, in a hushed silence, as their young protégés offered up some kind of validation for their parenting skills.

Young Eban Barnard sweated profusely under the heat of the makeshift lights.

Pressed into a woollen V-neck sweater knitted by his mother and strangled by an elasticated bow tie, he afforded himself a tentative look at the only other side-drummer in the company.

His best friend, Stevie Burns, was a model of anticipation, poise and purpose.

As they had been taught, Stevie held his sticks high in anticipation of the forthcoming trial, his eyes fixed on the music stand in front of them both. (As Mr Chambers, their new Primary Seven teacher, had prepared them to sight-read the arrangement for percussion.)

But Eban – wan and perspiring – had alarmed eyes only for the spindly snare drum stand and the vast blackness of the auditorium in front of him.

When their moment came, it took the seemingly benign form of *When the Saints Go Marching In*.

Given his past transgressions, here was an unmitigated opportunity *to shine*.

Sweat ran into his eyes and they smarted in the lights, but he drew on the memory of the countless sessions he'd practised on the living room furniture with his mother's knitting needles. There were four beats, just four beats, in the opening verse. *Anyone could do that*, he told himself.

"A trained monkey could do that," was what Mr Chambers had said.

Easy-peasy-lemon-squeezy.

Eban and Stevie struck their small snare drums in perfect unison as one. The actual surface, the taut stretched-skin head of the drum, was surrounded by a raised wooden frame. It was a narrow enough target. The trick was not to crack the stick off the rim, but to hit firmly and confidently, dead centre on.

"*Oh when the saints… dit- dit-dit-dit… go marching in… dit-dit-dit-dit… Oh when the saints go marching in… dit-dit-dit…*"

Eban's drum lurched worryingly on its rickety tripod stand.

He hit it again and the clamps holding it to the stand began to yawn open.

With every strike, the drum leaned a further notch. Soon it was lurching alarmingly at a crazy angle.

If he kept this up, the drum would almost certainly tumble off the stand.

In an instant, fast becoming an eternity, it was all so dreadfully, awfully clear.

Another sound thwack and he faced the humiliating prospect of his small snare drum leaving its mooring and tumbling, rolling, careering slowly across the wooden boards of the Ulster Hall stage.

Leaving him standing exposed and naked.

Equally awful was the option of standing stock still, immobile, arms by his sides, as the band played on. Like some defective retard who, presented with his moment in the sun, bottled it.

Faced with Hobson's choice, he opted for the latter.

He froze. He knew what they'd say: "Couldn't keep his end up"; "Let the side down..."

And in what seemed like time without ending, of excruciating mortification, he stood stock-still as a puzzled Stevie Burns assumed sole percussion duties.

A lifeless stooge in a vast expanse of public judgement, Eban wilted and his eyes filled with tears.

George Chambers stared at him, uncomprehending.

Stevie Burns played twice as hard.

Out from the depths of the darkness, he imagined he could hear sniggers. Whispers. Alex and his mates perhaps?

In that awful cauldron of indignity – illuminated in a sea of unforgiving, electric light and with nowhere to hide – Eban Barnard vowed never again to stand immobile whilst others beat the drum on his behalf.

13

"E.B... You'll be late for work!"

Emily knew that he'd arrived in late last night.

He hadn't come up to say goodnight, despite the fact that he would have seen her bedroom light on. She tried not to be upset by this kind of slight. She believed that it was not intended as such and had learned that to have even the most pedestrian expectations of romantic convention from Eban was to be disappointed.

Affection, yes.

In his own way.

But he always held something back. And that was alright with her. Because she knew that *she* did as well.

She was curious, however – less about where he had been, but rather what he had been doing when traipsing around his room into the early hours. Feverishly feeding paper into his printer, the printer-head buzzing back and forth. The paper tray emptied; then refilled immediately for the process to continue. Tramping into the kitchen for coffee. The kettle boiling. The clink of spoon in cup. Then returning. The office chair being pulled up to the desk again. Slapping on the computer keys once more.

Until the very small hours.

Living directly overhead was like living together.

But with a degree of independence.

She knew that his nocturnal machinations could not be work-related.

Eban had strong feelings about that kind of thing.

She returned with a piece of toast and rapped a knuckle lightly on the door, wary of bringing any of the others out onto the landing.

The door cracked a few inches, then wider. Eban's head emerged and looked furtively back and forth. Hair wild, eyes like saucers.

"What's the craic?" he said and coughed.

Loose phlegm gurgled up in his throat and sounded like it might involuntarily leap out from his mouth. He covered it with a tissue in time.

"Are you sick?"

"Yes and no."

"What's that mean?"

"Well, officially yes – I'm not going to work – but actually no… I've lots to do."

"Want toast?"

"Come in; come in." He gestured urgently.

He took the slice from her, holding it between his teeth and pulled her into the room, closing the door.

Emily had visited him here less and less in recent months and couldn't honestly remember when she had last stayed the night.

The room was ultra-tidy for first thing in the morning. He was pretty organised, all things considered. Tidier than her room, that was for sure.

The bed, which dominated the space, had been made up. Duvet pulled tight to all four corners, pillows plumped.

The large bay windows overlooked the back garden, at the centre of which stood an impressive oak. It was a magnificent specimen. Bare now, but with branches that grew up and out at every angle. Up to the sky and down to the ground.

Eban had recently told her that – in its current state – he simply couldn't believe that it was the same tree that would fill the entire space with such a glorious explosion of swaying, green profusion come May.

Instead, he said, the bare branches reminded him now of nothing less than the capillaries, veins and arteries of the human heart.

He had the window sashes up a fair way and the fresh winter air was bracing.

Emily figured that – what with his cough – he must be smoking weed again, but the ashtrays were pristine.

Facing the bed, on a wide Persian rug, was his media centre.

TV, VCR, CD and DVD players and a dock for his iPhone.

He had it rigged so that they all played through the speakers that bookended the arrangement. In front of the windows sat his desk, with PC and printer.

Across the room a reclining chair, and on every available wall, floor-to-ceiling bookcases.

It was a big, spacious, high-ceilinged room and he had optimised every inch of it.

On the desk sat neatly-piled printed pages. Several bright green folders were lined up to accommodate these and a plethora of newspaper cuttings, also arranged for inclusion in separate files. In the centre of all of this was an official-looking form that Eban had filled in by hand.

"Someone's been a busy boy," she said and made to move toward the desk for a closer look.

He sprang across quickly to block her, putting himself between Emily and the desk.

"Private!"

"Okay, okay; you just had to say." She was a little insulted but knew she shouldn't be.

She had no rights here.

Emily sat down in the chair whilst Eban gathered up his materials in a rather clandestine manner.

"Look… I think I should mention…" she said a little warily, "it was me who brought the mail in… again." She rolled her eyes.

Eban shared her disdain regarding their housemates' tardiness.

"Anyway… I couldn't help but notice the official-looking letter… something about Historical Enquiries Team? Isn't that the police or something?"

He spun around from the desk and glared suspiciously at her.

"I'm not snooping or anything—"

"Then don't!"

"I'm not, but… ummm… and there was a letter from the hospital… you're not sick or anything are you?"

"CHRIST!"

"Would you rather I'd left it for Rosemary? She'd have had a field day!" she offered in meek defence.

Eban had gone red in the face, and went to speak but stopped himself. Emily could see that he was grinding his teeth together so violently that the veins on his face and forehead became swollen, his jaws taut. Instead he simply gestured toward the door, indicating that she should leave.

"Charming…" she said, and moved to do so.

As she turned the handle, he spoke. His voice was thin and small.

"In case you're wondering… if I'm not around, I mean… I might have to go away for a little while."

"Is everything okay?"

She badly wanted to show him something. Concern. Warmth. At the very least, support.

"When has everything *ever* been okay?" he said sarcastically.

As she left, Emily passed Rosemary and Pascal talking furtively in the kitchen. Their tone dropped discernibly when they saw her.

"*Au revoir,*" Pascal called after her.

And then, to Rosemary, she clearly heard him say in his heavily accented English, '*There is one who kisses and there is one who is kissed.*'

14

Dan Watson's willpower had held out for just two days.

The presentation at the City Hall had been an unmitigated disaster on pretty much every level. The Chief Constable wanted a full report indicating how an event that should have been a PR coup for the PSNI and HET had turned into an unseemly scrum for money.

And all in front of the US delegation.

Nevertheless, he just couldn't seem to keep his mind on anything else but the open invitation two doors down the hallway.

Part of him felt pathetic and useless.

Another part felt that he knew exactly how to fix that.

In the short term anyway.

When Officer Totton responded to his request to 'drop in when you get a moment', she noted right away that his blinds were drawn and the dimmer lights were on low.

HET officers worked a rota system on conventional police duties, so she was in uniform, having just come back off a patrol.

He had placed the photo of his children and his wedding ring in the desk drawer.

He felt a little foolish.

"Ah, Helen. How goes it?" Christ, he felt like a schoolboy.

"Fine, Dan… fine. Have you given any thought to what we talked about?"

He was already up and halfway around his desk.

"I've hardly thought of anything else."

He paused when he reached her, momentarily hesitant. Then almost knocked her over in his hunger and haste. Hands everywhere, mouth gulping on hers.

She grabbed his ass with both hands, pulled his crotch into hers and held it there.

Rubbing against him.

Her hair came undone.

He was kissing her neck, her hair, her breasts.

"God... don't eat me alive!" She laughed.

He felt chastened.

"Sorry... sorry." He backed off a little.

"No, it's okay. I like it... I do... wait... wait a minute."

She unbuckled her utility belt and let it fall, clunking, to the floor. Handcuffs, torch, Taser, pepper spray.

"Maybe we should lock the door?"

Dan felt momentarily conflicted. But he knew he couldn't stop now.

"Yes, okay."

She crossed the room, turned the lock and returned, unbuttoning her blouse.

"Would you like me to eat *you* alive?" she said, smiling, her hands already on his belt buckle.

He was shocked but fought to hide it. "Yes... God yes," he gasped, but looked at the door with concern as someone walked past, down the corridor outside. "Maybe we should get a room; a hotel... someone might come."

She was already on her knees in front of him. Already had her hand down his boxers and was gently pumping him. Big blue eyes, looking up, compliant. With her other hand she reached up and spread her palm open on his chest. Scrunching his chest hair.

"Oh gawd..." he breathed and closed his eyes.

She pulled the shorts down fully and gently cupped his balls, squeezing them a little. He was scared he would cum then and there.

Think of something... anything! Had he had a shower this morning? Was it clean down there?

Now she was licking, flicking her tongue, before taking him in.

"Mmmmm," she moaned.

He rested his hands on the top of her head, closed his eyes and forgot about everything.

15

One of Cecil Herringshaw's proudest boasts was the lineage he claimed.

All the way back to Oliver Cromwell's Yeomanry at Drogheda.

He shared the same warts on his face as the great man himself, and drew attention to the fact.

Herringshaw had had a family coat of arms made up as a plaque, which was affixed to the gatepost pillars of his large detached home in Templepatrick, County Antrim.

The same crest appeared on his business cards.

It featured a leaping salmon and the red hand of Ulster in the bottom quadrants, with a shield of red and yellow halves bisected by a blue diagonal stripe.

He'd even had a number of ties made up with the rather garish design resplendent upon them.

As he sat reflectively puffing his slim panatela in the front seat of Ronnie Simpson's parked Mercedes, thoughts of duty and loyalty; of insurrection and purge wafted about him with the smoke he exhaled. To those who saw him, he brought to mind the image and gait of a Bond villain.

Mayor Simpson eased the electric window down a touch, partially raised himself with an effort from the leather upholstery and loudly farted.

"*Trumpetbum!*" complained the big man.

"My guts are at me, Cecil," said Simpson in apology.

Herringshaw looked straight ahead, without any acknowledgement.

The City Hall car park was emptying, save for themselves and a tourist information caravan. The big Benz stunk of leather, tobacco, aftershave and bad eggs.

Cecil Herringshaw loved these informal pre-meeting car park briefings.

It was where the *real* business was done.

Substance before the pretence of having to play silent subordinate to the Mayor for the public's consumption. Only right that the elected representative and first citizen at least *appeared* to be making the decisions.

Both men enjoyed a mutual admiration.

And both recognised their respective talents and the rules of their relationship.

If Ron couldn't secure agreement on the golf courses and clubs of County Down, then Cecil, who played off scratch, would offer to employ a different clubbing technique with the party in question.

Enough said.

Eventually Cecil spoke. "I think we'll have to keep an eye on our friend Watson, Ronnie. I'll tell you for nothing, I'm not best pleased at this Historical Enquiries malarkey. He's some fuckin' cheek announcing that Loyalist paramilitaries and security force collusion were part of their remit."

"Now Cecil, we've nothing to hide here," said the Mayor, smiling.

The luminescence from the dashboard display lit him up. Pristine white dentures glowed from an orange, sunbed tan. "And we'll not behave like we have."

The tone of Herringshaw's voice dropped menacingly. "Should I need it, I have a card up my sleeve, where *that* particular gentleman is concerned."

Ambulance and fire brigade sirens wailed somewhere off in the distance. Across the road, the good citizens of Belfast lined up dutifully, awaiting buses home from the daily grind, oblivious or indifferent to the vagaries of what passed as a democratic decision-making process inside the sober façade of City Hall.

"Looks like snow… early for this time of year. Do you think it will keep the flag protesters off the streets?"

"Things are shaky, Cecil… people are worried we're being sold out. They're at each other's throats out there."

"Aye… so much for '*a shared future*'!"

Simpson pushed himself up again, scratched his arse and surreptitiously smelled his fingertips by way of scratching his nose. He turned to face Herringshaw.

"If they're willing to pay for it, Cecil… if they're willing to pay for it, then a shared future is what we're going to give them."

16

The rusting gates of the Francis Hughes Community Centre in Da Rossa Estate, West Belfast were held partially closed by a shiny new link chain and heavy padlock. Slicked and greased with fresh lubricant, it was a stop-gap measure from the local authority against the young hoods who had been using the grounds for drinking and spliffing up.

The corporation felt that this modest effort offered a semblance of ownership and influence, deep within hostile territory.

But no-one here was fooled.

RIRA was sprayed on walls again as soon as it was removed. A weekly choreography that neither side looked like abandoning. This was where the 'Real' IRA drew on what limited support they could muster. The unreconstructed Republicans. Those who favoured the old adage, *Not a bullet... not an ounce* when the prospect of decommissioning was first mooted. Those on the margins who fed off the poverty and deprivation in the area. Those who still remained outside the sway of Sinn Féin, denouncing them as traitors and Brit-lovers.

The small man struggled with the tiny key, sausage fingers prematurely arthritic, pinching and stabbing awkwardly for the aperture of the lock. The mild tremors that pulsed through him, occasioning his body to shake unexpectedly, did not help his co-ordination. Gnarled, the skin dry and split, the knuckles uneven and misshapen from their savage pummelling of cement and brick.

In anger.

In release.

In the frustrated agonies borne of bitter disappointments.

Disappointments in men and in life and at the desperate hand that he had been dealt.

Joe Breslin sighed and stuttered an exasperated curse under his breath.

The speech impediment had developed many years ago during the early stages of his rehabilitation. It surfaced at times of irritation and anger.

His stooped stance further reduced his height, diminishing him so that he might easily be mistaken for a child from behind. Furrowing his brow in concentration, at last he managed to secure the lock.

He glanced around to ensure that he had turned off all the centre's lights, and pulling his baseball cap down low over his eyes, pushed his plastic lunchbox up into his armpit and walked with an awkward, pained, open-legged gait back to the council house where he lived with his mother and younger sister.

All things considered, it hadn't been a bad day.

His morning had begun when a small group of local children – all in possession of a different musical instrument – tugged, pushed and pulled at each other impatiently.

They peered through the fence at the ugly concrete building covered in Republican graffiti, then back to Joe expectantly.

"Joe! Joe! Joe! Let us in… it's freezin' out here!"

He shuffled over to do so as quickly as his broken body would allow him.

With a click, the lock turned and the peeling, squealing gates cracked open, giving way to the small torrent of laughing children who poured through them. Joe opened the centre's double doors, and before they swung closed behind him, turned on his heel, now inside looking out.

Da Rossa housing estate was a vision of awfulness.

Empty flats, breeze-blocked shut, windows scorched around the edges. A dilapidated ice cream van, rusting now, clown faces and cartoon characters a parody. Skinny, scabby dogs. Rubbish tipped out onto green areas. Used nappies and condoms. Empty, crushed beer cans and torn Rizla paper packets.

Tired, defeated people.

The children were dutifully arranging the plastic chairs in a performance circle. Discordant notes and snatches of musical phrases arose from the young people inside.

He felt like closing the gates against it all.

Keeping it out, if only for a while, whilst he and the kids lost themselves in the jigs and reels and the folk-stories behind them.

The days when the traditional Irish music classes occurred were good days for him. The children – often so cruel and dismissive of each other – seemed to treat him with a kindness, almost a reverence that might have been reserved for some poor fictional Disney wretch that they'd seen in *Beauty and the Beast* or *The Hunchback of Notre Dame*.

He was aware of course that their parents knew all about poor Joe Breslin, the man who had had his young life stolen away in his prime.

The days when music classes took place were special for another reason.

On alternate weeks, the black Volvo that pulled up to the door contained not just Dympna – the music teacher from St. Aloysius Primary School – but also Molly McArdle, the sightless piano tuner from the Workshops for the Blind.

Joe had only recently confided in his sister Anne that he thought – no, he was sure – that he was in love with Molly McArdle.

Yes, even if it had been only some four months from making her acquaintance.

Tears had rolled down Anne's cheeks uncontrollably and she had needed to leave the room before returning and discussing with her older brother whether he should share his feelings with the woman.

Joe said that he felt that Molly already knew, as they were getting on like a house on fire.

She'd asked him and he'd let her feel the contours of his face with her hands.

Soon, he thought, he would ask her out on a date.

Joe, Molly and Keano, her guide dog.

17

Eban knew that Rosemary and Pascal were not at home.

If you were so inclined, it was possible to discern the comings and goings of your housemates by the opening and closing of room doors, the footfall descending the stairs and the slamming of the front door. It was a tried and trusted method employed by both him and Emily when they wanted to enjoy each other and not be interrupted.

They were fearful that the noises of their lovemaking would travel and provide the others with some voyeuristic satisfaction or lazy gossip.

He looked again at the letter he had been dreading.

The letter he had been craving.

The letter that might once and for all bring it to an end.

Thank you for your correspondence dated 15th January 2014. We have received and processed your request for an investigation to be undertaken regarding criminal incidents which occurred on or around May 1970 in relation to an unnamed victim and are writing to you now to request that you attend a meeting with our investigative officers to further discuss the matter.

Please be present at our offices on Wednesday 5th February 2014 at 2.30pm, bringing this letter with you.

It was signed, *Sgt Samuel Coulter on behalf of Detective Inspector Dan Watson. Historical Enquiries Team, Police Service of Northern Ireland.*

For the umpteenth time he methodically went through

the contents of his folders, laying out the press cuttings in date order; arranging the correspondence in date order; looking again at the HET Terms and Conditions document and the sections he had highlighted in pink, blue and green ink. The yellow annotated Post-its, strategically ordered and poking out from between its pages. A seemingly endless amount of meticulous, painstaking research – and no small amount of anguished soul-searching – had finally brought him to this point.

He ached to be done with it.

Or just to have a confidant in all of this.

A second opinion.

Someone to vindicate what he was about to do.

But *that*, he knew – had always known – *that* would not be possible.

He heard Emily move around in the room above him. He desperately wanted her to enfold him in her perfumed arms. To reassure him. To fall asleep together again. Maybe for the last time.

They had not spoken since they had parted in anger. He had been dismissive and accusatory toward the only person who had shown any concern for him. And he could not explain the reasons why to her; could not seek mitigation on the grounds of diminished responsibility due to… *what?*

The failings of a feeble man, tortured by the horrors of memory and conscience?

It took only a few moments to convince himself that contrition was the driving motivation for seeking a reconciliation with her.

In truth, blood was already rushing to his semi-hard erection.

Memories of Emily naked but for a pearl choker and stockings; red polka-dot silk dressing gown spread out under her. Doing it standing up, against the wall, behind the door of his room. On the king-size bed, in the hotel in Portstewart, that weekend away together. When she was having her period and said that it would be more arousing for her.

He climbed the stairs quietly and tapped on her door.

"Emily… it's me."

There was a pause. Then the sound of objects being moved around. Cups, plates, glasses clinking.

Bless her, she's tidying her room, he thought. *She knows what an obsessive-compulsive freak I am.*

Eventually the door opened a meagre width. Emily peered through the gap, her dressing gown clutched closed at the neck.

"The house is empty," he whispered.

It was the standard shared code, the traditional precursor to their lovemaking. As potent as any foreplay.

"I should tell you to fuck right off Eban Barnard!"

Her voice did not match the admonishment. It was somehow tempered by the unanticipated, now-dawning promise of longed-for intercourse.

Eban recognised it. "Can I come in?"

She pulled a mock-disapproving face but swung open the door and stood aside, allowing him entry.

The room was how he'd remembered it.

Brightly coloured scarves and silk blouses were scattered here and there, draped over every available stand and surface.

In the corner stood a music stand, replete with sheet music for medieval madrigals. A lacquered wooden recorder was placed along a shelf there. A large ornamental mirror was placed against the wall. From it hung string upon string of every kind of necklace.

The unmade bed was covered in a detonation of clothes: skirts, sweaters, slacks, jeans. Dresses hung in see-through cellophane bags in the only wardrobe available.

Several coffee mugs sat around what little spare surface

space that remained. Stuffed into them were mouldering banana skins and orange peels. The whole room smelled of perfume, cocoa butter and talcum powder.

"Ahh… just as I remembered it," he said faux-sarcastically.

"Let's not go there right now," she warned. "If you think—"

Before she could say anything else, he had crossed the floor to her and placed his hand through the gap in her dressing gown and between her legs.

He pushed his index finger down the front of her panties. At the same time he placed his other hand at the nap of her neck and pulled her face toward him, kissing her deeply.

She gasped and they both fell backward onto the bed, knocking against the dresser. Hand cream and lipsticks clattered to the floor.

He took one hand away and tugged at his belt buckle. Emily joined him, pulling at his jeans, her dressing gown falling fully open.

She rolled on top of him and he let out a curse.

"Shit! Ouch!"

Eban reached behind him and removed a large purple dildo from amongst the sheets.

Then a dinner plate with dried gravy on it.

He looked at both, then at her.

Emily momentarily made an adorably penitent face.

"On the floor…" he panted. "On the floor…" and they rolled sideways, pulling the duvet and pillows down with them.

She had managed to work her panties off, pushing them down with her foot and pulling out of one leg.

He was kissing and sucking her breasts.

"Put me in," he rasped. "Put me inside you!"

He pulled her hand toward his crotch. She felt him enter her and push hard, moving her, sliding her along the wooden floorboards beneath them.

"Slowly," she gasped, pleading. "SLOWLY!"

But it was too late. He bucked and arched and bellowed as if in pain. Like he'd been seared with a hot branding iron, *"AWWW! S-H-I-T! F-U-C-K!"*

And then he collapsed his full body weight on top of her and lay there, breathing heavily.

She pushed at him, "Get OFF me... you great OAF!"

Eban rolled off her and lay with his face pressed down in a pillow. His body was rising and falling in small heaves.

They lay like that for some moments.

She thought at first that he was crying, and – despite a degree of awkwardness – slowly reached over to touch his shoulder.

At that moment Eban rolled over onto his back and she could see that he was giggling. Barely able, it seemed, to hold in the laughter.

Emily pushed herself up on an elbow and scowled.

A faint buzzing noise intruded.

Her thoughts turned to the battery-powered dildo that must be somewhere within the chaos of the bedding.

Eban looked at her and began rocking with laughter again.

She couldn't help it. A smile spread across her face.

She had to join in.

It was as if some great weight had been temporarily lifted from him.

From them.

It was the happiest she'd seen him in months, and she was surprised by how good it made her feel. She slid down back to the floor, lay flat on her back and giggled too.

They stayed that way for some time until the noise of the front door slamming told them that one of the others had arrived home.

Eban reached for the duvet and pulled it over them both in a defensive manner.

"I'm sorry Emily," he said. "Really... I'm truly sorry..."

He tried to control himself. His laughter seemed incongruous with his remorse. Emily didn't quite know how to react. Was he sorry for the way he had been treating her? Or sorry for his inexcusable selfishness in leaving her wet, aroused and unsatisfied?

"Well, so you should be!" she said in a manner hinting at her indignation.

"I *said* I was sorry…"

"It's easily said."

"No… saying sorry is hard…"

"It's not for me."

Well it should be… if it means anything!"

The mood had somehow changed.

Reverted back to what it had been before.

Imperceptible to both, they were speaking in low whispers now. An unavoidable habit that they had both succumbed to ever since their first illicit rendezvous under the same roof as the resentful, watchful Rosemary Payne.

She reached for a box of tissues, tersely pulling a handful free and passing them to him.

He took them and wiped himself.

She did the same.

"I'm assuming you're still taking responsibility for your own protection?"

The offhand, formal manner in which he said this was simultaneously hurtful and antagonising.

"A bit late… but nice of you to ask," she said sarcastically.

"Well…" He tailed off, nothing really to add.

She had already moved away and was pulling on a pair of jeans. He was buckling his belt.

Emily was still stung. "And what if I hadn't been… what then?"

There was movement outside on the landing, a creak and a knock on Emily's door.

It was Rosemary.

"Emily… I'm making tea; the fruit tea you like."

They both looked at each other.

It was a common tactic by the house matriarch to embarrass them.

"I'll be down in about five, Rosemary," she shouted and continued to dress.

"I have scones…"

"In about five minutes."

"Oh, *fine*," she said, with barely concealed disapproval in her voice; lack of entry to the room probably confirming Eban's presence. "Don't be long dear…"

Her footsteps moved off.

Eban sat down heavily on the edge of the bed, the springs creaking. He put his head in his hands. "Jesus… what a way to live!"

Emily took it personally. " I didn't ask you up here."

"Not *you*… *her* – *this!*" He gestured around him. "Look at us! Look at the way we live. Most people at our stage of life have children, families, friends, homes… *what's wrong with us?*"

Emily was taken aback by the scope and intensity of his outburst. "I have friends," she said somewhat defensively.

"Acquaintances maybe – workmates – but that crowd from the school don't *care* about *you!*"

She'd almost forgotten how cruel he could be. "Why are you so angry all the time? Why do you have to strike out at *me?*"

He sneered, "You're the one who goes in for counselling – what was it they told you? Hurt people *hurt* people."

"It's a fact," she rallied, but she was thrown by this.

Eban disparagingly referred to her sessions with Dr Amanda McCabe as treatment for her '*mental illness*'.

He looked up at her. "You're going to die alone, and so am I, because of the decisions we've made and the people we are!"

Emily was shocked at his callousness.

But like the few women who had come before her, she was also somehow attracted by his desperate hopelessness.

Pulled toward some need to '*fix*' him.

To save him.

"Eban, where does this stuff come from? Why would you be so—"

"You don't know me!"

"I've tried to know you."

Eban went quiet. He stood up and moved toward the door, avoiding her eyes.

She called after him, "It doesn't have to be this way. We've talked about… *alternatives*."

Eban swung around. "What… you mean moving in together? Don't start *that* again!"

Rosemary called up the stairs impatiently.

She wanted dearly to play cat to Emily's mouse. Wanted to see if she could smell Eban's lovemaking on her. "*Emily, TEA!*"

"It couldn't be worse than *this*," Emily said, pointing to Rosemary's voice.

"Couldn't it? We've known each other for how long – three years? We're adults: we behave like adults; we talk like adults, yet what do you really know about me?"

"That you're… different."

"*Different?* What does *that* mean? If you knew – *really* knew – me, you'd run a mile!"

"Oh come on…"

"I'm serious: what are any of us but the sum of our hopes and fears? When that's gone, what's left of us? I mean, what's left standing? Believe me Emily… I'm doing you a favour… you don't need more angst in your life."

His conviction was frightening and overpowering. Emily felt that she was diminishing in the face of it. "I know that you're not a bad person…"

"Oh do you… do you now?"

"I think so. Why can't you have some faith?"

"In what?"

"People… God…" She looked into his eyes. "*Me?*"

"Faith is the path of least resistance. It's an abdication. Try accepting responsibility. Try living a life with doubt instead." He hurled the words at her.

She was taken aback by his passion.

"I know you'll never be happy like this."

"You don't know me. If you did, maybe you'd be surprised."

The ambiguity with which he said this frightened her.

She vainly, desperately, ultimately inappropriately reached for something and found only humour. "You're too boring to be really bad!"

This seemed to make Eban angrier still. "*The banality of evil*," he said portentously.

Emily was surprised to feel scorn rush through her. This self-pity; this bitterness; this pomposity was all just too much. Making a spooky noise, she waved her hands mockingly. "Ooooooh, now you're *evil!*"

Eban opened the door and looked back over his shoulder. "Just remember: you're a long way from Wolverhampton."

He made it sound like a threat.

18

Sometime later, the pink weals on his rump now fading, Eban found himself once again drawn back to the wreck of McGrew's pub.

Stepping back further into the alleyway and away from the sheerness of the climb, Eban darted glances this way and that. He shielded his eyes from the low, early morning summer sun that shot piercing orange spears down the alley from the east.

Lines of over-full dustbins awaiting collection stood to attention like squat, untidy sentinels outside garishly multi-coloured back doors.

The house numbers painted onto the bins with broad, unwieldy brush strokes.

The doors' colours determined by the last job lot of emulsion purchased to paint the entire house inside and out.

Behind these doors, families were listening to reports of the previous night's riots and wondering what remnants of the evening they might encounter on the way to work or school.

John Parkes, his Sunday school teacher, had called them '*little fortresses of common love*'.

Eban wasn't sure why.

Just like the pictures at the start of *Coronation Street* on television, Parkes had said.

As he looked them up and down now, Eban half-expected to hear the plaintive refrain of the telly trumpet parp out its signature tune over the scene.

He wondered if they too had outside toilets in the yard, so that the seat almost burned your bare arse with the cold in winter.

Or no hot water, so that you bathed in a tin bath and your ma washed your hair over the sink, with a milk bottle full of hot water. A milk bottle full of cold for the rinse.

The rising heat from the summer sun warmed a yawning black cat. She stretched and stirred herself, half-interested in the smells and odours of family waste that peeped over the top of the receptacles.

By retreating another two steps backward and craning his neck, the boy could see the corrugated iron roof that enclosed the back yard of what had formerly been McGrew's Pub and Off-Licence, and colloquially known as 'The Wine Lodge'.

It sloped down toward him at a steepish angle, but was still flat enough to retain tin cans, a couple of old sneakers, a burst football and a bicycle tyre that had been thrown up there at some time or other.

It had stood like many others, bricked and boarded up since the night it had been attacked.

In the centre was his point of entry.

A Cyclops skylight.

Like a black scorched hole, scarred and blind in the very middle of the covering. The glass absent and the edges sooty and charred from the night when the Catholic Paddy McGrew and his family were burned out and the place ransacked.

It was to him, the portal to another world.

And it had become, without doubt, the most important, the most secret, the most liberating and the most beautiful thing in young Eban Barnard's troubled life.

Eban knew that by placing a dustbin at the foot of what

had been the back door jamb, he could elevate himself high enough to find footholds in the broken brick on each side.

Placing his school blazer over what seemed to be the dullest, bluntest glass, he could lie across the yard wall apex and pull himself onto the sloping roof.

Following the routine as usual, he lobbed his school bag up onto the roof ahead of him, and heaved and struggled to follow.

A pigeon fluttered up and off.

The boy also knew he should be at school.

He had his violin lesson today. What a mistake that had proved to be.

Following the fiasco with the drum, his parents had forked out for the hire of an instrument from the Belfast School of Music, but had instantly regretted it as Eban's best efforts suggested cat strangulation on an industrial scale.

Miss McInerney, the spinster violin teacher, would be looking for him.

But the confusion and chaos of the last two weeks seemed to render everything null and void.

Men and boys ran the streets late at night, shouting and screaming.

Gunfire sounded close at hand.

Grown-ups seemed distracted and preoccupied.

His parents, the neighbours, his older brother Alex, even his teachers spoke in clandestine whispers.

Terms like *petrol bomb*, *zip gun* and *rubber bullet* filled the playground.

Classmates traded in spent CS gas canisters and brass shell casings as currency.

The older boys boasted of carrying weighty, oil-stained canvas bags from house to house, where local men would nervously receive them.

Eban welcomed the grown-up preoccupations and the decline of the natural order of things.

It served his purpose.

He could disappear unnoticed.

Now he could hear the voices of the women on their way to the Ladybird linen factory where his mother worked.

He was most vulnerable at this point in his modus operandi.

He would have to be quick.

This was the crucial moment.

Whilst on the roof, which seemed to him to be high above street level, he was exposed to others. A neighbour might notice him and assume that he was after copper, lead or other pickings from what the McGrews may have left behind them in their haste.

Dropping down slowly, carefully now, through the skylight and into his sanctuary.

Lowering himself, until his foot made firm contact with an old upturned gas stove.

He knew from his other visits that there would be enough light coming in from overhead, and through the rips and holes in the corrugated metal sheets covering the windows, to tentatively negotiate the sea of broken glass and debris which now crunched underfoot.

Crates, kegs, smashed beer and wine bottles, old shoes, cereal boxes, palettes and charred wooden beams fallen from the roof.

The flotsam and jetsam of the McGrews' hurried flight from persecution.

Eban Barnard was in again, undetected.

19

Eban stood in the foyer.

It was a modern, high-ceilinged, marble-floored, glass-fronted structure. Open plan.

Glass-walled elevators with brushed steel doors hissed up and down, emptying people on the ground floor and welcoming other waiting groups to rise up and away with elegant efficiency.

It might have been the offices of any large multinational or conglomerate.

Indeed, the location was smack in the middle of Belfast's prosperous Waterfront district.

The Ministry of Truth looks better than I would have thought, he reflected, and smiled to himself a little to alleviate the nervous tension that had deprived him of any sleep the night before.

The left side of his face ached again.

His jawline pulsed with pain from his ear and radiated downward.

He'd first thought it a simple toothache. Then an inner ear problem.

Then perhaps some kind of sinus infection.

The cardio stress test he'd undergone some weeks ago suggested otherwise.

Decked out like an astronaut in training, electrodes stuck to his chest, he ran on a treadmill that gradually steepened its incline.

Although the pace of the machine was hardly demanding, he was bent over, sweating and wheezing, by the end of it.

The letter that Emily had noticed – from the Royal Victoria Hospital – had confirmed it.

Angina.

Now that he was officially diagnosed with heart disease, the NHS coronary care machine took over.

He was in the system.

He was required to meet with Mr Khan, the consultant cardiologist, to determine the extent of the narrowing of his arteries.

But all that would have to wait.

He unconsciously massaged his throbbing left upper arm again and looked around. Approximately half the people he saw wore police uniforms. But they somehow seemed to him to be of a softer, more 'civilianised' design. Smart white shirts and blouses, pencil skirts and sharp trousers. A minimum of insignia and paraphernalia.

He was struck by how young they all looked.

A large official crest was suspended high from the roof of the foyer. It read, *Police Service of Northern Ireland, Historical Enquiries Team – Policing the Past*, and featured a nondescript logo.

The sweat from his palms was beginning to soften and warp the cardboard folders he was carrying. He shifted them from hand to hand self-consciously. He looked around nervously to see if anyone was watching, then wiped his sleeve across his brow and looked at it.

It was sodden.

Such a smart, clean, anonymous building to house so much pain and hurt, he thought.

Then, almost immediately, a high door opened and an elderly, weary-looking woman emerged, bent over and sniffling into a handkerchief; supported by a younger man and woman. They were followed by a young woman police officer who looked suitably consoling and held open the door.

So I have come to the right place, he thought and moved over to the reception desk.

Taking off his overcoat and draping it over his arm, he addressed the officer.

"I have an appointment."

"Of course sir, might I see your letter?'

He pushed it across the desk and waited.

The policeman lifted a telephone. "A Mr Barnard for his 2.30 appointment... thanks."

He gestured. "If you'd like to take a seat over in the public waiting area someone will be right out to collect you."

For a brief second Eban thought he heard his own incredulous voice say, *'What fucking lunatic scheme is this?'*, and he thought about turning around and walking right out again.

Last chance.

No-one would ever know, much less care.

But he knew in his marrow that this was never an option.

Every road had led him here.

And here was where it would begin and end.

For better or for worse.

Eban moved over to a social area with pot plants, a coffee maker and a large wall-mounted TV with the sound turned down.

Three others sat there already, forming a tight huddle.

An older man looked off into the distance, seemingly having zoned out all and any activity around him. Whilst a younger man – perhaps his son – sat on the edge of the leatherette couch, his knee bouncing up and down in anxious apprehension.

He wore a denim jacket with a shirt and loosely knotted tie, suggesting perhaps a detour from a manual job to be here.

A young woman left the group and moved toward the coffee maker.

Eban noted that the sounds around him seemed strangely muted.

Barely audible piped music, the ping of the lift as the doors opened, the ringing of telephones off in the distance, voices. It was like being in some hermetically sealed bubble.

An Asian man glided past with a floor-polishing machine, its brushes rotating. But even this seemed strangely dulled.

Everything smelled faintly of furniture polish and disinfectant.

But behind that was the unmistakable odour of public toilets.

That masked smell he recognised from airport lounges and car salesroom lobbies.

The smell of fifty different kinds of faeces held back by lavender mist and spring morning dew.

Concealing to appeal.

Before he had time to sit, a hand on his shoulder made him jump.

"Mr Barnard? Sorry to startle you. Can I get you a wee cup of tea or anything?" The policewoman was smiling at him.

"No... no, I'm fine thanks."

"Alright then, if you'd like to follow me, Inspector Watson will see you now."

She led him through swishing double doors, and down carpeted corridors.

To either side of him he could see rooms full of library-style shelving, holding hundreds of files from floor to ceiling. Cardboard boxes with names and dates written on the side stood in piles on the floors. Others were marked, 'Forensic Evidence'.

As he moved down the corridor, a door opened momentarily in a side room where a stout man sat in front of a tape recorder, across from another man taking notes. Eban thought he heard the man say, "On the 17th October 1983, my father was abducted from his place of work by two men, taken to the Hightown Road outside Belfast and—"

The door closed again.

Eban noticed again how much he was sweating.

He'd dressed for winter in an insulated ski-coat that had seen better days. His woollen beanie and heavy crew neck sweater ensured the walk from the town centre to the offices was an uncomfortably overheated one.

He took out a handkerchief and dabbed the back of his neck. Laughing self-consciously, he remarked to the woman walking ahead of him,

"You probably think I'm one of those people who get nervous – guilty, I mean – around policemen... police*women*, I mean..."

"Och, no sir... not at all." She didn't look back.

"I've just got a bit of a cold."

They turned a corner into a long passageway.

Coming in the opposite direction was a plain-clothes office, his laminated identity pass clipped to his jacket. As they drew closer Eban noticed the man's eyes widen as he came level with him. It was at first a look of recognition, which then changed to one of naked astonishment. The man stopped and turned around as they passed, making no pretence at covert observation. He watched them, open-mouthed, as they disappeared down the passageway.

Eban's stomach lurched. *It's begun...* he thought.

When they reached Dan Watson's office he was on the phone.

Eban could see the tall man through the partially closed blinds on the glass office walls.

Watson looked up and Eban thought he heard him say, "Yes... he's with me now."

Watson looked again, this time squinting, trying to focus through the gaps. He said something else, urgently, furtively, that Eban could not catch. The policewoman knocked on the door.

"Come in."

She stood aside and allowed Eban to enter.

Dan Watson pushed his chair back to stand. His face drained of colour. He still held the receiver to his ear, "Christ… " he whispered. "It's like seeing a ghost."

He replaced the phone in its cradle unsteadily.

He pulled himself together.

"Sorry Mr Barnard – Eban – will you come in?" He nodded toward the officer.

"Jenny, will you tell the switchboard no calls? I'll let them know when."

She left, closing the door.

Eban entered, and placing his padded, threadbare overcoat over the back of the chair, sat down. He wiped his hands on his trouser legs and began to arrange the folders he was carrying on the table in front of him.

Watson still stood, rubbing his chin, seemingly perplexed.

Eventually he sat on the edge of the desk. Unexpectedly, an exasperated laugh of disbelief escaped him.

Eban sat back with a start.

Watson was shaking his head.

Eban was becoming irritated. "Is there something I'm missing here?"

Dan Watson held up both palms in an effort to placate him. I'm sorry. You've got to appreciate, after all these years… well… you just look so like *him*."

"Don't you think I've heard that before?"

"Have you?"

"Only all my life."

"Your brother was held in pretty high esteem around here."

Watson leaned back across the desk and pulled open a drawer.

Removing a coffee mug, he passed it to Eban.

Embossed on it was a photograph of Dan Watson and Alex Barnard, Eban's older brother. Both were smiling and in uniform.

Underneath this it read, in bold black letters, *Elementary, My Dear Watson!*

"He had that done for me when I made detective. He was one of the good guys, your brother; one of the best... oh, I'm sorry..."

He proffered his hand as an afterthought. "Detective Inspector Dan Watson. We've never actually met before, have we?"

Eban let it hang there for what seemed a long time.

When it became apparent that there would be no handshake, Watson self-consciously returned it to his pocket.

Eban felt that he had regained a modicum of control in what was fast becoming a prematurely unstable situation. "No, not that I'm aware of," he said, holding the taller man's gaze.

"He never really... well... mentioned you a lot. I mean..."

"No need to feel awkward, detective; we weren't close."

Watson seemed uncomfortable. "No, I just meant that he kept clear boundaries between work and home life; family – you had to back then, in this job."

Eban was becoming irritated.

This was not going as he had planned it a thousand times in his head.

His pulse was racing and he could hear himself say, more abrasively than he intended, "And a lot of good it did him. Still... times have changed for the better I take it? Pretty cushy number you have here, detective..." He gestured around the office. "Beats plodding the streets, eh? No danger you'll finish up like poor brother Alex."

Dan Watson was rather taken aback by the combative nature of Eban's attitude.

"Alex knew the risks, we all did – we all *do*. The dissident threat is still a real one."

Eban was tiring of the clichés already. His anxiety was causing him to accelerate the process that he had so patiently and meticulously planned for so very long.

It was almost as if someone else was in the driver's seat.

Somewhere behind his eyes, pulling the levers.

He could barely believe the words that were spilling out now from his lips.

Suddenly, irrationally and with real anger he said, "Look, Christ – spare me; this is the reason I didn't go to his funeral: so I wouldn't have to listen to all of this 'buried with full military honours' bullshit!"

Dan Watson was stung on behalf of his dead friend, but wasn't entirely sure how to react.

"Hey, hey, hey... hold on now! That's no way—"

"And here you are, all these years later, still banging on about duty and honour and—"

Watson resorted to professional detachment as he'd been trained to do. "Just calm down Mr Barnard. Can I get you a coffee; some water?"

It seemed like some kind of hiatus.

Eban breathed in deeply, closed his eyes and tried to compose himself. In full knowledge of what was yet to come.

If he was to see this through, he'd have to somehow hold it together. He mustered a steadier tone. "Have you read my letter?"

Watson hadn't finished. "Just so as you know, your brother died protecting the citizens of this..."

Eban closed his eyes again. He felt his shirt sticking to his skin.

Breathing deeply through his nose, he clenched his fists, out of sight below the desk, and tried again. "Have you read my letter?"

Watson talked over him. "...Province. He was an inspiration to the men who served with him and under..."

Eban's jaw set with tension. He raised his voice an octave. "HAVE YOU READ MY LETTER?!"

Watson too spoke more loudly. He was determined to finish what he had to say. "...AND IT'S BECAUSE OF MEN LIKE ALEX BARNARD, THAT—"

Suddenly, unexpectedly, an ice-cold calm flooded through Eban.

From where he knew not, but the quality of this newfound resolve was distinctly malevolent in character and purpose.

An unruffled look spread across his features.

He relaxed.

He smiled.

"Tell me, detective – what have my brother and the black taxi cab that brought me here got in common?"

Watson looked bewildered.

Eban waited for a moment. "No? Well, it's obvious: they both took five in the back."

He leaned back, smiling. Pleased with himself.

Dan Watson was incredulous. Oscillating somewhere between disgust and fury.

Eventually he spoke, close to a whisper.

"Is that supposed to be funny? Your brother died a hero."

Eban was ready for him.

He rolled up one of the newspapers on the desk into a tight rod. "My brother died on his knees, tending his rose bushes: three to the back of the head." He reached out his hand in front of him and aggressively slapped the paper down three times.

CRACK! CRACK! CRACK!

It was too much. Watson exploded. He jumped to his feet.

"FUCKIN' MURDERIN' SCUM! COWARDS! THEY SHOT HIM WHILE HE LAY FACE DOWN... DYING ON THE GROUND!"

He rounded the table and put his face close to Eban's.

His breath smelled of peppermints and halitosis. His voice lowered to a threatening hiss.

"Listen, you little prick: Alex Barnard was twice the man you'll ever be. If you didn't look so alike, I wouldn't believe you had the same blood running through your veins!"

Eban sighed in an exaggerated fashion, still not quite believing the self composure he was somehow enjoying.

"As I was saying, did you read my letter? I've filled out all the necessary request forms. I didn't come here for *this!*"

Watson collected himself. "Then why did you come?"

"You people investigate unsolved murders, don't you? I mean, that's what you do: bring 'closure'" – he sarcastically accompanied the word with a mid-air quotation sign – "to poor unfortunates who live their lives without answers. You make historical enquiries, no?"

"We help people move on with—"

Eban was briefly disgusted. "Crawling; digging around in the past, through the muck… it must feel like living in limbo land for you as well as them." He was suddenly jolted by a bolt of realisation. Of memory. It shook him.

"As well as… *me.*"

He recovered shakily. "Like I said… I didn't come here for this."

Watson saw him waver. "And like *I* said, why did you come?"

"For answers."

"To what?"

"The victim, for a start; what happened to the victim. Give me an address."

"I have someone looking into that. Your letter says serious assault; possibly murder. Well… which is it?"

"That's what I want *you* to tell *me.*"

"Well, it's a long time ago." Watson pulled a file across his desk. "No name... a date... a street... McGrew's pub. That's all you're giving us?"

"That's all I can give."

Watson felt back on home turf now. He stood up, gesturing to the door.

"Well Mr Barnard, you can take it that we'll be in touch if..."

Eban, who had been waiting for the right moment, played his trump card.

It was the moment he had visualised a hundred thousand times in his mind.

He was determined to do it justice. "But I haven't confessed yet. I came to confess."

Dan Watson was tired of being toyed with.

He had a full afternoon's agenda ahead of him and had become unsettled and unnerved by this ghost, this doppelganger of his late partner who had seemingly come here today for little other reason than to harangue him and fuck with his head.

"Confess? Confess to what?"

Eban Barnard stood slowly, pushing his chair away from him. He walked around the desk and leaned over the detective, putting his wrists together. Inviting invisible handcuffs.

"I killed my brother... and... he deserved what he got."

The big man couldn't believe what he was hearing.

Grabbing Eban by his lapels, he hoisted him clean off the floor, and knocking over a coat rack, pushed him hard against the wall, cracking the back of Eban's head in the process.

Sergeant Coulter, hearing the noise, knocked on the door.

"Everything alright sir?"

Watson regained control of himself and let Eban drop.

"Everything's fine," he called back with a shaky voice.

Eban brushed the creases from his shirt. Buttons that had popped in the altercation bounced on the desk. He rubbed the back of his head gingerly. "Everything's not fine though... is it, detective?"

Watson took a deep breath and cast around for some modicum of professional composure.

"Mr Barnard, given that I was one of the arresting officers of the scum that boasted of killing my friend – and your brother – Chief Superintendent Alex Barnard, I'd have to respectfully contend that you are full of shite, and that you're a liar, a sick fantasist... or both. They served time and were released under the terms of the Good Friday Agreement, more's the pity. There's nothing to consider; nothing to investigate. This charade is over."

Again he gestured to the door.

Eban was suddenly desperate again. He needed to make him understand.

"For God's sake, man – did you not read my letter?" he pleaded.

Watson was again in full control.

He opened the folder on his desk. "Your letter says nothing about your brother. You say on the forms that you want us to investigate the attempted murder of some fellow called..." He put on his glasses and squinted for effect. "Oh that's right: you don't have a name – someone who was seriously assaulted, possibly murdered in 1970."

"Correct. Unsolved, isn't it?"

"Yes, along with about a thousand others or more. Listen, I've looked into it; we've spoken to people... it was right at the start of things; very bad times, but you need to give me more, otherwise I see no good reason to—"

Eban became suddenly animated. "So you think maybe he didn't die...?"

"I can't answer that at this time, and you're not immediate family; in fact you can offer no reason for an interest in this case."

Eban looked crestfallen. Then he linked his fingers under his chin in a rather officious manner.

"I've paid my fee and filled out all the necessary paperwork. I'll take it to the police ombudsman if I have to."

Dan Watson realised that he really didn't need something like this getting out to the press. Especially from Alex Barnard's lunatic brother.

He rolled his eyes, "Look mate… what is it you want from me?"

Eban pushed the folders he had brought with him across the desk at the detective.

"Find out what happened to the victim. Hear my confession." He was beseeching him.

"That you killed your brother Alex…?"

Eban stared at him intensely. In silence. It was oppressive. Finally he spoke.

"*Arrest me!*"

"For God's sake man, think about what you're saying. It makes no sense, any of it."

"Please… I'm begging you." There were tears in Eban's eyes.

Dan Watson rubbed hard at his own eyes. "Alright. I must need my fuckin' head examined…" He paused for a moment, once again trying to balance this debacle in his own mind.

"Alright, out of respect for his memory we'll hear whatever bollocks it is you have to say. But only for your brother's sake, you understand? Not for yours, do you hear me? Not for *you!*"

He picked up the telephone.

"Gerry, set up the cameras and mics in Interview Room 1. There's a man here says he wants to tell us a story."

He put the phone down and looked hard at Eban.

"One condition: when you've done, you're going to meet with our psychiatric people for an evaluation. You're in need of some serious help my friend."

Eban burst out laughing. He threw his head back and roared. It was the funniest thing he'd heard all day. He gradually became aware of how that must appear to the senior policeman across the table. Eventually he gestured sideways with his head.

"And what about Harvey... my big white rabbit?"

20

When they entered the interview room, the harsh light from the overhead fluorescent strip was enough to make Eban blink and squint.

"Did you say interview room or interrogation room?" he said sardonically.

"We don't do that kind of thing."

Eban raised his eyebrows cynically.

"Here, I mean."

Watson had taken off his jacket which he hung on a peg behind the door, and was now rolling up his shirt sleeves. He'd brought with him a pillow for the small of his back, which pained him like a toothache when he sat for too long.

Eban, seeing this, crossed and hung his own overcoat on top of Watson's jacket. He returned to the table and began to arrange his files in front of him again.

Watson observed this uncomfortably. For a moment the policeman considered crossing back and removing his coat from under Eban's.

Maybe placing it on his chair back. But he knew how this would look.

Certainly insulting.

Possibly weak.

Instead he sat down and watched this enigma across from him busy himself in preparation for he knew not what.

He saw how the sweat stuck to Eban's clothes. Thought he caught a whiff of fetid arse crack from him. Wondered about fleas and lice; the parasites that may now be crawling from this man's rag into the very fabric of his Donegal tweed jacket.

He suppressed a shudder.

The office was a standard enough affair.

Almost identical to the one in which Eban had seen the fat man answering questions on his journey to Watson's room.

There was an elaborate recording device on the desk between them and a file of blue-lined A4 paper for Watson to make notes. Two biro pens, one red, one black, sat on top.

Eban thought that the conicaled, cushioned walls seemed acoustically designed to deaden or muffle noise, for some reason that he couldn't fathom. They reminded him of a padded cell.

Maybe just his imagination.

Because he had imagined this room and this exchange many, many times before.

In his dreams.

In his fantasies.

"What, no two-way mirror?" Eban feigned disappointment. Watson ignored him.

Instead he cleared his throat and pushed the record buttons on the desk machine. Then, looking at his watch, he made a note of the time on his pad and began, in a rather officious tone.

"Just to take you through the standard operating protocols, as a general rule, cases are examined in chronological order starting with the earliest – but there are some exceptions. We sometimes review cases out of sequence; maybe because an elderly relative is in poor health, or because a number of violent events are linked…"

Eban was not looking at him, but rather removing a pen and paper from one of his own folders.

He began to write.

"Say that again," he suddenly fired at Watson; more an instruction than a request.

"What?"

"The bit about violent events being linked."

"Well, you obviously heard me the first time."

Eban stopped writing and looked up.

Slowly, he smiled at the detective with what seemed to Watson to be some degree of perceived advantage. Like a chess player who has surrendered his piece, safe in the knowledge that he is three moves ahead of his opponent. Watching him, amused, like a cat with a mouse.

As cryptically as he could manage, Eban said, "You see, Detective Watson: you're making breakthroughs already!"

Dan Watson became aware that he was being drawn into some sort of mind game.

He found this irritating in the extreme.

"Yes, we make exceptions within stated protocols, or – as in your case – against all our better instincts and judgement, we may do someone a special..." He paused for effect. "Call it a *family favour*."

The sarcasm was not lost on Eban, who batted it back. "And I'm eternally grateful."

Watson returned to his procedural preamble rather wearily. He knew it off verbatim.

"In order to ensure consistent professional investigation standards, the HET has developed a process through which every case is taken. Firstly, Collection and Assessment. This includes the recovery and examination of existing records and exhibits. Secondly, Review. Here cases are examined to determine whether any further investigative or evidential opportunities exist. Next..."

He looked up from the notes he'd been writing as he spoke, and paused for effect and emphasis.

"... and in cases so deemed applicable and warranted, reinvestigation may be judged to be necessary. If the review finds any new evidence or possible lines of inquiry, these are followed up and criminal charges may be brought."

The detective was making it clear that he would remain final arbiter of Eban's petition.

Eban was beginning to become impatient. "Look, is all this really necessary? I'm interested in a resolution. In justice... I imagine you'd call it *'closure'*."

Watson carried on, undeterred. "In some cases a resolution could involve judicial proceedings. For all families it will include the provision of a written report addressing the specific questions they have asked."

"And my specific question is: *where is that man? Is he alive or dead?*" Eban was deliberately confrontational in tone. "And what do you propose to do to find out?"

Watson raised his voice a little to convey both authority and disdain. "The Historical Enquiries Team has full support from within the police service and maintains close links with other agencies including the police ombudsman for Northern Ireland, Forensic Science Northern Ireland and the Northern Ireland Office."

Eban shrugged his shoulders. "So what are we waiting for? Let's get started."

Dan Watson looked at him as he would an idiot child.

"Just so as I'm clear, Mr Barnard: you want us to investigate the serious assault or possible murder of someone currently unnamed... in 1970? If I authorise a team – a very overworked and under-staffed team, I might add – to take this on, will you drop this nonsense concerning your responsibility for the murder of your brother?"

Eban placed his pen on the desk, folded his arms and sat bolt upright. "Absolutely not!"

"Then I'm not sure that I'm prepared to help you with this."

For a long moment Eban said nothing. He glared straight at the detective with barely disguised rage. Then, disconcertingly, slowly, he began to smile.

As before, some inner calm that he had not thought himself capable of, until today, was seeping through him.

Dousing the fires.

Calming his nerves.

Eventually, he spoke.

"Oh come on Watson! Aren't you even a little intrigued? Won't you dig just a little? God knows what you think of me, but I'm not mad you know. What was it Sherlock Holmes said? *'Whenever you have eliminated the impossible, whatever remains – however improbable – must be the truth.'*"

He was beaming at the policeman now. Clearly enjoying the game. "*Elementary* really… *you* should know that."

Watson fought an urge to punch this man in the face. But Eban Barnard had never looked more like his dead brother Alex than at this precise moment. Worse still, Watson couldn't shake the feeling that this man was toying with him. Pushing his buttons for the fun of it.

It made him angry.

He abruptly shot out a long leg and kicked the wire wastepaper basket across the room. It clattered into the metal filing cabinet, startling Eban.

It had the desired effect.

In an eye-blink, Dan Watson came from behind his desk, drawing himself up to his full six feet three inches.

"*Suppose you tell me what the fuck you're playing at?*" He rolled his shirt sleeves further up in a menacing manner.

Eban was not cowed. "Suppose I do… will you sit still long enough to listen; to hear me out?"

Watson smiled. He loosened the top two buttons on his shirt, pulled down the knot in his tie and with deliberation, returned to his seat. He plumped the cushion on his chair and – pushing himself back – stretched out his long legs and crossed his feet on the desk top.

He made a little spire with his fingertips beneath his chin. "*Shoot.*"

"You might not like what you're going to hear."

"Goes with the territory."

Eban too adjusted himself in his chair, getting comfortable, settling in for a long session, warming now to his task.

"Are you a churchgoing man, detective?"

"Not particularly."

"Me neither…"

As he spoke he was taking out newspaper clippings from one of his folders and arranging them so as they now faced the policeman.

"… but that's where it all begins – or rather, *ends* – for me: in church."

Watson bent forward and read aloud. "*The Newry Reporter, August 1991.*" He looked up at Eban quizzically.

Eban spoke dryly, by way of explanation, "It's from my collection."

"First 1970; now 1991? Do you mind telling me…?"

Eban chuckled and pointed at him. "The *Historical Enquiries Team*… right?"

Detective Watson did not appreciate the pun.

Watson continued to read aloud. "*Groom-To-Be Defies 'Get Out' Order: One of the six Newry men who have been ordered by the IRA to leave Ireland by noon on Saturday says he is being wrongly accused and will not leave. With an apparent stalemate in negotiations, two local men have claimed sanctuary in Newry Cathedral and continue with their campaign to have the threat of IRA violence against them lifted.* I remember this; it was in all the papers… but what's it got to do with you, or with Alex, or this mysterious 'victim' from 1970 for that matter?"

Eban could taste vindication.

At last he had the captive audience that he had dreamed and schemed and ached and suffered for. He pulled his chair closer to Watson and leaned right across the table. He rested his upturned hands under the glare of the powerful desk lamp. And for a moment, he seemed to trace the deeply ingrained lifelines that criss-crossed his palms. As if he were searching for something there.

When he spoke, it was in little more than a whisper.

"I spent some time there, in that cathedral – with them, I mean; babysitting them, you might say. God knows they needed it…"

The reminiscence seemed to grip him and Dan Watson saw that this strange, troubled man was being transported by the recollection of things past.

When Eban spoke again it was as if he were talking to himself.

He looked right through the police officer.

Right through the walls of the room.

To somewhere he was compelled to return to.

"What is it they say, detective: *no good deed goes unpunished*?"

21

OUTSIDE NEWRY CATHEDRAL, AUGUST 1991

Sledger zipped up his Adidas top full to the throat and pulled his baseball cap down low.

He sucked air in through his nose, into the back of his throat, hocked up from deep within and spat.

The green phlegm resembled wallpaper paste.

He did a little dance on the balls of his feet, to keep warm.

The evening light had faded early.

Beside him stood a smaller man.

Similarly clad in green, gold and white sportswear, he dug his hands in his pockets and retracted his pink, shaven penis-head back into his shoulders like a tortoise foreskin.

Gold ear studs and neck chains on both men sparkled in the Lucozade street lights.

This was their third night on watch.

They stood below a savage wall mural asserting *From the Ashes of '69 arose the Provos*. Two enormous figures – balaclavaed and clutching AK-47s – made the point more forcefully than any words could convey.

Tootsie, the smaller man, craned his neck and looked upward at the glow illuminating the stained glass window, high in the basilica above them. Occasionally it revealed a momentary or passing contour. The objects of their attention moved in shadows and silhouettes across a square of light, set in the stone walls of Newry Cathedral.

Tootsie became animated.

"Was that one, Sledge; was it – *was that one?*"

The organ grinder grinned at the antics of the monkey. "I told you… calm the fuck down."

"Never mind calm down! They're fuckin' hoods!"

Tootsie seemed to consider something for a moment, and suddenly, with indignation, announced, "I was baptised in there you know!"

The heavyset man smiled. "I heard you were an altar boy."

"Certainly I was… what about it?"

Sledger turned to him and smiled slowly. "Altar boys take it up the arse."

Tootsie pulled a shape in front of him, all shoulders and neck pushing forward in mock bravado. "You're not too big for a slap!"

Sledger raised his eyebrows and grinned through nicotine-stained teeth, with 'as if' derision. "Away and get some sleep… you're hallucinatin' again."

"Away yerself! I'm on 'til two o clock. Seamy will take over from me then."

"Away home. They'll hardly come out now, after all their pissing around."

His tone dropped menacingly and he spoke as if to himself. "They know well enough what they'll get when they do."

"Who's gonna do them, Sledge… are you gonna do them?

The small man's rat-like features were earnest.

Excited. "*I'll* fuckin' do them if you want?

Sledger did a little dance on the balls of his feet again to keep warm.

He looked like he might be sparring with an invisible opponent. "Remember you tried to get us season tickets for the match at Parkhead against the Huns? Remember the length of the waiting list?"

Tootsie, puzzled, nodded his assent.

"Well…" Sledger rose up on his toes and stretched his neck, extending his head left and right. There was a cracking sound. "… *Get in fucking line.*"

The small man became animated again.

"Look… LOOK! There's one of the fuckers now!"

He pointed at the window and gesticulated wildly. He cupped his hands and shouted.

"Go on, you scumbag cunts… you can run but you can't hide. You'll have to come out some time!"

22

For five days now the nerves of Newry town and the surrounding environs of the border counties had been stretched snare-drum tight.

The usual suspects had mobilised.

Marginals, wannabes, hangers-on, under flags of convenience.

Rabble-rousers.

Wasters and chancers.

Young men with nothing better to do.

And genuine, 100% psychopaths.

All desperately seeking a catalyst.

All primed for a knee-jerk reaction.

All craving the catharsis of recriminatory violence.

Reckless excess was abroad and draped in the pseudo-credibility of '*community justice*'.

Local law and order was in limbo by decree of the Provisional IRA Army Council.

A virtual no-go area had been created.

And dozens of Sledgers and Tootsies had loudly declared allegiance to their community by perversely turning upon their own.

Incidents of insidious and actual intimidation had become commonplace.

Thanks to the strategic employment of 'suspect devices', a relentless, round-the-clock constriction of the arteries of roads, streets and estates surrounding the cathedral rendered the town virtually paralysed.

It was a parochial, insular, dirty little squabble and it required understanding as such.

In that regard, Eban Barnard, some forty miles away in Belfast – under-informed and out of his depth – was inadvertently about to make a *very* bad call.

"*You can't be fuckin' serious?*"

"Look Eban, I can tell you anything you want to hear, right? But the bottom line is, we're in over our heads here!"

"You're telling me!"

Philip Walters was getting annoyed now. He knew well enough what he was asking.

Barnard wasn't making it any easier.

He nuzzled the telephone closer into his shoulder with his chin and tried again to keep his voice low, but he couldn't help but sound somehow conspiratorial.

Did Barnard think for a moment that he wanted this shit-storm to be dropped in *his* lap?

For *his* staff to be locked down in some bloody cathedral, minding some shit-scared kids who had called down the wrath of the local heavies?

He sighed deeply and began again. Appealing now in more conciliatory fashion.

"Besides… isn't this *supposed* to be what community relations work is all about?"

It was the only card he had and he'd played it early, far from confident that Eban Barnard gave a good fuck as to what community relations work was supposed to be about.

Eban looked again at the urgent fax Walters had sent him.

The manager sensed an opportunity in the pregnant pause at the other end of the line and rushed to take it.

"*Families Against Intimidation and Terror* – they do good work, Eban; they run a support service for fellas who've been intimidated out of their own areas. The two lads holed up in the cathedral, they're both seventeen; they've already been beaten with iron bars and baseball bats in their own beds for God's sake!"

He didn't know if this was true but it sounded good.

Another silence followed.

In for a penny, in for a pound... thought Walters, and screwed up his face as he delivered the medicine. "There's something else... just so as you know: the IRA say they were committing *'crimes against their community'*."

"The *IRA*?! You didn't say anything about the IRA!"

Walters was sure he'd lost him.

Eban eventually spoke. "Well... were they?"He felt stupid. What did it really matter?

"There were originally six of them... I think they've all been tarred with the same brush."

"Not literally," Eban knee-jerked; then winced. "Sorry... bad joke."

Walters ignored it and pushed on.

"Look Eban, I appreciate this. There *will* be other people there with you. John Hickey, for one. You're relieving someone from a twelve-hour shift – some volunteers; community workers – then somebody will come to relieve you."

Silence on the other end.

"I've done *my* shift."

Still nothing.

"I really appreciate this."

All of Eban's instincts screamed *no fucking way!*

But as he looked around the grey-and-beige-induced brain death of his prefabricated hut, something desperate and primal in him cried out for change.

For animation.

For affirmation.

For excitement.

And besides, wasn't this why he'd come back from England in the first place: to make a difference?

"What was it like... in there I mean?"

"No problem, really – playing cards; sitting around; chatting. They're just kids..."

Eban heard someone enter the outer office. It galvanised him to make a definitive decision.

He heard himself say, *"I'll do it."*

"What?"

"I SAID I'LL DO IT, FOR FUCK SAKE! DO YOU NEED IT IN WRITING?!"

Walters tried not to be too obvious but his relief was palpable. He thanked him again, gave him some directions and hung up.

Eban absentmindedly worked an elastic band around his fingers several times, cutting off the blood supply and leaving temporary weals.

Jesus... this fuckin' place... he thought.

23

SHANKILL ROAD,
BELFAST, NORTHERN IRELAND
MAY 1970

By afternoon he'd finished the *Beano* summer special and two *Fantastic Four* comics. He'd ploughed through his *Uncle Creepy* and *Cousin Eerie* horror mags as well.

American imports, they would have proved expensive if purchased new, but Eban traded for these regularly at Smithfield Market secondhand bazaar.

The low sun was slanting in through the skylight.

Through the gaps in the sheeting and the bolt-holes pockmarking them. Shafts of light shone down and through, criss-crossing the interior, making it look like the deck of some kind of spacecraft.

He walked amongst them, putting his hands underneath the beams.

Enjoying the heat, the glow.

Since he'd been hiding out here, it had become his favourite time of day.

The light made him squint to look directly out onto the street.

To the right he could see the vast, dark mound of Black Mountain.

It was one of the most prominent features of the city, towering above most of West Belfast and reaching a height of some 1,275 feet.

He heard John Parkes, his Sunday school teacher, say that there had been flint and copper finds in the area. That the mountain had deserted farms and overgrown paths joining the fields and homesteads, and trails scattered all over it. On a clear day there were views of Strangford Lough, the Mournes and the Sperrins. Even of Scotland and Donegal.

To his left he could see the whitewashed walls of Jersey Street, Shankill Road Mission Hall, where he was sent regularly on Sunday afternoons and where John Parkes and his son John Junior gave witness.

The hall always caught the late afternoon sunshine, illuminating it spectacularly like some blazing sepulchre.

He liked John Parkes.

Liked the way people deferred to him. The quiet authority he had. His certainty of spiritual belief that rendered the man himself believable.

He was a solid, middle-aged man who always dressed in smart pinstriped suits, shirt and tie.

Psalm 91: *He that dwelleth in the shelter of the most high shall abide in the shadow of the almighty.*

His go-to scripture.

Eban felt safe when he heard John Parkes intone what seemed to him a contract.

A certainty.

A conviction.

The bald dome of his head was blotched with premature liver spots and one large purple birthmark in the shape of a country.

Or so the boys thought.

They argued whether it reminded them more of Africa than of South America.

They joked that his whole cranium was like a globe of the world.

Eban saw the man's head as resembling nothing less than the cratered surface of the pale moon itself.

He listened when John Parkes spoke.

In between the Bible readings and the catechism.

The colouring-in books of Old Testament prophets: Daniel in the lions' den; Elijah ascending into heaven in a chariot of fire; Noah in the belly of the great whale and the born-again sing-song of *I will make you fishers of men* and *Jesus loves me, yes I know*.

Somewhere in all of this Eban felt that there was something of value to be had.

To be discovered, cherished and learned from.

Stored away for when he might need it sometime in the future.

John Parkes was a local historian of sorts.

Fiercely proud of his roots and his community, he often told his young charges, "Be proud you're from the Shankill, boys and girls; in the Irish it means 'Old Church' and was otherwise formally 'the church of the white crossing': *Ecclesia alba de vado*. So when people ask you, you tell them, 'I was born at the crossing of the white church, in the shadow of the black mountain.'"

As a Presbyterian minister, he had raised a few eyebrows during this sensitive time by preaching in his Sunday evening service that they – his congregation – were as Irish as anyone on the island, and that their forefathers, Henry Joy McCracken and William Orr, were something called 'Dissenters', and how they had fought and died for that birthright.

Eban's eyes were growing heavy in the half-light of McGrew's pub with the remembering, and as late afternoon approached, he stepped gingerly and uncertainly between the detritus.

24

Anthony 'Anto' Gatusso hovered at the edges of the window, uneasily moving from one side of it to the other.

Suddenly, something engaged him in the street below.

"PISS OFF MOLLOY, YOU FUCKING PERVERT!"

He waggled a two-fingered V sign and spoke back over his shoulder.

"It's Tootsie Molloy. I think there's a team of them back in the shadows, but I can only see two of them under the light."

A tired, disembodied voice emerged from the depths of a frayed brown sleeping blanket, its zipper broken. It resembled a giant larva stretched out on a moth-eaten couch.

"You were told, stay away from the window."

But Anto wasn't listening.

Instead he bellowed again, *"YOU'RE A BIG MAN WHEN YOU'RE WITH YOUR PROVO MATES, MOLLOY. I'LL KNOCK YOUR FUCKIN' BOLLOCKS IN IF I GET HOLD OF YA!"*

"He can't hear you, Anto."

A woman's voice emerged from an antechamber side room which acted as the sacristy and smelled of candles and flowers. It was young and fragile and weary.

"Who's the other one?"

Anto still stood in the window, gesturing. "What?"

"Who's the other one with him?"

The young man cupped his hands at the sides of his face and squinted through the glass, pressing his forehead against it.

Suddenly he flattened himself tight against the wall, clearly scared.

"Oh Jesus, it's Sledger!"

Ruairí Connolly spoke again from the sleeping bag with drained resignation. "I told you: *stay away from the fucking window!*"

To one side an older woman placed soft drink cans, crisp packets and chocolate bar wrappers in a black bin liner. She looked exhausted.

Dotted around the floor of the room were unrolled sleeping bags.

A temporary cot had been arranged at the back for the senior citizen.

A tinny portable radio buzzed in the background, keeping the besieged up to date on events outside.

A middle-aged man sat at the long table that ran the length of the small room, shuffling a pack of cards. It was covered with magazines, overripe, mouldering fruit and overflowing ashtrays.

"Who's Sledger?" he asked without looking up, half-interested.

Sinéad Farran emerged from the antechamber, drying her long, fine brown hair between two small tea towels which were obviously woefully inadequate for the job.

She wore tight leggings and a leopard print top.

She crossed to where her fiancé lay and pushed her small bony ass into a space at his feet.

She was six months pregnant and just turned seventeen.

She looked haggard and pale. Sunken eyes set into brittle-bone fragility.

It was the vodka and fags.

The burgers and chips.

The E and spliffs on the weekend.

Her delicate blue veins showed through the taut, translucent sheath of skin they were wrapped in.

Ruairí's head and shoulders emerged from the sleeping bag. "A bad man."

Sinéad corrected him. "A *very* bad man."

Anto moved away from the window rapidly and crossed to the table.

He was an attractive young man, with jet-black hair – gelled and side-parted – and the classically Mediterranean good looks that he had inherited from his Italian father.

His large brown eyes perhaps hinted at a soulfulness or depth that was, in truth, absent.

He was animated now, wanting to explain all to the questioner, Conor McVey.

"Sledger used to run the punishments teams. His sister's house got done and her car got ripped off..." He looked sheepish. "So he's taken all this kinda personal, like."

The community worker, whose shift was coming to an end, looked at him disapprovingly.

"*We* didn't do it!"

Anto looked pantomime-offended, and toward Ruairí for validation.

"I told 'em mad bastards, I told Spud and Dinny to leave off of her. Leave well alone."

It was unclear who he was trying to convince.

Sinéad clamped her hair between the cotton towels and rubbed. "Spud and Dinny are probably in Kerry by now, drinking pints and laughin'."

Ruairí reached down and rooted around in the bowels of his sleeping bag. He produced a manky-looking brightly-coloured beach towel. It had dolphins jumping through hoops on it.

He threw it the length of himself and it wrapped around Sinéad's head and shoulders, almost knocking her sideways.

Anto sniggered.

She pulled it off angrily and glared at Ruairí. "That's where you two should be, instead of acting the hard men… instead of putting us all through *this!*"

Ruairí became agitated.

"Don't you be startin', wee girl. I'm telling you for the last time, me and him" – he nodded at Anto – "we did nothing wrong… nothing at all. Spud and Dinny turned up with the spondulicks. We didn't ask where they got them. We went out drinking with them, that's all."

He looked at the window and across at the huge, heavy wooden door that was the only way in or out of their incarceration.

"God knows, I wish they'd kept their hands in their pockets," he reflected ruefully.

Mrs Connolly, Ruairí's mother, was straightening the bedding in the cot that had provided her only fitful sleep since the beginning of the ordeal.

On the table beside this she arranged her various medications and plonked her false teeth into a glass of water, dropping a fizzing cleaning pill in with them.

Years of rearing a family of seven meant that she could quite easily zone out the banter flying back and forth between the young people further up the room.

Sinéad nodded in her direction. "Aye, your ma might believe that oul crap, but I didn't come down in the last shower."

Ruairí had risen and – now wearing his sleeping bag pulled up to the chest – was stumbling awkwardly toward a thermos flask over by the makeshift kitchen area.

"What's that supposed to mean?"

It sounded like a challenge. Like he might be ready to up the ante.

Anto, sensing this, got to Sinéad first.

He employed his best conciliatory tone, hands outstretched in supplication.

"What were we supposed to do? Turn down a few free nights' liquoring because we didn't know where they got the money from? Cop yourself on, Sinéad."

Sinéad was having none of it. She narrowed her eyes.

"You knew where they got it alright. Sure, didn't his ma tell me?"

She turned to speak at Ruairí's retreating back.

"He hides stuff in a shoebox, behind the hot water boiler. Four hundred quid in twenty-pound notes and two big lumps of hash."

She began to pull her hair back from her pinched face and tie it. "Aye, you thought I didn't know about that. Your ma tells me it all. She says you have her nerves wrecked."

Ruairí spun around threateningly.

"Shut the fuck up! That was from something else. I don't do houses and I don't joyride. And leave my ma out of it!"

Mrs Connolly went about her ablutions, indifferent. She did not hear, or did not care.

Sinéad rose to her feet, placing one hand on her hip and stabbing the air with a finger in Ruairí's direction.

"*Shut the fuck up?* Wait 'til I tell you, wee fella, I'm sitting here six months pregnant and you and Einstein and the rest of your dozy crew have dropped us all in the middle of *this* shit!"

She surveyed the room theatrically.

Anto and Ruairí spoke together in unrehearsed unison. "And don't we fuckin' know it."

They smiled wryly at each other, Anto crossing the room to exchange a half-hearted high-five with his comrade. They both wore tracksuit bottoms and hooded tops.

Their baseball caps lay on the table amongst the debris of their ordeal.

117

Sinéad, unimpressed, was intent on the last word as usual. "Aye, you *know*… but do you *care*?"

Ruairí suddenly seemed deflated.

Fatigue swept discernibly across his pale face.

For a moment he looked very young. He had in that instant decided that withdrawal from this arena of conflict was the smart play.

Eyes widening, he appealed to her.

"Look, you're doing my head in… how does any of this help? Do you not think I've enough to be worried about? You'll need my ma if I have to go away. *Your* ma would be no help with a wee baby."

Sinéad looked around the room, arms open, as if appealing to an invisible audience.

"Oh, so now he *is* going away. I wish he'd make his mind up."

She was stabbing a finger at Ruairí again. "If you'd told the Provos that a week ago, we wouldn't still be in here."

Unexpectedly, Anto exploded. He seemed to be verging on tears of anger. Or maybe fear.

"It's a *death* threat you heartless bitch… you know? *A death threat!*"

He put his finger to his temple and pulled the imaginary trigger.

The room went pin-drop quiet again. And again they became aware of the noise from outside. Unceasing vitriol directed at them alone.

Conor was the first to react.

He was full of mock bonhomie, believing this to be his job.

But he knew as well as anyone.

Maybe better.

He'd been listening more closely to the radio than the others.

Listening, every hour on the hour. And still no-one brave or stupid enough to take a decision on whether they were all technically trespassing on church property or not.

The diocese might still evict the lads from the cathedral grounds.

They were at a standstill.

In limbo.

"C'mon folks, everybody's tired… nobody's going anywhere. Your wee baby needs his da to be around. There are plenty of people – good people – out there who are prepared to stand behind you on this."

Ruairí and Anto exchanged a cynical glance.

They both turned their backs on Conor and Sinéad, who rubbed her eyes hard and flopped back onto the couch, deflated.

Anto crossed to the window and looked out tentatively.

"Oh aye? Well, where the fuck are they then? I can only see kneecappers out there. Where's the RUC when you need them? Those lunatics could come through that door anytime they felt like it."

All eyes turned to the heavy door with its cumbersome circular ornamental handle and slide bolt.

Sturdy, certainly, and capable of repelling intruders from a bygone age. But archaic and unreliable now.

Sinéad suddenly looked genuinely frightened and began to gnaw earnestly and agitatedly at her fingernails.

Mrs Connolly – who had heard everything but registered nothing – abruptly straightened and pulled a bed sheet up to her throat.

"Well… *I'm here*," offered Conor McVey pathetically.

Ruairí and Anto laughed sardonically.

Conor looked wounded.

Ruairí, seeing this, crossed to the man and placed a hand on his arm.

"Conor, we know you're a bit of veteran at this and all. Eamon O'Brien told us what you did in the 70s, with the civil rights crowd, I mean – mediation and all that…"

Sinéad noted the man's injury as well. "And coming here to sit a twelve-hour shift in this hole… not many would do it."

"Aye, fair enough… fair dues," said Ruairí and poured a cup of tea from the flask, handing it to the older man. He sat down beside him and pushed a packet of Jaffa Cakes across the table. He paused as if something had been bothering him, and then spoke.

"Look… I don't mean to worry you – maybe you haven't thought about this, mate – but don't *your* people live on our estate too? These guys could be up there right now, at your mother and father's house, smashing windows; burning…"

Conor's expression changed from one of self-pity to alarm.

Sinéad, recognising Ruairí's lack of tact, cut him short.

"Ruairí, give over!" she admonished.

Anto butted in, excited. This was something he knew about.

"Let me tell you about when they came for me."

He pulled up a chair at the table, happily anticipating an audience. "Let me tell you the inedible truth, as my oul man used to say."

Conor laughed – unconvincingly, but breaking the tension somewhat. "You mean the *inevitable* truth."

"No, this is hard to swallow, never mind stomach," Anto wisecracked.

Sinéad spoke with a hint of reprimand in her voice, but she was half-smiling. "Anthony…"

Anto ignored her and continued.

"Well, they didn't have much to mess up – our place is always a tip; the way our Maria looks after it, I mean. She's laying on the sofa reading some pop junk mag as usual; then the knock comes to the front door. 'My da's forgot his key again,' she says; 'let him in', but I'm already moving to the kitchen, toward the back door. Like, four of them kick it in before she knows what's happening – ski masks, boiler suits, baseball bats, the works – well, I'm away on it, so I am; not hanging around. She says the big one goes to the middle of the room, takes out a piece of paper and starts reading it. '*Third Brigade Provisional IRA find Anthony Francis Gatusso guilty*, blah, blah blah' – ya know what our Maria says? 'Wise up, Sledger.'

Anto burst out laughing at the thought.

"*Wise up, Sledger!* I love it... he's probably doing a redner under the mask. He thinks about slapping her, but just says, 'Tell Anto we'll be back later to pick up our pizza', then the fuckers all burst out laughing... I mean, I don't think that's so funny..."

Seemingly stung by this regularly used slight to his family name and origin, he looked at Ruairí for vindication. "Do you think that's funny?"

Ruairí just smiled.

Anto concluded, tailing off, deflated. "So before they leave, they do a good job of trashing the place anyway."

Conor McVey was far from reassured.

"No, no... they won't – they wouldn't touch *my* people. That has to be some rogue outfit operating out there; Sinn Féin would never sanction it."

Finding that no-one was speaking up in his support, he tried harder to convince them and himself. "Sure everybody knows the war's as good as over." He stood up from his seat and paced the room, shuffling the deck of cards all the while.

"You've all heard it on the radio and I brought you in the newspapers; we're trying to get Amnesty interested – *Amnesty International*, for God's sake! Everybody's watching; watching right here, to see what happens..."

He suddenly stopped and looked at the picture of the Mother and Child icon, high up on the wall above them.

"You're on sacred ground – church ground; *holy ground*, for Christ's sake!"

Anto sarcastically let it slip out of the side of his mouth, "Aye, dead on." He pushed himself back on the two legs of the chair and crossed his feet on the table top.

"Look, nobody gives a fuck about this... about us. Everybody thinks we're hoods. Everybody thinks we deserve what we get."

He laughed ironically. "*Sacred ground?* Do you think that means anything to that crew?" He gestured toward the window. "The war's over? Give me a break."

Sinéad buried her face in the towel and wept softly.

Ruairí glowered at Anto and made a gesture for him to cool it.

Conor McVey rubbed his wrist so that he might look at his watch covertly.

He was thinking to himself, *I've done my shift... now get me the fuck out of here*, but instead he announced unconvincingly, "Well, we're FAIT – we're Families Against Intimidation and Terror, and that's what we do; we won't let you down. That's why volunteers will keep a vigil with you."

His eyes dropped awkwardly – apologetically – down to the floor. "I'll be heading off in a little bit..."

They all suddenly looked at him in panic, revealing their bluster for the sham it truly was. McVey noticed it. "... But a fella called Barnard will take the watch from me."

Anto was first to recover himself and shot back, "Oh, well that's alright then. For a moment there I thought we were in trouble. Aye, you pop off on home now."

Again the noise outside seemed to rise and fall.

Sinéad balled her hands into small fists, the knuckles going white. The walls seemed to close in just a little more.

Ruairí looked around, and accepting the role of alpha-male, tried to break the tension.

"Anto, tell Conor how Tootsie Molloy got his nickname."

Anto, warming to this, smiled.

"Oh aye, that wee prick. When we were at St. Malachy's, well, our class used to go to the swimming baths every week. When Molloy was in the changing booths he used to look under the gaps at the bottom of the door, at women's feet…"

Anto looked around the group to monitor their engagement. Delaying his punch line.

"… *and jerk off!* Dirty wee bastard!"

Sinéad was smiling now and wiping tears from her eyes. Conor and Ruairí were smiling also.

"Tell him about the nail varnish," prompted Ruairí.

"Oh aye." Anto was in the groove now.

"So the cjit comes home and boasts about this – actually *boasts* about it to Sledger's entire mob. Of course they destroy him; make out he's queer and that, like. So he comes back in a month or so and says everything's alright now: he only wanks off to feet with nail varnish on them, so that way he can be sure that it's a woman, like!"

They were all laughing now. Perhaps louder and harder than the story merited, but grateful for the release of tension it provided.

Even Mrs Connolly, who typically feigned ignorance on such matters, allowed herself a titter.

"That way he figures to convince them he isn't bent and so they're to stop with the slagging!"

Ruairí pitched in for effect. "And so Tootsie was born."

Conor giggled guiltily. "And the moral; the moral of the story is…?

Sinéad provided it. "When you're in a hole, stop digging."

25

Newry bound, he was driving at a steady speed.

One hand on the wheel and one scanning the radio stations for news.

Pale green electroluminescence leaked from the dashboard, lighting the car's interior.

Night and a late summer rain were beginning to fall.

According to the reports he could pick up, the parish priest and the bishop of the diocese could not be contacted for comment regarding the standoff in the cathedral.

Much to his surprise, Eban seemed to be enjoying some sensation of associated celebrity.

The fella in the big picture.

That he himself was heading straight into the top news story of the hour.

To be part of it.

It seemed to afford him an opportunity for professional exasperation with the whole thing.

Eban spoke tetchily, aloud to himself. "Does *anybody* know who's in charge down there?"

The closer he got to the cathedral however the more his thoughts turned uncomfortably to the worst-case scenario.

He had earlier spoken to McVey on the phone.

Conor had told him, "It's mostly to take a stand really; the press have got interested. Nobody actually *believes* the guys outside will try to go in after them – 'sanctuary' and all that. It's a *church* for Christ's sake!"

McVey had managed to convey the fundamental human

rights angle of the ordeal to him and he reflected on this seriously for the first time that night.

Eban allowed himself a little buzz of liberal feel-good.

Perhaps Amnesty International *would* become involved?

Maybe he'd be asked for a comment.

They were all on the side of the angels, were they not?

Newry Town Centre – 3 Miles said the sign, suddenly thrown up in the headlights.

UVF – Kill 'em all... Let God decide was spray-painted across the bottom of it.

He had reached the Loyalist estates that skirted the town.

These dark hills and market towns were contested country.

The unwary traveller slid in and out of tribal boundaries denoted only by brightly coloured paving stones and ragged, flapping standards tied to lampposts.

He'd been strangely melancholic of late.

Still unsure that his recent return from London had been the right thing to do.

Listening to Van Morrison's *Into the Mystic* on his Walkman on the deck of the ferry as it choppily ploughed up Belfast Lough in the mist and rain.

All the pseudo-Celtic bullshit he had fed himself about the holy ground.

About the loss of homeland equating with the loss of self.

About the spiritual thirst of the exile.

Had he *really* meant any of it?

Or was it simply another device to squirm out of expectations, obligations, responsibilities?

Back from self-imposed exile.

Back to... *this.*

How quickly, how easily one forgets.

The rain now necessitated the use of his wipers.

A light mizzle turned to a steady fall.

Good, he thought to himself. *It might keep the lunatics off the streets.*

26

A chartered bus pulled up outside the cathedral.

Air brakes hissing and fold doors flapping.

Several men from outlying areas piled off in high spirits.

Drink had been taken.

They immediately made their way over to Sledger and Tootsie, who were standing around a roaring brazier, sparks disappearing up into the night sky.

Greetings and mock-unpleasantries were exchanged in the way that young men announce themselves to one another.

Sledger said something.

The group exploded with laughter.

It was an affirmation of pack order; invited, affirming and welcome.

They had kept up a level of agitation for the past few nights, increasing this with a wall of sound around the time that they expected those trapped inside might be considering sleep.

If bin-lids, bodhráns and whistles were again employed effectively, there would be no rest for the besieged.

They imagined all those gathered inside the vestry of the cathedral physically wincing as the metallic clanging began again.

They knew it would peck away at their nerves like some Chinese water torture.

Relentless. Incessant.

No-one was going anywhere.

The tense semi-silence that had fallen on the brightly lit vestry would increase a notch further.

27

Eban was stopped at the last set of traffic lights.

The spire of the illuminated cathedral was now plainly in sight.

He could hear the whistles, the shrieking and the clattering even from this distance.

Even with the car windows up.

He turned off the radio.

The noise sounded strangely primitive, barbaric, otherworldly.

His stomach clenched.

This was front-line stuff.

Not normally his territory.

People get hurt, he thought.

Now he could see a crowd.

Not huge, but more than he had expected.

Beside them a TV crew were setting up for an outside broadcast.

During the day the police had been there and thrown up a light cordon of aluminium barriers around the cathedral and its car park area. But now they didn't seem to be trying too hard.

One armoured Land Rover sat in a poorly lit corner of the car park, at a distance from the crowd.

Its occupants wary no doubt, of providing an easy target.

Eban pulled the car to a halt beside them.

The back door opened and two officers alighted, putting on their caps and pulling down the flak jackets that had ridden up while they had been sitting in the back of the vehicle.

Rolling down the window, Eban smiled and tentatively offered his council identity card, half-expecting them to laugh.

The two seemed disinterested, exchanged a few words and pointed to the main area where the crowd had gathered.

He pulled into the main car park.

Climbing out of the car, he moved around to the boot, lifting out two swollen plastic carrier bags full of groceries.

An increase in the volume of abuse momentarily startled him.

Something had happened to incite them.

The crowd were much closer to the cathedral entrance than he'd originally noticed, and he was taken aback by their intensity of purpose.

Then in horror, he realised.

The abuse was immediately audible and clearly directed at him.

"Stop protecting that fuckin' scum!"

"If you're goin' in… then send the bastards out!"

He panicked.

Felt disorientated.

Spun around quickly.

Then, moving fast – by fear more than design – bumped his groin sharply into the wing mirror of his car.

He doubled up momentarily as it had the effect of winding him.

Tins of tuna and packs of eggs fell loose, clunked and cracked on the tarmac.

A collective jeer went up, the volume of which again took him aback.

Suddenly feeling sick and exposed, he inexplicably managed an automatic smile between embarrassment and incredulity.

They can't be shouting at me? he thought in disbelief.

Stumbling away from the vitriol, he noticed a handwritten sign reading *Vestry*.

Quickly pushing open a small doorway leading to a set of dimly lit, winding stone stairs, he half-jogged up them, only to be stopped in his tracks by an enormous, solid wooden door at the top.

Out of breath, he was surprised to note that he was already wet and sticky with cold sweat.

Eban paused momentarily to compose himself before knocking.

Thirty-two years old and wheezing like a retired asthmatic. *For fuck's sake... get a grip!*

28

INSIDE THE CATHEDRAL VESTRY
12.02AM

Eban Barnard's knock on the heavy oak door seemed to explode around the room with exaggerated volume.

Gradually, the large metal handle rattled and grated as it turned.

All turned in trepidation toward it as it creaked slowly and tentatively open.

Ruairí leapt forward brandishing a heavy candleholder in both hands.

He screamed angrily, "Christ, Anto – I warned you to keep it LOCKED!"

Sinéad allowed a feeble whimper to escape her lips as the young man moved defensively in front of her.

The door opened with a long, low creak and a bemused-looking man in his early thirties, wearing chinos and a tweed jacket, tentatively pushed himself through the gap.

He appeared a little crumpled, perhaps even defeated.

And across his eyes there rested something like a shadow.

As if he were still not reconciled as to the reasons for whatever disappointments life had dealt him.

He was carrying a small holdall and two plastic bags full of provisions, and appeared to be out of breath and sweating.

His shoes squeaked comically as he crossed the polished wooden floor.

He spoke apologetically. "Umm… sorry, I didn't mean

to…" Eban held the bags aloft and smiled weakly. "Is there a Conor McVey here? He sent a list – shopping and that. I'm here from the peace and reconciliation people… to take over the night watch…"

Anto sat back down in his chair. "Christ, it's the cavalry."

Ruairí set his cudgel down and took the bags from Eban, who rubbed his hands in an attempt to promote circulation.

"Nahh, it's only the Pony Express," he said sarcastically and began to rummage through the contents.

Conor McVey walked toward Eban, hand outstretched. "I'm McVey; we spoke on the phone. You must be… is it *Eban Barnard*? You're very welcome."

"I'm afraid the barbarians are still at the gates." Eban could think of nothing else to say. It came out sounding stilted.

Mrs Connolly had stirred from her cot and – perked up by the prospect of entertaining guests – was collecting up tea mugs for washing.

She glared admonishment at Anto and Ruairí.

"Never mind them fellas Mr Barnyard; they'll cut themselves on their tongues one of these days. Will ye have a wee drop a tea?"

"Lock the door." Sinéad was oblivious to all else and stared at the open, unattended portal.

Mrs Connolly scolded her, "Will you let the man get his coat off first?!"

Eban spoke. "No, she's right… I was stopped at traffic lights a good half-mile away. I could hear the shrieking and clattering from a distance. It sounded bloody primal. They're like some medieval mob out there!"

Conor had his hand in the small of Eban's back and was trying to guide him toward the sacristy. "Ahh… could I just have a quick word?"

Sinéad was suddenly, anxiously interested in news from the outside. "How many?"

Eban, ignoring Conor, turned back toward her. "Big – there's a big crowd gathered out there, and a TV crew…"

Sinéad dropped her hands to her pregnant bump, where she rotated a silver ring repeatedly around her finger. "And police…?"

"A few… but they only seem interested in the overtime."

Conor raised his voice a little, adopting a more authoritative tone.

"Barnard – Eban – look, I'll have to ask you to—"

Sinéad moved toward Eban, tugging his coat sleeve.

Her eyes were wide. "What were they shouting? What did they say?"

Eban's adrenaline was still up.

It fired again as he recounted the incident. "I don't mind telling you, I panicked… it was scary… '*Fuckin' scum! Send them out!*' – I nearly fell over. Thank God I kept moving; I thought they were going to lynch me!"

Sinéad backed away from him, lay down on the couch and pulled herself into a semi-foetal position.

Conor McVey had heard enough.

He bellowed at Eban. "FOR CHRIST'S SAKE, MAN, YOU'RE SUPPOSED TO BE HERE TO HELP!"

The colour drained from Eban's face in a moment of realisation followed by contrite self-awareness. McVey had his hand on his back again. The beleaguered custodian regained his composure, hissing at him, "I need to speak to you alone… NOW!"

He gestured toward the antechamber and both entered, pulling the chintz curtain that acted as a separator behind the two rooms. Of those remaining in the vestry, only Mrs Connolly spoke.

"You can make your own bloody tea, mister!"

The sacristy was a small room, overly packed with vases,

candles, crockery, religious artefacts, PE equipment and a few theatrical props and pillows in a large wicker basket.

There had been an attempt to impose some kind of order on this untidy storeroom, but all had come undone since the arrival of the refugees.

The space was lit with paraffin lamps, bathing it in a warm orange glow.

A small wall-mounted sink and toilet were hidden behind another hung sheet acting as a partition. Two blue-and-white striped deck chairs were arranged opposite each other.

Conor McVey motioned for Eban to sit in one before sitting himself and leaning forward.

He was still obviously irate. Keeping his voice at a conspiratorial hush, he spoke. "Who the hell do you think you are?"

For a moment Eban considered standing up and walking straight back to his car.

He regathered his poise. "Look, friend, I didn't mean to get off on the wrong foot with you here…"

McVey was somewhat chastened and reined himself in. "Let me be clear: I… we appreciate this, right? There will be other people here. You're relieving my shift; then somebody will come to relieve you. Okay?"

McVey's face was still close to his.

Eban drew back a little, still faintly ashamed and a little disorientated with all that had happened since his arrival at the cathedral.

Conor spoke again. "You got the letter from FAIT… right?"

Eban remained silent. It was starting to get awkward.

McVey was becoming exasperated. "You do work in community relations, right?"

Eban said nothing and began to rub his temples.

"Well, for God's sake, say *something*."

Eban finally spoke, honestly if a little defensively.

"Look, friend, I can tell you anything you want to hear, right, but the bottom line is: *I'm out of my fucking depth here!*"

"Well, they've been in here almost a full week now. So what did you think was going on here exactly?"

"They told me – I thought – that I had to babysit some Catholic kids who had called down the wrath of the local heavies."

Conor McVey sneered sarcastically.

"Why don't you set up a soup kitchen while you're at it? Give out a few blankets and condoms and maybe teach us how we shouldn't keep coal in the bath."

Eban felt wounded. "I don't think that there's any need for that... to speak to me like that I mean."

There was an awkward silence. It seemed to last forever. It was broken by McVey who sighed heavily, his whole body suddenly seeming to collapse in on itself.

Eban noticed the change in the man. "Are you okay? You look shattered."

Conor melted somewhat. "I'm sorry. No sleep."

Unfortunately, Eban Barnard's propensity for ill-advised jokes to lighten the atmosphere at inappropriate times was never far away. "Guilty conscience?" He smiled.

An ice-cold, side-on glance from the beleaguered McVey told him how far off the mark he was.

"Coffee," he said. "And lots of it. Caffeine – or you could try to get some sleep. Good luck with that!"

Eventually he extended his hand. Eban shook it.

"We do our best for fellas like these."

He nodded at the babble of voices rising in the main room. "Those intimidated out of their own areas. The two lads in there are still in their teens... they went to work last week when they were told not to. It all kicked off after that."

Eban spotted an opening to redeem himself. "Christ... they're lucky to have a job around here at all."

McVey's lack of response suggested that he might just have taken this as another patronising remark. "They work in a scrap metal yard."

Eban pushed on. "The radio – the IRA – says they were selling drugs to kids... were they?"

Conor McVey guffawed aloud.

"That's rich, coming from them! It's the paramilitaries who control the drugs! Anyhow, I don't believe it; sounds like a handy excuse to me. This has more to do with laying down the law; setting an example; pissin' on their territory... marking it out."

"And the church...?"

McVey looked vexed and bent in lower, hushing his voice.

"The parish priest, Cudden, and the Cardinal himself... well, they mysteriously can't be contacted. Suddenly nobody knows who's in charge down here. There's something – I don't know – *sinister* going on. The rest of the church is locked; closed off to us. What you see is what you get."

"Where's the ecumenicists when you need them most, eh?" said Eban acerbically.

McVey wasn't laughing. His tone was grave.

"Let's be clear about this: they know what they're doing. Their failure to get involved is something less than a neutral act. No condemnation of the mob's actions... no moral leadership to the community... it's being taken as tacit approval."

Eban hadn't expected that. A sin of omission. As so often in the past, moral ambiguity; ethical ambivalence from the men in black had fashioned a vacuum. And hatred had rushed in to fill it.

"But we're – they're – safe while they're in here... right?" he asked anxiously.

Conor McVey paused longer than Eban would have liked.

Then, as if to convince himself as much as Eban, "Sure... sure... *sanctuary* and all that..."

Eban looked unconvinced.

McVey continued, speaking so as he might hear himself say the thing aloud again. "I mean, it's a church for fuck's sake!"

"Strange... that's what my boss said."

Both men looked directly at each other.

There could be no disguising their discomfort.

Each wondering what precisely they had got themselves into.

The moment was broken by Ruairí, who had been listening at the curtain, unseen.

He seemed to be relishing their disquiet.

He stepped into their space. "This is front-line stuff, gentleman: people get hurt; vigilante justice holds sway."

He announced this with the swagger of a documentary-maker.

He was clearly enjoying himself.

Eban noted that he was more confident, more articulate than he might have expected.

And how his striking blue-green eyes burned with intensity and an intelligence that may or may not be malevolent.

Conor looked embarrassed. "Sorry Ruairí, I didn't see you there."

"People are wondering what all the talk is about. You're making them nervous."

"Then I suppose we should introduce Mr Barnard to his charges for the evening."

Conor and Eban stood up and all re-entered the main vestry area.

As they pushed through the curtain, Eban felt a tug on his arm. McVey had pulled him momentarily back. He whispered quickly in his ear, "You might keep an eye out for young Sinéad. She's well on in her pregnancy. I've been trying to get her to go home, but she won't leave him."

Ruairí jumped up on the couch and gestured at the two men.

"Ladies and gentlemen, the troubleshooters...I give you the Lone Ranger and Tonto of conflict resolution."

Sinéad scolded him. "You'd think you would need all the friends you could get right now."

Ruairí appealed to the men in mock solemnity. "You *are* fighting against dark forces, are you not?"

He jumped off the couch, and finding a half-deflated football in a corner of the room, flicked it adroitly over to Anto, who trapped it on his knee and began to juggle with it.

Conor busied himself orientating Eban.

"Coffee and tea-making over here... sleeping bags in here... toilet just in here..."

He lifted his coat from the seat back. "Well, I'll be off."

Again, there was a hollow silence.

McVey was already moving toward the door.

Walking backward, almost tripping over an Adidas kit bag, he announced to all assembled, "Eban here will make sure everything goes fine. Len Kennedy will be along in twelve hours for the next shift."

Eban blurted out, surprised, "Twelve-hour shifts! Whose fucking bright idea was that?"

Everyone stared at him. McVey glowered. "I thought we already had this conversation?"

Eban again seemed contrite. He gathered himself. "Right... you're right."

"See me to the door Eban, will you?"

He grabbed up some belongings and pushed them deep into a rucksack.

The two young men, Sinéad and Mrs Connolly had silently drifted toward the entrance.

They stood in a little semi-circle.

There were collective goodbyes to Conor McVey, with

hugs from the women and affirmations from the council worker to 'stay strong'.

Eban slid back the long latch-bolt. It grated with a metallic screech.

Anto shouted from behind them, "Still, it could be worse, eh Conor? I'd hate to be an Orange bastard stuck in the middle of all of this!"

The comapny immediately broke into laughter. Eban alone did not find it funny.

He hissed his concern to the departing McVey.

"What did he mean? What did he mean by that?"

Conor smiled. "Relax. He's only winding you up. If you knew him… look, you'll soon get to see what he's like. Now I need to get some sleep… this lack of any decision from the diocese – to evict them or not from the church grounds – it's doing my head in."

Eban felt panic rising. "What if the clergy show up when I'm here? Sure, they'll take no heed of me."

Conor McVey was strangely Zen-like at the prospect of his own bed. "Don't panic… don't worry… remember, this is largely a morale-boosting exercise for them."

He nodded back over his shoulder. "Keep their spirits up, but be careful…"

Eban's eyes widened in alarm.

McVey noticed. "I mean *sensible*; be sensible – keep the door locked and keep strangers out in the hallway. One door in; one door out."

With that, he was gone.

Eban swung closed the huge door behind him and bolted it.

It took a considerable effort.

It was fully seven feet tall and set solid into the arched stone surround that framed it.

He turned with some trepidation to face his new roommates.

Ruairí Connolly looked directly at him, puffed out his cheeks and exhaled resignedly.

Eban looked toward Anto, who rolled his eyes and looked heavenwards.

Taking a deep breath, Eban Barnard rubbed his hands together in a mock-efficient, businesslike manner. He shot for casual bonhomie.

"It looked like rain earlier; might keep the thugs off the streets, eh?"

"What, you think the Provos don't have umbrellas?" said Ruairí.

"Aye – green, white and gold ones," added Sinéad.

"Semi-automatic ones," offered Anto.

Eban crossed to the window and pulled aside a makeshift paper blind so as to look out. Suddenly there was a surge of baying and howling from the street below.

Eban reeled back ignominiously and stumbled, catching hold of the table for support and sending cups and saucers flying.

Mrs Connolly had recommenced chain-smoking. She said wearily, "Don't go near the windows. Anyone will tell you that."

They all added, in mocking unison, "Yeah, don't go near the windows."

Eban felt stupid.

"Right... of course... don't go near the windows."

He looked at his watch. "Christ, it's after twelve. Do these people not have somewhere else they'd rather be?"

Anto offered cold comfort. "The bars and clubs are closing now. There'll be some hijinks from here on in."

Mrs Connolly stubbed out a butt and rubbed her eyes with the heels of her hands.

"They'll be out with the megaphone again soon. The filth they scream up here at us... I hate that the most." She nodded at Sinéad. "She shouldn't have to listen to that."

The uniformly grim prospects ahead of them forced Eban to reach for something.

Anything.

"Still, as long as the police are there, we're alright. I mean, they'll keep 'em in line, eh?"

Anto flashed amused surprise. *"You're* a long way from home."

Ruairí was pulling the sleeping bag up under his chin.

"The feds go about two or three o'clock; sometimes earlier if there's trouble somewhere else. Did nobody tell you that, mate?"

There was a piercing howl of static and white-noise feedback from the megaphone in the street below. A chant started up. Feral voices.

"Connolly, Connolly, Connolly… out, out, out!"

Eban reached into the overnight bag he'd brought and took out a wrinkled handkerchief.

He began to dab his brow.

"No. Nobody told me that."

29

THE HISTORICAL ENQUIRIES OFFICES,
POLICE SERVICE OF NORTHERN IRELAND
BELFAST, 2014

Sergeant Sam Coulter stood outside the door of Interview Room 1, observing, unnoticed through the glass door panel, the two men who sat opposite each other.

His boss, Dan Watson, sat with his back toward him.

Hunched over, occasionally looking up from his notes.

Pausing with his pen held above the pad. Seemingly in deep concentration, never interrupting the steady stream of words pouring from the other man across the desk.

Coulter could see the man's face clearly.

Knew who he was and ostensibly why he was here.

His aspect was a portrait of absorption. Animated and intense.

Coulter marvelled again at the similarity of his features with those of his brother, Alex Barnard.

They might have been twins.

He looked at his watch.

They had been at it in there for pushing two hours without a break.

It must have been something that had captured Dan Watson's imagination, for the Detective Inspector was disinclined to remain sitting for any amount of time due to the discomfort he experienced with his back.

Although his professionalism dissuaded him from breaking

the punter's flow when it was established, Coulter was about to knock on the door and enquire whether his boss wanted him to stand in for him while he took a break.

A polite cough of introduction from behind distracted him.

He turned around to see Officer Helen Totton standing with a tray holding cups, saucers and a coffee pot.

"I just thought I might get a quick word with him," she ventured.

Coulter didn't like the woman.

Ever since she'd arrived in their unit, it seemed to him that Helen Totton had been overly familiar.

Too self-confident.

Had pushed herself forward at every occasion and paid a little bit too much attention to her appearance.

Now there were the rumours beginning to circulate about her ambition to fast-track her career. To become overly friendly with senior officers.

He moved past her and gestured that she should follow him. "Don't interrupt them."

She seemed disappointed.

"Any idea what all the fuss is about?"

"Fuss?"

"Well, everyone says that the punter is the brother of an old friend of Dan's. His former chief, in fact... Alex Barnard?"

Coulter had been long enough in the game to recognise that she was fishing.

"What about it?"

"Nothing... just... I dunno... they've been in there a long time."

"That's not unusual."

"I'm working late, so when Dan is done could you let him know I called by?"

Coulter hated her easy familiarity. "Detective Inspector

Watson will be going home when he finishes up. Mrs Watson is expecting him."

He felt that she banged the tray down on the kitchenette counter with just a little too much gusto.

Helen Totton returned to the staff rest room and sat flicking through the in-house magazine until the last of her colleagues had left.

When the room was empty, she dug into her tunic pocket and produced a cheap, disposable mobile phone.

She activated it and pressed speed-dial.

The line clicked at the other end.

"Cecil, it's Helen... they're still in there together. No... nothing. Yes, yes of course."

She hung up and pocketed the mobile, replacing it in her hand with her own iPhone.

She activated the camera so as to view her own image on the screen.

Producing an ice-pink lipgloss holder, she pouted and reapplied.

30

Emily watched the children dutifully line up in the playground and file in holding hands, two by two.

The juniors in some ways presented the greatest challenge to her and her colleagues. But they offered the greatest rewards.

These little people, still forming as characters; still with so much potential, representing so much hope for the future.

But as Emily watched the dry leaves blow around the empty yard, hopeful was not how she was feeling.

Rosemary had got to work on her over recent days, rendering Emily gloomy and self-critical about her life in general, her displacement from the certainties of her home country and her lack of luck in love. When she pulled that mother hen routine, Rosemary seemed to assume she was acting in *loco parentis*. She spoke to Emily like she was a child, particularly in regard to the matter of Eban Barnard and his visits to her room.

"He's only using you, dear; I've known men like that all my life."

Nothing could have been further from the truth, thought Emily.

She was unaware of any relationship involving the older woman.

For all she knew, Rosemary Payne was still a virgin.

Sometimes she felt that Rosemary might have feelings for her that went beyond acceptable levels of matronly concern.

She endured these lectures partly for reasons of house politics and partly as a kindness to the woman (as she sensed that Rosemary somehow needed to play the role of the worldly-wise veteran), but always made sure that their conversations took place in the communal area of the kitchen and never in the privacy of each other's bedrooms.

As Rosemary droned on about damson jam, *Woman's Hour* and the menopause, Emily would remove her glasses and set them on the table. Such was the paucity of her eyesight that this simple act rendered the speaker unrecognisable.

A dull blur overset with colours, swirls and floaters drifting across her field of vision.

It helped her to 'zone out' of any exchange she considered unpalatable, and offered a respite to the effronteries of the real world.

Her secret concern was that she was retreating there much too often.

Emily re-entered her classroom.

The walls were covered in brightly-coloured drawings and posters.

Paint and glue pots sat around the table tops with sand trays, a fish tank and a cage containing Herbie the hamster.

She instructed the children to form a close ring around her at the centre of the room and be seated.

Her enraptured charges obliged.

Jill, the classroom assistant, was busy at the sink washing out paintbrushes.

Emily picked up the book she had been reading before break time and motioned the children to lean in closer, speaking in an intimate whisper.

"And that is why sea lions and turtles, to this very day, still share their secrets – and their picnics – on the shores of the enchanted sea, under the marble moon."

She opened the book wide and showed it around so as the children could see pop-up characters inside.

"Alright children, that's today's story. What we are going to do for the remainder of the day is something called 'things and people', and this time instead of all those lazybones sitting still and listening to me, this game means that everyone has to take part."

A little boy raised his hand. "Miss, I need a wee."

"Alright Nicky, Jill will take you."

The woman had already left the sink and was now shepherding the child to the door.

"Alright everyone." Emily clapped her hands for efficiency. "Gather round; gather round."

The children had long since become used to her English accent, the Brummie softened to the point of being almost unrecognisable.

Emily opened a box.

"Now what we have here are some objects… let's see what we have, shall we? What's this? A letter, a milk bottle – yes that's right, Steven – an umbrella, and this is a thermometer for taking your temperature. And what's this?"

They all responded in unison. "A hammer, Miss."

"That's right; a hammer, a parcel and a compass… now let's see who is on these cards as I turn them over…"

The picture cards variously featured a workman, a postman, a soldier, a milkman, a city gent and a doctor.

"Okay," said Emily, "who will go first?"

Little arms shot up into the air. "Miss! Miss!"

"Let's see… Janet, who does the hammer go to?"

"Workman, Miss."

"Very good, Janet. Hannah, who does the thermometer go to?"

"Doctor, Miss."

"Excellent, Hannah."

Little Nicky had returned from the toilet and sat on the fringes of the circle.

"Ah, Nicky – who does the parcel go to?"

"Ummm… the policeman, Miss."

"Take your time Nicky…" Emily held up the card with the postman on it encouragingly. "Try again."

"Miss! Miss! Miss!"

Hands punched the sky. This competitive streak amongst those so young never failed to unsettle her.

The boy was adamant. "Policeman, Miss."

Emily was becoming a little wary of where this was going. "And why is that, Nicky?"

"Because it's a bomb, Miss."

The others went quiet save for a titter or two.

Emily had been here before with these children.

It was profoundly disturbing. "No, it's just a parcel, Nicky. What about this?"

She held up a milk bottle.

"Policeman, Miss."

Emily was allowing her mood to sour her day.

She heard herself say, with a marked degree of tetchiness, "So the milk bottle goes to the policeman; why not the milkman?" She held up the picture card.

"Cuz they take them off of him… to throw at the policemen, Miss."

Hannah chipped in. "Petrol bombs Miss; they're called petrol bombs."

"What? Yes, thank you Hannah. I just… ah… everyone back to their desks and get their colouring crayons and books out please."

She looked around for the class assistant. "Jill… could I have a quick word?"

The woman had been arranging library books in a corner of the classroom. Emily heard her voice rise in a faintly hysterical whisper.

"Jill, did you see that? My God, what age are these kids –

147

four; five – and it's Nicky Patterson again! Jill, I'll have to speak to Mrs Andrews about this… she should know these things go on."

The older woman looked tired and wholly nonplussed. This was well above her pay grade.

"Oh, I think you'll find she knows already."

Emily wasn't sure if she detected a hint of mockery.

She was about to leave it there when Jill said, "I've heard my own two at it, singing *If I had a penny rope, sure I'd hang the friggin' Pope* – what can you do? They see it all around them."

She had moved across to the sink and was wringing out a towel. "And most of the kids in this school, they're from fairly well-off families. Sometimes it's what they don't say, but it's still there all the same."

Emily felt like sitting down right there in the centre of the classroom and crying.

They never trained me for this, she thought for the umpteenth time.

Yet none of this came as a surprise particularly.

She was just having a bad day.

Jill noticed her wilting. "Now they've got their crayons out; for God's sake don't let them draw flags and emblems!"

Both women laughed, though neither really enjoyed the humour.

31

OUTSIDE NEWRY CATHEDRAL, AUGUST 1991

In a far-off corner of the cathedral car park, a man in a standard-issue BBC outside broadcast jacket made some finishing adjustments to a tripod stand holding a square halogen light.

Beside him his colleague twisted some knobs for level on a recording device hung around his neck. He did so with some difficulty as he simultaneously endeavoured to keep hold of a shaggy mic attached to a long boom stand, whilst fiddling with his headphones.

Councillor Terry Molloy squinted and held his hand up to shield his eyes as the lighting rig hummed into life.

"Jesus, it's like being back in Castlereagh interrogation centre," he said.

Everybody laughed without irony.

A veteran of the movement, he'd been identified early on by the Army Council as elected representative material, and was one of the first to be schooled by Danny Morrison and the party media training initiative.

Licking his palm and smoothing his eyebrows, he patted his bald spot somewhat self-consciously.

Sledger and Tootsie hung back in the shadows watching, scarves pulled up to cover their faces.

Terry Molloy slipped effortlessly into gear and was off.

"Of course I can't speak for the IRA, but what people need to understand here is that the organisation is only acting on the wishes of the community. The police are not welcome here, we all know that, but people are being run over by car thieves; pensioners are being beaten up in their homes… parents have asked the organisation to punish their own sons – even shoot them – because frankly… well, they can't do anything with them. From what I'm given to understand they're not shot straight off; it starts with a slap or a beating. But if they persist, then they get put out of the area. Now *we* in Sinn Féin of course could *never* sanction such action, but this unfortunate situation, whereby these two men have taken so-called sanctuary in Newry Cathedral, well… it's been created by the men themselves…"

Sledger watched in unbridled admiration.

"Fuck, your brother could talk for Ireland."

Tootsie beamed proudly.

"That's what he does, Sledge… *He* does what *he* does, and *you* do what *you* do."

Councillor Molloy rounded it off, cracked familiar with the crew and joined his audience.

He was clearly pleased with himself.

"BBC, nine o'clock news tomorrow. It's a voice-over job but the message will still get across."

Molloy was referring to the broadcasting ban that was still in force for Sinn Féin spokespeople.

"Christ, those actors in Belfast must be shittin' themselves with all this talk of a ceasefire. They'll all be out of a job!" Tootsie was buzzing.

Terry Molloy ignored him. "D'ya like the Armani?" He gestured to his sharp suit.

Tootsie nudged Sledger knowingly. "I'd like to see the receipt!"

Terry Molloy pulled on his lapels. "Party issue… we know a man, who knows a man."

His younger brother was laughing, basking in the notoriety that had somehow become celebrity.

"Funny, I thought I saw a story about them on the six o'clock news as well… warehouse fire and theft… but I didn't see any mention of you on that."

The councillor's mood darkened. He was not amused. Instead he slapped Tootsie down with guilt drawn from demeaning domesticity.

"Were you thinking of calling around to see your sainted mother any time soon?"

"Ach, not now Terry. Save it, eh?" Tootsie was suddenly sheepish and awkward.

"You treat that house like a fuckin' hotel, you dump yer dirty Y fronts for washing when it suits you and expect that woman – a pensioner, mind – to take a scrubbing brush to them."

"Not *now!*"

Sledger pulled his scarf down from his face for the first time. He was grinning widely.

"She's an oul woman… you treat her like a skivvy."

Tootsie was cornered and contrite. "Tell her I'll be round at the weekend."

"Aye, for your Sunday dinner, hung over and stretched out with the papers on the sofa, scratchin' your arse and nobody can look at you twice."

"Lay off Terry, right!"

Molloy turned to the big man. "Sledger, will you slap him or will I?"

Before he could answer, Molloy grabbed his brother in a friendly bear hug and play-wrestled him into a headlock. Tootsie took it in the knowledge that this indicated the end of the lecture.

Molloy nodded up at the window in the cathedral wall. "What's the latest?"

Sledger pulled his scarf back up. "No change."

"Look Sledger, now I've a chance to talk to you…" He

dropped his voice conspiratorially. "You know this has all been kicked upstairs, right? Army Council, I mean... top flight... you get my drift?"

Sledger was dismissive to the point of insolence *"And?"*

"It's just, if we go in after them – and I say *if* – it will come from them and not before."

The big man straightened and pushed out his chest.

"If I'd wanted to go in of my own accord it already would have happened, and we wouldn't be stood here like two hoors at a hockey match talkin' about it."

He pulled up his jacket to reveal the butt of a 2.2 handgun tucked into the waistband of his trousers.

Molloy went apoplectic. "Put that a-fuckin'-way! Jesus, there's a film crew just down the road! The war is as good as over; hadn't you heard?"

Sledger just smiled, unperturbed.

Again Molloy's voice dropped to a whisper. "I take it you checked that out... through the quartermaster and that?"

Sledger was now cockily chewing gum. "Relax, will ya? It's not like you've never seen one before... Armani or no Armani."

Molloy went for the charm offensive.

He moved closer to the big man and leaned into him. "Sledge, listen... if they should come out and I'm not here, whatever you do, *don't* whack either of them, right? We've a safe house to take them to, they'll go up in front of the lads and whatever happens will happen after that... *only* after that, do you get me?"

Sledger said nothing.

"Sledge, it's *important.*"

"I'm not promising nothing," he said sullenly.

Molloy was becoming agitated.

"Sledger, listen: I am fuckin' deadly serious here. Do NOT, under any circumstances, act of your own accord if you know what's good for you. He's Frankie Connolly's brother for Christ sake!"

Sledger suddenly exploded, causing the councillor to step back.

"Frankie's dead! What about this community? What about my sister, her house robbed and wrecked; her car fuckin' totalled?"

"Frankie Connolly died for Ireland. This community will do whatever the fuck we tell them to do, and your sister... your sister has three kids to three different men!"

Calculated or not, it was an insult requiring satisfaction. Both men took a step toward each other.

It was Tootsie Molloy who stepped in between them.

"Ya see... ya see what they're doin'? They're getting yez at each other's throats!"

Terry Molloy was most enthusiastic to grasp the opportunity that his brother's intervention offered. He held the palms of his hands up to Sledger in a placatory gesture. "Is he worth it, is all I'm saying?"

Sledger's blood was up.

He sought some form of compensation. "And Gattuso?"

Terry Molloy was happy to comply.

"That greasy wee toe-rag deserves everything he has coming to him. You can fill your boots where he's concerned."

32

Eban sat at the table, studying an unfinished game of chess left there.

He assumed that Conor McVey had been one of the players, but looking around him, couldn't believe that any of his fellows made up the opposition.

He began to feel uncomfortable on the hard wooden chair he was perched on, fidgeting and with no real sense of time passing; keen to look at his watch without prejudice.

Everyone seemed to be involved in some elaborate play at pretend nonchalance.

Sinéad feigned reading a magazine, whilst Anto's long body was stretched out horizontally, his head supported underneath his folded hands.

Eban could see that he was not sleeping.

Simply staring straight ahead at the skirting board.

Ruairí repeatedly threw a tennis ball against the wall and caught it on the rebound.

He knew that the metronomic thump must be an irritation to the others, but as if in defiance, stared hard and intently at Eban, daring him to reprimand him.

Mrs Connolly had left an hour ago, for respite and for provisions.

So soon into my watch and we've already run out of things to say to each other, Eban fretted to himself.

Ruairí missed his catch and the break in rhythm seemed to galvanise him into engagement.

"Why is it – I mean, is there a word for it when you're thinking about something; I mean, when it's on your mind all the time and suddenly it's everywhere you look?"

Anto turned his head to look at him, puzzled. "Like what?"

"Like babies."

Ruairí seemed still to be staring intently, even intimidatingly, at Eban.

Without looking away he reached out beside him and held up a magazine showing the picture of an infant.

He slapped it down again on the floor.

Both young men looked across at Sinéad, who kept her head low, buried in the magazine.

Ruairí switched his gaze to her.

"I swear to God: TV ads for nappies; Calpol; pregnant women everywhere…"

Anto tried to be supportive. "Like when I got them Adidas Commandos… next thing, everybody's wearing them…"

His confederate grinned at him, knowing he was playing deliberately stupid so as to make the better foil to Ruairí's jibe when he decided to launch it.

"No, but I mean… on the TV; everywhere!"

Eban could sense that the young men were circling Sinéad, bored and about to savage her for some easy sport at the kid's expense. Not knowing how to defuse this, he gestured at the chessboard and blurted out, "Someone's in check."

Sinéad, who had been following the foreplay to the pending attack from behind her magazine, grabbed the lifeline desperately.

"Ruairí and Conor keep a game going between them. He's good, our Ruairí."

Eban was unable to conceal his surprise. He looked at Ruairí and arched his eyebrows. *"Really?"*

Sinéad seemed proud. "He'll give you a game if you want... won't you, Ruairí?"

The young man ignored her, continuing to stare at Eban. She raised her voice. "RUAIRÍ!"

Still nothing but that intense stare.

Eban felt transparent, like Ruairí was looking right through him.

He looked at his watch to break the spell.

Anto saw this.

"Looking at that won't make the time pass any faster, pal... especially on the night watch."

Eban let a laugh escape his lips. He stood up, rubbed his numb buttocks and seemed to be reaching for a memory.

"Ah, *the watch before the city gates depicted in their prime, golden light all grimy now...something...something... the something Captain and his squad of troopers standing fast.*"

It was the most he'd said for a long while. Anto was perplexed. "You what?"

"It's a poem; a song... about a painting by—"

Ruairí suddenly cut across him, barking out aggressively, "Rembrandt... it's by Rembrandt; the Dutch masters, right? Do you think we're all stupid around here?" he sneered.

Anto grinned from ear to ear, beaming with pride.

"He was the smartest in our class; wins all the pub quizzes. Ruairí, what was it you told us to say if the Provos get hold of us... if they question us, like?"

"I'm Spartacus."

"That's it – that's it! *Spartacus.*" His dark features pulled into a puzzled frown. He looked at Eban, puzzled. "Who *is* Spartacus?"

Ruairí suddenly leapt to his feet, and standing on Eban's chair, climbed up onto the table top. He affected an orator's pose: eyes closed, thumb in belt loop, the other hand outstretched mid-air.

"Rise my sisters, clouds eternal, shining bright with morning dew,
from the roaring ocean's bosom, to the sky the world to view.
Let us see the distant mountains and the holy earth below,
Where we irrigate the cornfields and the babbling rivers flow.
While far off, the breakers thunder, 'neath the sun's unwearied rays,
Make yourselves like human beings, and to the earth direct your gaze…"

He bowed low at the middle and all applauded and laughed, relieved by the unexpected nature of the distraction.

"Aristophanes' ode in praise of Socrates. Are you impressed Mr Barnard?" inquired the young man.

Eban was taken aback and nodded enthusiastically.

"Well, you shouldn't be." It didn't sound self-deprecating. More like an admonishment to Eban for drawing upon easy clichés regarding his charges.

"My da taught our Frankie and me that when we were kids. They used to get us up on the kitchen table at parties to recite it; it's my party piece, you might say. Trained monkey stuff."

He leapt down from the table and scooped up a sleeping bag.

"And with that, ladies and gentlemen, I'm off for some kip."

He disappeared through the curtain and into the sacristy.

Eban was left open-mouthed.

Sinéad smiled. "Don't mind him Mr Barnard, he's a sarcastic git most of the time."

Anto could not let this slight on his absent captain pass.

"Aye, it's you has him that way, so it is."

Sinéad turned on him threateningly, seemingly emboldened by Ruairí's absence.

"Don't start with me, wop!"

Anto bristled but did not speak.

Again Eban sought to break the tension.

"So how is it that Mrs Connolly is able to come and go as she likes; I mean, through the crowd outside?"

Sinéad answered. "Ruairí has three wee sisters that need looking after. It's only because of the goodness of Ruairí's Aunt Mary that Mrs Connolly can be in here at all with him."

Anto sneered. "It's because of Frankie."

"His brother?"

Sinéad picked up the thread. "Sledger and them, they worshipped Frankie. He was a top man in the organisation; they've a wall muriel of him in the estate and everything."

Eban didn't correct her.

Anto was dismissive. "A lot-a-good it did him."

Sinéad seemed stung.

"He died on hunger strike… he's a martyr. He died for what he believed in…"

She looked at the young man, who had begun to do press-ups, and said caustically, "What do you believe in, Anthony?"

"Getting my end away and getting out of my head, and don't ever fucking forget it, right?"

She turned to Eban,

"You see Mr Barnard, that's the quality of the people you're in here with. That's why we're in here in the first place. Ruairí could have made something of himself, with his family connections and that. It's hanging around with wasters like that" – she turned her nose up like a bad smell was coming off him – "that held him back."

Anto pushed himself up and began a cycle of squat thrusts. Slightly out of breath, he countered, "Oh aye… sure the Provos just love Ruairí! That's why they've been waiting for months to do him… *do him good.*"

Sinéad crossed her arms and moved her head from side to side. "It's you and the other two they want; it's not Ruairí."

Eban could see things accelerating, but was not adequately following. He appealed. "Slow down… I don't understand."

Anto was breathing more heavily from his exertions. He stopped and hunkered down.

"Look mate, Ruairí has been a disappointment to the lads ever since Frankie died. He's no interest in them and tells anybody who'll listen what bastards they are. Because he's smart, like; he really gets under their skin – they had him all fitted up for a Sinn Féin rising star in a couple of years. He told them to stuff it. Don't listen to her… they fuckin' hate him!"

Eban had heard something that piqued his interest. "And his brother… was he close to his older brother?"

"Hated him… when he got older, like, and realised what was going on. Before that… well… we all thought he was the bee's knees when we were kids… like you do with hard men."

Sinéad threw a magazine across the room, narrowly missing him. "That's a load of crap Anto; you're making it up cuz you're scared yourself."

Anto lifted the magazine, rolling it up into a tight tube. He rolled it tighter and tighter as he spoke.

"Scared? Yer fucking right I'm scared! I went along with Big Jamsey when he got done – for support, like; to phone the ambulance afterward. Let me tell you how it works, in case you didn't know. You agree a rendezvous and time – punishment by appointment. Jamsey's usually a cocky bastard, but he was a bag of nerves that night, slugging on vodka all day. We have to wait patiently until the back door of the club swings open; four come out with masks on, but you know who they are anyway. Two grab his arms and legs, while the third holds the gun to the back of his knee. The fourth is keeping watch. *Bang! Bang! Bang! Bang!*"

He slammed the table with each word, making the others jump.

159

"Both knees, both thighs."

Sinéad seemed cowed. "Okay Anto… that's enough."

The young man ignored her.

"They sprint off and leave me to get him to the hospital, and like there's blood starting to collect in pools under him, and he's laughing, the mad bastard – *laughing!*"

"Enough!"

"He didn't laugh for long, though. You see, it can go wrong, Eban. Bone or nerve damage if they're a fraction out or the gun's too high a calibre. Jamsey was a great hurler; could have played for the county – have a look around the area on your way out of here tomorrow, Eban; see if you can count the young fellas under thirty getting around on walking sticks."

Sinéad screamed, "ENOUGH!" She was close to tears. "I'm gonna wake Ruairí and tell him what you've been saying!"

"It's Ruairí I'm scared for most! They're bound to do a crucifixion on him: hands, feet, knees and elbows, and maybe with breeze blocks dropped on him instead of the gun."

"SHUT UP!"

"You wouldn't do it to an animal."

"SHUT UP! SHUT UP! SHUT UP!"

"HE'S *MY* BEST FRIEND!"

"YOU'VE A FUNNY WAY OF SHOWING IT!"

"IT TAKES TWO TO TANGO!"

Anto stopped abruptly, as if he had said something he did not intend to.

He looked to Eban to see if anything might have registered.

Sinéad's face was purple.

He spoke directly to Eban, nodding in Sinéad's direction. "I can't look at *her* anymore; I'm going for a lie down as well. Do you think you'll be safe enough on your own with her, Eban? She's a man-eater…"

Eban found himself blushing as Anto followed Ruairí into the sacristy with a blanket.

Sinéad called after him, giving him the finger as she did.

"Fuck off, dago; you smell. Have a wash; do us all a favour for Christ's sake."

Then there was quiet.

The racket from outside seemed to have abated somewhat.

Maybe they were getting tired.

After the malice of the exchange, both Eban and Sinéad drank in the hiatus, each content to dive into their own thoughts.

Eban Barnard had been shocked and unsettled by what he had heard.

Not because it affronted his sensibilities.

Quite the opposite.

This intimidation. This bullying. It was all too close to home.

The feeling was back, and it was strong.

The powerlessness.

His weary mind turned to a brilliant blue sky and the tinny jingle-jangle tune of an ice cream van.

Arriving home from his first job.

His first pay packet in his hip pocket.

A rite of passage realised.

He'd frozen at his parents' garden gate.

There, halfway up a ladder, a pair of puffy, white, hairy arse cheeks cracked over a denim jeans waistband.

Some tattooed thug was tying on red, white and blue bunting to the drainpipe outside *his* bedroom window.

Looking into *his* room.

It was the Loyalist marching season and this wanker hadn't even asked permission.

Instead he had just planted his ladder in the middle of his mother's begonias and was peering now into young Eban's inner sanctum.

His *Thunderbirds* pyjamas.

161

His *Charlie's Angels* poster.

The soiled tissues.

The titty mags.

He wanted to scream at this braindead usurper, *'You don't know me... I'm not one of you. Take it down; take it all fucking DOWN!'* To grab the ladder and shake it until the fat fuck crashed to the ground.

But of course, that would not happen.

No-one would say or do *anything*.

Not if you wanted to keep your windows intact, you didn't.

Later that year, he wretchedly watched the same fat fuck from his bedroom window, bouncing up and down on the bonnet and roof of his first car.

The little secondhand yellow Vauxhall Chevette stove in like a metal eggshell.

He had sat there for the third night running, observing the crowd banging bin-lids and smashing car windows, intending to lure the police into the area.

To provoke a conflict.

He fell on his bed, bent double; felt real pain, anguish, biting his fist and grabbing at his guts with the dreadful futility and frustration of it all.

Mob rule.

Gun law.

Then as now.

Nothing's changed.

Eban rubbed his eyes absentmindedly.

When his vision cleared, he found himself looking at Sinéad across the room.

She appeared so young and fragile.

A pretty girl. Too young to be a mother. Still only a child herself.

Her baby, like her, an unoffending soul ravaged by the indifferent lottery that determined place and time of birth.

By choices made… and by no choice at all. *No place to bring up a kid*, he thought.

Sinéad saw him look at her.

Her handbag rested on a chair and she pulled it closer with her foot, reaching in to take out a pack of cigarettes. She proffered the box to Eban, who refused. Lighting up, she tossed aside the lighter and smiled at him. "Well Mr Barnard… two's company, eh?"

Eban swallowed dryly and spoke.

"Yes, right… is *that* a good idea?"

He motioned at the cloud of smoke she had blown into the air, now hanging above her head, and then patted his gut. "I mean…"

Sinéad's shoulders slumped.

"Oh Gawd… don't *you* start. I can only smoke when *she's* not around. Look, you might as well know: I didn't want this kid, right. I'd have been on the boat but the Connollys have this big religious thing going on. I mean, that's one of the reasons we're all in here in the first place. But the bloody priests don't want the two of them here either… oul Ma Connolly just won't admit it to herself."

"I'm sorry, you're right… it's none of my business."

Sinéad took another long pull and threw her head back, tossing her long hair.

Defiant.

Exhaling the smoke directly at him.

Luxuriating in it, in what Eban thought was a provocative, almost promiscuous gesture.

He caught the smell of nicotine infused with her breath and the vapour that had been deep within her now entered his own nose and lungs in what seemed a wilfully intimate act.

She pouted. "Besides, I thought you were a man of the

world. I can't keep calling you Mr Barnard… what's your first name again? "

"It's Eban. Most people get it wrong."

She crossed her legs, " Oh, *Eban* – very posh… like a film star, or a lord."

"Hardly. I grew up in a place much like yours."

"Just on the other side, eh?"

"We moved around a lot. When I was kid, in the 70s, it was bad then… random car bombs; the lot."

He felt surprised by how freely he was speaking with her.

"When has it *not* been bad? Just depends whether it comes to *your* door or not."

"I suppose you're right."

She pulled her hands through her hair. "The 70s you say? You're giving away your age there Eban. Still, you look quite well on it… for an older man I mean."

Eban was sure now she was flirting. He felt flattered but suddenly self-conscious. "Oh, I don't know… I could loose a bit around here."

The minute it escaped his lips he felt like an idiot. Like some coy adolescent.

She saw it.

"You and me both." She patted the bump in her belly, placing him at ease again. They both laughed.

"Are you a married man, Eban?"

"Separated… she's in England."

"These things happen."

She waited a moment, slowly rotating one big hoop earring between her thumb and finger.

"Do you miss her?"

"No, not really. She got to know everything about me; then force-fed it back to me… some of it was hard to swallow."

He heard himself say this and again marvelled at how candid he was being with this young girl, a stranger until only hours ago.

"You should keep to your own, Eban. The English... they'll never understand; they've never wanted to. We're all bogmen to them."

Eban felt a wave of recrimination rise in him and was momentarily swept up in it.

"I can hear her like it was yesterday: *'Are you happy now?' 'Is this what you wanted?' 'Are you making a difference?'*"

He was chastened by how bitter he sounded, and sought to draw back. His voice dropped. "Anyway... we all have our demons..."

Sinéad pointed a finger at the wall where a large crucifix hung. "Well, you've come to the right place."

After a silence she asked, "So who keeps you here in this shit hole? Girlfriend?"

"There was someone... it's complicated."

"Isn't it always?"

"I'm not gay!" He winced. Why did he feel the need to say that?

She laughed, surprised. "I never said you were. Parents?"

"Both dead."

"Don't tell me: you were an only child."

Eban was suddenly conflicted. For the first time since they had begun to speak he sounded faltering, hesitant, awkward.

"Yes... well... no. I had... I *have* an older brother."

Sinéad seemed amused. "Well, make your mind up."

He shot back aggressively, "I have a brother. His name is Alex, alright... okay?!"

Sinéad was taken aback. "Jesus, don't eat me! You're just like Ruairí when they talk about Frankie. Nobody can look at him sideways."

Eban frowned, disappointed in his lack of self-control. "I'm sorry."

But Sinéad had moved on already. Now she was laughing. Maybe that was why he liked her. "We have twelve in our family. How would you like breakfast time in our house?"

"I've never had those kinds of… connections."

"Is that why you went to England?"

Eban looked at her open, honest face. Somehow it had become younger, fresher. Like some of her cares had for the moment left her, if just for a short while. Maybe just for an instant.

He smiled. "Christ, you ask a lot of questions."

"I like people. So, is that why you went to England?"

"Amongst other things. Sometimes it feels like I've been moving around forever. Do you know something – I've never owned a bed that I've slept in; isn't that crazy? At my age, I mean!"

He laughed wryly to himself, but she could see a glimpse of something broken inside. She teased him, "So you're a bit of a ladies' man then?"

Eban ignored her. This back-and-forth banter had passed on to something more personal, more confessional for him now.

"I try to remember all the bedrooms I've slept in – where the door was; the window – to get to sleep at nights… like counting sheep, you know?"

Sinéad stubbed out her cigarette. "You have trouble sleeping as well?"

He smiled and nodded at the sound of snoring coming from the sacristy. "We can't all go out like a light."

She fished in her bag for another cigarette. She looked older again.

"I've to take tablets, with my nerves, except I've had to stop… with the baby and all, although God knows I could be doing with them now."

"Do you need them to sleep?"

"I need them for the dreams. I have bad dreams… worse since I got pregnant."

She stood up and walked across the room, then reached across Eban to pick up a box of matches. He smelled her strong perfume, her shampoo. When she sat down again, it was next to him.

"Ruairí doesn't get it… he doesn't understand how nice it can be to snuggle up to somebody… how it can make you feel safe."

Eban drew back instinctively, immediately. He tried to make it seem casual, walking around behind her chair.

"What do you dream about?"

"Well, it usually starts off nice… like when I was young and my da was still around. I felt safe then… before he went for work in Liverpool. First the phone calls stopped; then the money he sent back stopped too. There's some talk that he has another wife and kids over there, but we haven't seen him in years."

"And that's what you dream about: your father?"

"Only in the beginning… it's always downhill after that. It's mostly about babies now, but…" She hesitated, looked guilty. "Not in a good way."

"That's to be expected. You're probably just anxious." He felt comfortable again in the role of protector, counsellor.

Sinéad was becoming upset. She pulled a balled-up tissue from her sleeve.

" No… no, it's more than that. You see when I was a kid – about nine or ten, like – we lived on the old Glenn Estate… do you know it? It made where we live now look like Beverly Hills!"

"I've heard of it. They knocked it down didn't they?"

"My ma was hard pressed with the twelve of us and that, so we'd to make our own way most of the time. Anyway, one morning on my way to school I saw this movement – looked like a shadow at first; a shape off in the distance, coming toward me, like; through the empty houses; down the alleyway... gettin' bigger. It was summer – hot, you know, even that early – it was comin' through like a heat haze; shimmering and that. I was always petrified of rats, but this was worse..."

She put her hand to her mouth, emotional. "Far, far worse."

Eban felt a morbid fascination. He gripped the back of her chair. "Go on."

"Dogs used to run wild around there – strays... half-mad. I saw them coming right toward me but I couldn't run... couldn't move... just stood there. About ten of them, and the leader of the pack out front, ahead... he had something in his mouth. It was flopping around from side to side; he held it high like a prize... at first I thought it was a kids' doll, but when they got close I could see it was a cat... a skinned cat. It was still moving... still alive!"

"My God... that's awful."

"But that's not it, you see – it's worse. In the dream it's a baby... *it's always a baby!*" She broke down, sobbing.

Suddenly a wail of feedback and megaphone noise rose up from outside. It made them both jump in shocked surprise. A voice, timid and broken, spoke haltingly; uncertainly.

"Ruairí? Anto? Are you there, lads...?"

Anto's head poked into the room from behind the curtain of the antechamber.

A look of confusion on his face.

The voice came again, fighting with the megaphone feedback.

It was agitated.

Complaining.

Protesting to someone. "I know... I KNOW! I *am* doing it!"

Ruairí and Anto suddenly shot through the curtain, dashing into the room in a state of disorientation.

168

Ruairí, who had been cleaning his teeth, trailed a line of spit and suds.

Anto, who had one leg in, one leg out of his trousers, bounced around like he was on a pogo stick. He careered toward the window but Ruairí pulled him back.

"That's… that sounds like…"

Ruairí confirmed it. "Dinny. They've got Dinny."

Below the cathedral window, Sledger and Tootsie flanked the bent and crumpled form of Denis Clancy.

A small man.

The runt of the gang.

He looked frightened, his clothing ripped and dishevelled.

Congealed blood had formed around his ear so that he struggled to hear his captors.

Sledger violently yanked his head back by the hair. "Just like we agreed, cunt!"

Dinny yelped in pain and fear, then cried out again mournfully, "Ruairí… Anthony…" He broke down in great heaving sobs.

Tootsie slapped him hard in the face. "Is *that* the way you want to play it?"

Sledger put his mouth to Dinny's good ear. "You saw your mate Murphy… is that the way you want to finish up as well?"

Dinny whispered, "No…"

Tootsie slapped him hard in the face again. "What? SPEAK UP!"

"NO! NO!" the boy cried.

"Not to us… to *them*," said Sledger, pointing up at the window. "Now try again."

Dinny swallowed hard. "Lads… it's no good… it's all over… they want you to—"

Another violent slap from Tootsie corrected him.

"*I*… *I* want you to come out. So does Spud. It's all over…"

169

Sledger smiled and jabbed the boy in the back. "And Clancy... tell them we know that *he* put you up to the whole thing."

Dinny began crying, pitifully, like a child. "Ruairí," he wailed, then turned to appeal to his captors. "I can't... I can't say that..."

SLAP!

"It's not true..."

SLAP!

Dinny was crying hard again.

He gestured for the megaphone. "Okay, okay... give me that..."

Sledger handed it to him.

Raising it shakily to his mouth, Dinny shouted, "Ruairí, listen... I'm Spartacus, do ya hear me? *I'M SPARTACUS!*"

The big man slapped it from his hand smartly.

The device hit the ground with a clunk, rolled and howled high-pitched feedback.

Denis Clancy bent low at the waist and cowered wretchedly, covering his head with his arms. Sledger looked at him, shaking his head incredulously.

"You stupid wee bastard."

Both men linked the boy's arms.

He collapsed in fear, as if poleaxed.

They pulled him backward, dead meat, his heels dragging on the cobbles, out of the street light and into the shadows.

33

Eban Barnard was feeling drowsy in the airless heat of the late afternoon.

At this time of day he usually made his way up into what he took to be the McGrews' daughters' bedroom.

Pop posters of Donny Osmond and David Cassidy and pictures of kittens were still taped to the blackened walls.

It was there that he kept his most exciting find of all.

A battered and dented slide projector.

The slide mechanism itself was bent and unusable. But the fire had melted a celluloid slide onto the metal frame, fusing it over the thick glass projector lens.

The boy knew that when the light from the late afternoon sun came through the skylight in a particular way, it was possible to illuminate the slide if held at the correct angle.

This produced a blurred and stained, upside-down image of a whitewashed country cottage surrounded by trees and hills.

Two figures stood at the gate, but try as he might, he could not make out their features.

Eban was able to project this onto an untouched patch of the white wall opposite, where, with a charred piece of wood, he had roughly sketched out a square to suggest the perimeters of a screen.

Here he would stare at this inverted, ghostly image for a long, long time.

It seemed to him that it was being beamed from another world.

From long ago in the past.

Accessible only to him and only through this medium he had created all on his own.

The stench could be near overpowering at this time of a summer's day as the heat rose.

Gallons of rancid wine, spirits and porter spilled arbitrarily during the looting, now rotting and filling the air with a caustic smell.

Like stale vinegar.

Despite this thick wall of stench, Eban immediately recognised the pungent odour of his own two-day-old faeces cutting through it and blushed.

At the time he'd been so excited by this primal act.

The sheer *badness* of it.

To crouch in the centre of someone's living room and defecate.

Knuckles white.

Squatting and squeezing out the stool.

He had looked around the room and noticed the broken vinyl records still in their sleeves: *Jim Reeves, The Christmas Polka*; *The Best of Hank Snow*; *The Romance of Engelbert Humperdinck*.

The glossy women's magazines.

The shattered furniture and kitchen appliances.

The browned and curled photographs of the McGrew family at the beach on holiday.

Or leaning over a barred gate in some country field.

He had never known them.

Had heard little of them or their misfortune.

But he had felt instantly ashamed of mocking their calamity in this way.

Further mortification ensued at this time with his inability to find anything to hand – other than the magazines and photographs themselves – to wipe his arse with.

Now, however, the smell prompted more immediate concerns.

As the boy tended to spend the whole day ensconced within the gutted shell, when time dragged on and hunger pangs stirred he had taken to picking though his packed school lunch.

The combined smells of warm, soft, overripe black banana sandwiches and fetid faeces was a difficult one to stomach.

It might have been worse again, though.

If his mammy had given him sugar or brown sauce on buttered bread he would have had to toss them away.

However, an acute fear of attracting rats into his sanctum kept the sandwiches sealed within their transparent plastic lunch box.

He moved warily across the room and up the blackened stairs to escape the stench.

The front bedroom was his favourite vantage point.

Behind the warping, undulating metal sheets which covered the windows.

Seeing all, but remaining unseen.

He looked down over Snugville Street and its environs in an imperious manner.

His surveillance encompassed the laundromat (colloquially known as 'the washers'), Sammy Kidd's corner shop and all the house fronts of his neighbours.

Women like his mother, out polishing steps, window sills, even empty glass milk bottles, ready for collection.

As if this outer solicitude somehow reflected a standard of unimpeachability that must not be compromised, even in the face of violence, poverty and hardship.

Occasionally a heavy lumbering army vehicle would growl

by, the noise rising to a shrill squeal as the squaddie changed up gears.

Eban wriggled and settled himself comfortably on his school bag, which acted as a cushion of sorts, atop the upturned beer keg he'd placed next to his lookout post.

After a while, he fell into a light sleep.

34

Anne Breslin waited for her mother and older brother to go upstairs before taking the letter from her handbag.

She unfolded it and smoothed it out on her lap.

In the translucent picture window of the official brown manila envelope it said, *Mr Joseph Patrick Breslin – Confidential*.

Despite acting as primary carer for him and their mother for most of her adult life, she was not normally in the habit of opening her brother's mail.

But something about this letter worried her.

And besides, Joe had been so up-and-down since the doctors had changed his medication. (Something about oestrogens and testosterone receptor blocking agents, they'd said.)

The last thing she wanted for him now was any additional worry or stress.

Still, she hated doing anything that demeaned his dignity or detracted from his sense of independence and self-worth.

God knows he'd had enough to deal with on that score.

Anne thought for a moment about leaving the mail unopened in the usual place.

On the hall table, behind an old photograph of Joe and their mother.

Him barely twenty, in denim dungarees and bovver boots, a shock of frizzy red hair.

Her gazing up at him lovingly, the apple of her eye.

Slipping a broken nail under the flap, Anne decided that she would explain that she'd opened it without checking the name first, as she was expecting something from the tax people.

Her intuition had been correct.

She knew that when she saw the Historical Enquiries Team letterhead.

Dear Mr Breslin,

A formal request has been received by us to investigate the incident which led to your assault on the 7th of May 1970 at Snugville Street, Belfast. As you are aware, no-one has been apprehended for this crime.

However, the request comes from a party who is not a member of your immediate family.

Therefore, as is required, I am writing to you now to enquire as to whether you would like us to proceed with any further investigation, and if so, grant us permission for this to take place.

Please contact us via the details provided below to make an appointment to discuss this matter further.

Sincerely,

Sgt. Samuel Coulter on behalf of Detective Inspector Dan Watson, Historical Enquiries Team, Police Service of Northern Ireland

Anne's blood ran cold.

She had long feared that something like this would one day come across their doorstep.

She heard the floorboards creak above her in Joe's bedroom.

She heard her mother turn over, slowly rising from her late afternoon nap.

They were a tight family.

Close. Insular.

Just the three of them since her father had died.

Too long ago now for her to remember him.

They were slaves to routine. To habit.

As long as nothing shook them out of their daily customs and schedules, then somehow the world could not intrude.

She heard Joe's faltering steps move across the landing to the bathroom.

Time for his injections.

Time to change his dressings.

Wounds, weeping.

Even after all these years, she thought. Still weeping.

Molly McArdle, the blind piano tuner, was coming to meet the family this weekend.

Anne and her mother had dared to believe again that there still might be someone for Joe.

Even yet. Despite everything.

As thrilled as she was for him, she struggled with her dread.

She had found his old scrapbook, taken down by him from the loft again and hidden behind the radiator in the hall.

The cut-out-and-pasted letters across the front.

Like some ransom note.

Delores.

Anne knew what it contained.

The photos, the love letters, the old Valentines cards from his once-fiancée.

The woman who had failed to stand by him.

Who had broken his heart after *they* had broken his body.

She feared for her brother.

"If you don't let someone in, then they can't hurt you," she had told him.

177

It had been her own mantra.

Her own code of conduct for survival.

But it had left her alone. Unmarried. Childless.

She could accept all of it as long as she believed that it had been her own choice.

And as long as she had her family. Mam and Joe.

But Molly McArdle was coming… and there might yet be hope for Joe.

Dear, sweet, broken Joe.

Anne moved through the kitchen – picking up the oven lighter on the way – and out into her mother's back yard.

You couldn't call it a garden. Mostly cement slabs contained by wooden fences.

Identical back yards behind and to either side.

Dogs barking, kids playing, couples fighting, music blaring. It was always the same.

Mrs Breslin had placed a few potted plants here and there.

A rudimentary, ornamental concrete fountain and bird bath lay long unused. Built by the former tenant. There since the Housing Executive had moved them in.

Moss-green stains deeply etched into them.

Tall plastic bins – blue for recyclables; brown for organic; black for everything else – stood in a line.

She opened the lid on the first one, clicked the lighter and held it under the corner of the letter. It caught quickly and she had to release it for fear of burning her fingers.

Instead of falling into the bin, the letter, curled and charred and blackened, was caught by the wind.

Anne watched as the paper disintegrated in the air above her, fell to the ground and blew around the tartan carpet slippers Joe had given her at Christmas.

35

Cecil Herringshaw was not a patient man.

Especially when he had gone to considerable lengths to arrange things just so.

Well... not to put too fine a point on it, he expected bloody results.

Helen Totton had enjoyed special dispensation from the Herringshaws and needed to start producing.

After all, she was his ex-daughter-in-law.

After her marriage to his pipsqueak, good-for-nothing son Jamie broke down, well, he'd kept the channels open.

Held out an olive branch.

He was an influential man.

On the Policing Board; member of the Ulster Scots Agency; on the boards of the Housing Executive; the Broadcasting Authority; the Environment Agency.

Shit, there were very few quangos in the province that he hadn't sat on or influenced in some shape or form.

He'd suggested some ways in which she might still be of use to him.

He had always liked her.

Liked the way she flirted with him.

If he had been twenty years younger, well... she would never have gone looking for some extramarital from *his* bed.

Jamie was an idiot.

Drank too much.

Stayed out all night with his rugby buddies, behaving like he was a single man.

The divorce broke his mother's heart but in the end Cecil didn't blame Helen one little bit.

They had no kids. That was a blessing.

God only knows what that halfwit would have sired anyway, he thought.

It was Cecil who had orchestrated her movements through the PSNI.

Who had arranged for her transfer to the HET.

Who had anticipated Dan Watson's professionalism and rigour when interpreting his brief in the new dispensation.

The new, *shared* Northern Ireland.

Not like back in the day.

It was a long time ago now, but he remembered *that* particular meeting very well.

Late at night.

In the committee back room of some suburban lawn bowling club or other.

Who would have ever thought of it?

All very hush-hush.

Cecil, some spook from MI6, a couple of army bods, a very nervous senior civil servant from the Northern Ireland Office, an elder of the Unionist party and two top-ranking Loyalist head-bangers.

Terrorise the Terrorists.

That had been their tactic.

Hit them where it hurts.

Show them that we're fuckin' mental!

He knew, in short, that meant atrocities.

The Loyalist paramilitaries had worked out that if the Provos couldn't protect their own people, then the fear of sectarian murder attacks – in reprisal for IRA operations – would begin to take its toll.

'A reactive deterrent' they had come to coin it, in the parlance of Ulster euphemism.

Soft targets: bookie's shops, crowded bars, unsuspecting lovers in parked cars.

Catholics shot; two, four, six at a time.

And anyone else who got in the way.

You shoot one, we shoot four.

They claimed it as a legitimate tactic of war… *legitimised* it.

And it worked.

Brought those Fenian scum, if not to their knees, then to the negotiations table.

Ended the war.

And for what?

Joint government.

A shared future.

The RUC scrapped.

Orange marching routes banned.

The flying of our own flag in our own country curtailed.

Millions spent on enquiries and commissions.

Public apologies from a succession of whinging British Prime Ministers.

All of whom were probably out walking their Labradors in the Home Counties when we were being murdered in our beds.

'*Careful, Cecil,* he thought. *Mind the old blood pressure… you've been warned.*

Herringshaw smiled to himself. When he shuffled off this mortal coil, he'd be taking a lot of collateral with him.

He knew where all the top brass bodies were buried, for sure.

Knew who had been up to Kincora Boys' Home, having it away with guttersnipes and waifs.

Had been Chief Procurer for undersecretaries, bishops and senior civil servants.

Arranged lavish parties in remote Fermanagh country houses.

Watched them on CCTV as, two and three at a time, they held the innocents down and rutted them mercilessly.

For a man of his ruthless guile and reach, Dan Watson had been just too easy.

The old 'honey trap' rarely fails.

He was up her faster than a rat up a drainpipe!

A man his age.

In his position.

Contemptible.

Mobile phones; wonderful things.

Cameras.

Videos.

Who knows what else?

A resourceful girl like Helen Totton.

Build up a portfolio. That's what he'd told her.

No need for bluntness or crudity.

Approach it all professionally.

Money in the bank.

And when the time comes…

When Detective Inspector Watson wants to try for Chief Superintendent Watson…

Well, we'd just have to see about that now, wouldn't we?

But more immediately.

More pressingly.

What if he intended proceeding with investigations into security force collusion?

Well, how would Danny-Boy like pictures of his sorry cock and balls plastered all over Facebook for his wife and kids to see?

Top Cop Goes Down On Unknown Woman Police Officer While Dressed in Full Regalia.

In a Hilton hotel room.

Following some awards ceremony.

A few whiskies too many, Dan?

Christ,he'd even let her film it on her phone!

"For later," she'd said. When she was alone, so she could call him and play with herself.

What a fuckin' ego!

The man wasn't fit to wear the uniform.

Bring back the bloody B-Specials.

It had all been going so well.

And now this.

It was the not knowing.

What the fuck was Alex Barnard's brother doing locked in a room with Watson?

What in the name of God were they talking about?

And why wasn't that stupid wee whore doing what she was put there to do?

Cecil thought about ringing her again, but decided against it.

She'd be in touch when she had something.

She was good like that.

"Just get in the room or get lover boy out of it. Failing that, get a look at those files," was what he'd barked at her.

"Either way, I need to know what they're talking about!"

36

Anto spun away from the window and stalked around the room in a rage.

He resembled a caged animal.

Stripped to the waist, his wiry body tensed, his muscles like cables, tightened and protruding.

His tattoos swelling.

Eyes wide in fury and fists clenched, he paced the length of the walls looking for something to punch.

To hit out against.

Finding nothing but brick, he yelled at the top of his lungs, 'ARAGGGHHH!", pushed his fist into his mouth and bit down hard to staunch the emotion.

Eban Barnard pointed lamely with one hand at the gunmetal-grey coin box mounted on the wall; the other rummaging for fifty pence coins in his pocket.

"Shouldn't we phone someone… let them know?"

Sinéad shook her head. "Disconnected."

Ruairí didn't move. He looked puzzled. "My ma… she must have known. Why didn't she tell us?"

"She told me," Sinéad whispered, almost to herself.

She sounded frightened.

Ruairí spun around enraged, incredulous. "She told *YOU*?"

He stood over her threateningly. "What exactly did she say?"

Sinéad took a sheet of A4 paper from the waistband of her leggings and unfolded it.

It bore a black-and-white picture of Ruairí. "She didn't want you to see this, or know about Dinny and Spud."

All three men moved around the table to look at the poster.

Ruairí read it aloud disdainfully. "*Wanted for Crimes Against the Community.*"

He laughed ironically. "That's a joke... fuckin' hypocrites!"

Sinéad explained. "They're all over the town... sent them to the papers, and the TV."

Anto seemed disappointed. "Didn't they do one of me?" he asked, perplexed.

Eban wanting something to contribute, could only manage, "It's not a very good likeness."

Ruairí turned on him. "Is that all you can say? Is that all you've got to offer?"

"What do you want me to say?"

Anto craned his neck and looked again. "He's right... doesn't look like you."

"Read the back," said Sinéad.

Ruairí turned over the sheet and read.

"*Statements from gang members Brian 'Spud' Murphy and Denis Clancy confirm their involvement in a catalogue of crimes and antisocial behaviour, identifying Ruairí Connolly as the gang leader and Anthony Gatusso as his lieutenant.*"

Anto was again perturbed. "If I'm a lieutenant, how come they don't have a picture of me on it?"

"Enough, Anto!" Ruairí snapped.

Turning to Eban, he asked, "Is this gonna make a difference... I mean, to your lot?"

"I don't... *my* lot?"

185

"You know: the dinner party crowd; the chattering classes… will yez give up on us now?"

Eban seemed surprised. "I think most people thought you did it anyway."

Anto and Ruairí looked at each other.

For a moment Eban thought they might punch him to the ground and stamp on his head. Instead, they both exploded with guffaws of laughter.

Anto was disbelieving. "You mean they don't care whether we did it or not?"

"I shouldn't think so."

"Just as long as we don't rob *their* houses, right Eban?" Ruairí was scathing.

Anto fell back into his chair, cackling. "Yeah, let us know when you'll be taking your holidays, will you Eban?"

Both were convulsed with laughter.

It was incongruous given what had just taken place.

Eban recognised it as a coping mechanism.

A pressure valve release.

He began to laugh as well.

Sinéad pulled the plug. "Dinny's not laughing."

The hilarity trailed off.

Anto took it like a slap in the face.

He called to her defiantly, "Yeah… what would *you* know about it?"

She shouted back at him, "You're not on the poster cuz yer head's too big for the fuckin' page!"

2.47am

Eban wondered if he should try to get his head down or whether there was much point now.

It would be dawn in a few hours.

He would be out of here and back to South Belfast with its

wine bars and convenience stores. Its boutiques and ethnic takeaways.

He could grab a pint of milk and a loaf and maybe be in bed by midday, with the curtains drawn and his ear plugs in.

He smiled to himself.

Never had the mundane and the familiar had such appeal.

He might phone in sick and stay in bed for the rest of the week.

Why the fuck not?

Perks of public service.

Let them all go fuck themselves!

Sinéad was asleep on the couch, only her hair visible above a tartan rug.

Anto sat at the table, face down.

His forehead resting on his forearms.

His breathing was rhythmic, save for the occasional gag or snore.

His back rose and fell in time.

A small pool of drool had gathered at the side of his open mouth.

Ruairí had disappeared into the sacristy some time ago.

The radio was on low in there.

Tuned to some all-night station for insomniacs and shift workers. *Like me*, Eban thought.

"*Psssst…*"

The sound came from the direction of the closed curtain.

When he looked up Eban saw Ruairí Connolly beckon him over before the drape closed again.

Passing through the curtain he found Ruairí seated in one of the deck chairs.

He was swathed in tartan blankets.

He had his feet raised on a stool. His hood pulled up over his head.

He looked comfortably settled in.

The small space was lit by two paraffin storm lanterns which bathed the room in a warm orange glow.

It seemed inviting of intimacy and introspection.

A confessional.

A haven against what had gone before.

An oasis of calm.

Eban Barnard felt exhaustion swell up in him.

It flooded his brain and forced together his eyes.

Perhaps it was the womb-like warmth of the small room.

Perhaps the distinctive smell of the heated paraffin, something he always associated with his childhood.

When Ruairí Connolly indicated that he should join him in the other deck chair, Eban didn't hesitate, gathering up the end of the rugs there and enveloping himself in them.

When he had snuggled down into a comfortable position, he looked across at Ruairí.

"I always hate this time of the morning. Too late for yesterday... too early for tomorrow."

The young man said nothing.

Eban tried again. "I feel like we should be on the deck of a ship."

Ruairí twisted his mouth into that ironic smile that Eban had already become familiar with. "I might be on one soon enough."

There was an awkward silence.

"England?"

Ruairí tugged his hood back so Eban could now see his face properly. He thought for a moment that the young man might have been crying.

"Scotland. I'd like to go to London but she has an aunt in Dundee. If things don't... well... I'd probably head for there."

"Will you miss it... home I mean?"

Ruairí's face hardened again. "Did I say I was leaving?" he shot back angrily.

"I just meant—"

"Anyway, what's to miss?"

"You're asking the wrong man. I was away myself for ten years."

"But you came back."

Eban was remembering his own exile, but his fatigue had softened his memory.

It made him wistful.

"Yes… I came back. Believe it or not, I came back for the people… for the Mourne mountains and the Antrim coast… for the potato farls!" He laughed to himself.

Ruairí wasn't buying it. "Home's an imaginary place. You were homesick for some place that doesn't exist."

"It's the people that make a place a homeland."

Ruairí pushed himself up in the chair and pulled his arms out from under the rugs.

He fixed Eban with a withering glare of cynicism and disdain. It wasn't the first time that Eban Barnard had misread him this evening. "The people! Are you fucking serious?"

Eban was backpedalling again. "Well… I only meant—"

"Don't give me that 'into the mystic' crap. I got all that from my da. The best people in the world; the fourth green field; the faith of our fathers… any green fields around here have burnt-out cars in them."

"You're young; you've never been away. Sometimes you have to travel to find out where home really is."

"And you're sitting there now, telling me that you'd rather come back to this hole than be swanning around the West End with some blonde on your arm or catching the tube on a Saturday to see Arsenal play? *Are you fucking mad?!*"

Eban was floundering. Falling back on his older, man-of-the-world persona, he wasn't confident.

"It must seem that way to you, and I know that there's still a lot wrong with this place… but home's home."

"You're breaking my heart."

"Look, I know there's more to it than that; than I'm making it sound. If I'm being honest with you, sometimes I think that when I'm there I want to be here, and when I'm here I want to be there."

Ruairí pounced immediately. "Then get a job on the Larne-to-Stranraer ferry!"

Abruptly, he laughed at his own retort.

Eban did too.

It seemed to create a brief respite in what had quickly established itself as a generational chasm, across which both looked on the other with mistrust and trepidation.

Eban smiled. "Okay, sure – a young man could have a great time across the water."

Again, Ruairí bristled.

"I didn't *say* I was going… besides, how much craic will I have with a ready-made family?" He nodded at the room next door.

He turned around fully to face Eban.

As if he had something to say that needed to be understood.

"If I do go, it'll be on *my* terms… not for her…"

He was becoming angry.

"… and not because I'm gonna run from Sledger and that scum… just so as you know."

He dug into the folds of his sweatshirt and from beneath the blankets pulled out a small pack of rolling tobacco. He adroitly rolled a cigarette, lit it and offered it to Eban.

Eban caught the whiff immediately. "Is this what I think it is?"

"A little of what you fancy does you good."

He hesitated. "Ah… I'm not sure. It's been a while."

Ruairí felt the balance swing back to him.

. "Listen, dope will get you through times with no money, but money won't get you through times with no dope. How

190

d'ya think we've managed to stick this place for over a week without losing the plot completely?"

He proffered the joint again to Eban, who took it and slipped back down in the chair.

The young man seemed to embrace a more affable manner now that the ritual of passing the hash had begun.

"What exactly was it you did over there anyway, Eban?"

Eban took a draw on the joint and tried hard to appear nonchalant. "Ah, they don't pay me for what I do; they pay me for what I know."

Ruairí smiled again.

This guy was easy. "The money's crap then?"

Eban couldn't help but laugh at his rapid-fire wit.

He could feel the marijuana hit immediately. Like an old friend who had been away for a long time.

He handed the joint back to Ruairí.

"I was a teacher. Kids about your age; inner city."

He closed his eyes to help himself remember. "Christ, they used to torture me for my accent."

Ruairí seemed eager to talk about something removed from the shit storm he found himself in. Happy to go piggyback on someone else's reminiscence.

"What kinda things did you get up to over there?"

"Well, I used to hang around with these guys from home, who were in a band over there. They found me somewhere to live in Cricklewood, near Kilburn. Big Irish community. Rent allowance, social welfare payments... the quids from gigs were nothing more than tokens for blow, beer and pool for those boys."

"Sweet."

"Nobody seemed to bother about religion there. If you came from the North, then other expats seemed to get it that it was kind of uncool to introduce anything into the conversation that might offend or embarrass anyone, like."

"They must have knew you were a Protestant. I mean, fuck sake... look at ya!"

Eban understood now how the young man liked to parley.

By always trying to get a rise out of the teacher, the priest, the authority figure.

He'd known kids like this when he'd taught in Neasden.

They were invariably the smartest in the class, but always unremitting ball-breakers!

He ignored the bait.

The joint moved back and forward between them.

"The only people who bothered about any of that were the sad ones who congregated in the pubs on Saturday nights. You always knew them: covered in cement dust from the sites and holding sodden fish suppers. They were like rubber men... gyrating with the drink... when the rebel songs started up, tears ran; thin lines through the dust and dirt on their faces."

The weed had loosened him up.

He attempted a passable Cockney accent, "'Fuckin' Paddies innit,' the barman used to say. 'To listen to them, the only thing they won't do for their fuckin' country is live in it!'"

"And nobody ever tumbled you for an Orange bastard?"

"Hey, easy on!" Eban feigned offence.

"I'm only messin' with ya."

Both men seemed comfortable in each other's company for the first time.

"There was this one night." Eban smiled at the memory. "I was on my way back from last orders. The band in the lounge bar struck up *The Soldier's Song*. Well, you know how it works: everybody drew their conversation to a close and rose to their feet; stood to attention, hands over their fucking hearts. The works! Well, it threw me a bit – Ireland's national anthem for fuck sake, right here in the middle of the great metropolis, the mother of Parliaments, heart of the empire!"

Ruairí seemed unimpressed. His trademark cynicism returned. "It makes me proud. What did you do?"

"Well, that's it… what *do* you do? I'm balancing three pints and two shorts; to stand still and look at the floor was the wisest option and one I took gladly."

"You bottled it. Some Prod you are."

"Maybe… anyway, the music ended and a cheer went around the bar. When I was passing the lounge door I looked in. The band were still on stage. The Boys of Erin; I never forgot that… they'd been stoking the punters all night with rousing ballads of uprising and rebellion – well, didn't they all look lovely in their crushed velvet lounge suits, lace-fronted shirts… *and turbans!*"

"Fuck off!"

"I'm tellin' ya – every last one to a man… *Sikh!* Listen, Ruairí: that town has a way of fucking with your certainties."

They both laughed.

Ruairí proffered the joint again. "So why are you back here?"

Eban stiffened somewhat. His mood changed. "Unfinished business," he said tetchily. "*My* business."

He took the joint hungrily and pulled hard on it.

The young man seemed offended. As if a growing familiarity had suddenly been extinguished.

He lashed back. "Chill… I don't give a fuck."

Eban was immediately disappointed with himself.

Embarrassed at his careless abandonment of something that he had been building.

He tried to make amends. "Sorry. Look… maybe… I… you see, I'm… I come from a pretty rough area myself – Loyalist area, I mean – and sometimes—"

Connolly was having none of it. "Now everybody's a war baby. How'd you like to be where I'm sittin' right now?"

Eban came down with a crash.

The exhaustion flooded back in.

The awfulness of the situation they found themselves in had not alleviated one iota.

He yearned for sleep.

Instead he was trapped somewhere in a world of half-wakefulness.

A twilight zone of blurred lines.

He hadn't really noticed the radio playing in the background until now.

It had been cackling away with a playlist for long-distance lorry drivers and nighthawks. But now the room seemed to be filled with some plaintive Irish ballad.

The uillean pipes swelled in a mournful refrain.

He felt an overwhelming need to clarify.

To be understood.

He tried again.

"If you would just let me explain… it's difficult for me to explain. You try to find *good* things… I mean, sometimes… sometimes there can be beauty; sometimes there can be *more*, you know? We lived on the peace line, near where the city ended and the countryside began…"

It was clearly difficult for him. He had to close his eyes.

To concentrate.

To force back the memory.

"There isn't much good to say about it really, but one winter, after the whitest winter and close to the thaw, four horses clip-clopped by my bedroom window, down from the hills; through fields… they woke me from my sleep."

Eban put his face in his hands and rubbed his eyes, the better to focus.

"They were ponies really… they echoed down the empty tarmac, under the glare of street lamps… all brown. They shimmered… all black… they shone in the neon light."

It was as if he were alone in the room.

As if Ruairí Connolly need not be there to listen.

He was talking to himself.

"Indecisive at the junction, I heard them stop... then turn... then wait... then move off far into the distance, out of hearing... out of sight..."

Eban paused.

He looked puzzled.

As if trying to make sense of something.

Ruairí could see that the older man was close to tears.

Abhorring such weakness, he pounced.

"Here." He reached out for the joint. "Give me that back!"

Eban flinched.

"Who pushed your wacko button?" he said disparagingly. "I mean, so what? *So-fucking-what?*"

He was merciless.

"Let me tell you a story – and you can ask Anto if you don't believe me. When I was a kid, I liked horses too. Oh yes... used to go up and feed the travellers' nags up on the halting site all the time. Eventually, they moved on, but they left an old donkey – left it to die, I expect. Scrawny oul thing it was – bag o' bones – but every day, rain or shine, I was up there brushing its coat, bringing it carrots and sugar and that... until I got up there one Sunday morning – morning of my confirmation as it happens – and somebody had put an iron bar through its eye and out through the back of its head – AN IRON BAR THROUGH ITS FUCKING EYE!"

He stood up and bent low, level with Eban's gaze.

Spitting words into his face.

"Now you tell me: why would anybody want to do that?"

His anger was withering. "*The people...* you came back for *the people?* Cop on – they eat their young round here!"

The older man cringed.

There was nowhere to hide.

Not in this young man's realm.

His blowtorch scrutiny of things.
His unforgiving edifice of suffering and pain.
Eban was diminished by his unrelenting cynicism.
He broke his gaze and looked at the ground.
A whistle blew somewhere.
The relentless tattoo outside started up once again.
The walls closed in a little tighter.
Eban Barnard felt like he might scream.

37

As she stood in the supermarket checkout queue, Emily Atkins' mind wandered.

Since parting acrimoniously with Eban, she'd hoped for an opportunity to speak with him again. To revisit some of the things he'd said.

The more cryptic he had become, the more she had poked fun at him.

But it was unlike him to put so much out there.

Cryptic or not.

Clearly he had been brooding on something.

Trying to push her away.

Keep her at arm's length.

That was not unusual.

But all these enigmatic references to some 'secret' Eban.

One, he said, not worthy of knowing.

Of trusting.

Of loving.

Had he been asking for her help?

For her intervention?

In the only way he knew how?

It troubled her.

The class lesson earlier had got away from her.

She'd somehow allowed herself to be rattled.

It annoyed her.

It was something that she'd prided herself on.

That she'd become acclimatised to.

The sometimes naked sectarianism of Belfast.

She'd lived and worked here long enough now to know how to roll with the punches.

Were her feelings changing?

Was she coming to the end of something?

And perhaps the beginning of something else... somewhere else?

Emily had phoned home earlier, ostensibly to check as to whether Rosemary needed anything from the supermarket.

But really in the hope that Eban might pick up.

When Rosemary did, she had to feign indifference through generalities.

"All alone today?" she asked the older woman.

"Yes... Pascal came in around lunchtime, then he left again."

Rosemary made no mention of Eban.

Deliberately so, thought Emily.

If she wanted information regarding him, she'd have to come straight out and ask for it. And that would invite Rosemary Payne's disapproval and perhaps another lecture.

"Any mail for me?"

"None."

"Would Eban have perhaps picked it up early and put it under my door?"

It was an adroit manoeuvre. Rosemary Payne paused. As if she was considering. "No, I shouldn't think so... he's been gone since early this morning."

"Oh." At least Emily had established that he was not at home.

And then, unexpectedly, she was given more.

"That thing he calls a briefcase is still in the hall, so wherever he's gone, it's not work."

Rosemary said this in a manner that was designed to make mischief and incite mistrust in Emily.

Instead, it just worried her.

In the light of his manner recently and the clandestine nature of his behaviour regarding the correspondence from the Historical Enquiries Team and the hospital – Emily felt an unreasonable dread that Eban had involved himself in something that he could not control.

But she had not an inkling what that might be.

She looked down at the wire basket looped over her wrist and forearm.

A sorry selection of items sent her spirits dipping further.

One half-pint of semi-skimmed milk; one yoghurt; two bananas; the latest issue of *Marie Claire*; one small tub of cottage cheese; one packet of Jaffa Cakes and one packet of fig rolls.

A life, she thought lamentably.

The queue shuffled up one.

Across from her, the parallel checkout became free.

She saw this and moved over to take advantage.

Suddenly, from nowhere, she bumped forcibly into a young mother berating two small children.

The woman lost her grip on a large bottle of ketchup, which tumbled to the floor before exploding with a pop and showering her lower body and her children in red gunge.

She glared at Emily in what seemed an endless impasse. "Oh my God – can't you watch where you're going?"

Emily blushed, contrite due to her daydreaming, but felt that the woman was at least as much to blame as she was.

"I'm sorry, but *you* bumped into *me*. I'll pay for it though."

The woman seemed to bristle further on hearing Emily's English accent. The children were beginning to cry.

"Oh, *I* bumped into *you* did I? I suppose you've got some God-given right to jump the queue ahead of us all. We only live here after all!"

Emily was stung by this.

The children were wailing loudly now.

199

Other shoppers had begun to look over.

"I live here too," she said, somewhat weakly.

The woman seemed to be warming to the confrontation in proportion to Emily shrinking from it.

"Oh, do you now? Youse people make me sick: comin' over here, taking jobs... God knows there are few enough of them as it is. Take yourself away off to where you came from."

Emily dissolved.

It was so unexpected, the woman so abrupt, the children wailing and the shoppers craning their necks. The last thing she needed was a public confrontation.

Without a word, she simply set down her basket and began to walk tearfully toward the exit.

The woman was shouting after her, "You come over here; you think you know everything... you think you own the place... you just make matters worse."

The checkout girl and another woman in the queue came to Emily's defence.

"Here, that's enough, you."

"It was your fault as much as that wee girl's."

"There's no need for talk like that."

But Emily was already outside the store.

Leaning against the wall.

Gasping in air.

Fighting back tears.

An ambulance rushed by, its siren screaming like a banshee.

It seemed to momentarily open up a vortex to the past.

Of TV footage of death and carnage.

Syria... the Ukraine... Belfast?

And all Emily could think about was how the woman and the children appeared to be splattered all over with blood and gore.

38

INTERVIEW ROOM 1,
THE HISTORICAL ENQUIRIES OFFICES,
POLICE SERVICE OF NORTHERN IRELAND, BELFAST

Detective Inspector Dan Watson continued to note down anything he felt was relevant.

But looking now at the page of foolscap in front of him, he could see that he'd filled barely half of it.

This agitated man across the desk just seemed to drone on and on.

He had begun by listening carefully, attentively, genuinely, for anything that might shed some light as to why he was here.

Maybe some mention of his brother – and Dan's former colleague – Chief Superintendent Alex Barnard.

Perhaps some reference to this man who had been assaulted in 1970, and who he seemed so animated about.

Instead Eban Barnard seemed fixated on conveying every last detail of his period 'babysitting' a couple of reprobates in Newry Cathedral in 1991.

But *why*?

He still could not make any sense of it.

His back was hurting.

It was inevitable that his mind would begin to wander.

His mobile phone, on vibrate and pressed against his thigh, didn't help the situation.

He knew it was her.

The first time it had buzzed, he had cannily slipped it out for a look under his desk, unnoticed as Eban Barnard carried on with his ramblings from the past.

She had sent him a photograph of herself, topless.

Her police cap pulled across at a jaunty angle.

He recognised it as one he had himself taken and previously emailed to her.

On one of their nights spent in the Belfast Hilton.

Now, as he sat here listening, every time the phone buzzed in his pocket he knew it was her and his cock tingled and grew hard.

He was aware of the risks he was taking.

Aware of how completely and utterly insane this whole affair was.

Aware of all that he might lose if things got out of hand.

Came to light.

He knew all of this but it did not help at all.

In fact it made it worse.

Much, much worse.

The higher the stakes...

The thrill... the sheer abandonment to lust and to wanton risk-taking.

The reckless, needless, unjustifiable self-destruction.

The excitement of being desired and of desiring again.

The greedy, animal sex.

It was like a drug.

Like a death wish.

And he couldn't get enough of it, or of Officer Helen Totton.

He'd had four texts from her during the interview.

All of them wanting to meet him in the records hall.

Between the long corridors of racks and sliding shelves. Between sections U through Z. Where the room was in shadow and passing footfall was rare.

Where they had groped and tongued hungrily at each other on a number of occasions.

More thrilling for the fear of interruption.

Of discovery.

He would put his hands on her hips and draw her to him, as she looked up, wet lips parted.

"Supposing I was to tell you you're in breach of about ten professional behaviour guidelines…"

"Supposing I was to cry and put my head on your shoulder…"

"Supposing I was to let you…"

"Then supposing I did… this?"

In her texts she wanted to know what he was doing in there.

What they were talking about?

He could see her at the door. Bringing tea and biscuits.

Turned away by Sam Coulter.

Did he know something? Were people beginning to talk?

Fuck them!

Let them do their worst.

Eban Barnard was still talking though.

He would allow him to finish.

Treat the whole thing professionally and let the man talk himself out.

Maybe that's all he had come for.

But why the whole sorry story of the Newry Cathedral siege?

It had been well covered by the press, but that was years ago.

And why say he'd killed his brother?

Why request an investigation of some incident in 1970?

Why, why, why?

Maybe there was no answer.

Maybe he was a nutter.

Whatever.

Let him have his tuppence-ha'penny' worth.

And when he'd exhausted himself, toss him a scrap to send him on his way.

Based on the little information that Eban Barnard had provided, he'd had some of the team look into any serious assaults round Shankill Road, May 1970.

Given the level of activity on the streets then, he'd expected a deluge of incidents.

In fact there were relatively few.

Records were sparse from those chaotic, insane early days of the conflict.

And Barnard's 'McGrew's Pub' angle checked out.

There were incident records and hospital reports from the Belfast Mater.

A young nineteen-year-old Roman Catholic man – Joseph Patrick Breslin – had been seriously assaulted during rioting activities and left for dead.

Found in the ruins of the disused, burnt-out pub.

Watson had asked Coulter to track him down if still alive and inquire as to whether he –based on an appeal from a non-family member – would be interested in reopening the case for investigation.

Coulter checked addresses, found him residing at the same abode and duly wrote with the request.

If Eban Barnard could legitimately explain why he was interested in this case, and would agree to drop all this nonsense regarding his brother, then maybe Watson might throw him a bone on the survival and identity of the individual he seemed so interested in.

If nothing else it would be a mercy.

The poor bugger sounded in pain.

About what, he didn't know, much less care.

The phone buzzed again in his pocket.
Christ, she was one horny bitch!
Eban Winston Barnard talked on.

39

THE CARDINAL'S RESIDENCE, DIOCESE OF DROMORE AUGUST 1991

There were three figures seated around an ornate oval table.

They sat in shadow, the dimly lit lamps barely penetrating the gloom of the chamber.

The two petitioners appeared to flank their superior.

Or so he seemed, by virtue of the high-backed, immaculately tooled and carved oak-and-leather chair that he sat in.

It resembled nothing less than a throne.

The heavy man sat back, deep into its recesses.

He rubbed at his temples beneath a shock of unkempt steel-grey hair.

It was clear that he had been disturbed from his slumbers.

Tall, well-stocked floor-to-ceiling bookcases covered every wall in the room save for those housing the doorway and the black slate fireplace.

An imposing portrait of the Sacred Heart of Jesus hung above this, the Christ gesturing toward that odd little red mound, surrounded by thorns and blazing with celestial light.

The first priest cleared his throat and spoke.

"Eminence, we must consider the bigger picture."

His confederate followed swiftly. "Hearts and minds, Eminence... *hearts and minds.*"

The Cardinal pinched the bridge of his nose where his spectacles had previously rested.

"My God, I feel like Pilate going before the mob." He seemed perplexed. "This is really too much..." he protested.

The first priest saw an opportunity. "Then give them Barabbas!" he exhorted.

Again his colleague spoke. They were clearly a well-rehearsed double act on matters of lobbying. "And on a simple technicality – the building... we are not insured, Eminence."

The Cardinal seemed thoughtful. He turned it over in his mind for a moment. "People are watching. Only today I saw it on the television news. Public opinion and all that."

"The world has no interest, Eminence. It is a storm in a tea cup," said the first priest, careful to ensure that this did not sound like an admonishment.

"The clergy at the cathedral gave full access to the men's families. But they became concerned that their supporters were coming and going in a way which was incompatible with the cathedral's role as a place of worship."

"It is also the effects of the activities of their supporters on cathedral routine," said the other.

"The focus of the campaign has changed, Eminence."

"When the two men entered, they were asking protection and sanctuary be provided by the church against threats to their lives. As the situation has deteriorated however... well... the premises have been used as a faculty from which to plan and run a campaign by non-church groups."

"You asked us for counsel, Eminence, and we are now of the view that the men and their families must choose... choose between running such a campaign and having the protection of the church."

"Remember your flock – your *own* people... these are difficult times for the church," added the second.

They worked him like two sheepdogs.

Nipping and snapping at his heels.

Driving him toward the open gate.

The Cardinal leaned forward in his chair.

The priests could see from his expression that they had misjudged the extent of their immoderation.

"Do not suppose to lecture me on the challenges facing Mother Church..."

Both were contrite. "No Eminence," they whispered.

"... nor on the hearts and minds of Christian people."

The first priest stole a cautious glance at his comrade. It seemed to say, 'tread warily'.

"Of course, Eminence."

"Again – who is the parish priest caught up in all this down there?"

"Father Cudden; a very..." – the Priest chose his words carefully – "able communicator, Eminence. We are in constant contact with him."

The stout man sighed heavily and shook his head. "This is a very delicate conundrum."

"But a civil matter, Eminence; ultimately a civil matter nonetheless."

The Cardinal lifted his spectacles from atop a sheaf of papers, and squinting at the pages asked, "And the petition?"

The first priest was caught momentarily unawares and scurried hastily through his notes.

"Ahhh... let me see... from the county of Tyrone; a Father Frank Connolly. An uncle, I believe. A peripheral concern, Eminence... left his best behind him in the Missions."

He allowed himself a smile of smug superiority.

The Cardinal, seeing this, reached across the table and snatched the priest's cuff. He turned the man's hand over, palm up.

"And *your* best, Ambrose – where might we locate it, eh? In the Blackfriars library or the reading rooms of some theological college, nursing a sherry or a fine cognac perhaps?"

The man was instantly ingratiating in his clarification. "Eminence, I simply meant—"

"Quiet now," the Cardinal interrupted. "I'm tired and I have devotions later."

The two Priests began to shuffle and gather their papers together. The second tentatively pressed home his brief. "And your decision, Eminence?"

The Cardinal retuned to massaging his temples wearily.

"We all three know what will happen to them on their expulsion. The absence of war does not guarantee the peace."

"These things are happening every other day, Eminence." He made it sound paltry. Of no significance. He made it sound like the most natural thing in the world.

"Have these two young men attended confession... sought forgiveness?"

The two priests spoke in unison. "No, your Eminence."

He sank back into the recesses of his chair. "The ignorant neither forgive nor forget; the naive forgive *and* forget; the wise forgive but *never* forget."

The priests sensed an opportunity.

"These young thugs... they urinate in the flower beds..."

"Condoms in the sacristy... they mock us."

"And what of compassion?" asked the Cardinal, as much to himself than the men.

"The compassion of our Lord Jesus Christ and the Holy Mother Church is infinite," intoned the first. The second fingered his rosary and nodded in agreement.

The Cardinal was silent.

The men gathered up their briefcases and moved toward the door.

The Cardinal called after them. "Be in no hurry to turn them out. There is no witness so terrible, no accuser so powerful as the conscience which dwells within us."

He rose and tied the belt of his silk dressing gown around his girth.

"You shall have my decision in the morning."

40

INSIDE THE CATHEDRAL VESTRY
5AM

Anthony Francis Gatusso seemed to possess the ability to move between states of high excitement and anxiety, to complete comatose REM repose at the drop of a hat.

If people did not know him any better, they might have assumed that his capacity to slip into sudden dreamless sleep suggested the clear conscience and easy demeanour of a complete innocent.

Now he sat propped up on his elbows inside his sleeping bag, blowing smoke rings into the air above his head. Seemingly oblivious to his plight and to all those around him.

Eban's eyes stung from the smoke and the exhaustion.

He flicked through the well-thumbed copy of *The Pan Book of Horror and Ghost Stories* that one of his predecessors had left behind.

The cover showed a severed head in a bucket.

Looking at Anto, he wondered at his charge's apparent indifference to his plight.

He wondered how that might feel?

No baggage. No regrets.

Burn it all fucking down. Laughing all the while.

Ruairí sat on the couch, going through Sinéad's rucksack, apparently looking for something. The girl emerged a little unsteadily from the toilet area, wiping her mouth.

Eban surmised that she had just thrown up again.

The outside noise seemed to have abated somewhat.

There was an almost peaceful silence, the first time he had consciously noted this since his arrival.

The radio droned on, on low volume. Talking heads mumbling incoherently.

Suddenly the moment was shattered by the blaring, self-important theme tune that indicated news at the top of the hour.

Anto reacted first. "Eban, mate... turn that up will ye?"

Eban reached across and twisted the dial. It was BBC Radio Ulster. The local bulletin.

"Latest reports from the cathedral siege in Newry indicate that community spokespersons have rejected efforts by intermediaries to lift a rumoured exclusion order on local men Ruairí Connolly and Anthony Gatusso. Sinn Féin, in a statement, called on all the people of the area who had suffered as a result of these individuals' actions to rally behind the groups and organisations who had declared their intention to 'cleanse the area of all hoods'..."

No-one spoke.

No-one needed to.

By the time the weather forecast had begun and before Eban could turn down the volume, all had in some way made their peace with the updated news.

The forces reigned against them had conceded nothing.

Instead they had ratcheted up their campaign another notch.

If either of the men were wounded by this, they did not show it.

Ruairí Connolly's face was a stone mask of concentration on nothing in particular.

Anthony Gatusso continued to blow smoke rings.

Only Sinéad Farran seemed moved by the reports.

She winced as if someone had struck her across the face and returned to ravenously gnawing on her fingernails.

Eban was lost for something to say.

Instead he moved over to the large stained glass window and looked below.

Ruairí saw him. 'Eban, stay away from the window."

Suddenly, unexpectedly, the room detonated.

Four hammer-blows fell heavily on the outside of the door.

Boom! Boom! Boom! Boom!

For a moment the whole interior seemed to sway like a ship in a storm, then right itself again.

All three young people looked instantly terrified.

First at the door.

Then at Eban.

He felt the weight of their fear and expectation and it rocked him back on his heels.

Sinéad grasped at her belly. In terror. In protection of her unborn.

Eban moved slowly, tentatively, falteringly toward the door.

He paused before placing his hands on the large metal bolt that held it closed. Leaning forward, pushing his whole weight against it.

"Who's there?" His voice was shaking.

"It's me, Mr Barnyard; Ruairí's mother. I've some groceries!"

The relief was real.

All physically deflated. As if a stopper had been pulled on them and the air rushed out.

Anto cackled with mock bravado.

Ruairí said, "*Christ, Ma!*" rebuking with his tone.

Sinéad let out a little whimper of respite.

Eban smiled and pulled the loose sleeve of his shirt across his brow.

He took a deep breath and with both hands began to slowly slip the heavy bolt back.

It squealed with grating compliance.

"I've someone here with me." Her tone held enough uncertainty to freeze Eban's actions instantly.

Both Ruairí and Anto bounded toward him, shouting, "NO, EBAN… NO… HOLD IT!"

Eban stood like a statue, petrified.

Eventually he found his voice.

"Who's out there?"

A conciliatory voice responded.

"It's Father Sean Cudden, son – the family priest – and Councillor Molloy. Look… *we want to help.*"

Eban was momentarily perplexed.

His thoughts were colliding.

All the actors in this tableau seemed to know one another.

To know what was going on.

Except, that was, for him.

He had felt at a constant disadvantage since he'd arrived.

It had irritated him.

It had made him impatient.

As if this whole affair was some elaborate choreography being played out by performers who knew well their parts. Knew the boundaries. The acceptable and unacceptable modes of behaviour. The lines that could and could not be crossed.

It made him angry, and in this moment of fear and panic and hesitancy, he greedily fed off it. Righteous indignation replacing indecision and dread expectation.

He needed to take control of himself and the situation.

He did so by ignoring those around him for the first time since he'd arrived and – taking a deep breath – continued slipping the bolt back slowly.

Bracing his shoulder against the wood.

Cracking the gap a little.

On the other side of the door stood Councillor Terry Molloy, still in Armani pinstripes.

Beside him a stick-thin man, head-to-toe in black.

An almost spectral figure, wearing clerical garb, completely bald and with piercing blue eyes.

Mrs Connolly had her gaze cast down to the floor. A reluctant stooge and penitent. A Trojan Horse.

Eban stepped away from the portal, allowing them entry.

The priest quickly swept over the threshold.

He wore a full-length cassock in the traditional style, buttoned from neck to hem, and clenched a rosary wrapped tightly around his knuckles.

Sensing the indecision in the company, and seeing his chance, Father Cudden immediately claimed authority over the circumstances.

"Ahhh, Mr Barnard, isn't it? I'd like a word with *you*."

He made it sound officious.

Accusatory.

He abruptly motioned to Eban to follow him to the corner of the room.

There he stood, arms folded and demeanour solemn, inviting a conspiratorial parley.

Terry Molloy followed a few steps behind him like a bullwhipped puppy.

Eban noted this as it seemed somehow absurd. Incongruous.

Ruairí Connolly moved as inconspicuously as the cramped conditions would allow to the fringes of the gathering.

The priest spoke first, reinforcing the notion that he was indeed on home ground.

"I'll come straight to the point, Mr Barnard. In the absence of any senior church authority here, I have been asked by local residents to bring this situation to a swift conclusion."

Eban somehow sensed that the man was bluffing. That he was acting unilaterally. He gathered his courage and spoke up to call his bluff.

"I've been given strict instructions not to leave these lads unaccompanied until my colleagues arrive tomorrow morning."

Cudden let out a snort of derision. He looked across at Councillor Molloy and both smiled with intent.

"The presence of these two *lads* in this cathedral is a blasphemy, pure and simple... and as for *that* one" – he gestured with his head toward Sinéad – "carrying one of their litter out of wedlock... they shouldn't be here and that's all there is to it!"

Eban was taken aback at the man's bitterness.

At how he spat out the words.

He felt he should say something in Sinéad Farran's defence.

"Steady on Father... Suffer little children, eh?"

The priest, who had been looking around the room with an expression of extreme distaste, suddenly focused on him. The man was seething. His stone-cold blue eyes boring into Eban.

"Is that supposed to be funny?" he demanded.

It sounded like a challenge.

In that moment, Eban was positive that he abhorred this individual.

For he recognised in him the kind of man he had come to revile throughout the entirety of his frustrating life in his sorry homeland. The browbeater, the tormentor, the oppressor, the bully.

"I see very little to laugh about here." Eban's mouth was like a sand box, but he said this with an unmistakable tone of defiance.

Of challenge.

215

Of confrontation.

It was not wasted on the priest.

He theatrically took a step backward and methodically looked him over, head to toe, with all the qualities of a bone-deep scan.

"Do I know you?" he remarked, running his long, bony fingers over his smooth pate.

"I doubt it, but I think I know you... or the likes of you."

Molloy stepped in threateningly. "Careful, friend... you're out of your depth here."

The priest leisurely raised a hand to placate Molloy, the man now searching for and drawing from some well of pseudo-magnanimity.

He turned to Eban, grinning.

"Look, what we have here are two bad boys, right? Now myself and Councillor Molloy have had a word with..." he paused for effect, "certain interested parties, and they tell me that if these two come out now and take their medicine like men..." – he shrugged – "then that will be the end of it."

He smiled like a polecat and shrugged and raised his open-palmed hands in offertory.

The most reasonable man in the world.

Eban's face flushed. He clenched his fists by his side.

"Am I to understand that you are negotiating on behalf of the IRA?"

Again Molloy moved forward threateningly. "Oh, is that the way you want to play it?"

Father Cudden held out an arm, barring his way. He spoke like he might to a child.

"Terrance, huusssh now... shuusssh... that's a good fellow."

All the while, he never broke his mesmeric stare on Eban, his tone more pragmatic now.

"Look, didn't I baptise one of them myself? All I'm saying

is… it would be over very quickly and things would be back to normal again – sure, isn't that what we all want here?"

"I don't think it's what *they* want."

Eban nodded to Ruairí, who had now moved closer to the three men. "Is that what *you* want?"

The priest could see that his opening gambit was not working.

He had not expected this night watchman, this babysitter, to prove so obstinate.

His agitation was showing and for a brief moment the mask slipped.

He leaned closer to Eban and spoke in a lower tone, conspiratorially. "Look… sure, what's a bullet in the leg? They'd be out of hospital and home in a couple of days and—"

Ruairí was standing close behind the priest now. With all the sarcasm he could muster, he spoke.

"*Huh… Man of God.*" He made it sound like an indictment.

Cudden spun around, outraged. "*What?* What did you just say to me?"

Eban stepped in front of Ruairí. "Will you do it, Father? Will you do it yourself… will you pull the trigger? Would you like that?"

"What's that supposed to mean?" Cudden was stung.

Unnoticed by the men, Mrs Connolly had also made her way to the fringes of the group.

She had been listening. Knowing her place.

Waiting to announce her presence when appropriate to do so.

But on hearing the priest's comments she elbowed her way into the centre of things, where she fixed Cudden with an accusatorial gaze.

"Yes, yes he would… I wouldn't put it past him!" she announced, emboldened by this turn of events. She stabbed a finger into the man's chest.

"You – you call yerself a man of the cloth?"

She turned to face Molloy now.

"And you – you're supposed to be for the working man… murdering fathers and cripplin' teenagers!"

Her unexpected outburst served as a catalyst.

Without doubt, the tide had turned.

All knew it.

The momentum was for the first time with the besieged.

Ruairí was momentarily dumbstruck.

Seeing his mother – a devout, lifelong Catholic and obsequious, unquestioning devotee of the clergy – so readily take on this small-town demagogue galvanised him.

He placed his face close to the priest's.

The merciless tension was at breaking point.

"Is that it, Father… you'd like to do it yourself, would ye, eh?"

Father Cudden didn't flinch.

Instead, he was savouring his anger. Rolling it around his mouth and over his tongue.

He slowly smiled. His malevolence palpable.

When he spoke, it was in a low, malicious hiss. *"That's right… yes; yes, maybe I would."*

Fionnuala Connolly looked like she'd been slapped hard across the face. An oppressive presence seemed to fill the small room.

"God forgive you!"

Ruairí did not step back. He stood on, breathing heavily, almost nose to nose with the priest. He whispered something. It was hardly audible.

"False prophet."

Again the priest smiled. He changed tactic again, assuming the authority of his station.

"Look, I'm telling you for the last time: they can't stay in here. This is God's house!"

"The Cardinal says we can." It had escaped Eban's mouth before his brain had engaged, for he did not know this to be true.

Father Cudden's smile grew broader. He instantly saw the bluff for what it was.

"The Cardinal is saying precisely nothing... nothing at all... and when he does I'll show him a petition with three hundred parishioners' signatures all wanting you... *abominations* out of their cathedral."

Eban's dread was rising.

The priest seemed to possess an almost supernatural presence, foul and intimidating.

Despite this he steeled himself and rallied.

"I've heard enough, Father... you'll have to go now."

He moved to place a guiding hand on the small of the man's back.

No-one budged an inch.

Unnoticed, the noise from the crowd in the street had picked up and at that moment seemed to surge. The swell seemed to energise the priest. To infuse him.

He looked directly into Eban's eyes, withering him.

"Take your hand off me," he snarled imperiously.

Abruptly there was a noise on the other side of the door.

All eyes turned, drawn in that direction.

A dull, low thudding.

Like someone was kicking against it.

It was clear in that moment that the bolt had not been sufficiently engaged.

Each hit loosened it more.

Making it shift a little each time from its position.

Two blows more and it would unfasten.

Mrs Connolly was the first to react.

She moved toward it.

Hand at her breast. Fearful. Petrified.

219

"Who is it?Who's there?"

She looked over her shoulder to the others for guidance.

Eban felt drained, but somehow exhilarated.

Strangely resigned.

Almost fatalistic.

Felt like he wanted all this to be over.

Wanted to confront whatever had been stalking them that whole night.

Maybe their whole lives

"Open it, open it for Christ's sake!" he heard himself moan.

Anto came to life. "NO! IT'S A TRICK; THOSE FUCKERS HAVE SET US UP!"

The stress in the room seemed to cause it to creak and moan.

The wooden timbers cried out and the floorboards seemed to blanch.

A pained, spiralling banshee wail broke from Sinéad and rose into the air.

It began as a whimper and ended as a siren.

"Noooooooooo… don't let them in!"

She clutched defensively again at her unborn child.

Terry Molloy pushed by Mrs Connolly, sliding the bolt back fully and violently throwing the door open.

It crashed against the wall, shaking loose puffs of white plaster and masonry.

Both women screamed and pushed back flat against the opposite wall.

Anto had armed himself with a billiard cue, whilst Ruairí had picked up a bread knife.

They crouched, coiled, waiting… waiting… nothing.

Then footfalls scurrying off down the stone stairway.

Laughter and shouts fading away… off into the distance.

The scene was fixed. Unmoving. Like some medieval montage picked out on a tapestry.

As if no-one knew what to do. What to say.

Ruairí spoke first "It's alright... it's okay, it's kids... it's only kids."

The hex had been broken.

Eban reacted more quickly than anyone, his body language decisive.

"Father, I think you'd better leave. Anto, get the door locked after them."

Father Cudden screwed up his face with disdain and barely concealed revulsion.

"Oh, we're going... the stink of this three-ring circus is turning my stomach."

Mrs Connolly's adrenaline was racing.

Denunciation from the pulpit be damned. She turned again on her parish priest.

"You've some cheek... you've locked us out of every other room; a pregnant girl with only a sink to wash herself in... I was married in this church but it'll be a cold day in hell 'til I'm back at Mass again in it, I can tell you that."

Councillor Molloy couldn't resist a parting barb. He spoke over his shoulder. "No amount of soap and water will scrub her clean."

Cudden moved toward the door, pointing at Ruairí and Anto as he did.

"I want them out of here and on the boat out of this country."

The two men exited.

Anto ran to the top of the stairs, shouting after them. "Molloy, tell your brother he's a fucking pervert!"

Unseen, from around the curve of the staircase came the echoing, incandescent reply. "Say it just once to his face; just once you greaseball bastard. JUST ONCE!"

Anto chuckled to himself, happy in the knowledge that he had gotten to the man. That he had riled the Molloy brothers and that the message would go back to Tootsie.

Laughing, he locked the door again and turned to find all inside glaring at him disapprovingly. The young man appealed theatrically, incorrigibly, shrugging with arms outstretched.

"Whaaaaaaaaaaaaat?"

The group fell into laughter.

Desperate, eager, insane laughter.

The laughter borne of abject relief.

Of being shot at with no consequence.

Of teetering on a precipice but falling backward.

After several breathless minutes the general hubbub ensued as each recounted what had just happened, all at the same time.

Eban felt somehow vindicated. Like he had been tested in fire and had by some means come through. He felt closer to his confederates than before.

Bizarrely, more close to them now, these strangers, than to anyone at that moment he could remember.

"Well, that's the Cardinal against us for sure," he said.

Anto was stoked. He tugged hungrily on a cigarette and blew out. "That's no loss. He was always against us anyway."

Similarly, Ruairí was enthused by the residue of adrenaline. He playfully counted out on the fingers of his hand.

"Let me see: the Roman Catholic Church… the Republican Movement… is there anybody we haven't offended recently?"

Only Mrs Connolly and Sinéad seemed sober. The older woman was gathering up dirty clothes again.

"I'm gonna speak to those children's people… running wild at this hour of the morning… do they think this is a playground for their amusement or something?"

She was preparing again to leave on the laundry-and-provisions run.

"I'll pick up some sandwiches when I'm out."

Sinéad pleaded, "No bacon sandwiches, Mrs C… they're cold by the time they get here."

"What do you want me to do, hold them under my oxters?"

"I know, but the fat, it…" She pulled a face. "What is it, Ruairí?"

"Congeals."

"Aye – the fat congeals and it turns my stomach."

The girl raised her hands to her mouth at the thought of it and exited for the toilet.

Mrs Connolly looked concerned. "Ruairí… away and see if the wee girl's alright."

Ruairí raised himself up from the couch, but it was Anto who pushed him down again and followed the girl out of the room.

41

Pascal Loncle was flossing, gargling and spitting.

His bedroom was the only one in the residence that had its own small enamel sink attached to the wall, rendering his need to tarry in the common areas of the house mercifully brief.

He even had a working fireplace, should he choose to activate it, but preferred a fire screen featuring a colourful bouquet of flowers picked out in fine latticework.

As was his wont, he kept the curtains pulled back and tied on clear evenings, well beyond dusk. The exhibitionist in him enjoyed the slight frisson of performance as he moved languidly in his silk dressing gown across the reflecting, dark rectangle.

Sometimes belted.

Sometimes not.

Pinetop Perkins played low, almost imperceptibly on his iPad speakers.

He dabbed his mouth dry with a cotton flannel and poured himself a Laphroaig single malt whisky before settling into an easy chair. Crossing his bare legs, he dangled a tasselled slipper from one foot whilst reading Peter Silvester's *The Story of Boogie-Woogie: A Left Hand Like God*.

It was his secret passion.

Everything about Pascal Loncle screamed 'cultured man of the world'.

His dress and general demeanour was that of a much older man, and he would have appeared ridiculous had he not carried this off with such swagger and aplomb.

He favoured Harris tweed jackets, gabardine rainwear, herringbone waistcoats and cravats. He wore his thick dark hair heavily pomaded and slicked back.

He was rarely without a tightly-rolled black Swaine Adeney Brigg umbrella.

For a Frenchman he was quite the archetypal English toff. This was no accident.

His father, Dr Henri Loncle, was a successful consultant paediatrician and dedicated Anglophile.

It was he who kept his only son in the manner befitting a scholar, a gentleman and an artist.

In return, Pascal realised that it would be imprudent of him to discuss his love of boogie-woogie piano or reveal his honorary position as president of the Jerry Lee Lewis Appreciation Society to his patron.

Instead he was happy to trot out uninspired renditions of Debussy and Beethoven at the *petit bourgeois* dinner parties his father would throw for friends when Pascal was visiting at home in Rennes.

Above all else, he was required to keep up the tiresome charade that perhaps one day he would provide his father with a grandchild.

This involved elaborate stories of fictitious episodes with imaginary girlfriends.

For Pascal had realised from quite a young age that his father would never accept his love of other men.

Unbeknownst to them, both Rosemary and Emily had regularly featured in his fictions. Familiarity with their circumstances, their routines, their characters and even their undergarments airing on the clothes horse in the kitchen had provided him with many plausible inventions and embellishments.

Mon Dieu, that Rosemary woman is a grotesque! he now thought to himself, and shuddered.

Perhaps the most awful downside of his pretence was having to endure her dull advances and nervous, lumpen innuendos.

She clearly adored him.

He winced at the thought and reached for a mandarin orange from the bowl beside him, thoughtfully and meticulously beginning to peel it with long fingers and well-manicured nails.

He felt better disposed toward Emily.

She seemed to him to be someone who went through life believing that she was herself of little worth, and so chose positions and partners that were beneath her. As if she deserved little more.

And this would seem to make clear her inexplicable interest in Eban Barnard.

Surely she realised that she could do better?

Pascal felt somewhat guilty when occasionally pretend-flirting with the woman.

It was improper to even partially lead her on in any small way.

It was a cruelty.

But it had seemed important to him to maintain the charade, even here in Belfast.

It helped him efficiently compartmentalise his feelings and provided a regular psychological workout in dishonesty and charade for the necessary deceptions at home.

As for Barnard.

He had no strong feelings one way or the other.

The man was an enigma to him. Keeping himself to himself from the time they had met. Not rude exactly, but bordering on brusque, and always seeming like he wanted to escape back to his own room and away from the social areas.

Pascal could hardly blame him for that.

He himself did much the same thing, but always with a parting witticism or compelling reason to excuse his taking leave that rendered him ever the charming continental.

Eban Barnard invariably just stood up and left.

Often as a reaction to your entering the room.

Social graces were not his forte.

Barnard, he speculated, had not been an unattractive man in his day.

An intelligent, even soulful demeanour.

Easily 6'1", but morbidly stooped now to 5'11".

He had gone to seed.

Perhaps for some good reason.

Some life event, or maybe a woman.

Only once did they exchange anything approaching empathy.

Pascal had commented on a novel by a French author he had seen Eban reading at the kitchen table. *The Erl-King* by Michel Tournier.

He had expressed an interest in borrowing this, and some days later Pascal had found the book outside his door.

On opening the paperback, a black-and-white photograph that Eban had evidently been using as a bookmark fluttered to the floor.

Pascal imagined it would have been taken in the 1930s or early 40s.

It showed a strikingly attractive young woman, her hair piled up high in the Hollywood film star style that was popular at that time.

She wore a high-necked dress with a collar of false pearls and flashed a stunning smile of strong, white teeth.

A black line cut the picture vertically in half.

It was clearly an amalgam of two separate portraits.

On the other side, a young man in military uniform.

Jet-black hair, Brylcreemed and side-parted.

He had an open, honest face which he set bravely and optimistically toward the world and any trials that lay ahead of him.

Pascal had returned this photograph to Eban Barnard almost immediately and – standing at his bedroom door – sought to engage him on the identity of those depicted within it.

As he suspected, Eban acknowledged both as his parents.

At first he seemed quite coy and reticent, but as Pascal applied his considerable charm, the man opened up somewhat and seemed to enjoy the opportunity to speak about them.

He said that his mother had been 'a bit of a looker' and that the black-and-white photograph did not do justice to her fabulous auburn hair.

He identified the uniform that his father wore as RAF.

Pascal was impressed.

"Oh, your father was a fighter pilot?" he asked.

Eban had laughed. The only time Pascal could remember him doing so in his company.

"Yeah… *pilot*… right. As he would say himself, 'piling it here and piling it there'… no, sadly he was ground crew."

Both laughed.

Only then did things take a turn for the worse.

Pascal had asked Eban if he were an only child like himself.

A shadow seemed to pass over the man's face, and he involuntarily took a step backward from the doorway and into his room.

"Enjoy the book," was all he said, before closing the door in the Frenchman's face.

Just before this, and looking over his shoulder into Eban's

room, Pascal had noticed a baseball bat leaning against the wall in the corner.

When he related the exchange to Rosemary Payne and inquired of her whether their housemate played the sport, the woman tittered behind an upraised hand.

"Oh Pascal dear... you're so trusting. Don't you know that there were 753 baseball bats sold in Northern Ireland last year and not one registered baseball team?"

"*Et alors?*"

She leaned in uncomfortably close, tutting. "I think he employs it for 'home defence'... you can take the man out of the ghetto, etc.... you know?"

Pascal didn't know and didn't want to know.

He looked up at the ski poles standing against the wall, behind his own bedroom door.

Soon he would submit his thesis, and following a surely successful *viva voce*, he could at last be with his darling Michael.

Wonderful, dangerous, flamboyant, hot, sexy Michael from Berne.

They had met last summer when Pascal was touring art galleries in Vienna and – after a whirlwind romance culminating in an explosive consummation in a mountain cabin in Klagenfurt – he had fallen irredeemably, head-over-heels in love.

Only with Michael could he be himself.

Rolling cigarettes on his chest in bed the morning after. Tobacco getting caught in his damp chest hair.

Laying naked on the sheets, getting hard awaiting his return from the bathroom.

Locked in motion, licking the salty sweat from his face, from his underarms.

Soon they would be together again for skiing at La Plagne.

Through letters, emails, phone calls and Skype, there had been talk of moving together to Sitges near Barcelona.

229

And so his days of exile in Ireland would be over.

But before that… his 'coming out' party. To his housemates at any rate.

In the three years he had been at 15 Donnybrook Avenue, Belfast 9, he had thrown dozens of small dinner parties but never once invited any of the others.

Soon he would shock them all by throwing one of his most lavish and announcing to Eban, Emily and Rosemary that he was a raving, steaming, rampant, proud homosexual.

It would be worth it to see the look on Rosemary's face.

He smiled to himself and stood up, crossing to pull the blinds before retiring.

The main front door remained unbarred as Eban Barnard had yet to return.

In the street below, across from the house, sat the silver BMW 6 Series he had passed on his way in some time ago.

In the front sat two men.

One wearing a denim jacket, the other a bright red hooded top.

The man in the denim jacket had smiled at him.

Pascal thought he looked quite handsome in a sort of 'Action Man' way.

Closely cropped hair, wide forehead, strong jaw with stubble.

Like some sexy army squaddie.

That was some three hours past.

As he looked down he caught some movement in the front seats.

That's an awfully long time to be sitting out there together… maybe they are lovers; perhaps one of them married and conflicted over his sexuality, he thought.

Il n'est rien de réel que le rêve et l'amour, he momentarily mused, before pulling the drapes closed, turning out the light and climbing into bed with faint fleeting notions of a fantasy threesome.

42

"It's the legs that go first, they say."

"The mobility."

"That or upstairs."

"The wits."

"The common sense."

At eighty-five years of age, Eileen Breslin had heard it all before.

As she pushed her trolley around the Iceland frozen goods supermarket, clutching her stash of discount coupons held together with an elastic band, she stopped for a word here and there with the shelf-stackers and her fellow shoppers.

She had to be selective in her purchases of course.

Only the less bulky items. So no heavy tinned goods or large glass bottles.

HP Sauce; Zoflora disinfectant; a Veda loaf; those Hovis digestive biscuits that Joe liked.

She'd have to go to Tesco's for them.

Then to the Post Office to pick up her pension. (Mustn't let it lie or build up to a noticeable sum. You never know… they might take it back off of you.)

Then to Dan Gilroy's for her cut, mixed soup vegetables.

Then home again.

The walk to the bus stop.

The 'wee dander' around the shops.

It was at the very hub of her well-being.

It got her out of the house.

Got 'a bit of fresh air' blew around her.

It helped tire her out. Helped her sleep better.

It was about independence.

'*Not being a burden to no-one*' became her mantra.

But most of all, it was about getting her day in.

Long, unending days when nothing seemed to happen.

No-one seemed to call.

Well, maybe you might see the young parish priest two or three times a year.

And someone might drop by to collect your envelopes if you couldn't make it to Mass.

There were the soaps.

And the Hallmark channel. But all they seemed to show were repeats these days.

And her books.

Her reading.

Where would she be without her books?

Maeve Binchy, Cathy Kelly, Marian Keyes.

It wasn't that Anne was inattentive.

A bad daughter.

Not at all.

A better daughter you couldn't want or wish for.

Anne made sure she wanted for nothing.

A hard worker too.

She stayed on late working at those council offices so many nights, and for no thanks.

But she wasn't a girl you could talk to.

Really talk to.

She kept so much bottled up inside her.

Too much.

Like her father, God rest him.

It wasn't healthy.

Maybe it was why she had never married.

But they never talked about *that*.

When they did talk, it was mostly about Joe.

Sure, wasn't Joe worse off than any of them?

It kept her going.

She needed her wits about her to look after poor Joe.

Couldn't go under until she was sure he was sorted out.

She knew that a fall or stumble at her age could end in disaster.

A broken arm or hip and... well, she would no doubt go downhill very fast after that.

And who would be there for Joe then?

Couldn't expect Anne to do it.

Wouldn't be right.

She walked slowly, scouring the ground in front of her for raised manhole covers or uneven pavement slabs.

Amazing, the pound coins and 20ps you'd find lying at your feet just by looking down.

She would go to see Dr Kelly and maybe the chiropodist later in the week.

She could pick up Joe's prescription for his medicines, get her ears syringed and her feet done and it would get her out and about.

A bit of fresh air.

Put the day in.

Joe still went through a powerful amount of dressings.

And now he had a notion of some wee girl again.

After all these years.

She wanted to ask Anne if it was a good idea.

To be opening up all that hurt again.

About marriage and children and families and whatnot.

After how things had finished with Delores and how depressed he'd been after it all.

Knocked him right back, it had.

Had to see the 'big doctor' about depression and all sorts.

Anne just said that Joe was an adult and deserved a life as much as anyone else.

Sure, didn't she know that already... but that wasn't the point.

She wasn't a mother.

She didn't understand.

It would be good to get back in.

Get a bit of dinner on for the both of them coming in.

Have a cup of tea and a lie on the sofa with the rug around her.

Watch *Loose Women* and maybe nod off for the afternoon.

43

INTERVIEW ROOM 1,
THE HISTORICAL ENQUIRIES OFFICES,
POLICE SERVICE OF NORTHERN IRELAND, BELFAST

The evening shift had signed in.

The morning shift had signed out.

And still this man talked on.

Dan Watson had given Alex Barnard's brother the benefit of the doubt.

He had gone the proverbial extra mile.

He had forgone his fish-and-chip supper from the café across the street.

He had crossed his legs rather than take a piss break.

And he had ignored the considerable charms of Helen Totton, who was clearly up for it by dint of her numerous appearances at the interview room door and her several suggestive text messages.

Enough was enough.

He waited for a pause in Barnard's story.

None seemed forthcoming.

He marshalled some gravitas to his tone.

"Right Mr Barnard, I think I've heard enough. Thank you for taking the time to apprise me of your story regarding the two youths in Newry Cathedral. I've given you the better part of three hours and honestly I have to say that we seem no closer to understanding why you came in here in the first place, or what any of this has to do with Alex Barnard."

Watson rose to his feet, shuffling the pages in a manner conveying finality.

Cut off in mid-sentence, Eban Barnard just stared at him open-mouthed.

"I'm sure you've got somewhere to be right now… I know I have."

Eban whispered, almost imperceptibly, "You gave me your word."

Watson continued tidying things up and appeared not to hear him.

"However, we could have some information about that 1970s assault that you may be interested in."

Eban lashed out with his right foot, kicking angrily against the desk. A stapler and a Sellotape dispenser fell to the floor.

"YOU GAVE ME YOUR WORD!" he exploded at the man.

"AND YOU SAID YOU'D EXPLAIN WHY YOU'RE DEFAMING ONE OF THE FINEST POLICE OFFICERS I HAVE HAD THE PRIVILEGE OF WORKING WITH!" Watson was surprised at how quickly he'd lost his temper. This man had a way of getting to him.

The door opened and Sam Coulter stood halfway into the room.

"Everything alright sir?"

Watson flushed, a little embarrassed, but was determined to press on with his resolution.

"Yes Sam, sorry… Mr Barnard will be leaving now."

"You gave me your word." Eban seemed hurt, crestfallen.

"Will you show him out please?"

"But I was almost done," he protested. "Don't you see? I was almost at the point I wanted to make – about me… about Alex… about all of this…"

"Go home Mr Barnard, and think long and hard about your brother's life and his sacrifice… his *legacy*."

Eban sat bolt upright.

He seemed unaware that his hands clasped and released, clasped and released the arms of the chair repeatedly.

"Well if it's his legacy is so important to you, let me finish. Let me finish what I started."

Watson looked unconvinced.

Coulter hovered awkwardly.

Desperate, Eban seemed to be suddenly fighting for his life.

"Or I swear to God, I'll drag his name, his reputation, everything you" – he nodded at Coulter – "and you ever thought honourable about him, through all the muck and the mire of this godforsaken hole of a country."

Both policemen looked stunned.

It was as if Alex Barnard himself was sitting before them. Threatening them with the destruction of his very own memory.

"How would you do that?" asked Sergeant Coulter quietly. He had now come fully into the room and closed the door behind him.

"By taking all this to the newspapers."

"All *what*?"

Eban closed his eyes tightly in frustration and pressed hard against his temples with the palms of his hands. "

"That's *precisely* what I've been trying to tell your genius inspector here!"

Coulter looked across at Watson, who rolled his eyes heavenward.

"How you killed your brother? "

"Yes," croaked Eban. "*Yes.*"

There was a long silence in the room.

Eventually Watson spoke.

"I'm busting for a pee. When I come back you've got a half-hour, you get me Barnard? Thirty minutes; no more."

Eban seemed to be wiping tears from his eyes.

"Sam will sit in with us – d'ya hear me, Sam: thirty minutes; you can time it. All this… *nonsense* is brought to a conclusion by then… or never."

With that Detective Inspector Watson left the room and headed in a hurry to the toilets.

On his return, Helen Totton was waiting at the bend of the long corridor.

Watson unconsciously sucked in his gut and flared his nostrils. He grinned at her and feigned an exaggerated apology.

"Sorry… sorry hon, I couldn't get away. I've been stuck with this creep all evening. How you been doin'?"

She furtively looked up and down the corridor before slipping an arm around his waist and leaning into him.

"I thought your shift finished hours ago?" he breathed.

"Didn't you get my texts?"

"Yeah, but like I said, this guy Barnard is a nut job."

"Then kick him out."

"Not as easy as that… look, I've gotta get back in there."

"Why?"

"Why what?"

"Why isn't it as easy as that?"

"Well, you know he's Alex Barnard's brother, right?"

"Your old boss?"

"Yeah… well, he's convinced he murdered Alex!"

She furrowed her brow quizzically. "Wasn't Alex Barnard…?"

"Yeah, South Armagh Brigade… so we're trying to get to the bottom of all this."

"Maybe he's just looking for attention?"

"No… no, it's more than that… says he can ruin Alex's reputation… his memory…"

"Why would a brother do that?"

"Your guess…"

"Didn't Sam mention some assault case way back in the 70s?"

Watson paused. The detective in him caught the overly curious nature of her inquiry.

She saw it and smiled, withdrawing her interest, changing the subject. "Anyway…"

"Anyway, I'll be done in about thirty minutes. You up for a drink?" He squeezed her buttocks together with one big hand.

"Is the Pope a Catholic?" She playfully tweaked a nipple through his shirt.

When Watson had gone back in, Officer Helen Totton returned to the staff social area and immediately located her throwaway mobile phone.

Hitting the speed-dial, she briefly apprised Councillor Cecil Herringshaw of all she had been told and what she had not.

The man at the other end moaned aloud.

A low, bovine rattle.

It was exactly as he had feared all along.

44

INSIDE THE CATHEDRAL VESTRY
6.02AM

Pink fingers of cloud were beginning to spread across the early morning sky.

The barbarians still at the gates.

But another night survived.

They had been laughing amiably at Eban Barnard's ignorance of Mother Church.

Initially startled by the loud ringing of the Angelus bell at 6am, their new compatriot – believing the chimes to signify the top of the hour – had reduced them to paroxysms of laughter by trying to set his watch to the strikes.

Ruairí had silently nudged Sinéad, who in turn elbowed Anto.

They watched Eban's bemusement turn to confusion as the chimes reached fifteen and counting.

All three could hold it in no longer. They exhaled with gales of laughter.

"Yeah, that's right Eban – eighteen o'clock!" mocked Anto.

"Have you never heard of the Angelus, Mr Barnard?" asked Ruairí a little too snidely.

"You should be on your knees Eban," laughed Sinéad.

"Aye... you'd know all about that Sinéad," Anto shot back.

"Fuck you, dickhead!" came the knee-jerk response.

"Anytime; anytime..." he goaded her.

Ruairí ignored both of them. "So what's it like, Eban?"

Eban felt wary. "What's what like?"

"Being an Orangeman?"

The other two sensed a change in Ruairí's tone and stopped jousting.

Eban felt instantly defensive. "Who says I'm an Orangeman?"

Anto smelled blood. "Well, you look like one."

"What's an Orangeman look like?"

"*You.*"

Eban felt a little hurt.

After the earlier dramas he had come to believe that he had earned a reprieve from this kind of adolescent blood sport.

"Can you see the horns from there?" he retorted defensively.

Sinéad chipped in. She circled the seated Eban, apparently looking for bony protrusions.

"Yeah, something like that. I wouldn't be great on Protestants myself. What was that song we used to sing when we were kids…?"

She cleared her throat and sang in a high-pitched, fragile voice.

The tune, a nursery-rhyme cadence.

"*Proddy-woddy-green-guts never said his prayers, grab him by the leg and throw him down the stairs.*"

"Charming," said Eban, not bothering to conceal his sarcasm.

"You're welcome," she replied, tartly.

Eban could see they were goading him.

Whether out of boredom or malice he was unsure. But it irked him and his response was to take the offensive.

"Well, as it happens, you're not far off… the closest I got to all of that was the Pride of Ibrox Flute Band."

Ruairí sat off to the side, alone.

He had been bemoaning the tardiness of his mother's return with their breakfast, but this seemed to get his attention.

He looked more closely at Eban Barnard as he spoke, but said nothing himself.

Anto too had become more interested. "You mean the flip side of those losers outside?"

He was referring to the Volunteer Robert Sands Republican Flute Band, who had periodically joined the protesters outside. They would lend their support to the siege by striking up with gusto, –*The Merry Ploughboy*, *Kevin Barry* and *The Soldier's Song*.

Eban smiled, pleased at their interest. "Exactly."

"Fuck… I wouldn't have pegged you for one of *them*."

Eban was warming to what he took to be a newly-achieved street credibility among his charges. He drew his chair up closer to the young men.

"Well, there were two reasons why you joined an Orange band back then. One was it was the closest thing to being a musician that any of us were likely to get. And two, for the women – the girls, I mean."

Anto's libido was nudged. "Oh aye?"

"Kick the Pope bands, that's what they were called – blood and thunder. But that's the bands that always attracted the wee Millies."

"Millies?"

"Mill girls… from the time when there was work in the linen industry – in the mills. They used to dance in a straight line across, behind the band leader with his flailing mace; ahead of the side-drummers. Hard young girls, waving their mini Union Jacks and tight wee arses in tartan trousers."

He laughed at the memory.

"It was the closest thing to groupies we could imagine."

Anto seemed intrigued. "*You* were a drummer?"

Eban puffed up. "Leading tip… but it couldn't last."

"Did you pack it in?"

"Well… I mean… some of the older members of the band were bloody certifiable, and everybody knew they were… *connected.*"

Anto seemed intrigued. "Any time I've seen it on the TV – the Twelfth of July I mean; the big day – it all seems a bit mental to me."

Eban knew what the young man meant, but didn't know how to answer him.

Of course it must have appeared like some kind of malign drink-sodden circus to someone like Anto or Ruairí.

The Glorious Twelfth.

For him it had all come to a head one particular Twelfth of July.

Coming back from the field, the word went around that the customary, ritual baiting of the Taigs was imminent.

The band would come to a temporary halt outside Donegal Street chapel.

The police escort would turn a blind eye, and the lads would pump up the volume.

Sidney Tweed, the drum major, would pass amongst the ranks of the young drummer boys, exhorting them through gritted teeth, bulging veins, eyeballs popping, to *"Play up! Play up! Let the papist whores hear ye in Rome!"*

In reality, the closest thing resembling a Catholic or Republican stood five hundred yards back from the road, behind the massive canvas screens that the British soldiers had erected.

They were grateful for the advance notice though, because down reined the old 'Belfast confetti': razor blades and Stanley blades slipped into cakes of soap and dug into potatoes.

Olympic shot-put records were about to be rewritten.

The others in the band would turn their drumsticks around to the fat end and blatter and blatter… blisters, skin and blood flying from the friction burns.

And when it was all over and their drum skins were burst and battered, the band returned, drenched in sweat and soaked in the certainty of their own superiority.

"We are the people!"

Ruairí Connolly had been taking it all in silently. At last he spoke.

"You're quite the closet Loyalist, aren't you Mr Barnard?"

Eban was knocked out of his reverie, surprised, a little thrown.

"Not really... not at all actually." He reddened.

Ruairí sneered at him. "Don't you have the courage of *any* convictions?"

Anto's antennae twitched with the entry to the fray of his friend. "Yeah... why *did* you pack it in Eban?"

Eban felt a little as if they were circling him like hyenas. He'd felt this way since they had begun joshing with him, but something had perceptibly changed in tone. He sought to draw back. Retreat.

"I'm just saying... none of it made sense any more. Walking back to the Orange hall in silence to a single beat on the one surviving drum... I felt ridiculous. Blue cap with orange plume, white shirt, red trousers with black stripes down the side, like a fuckin' clown... things were never the same after that. I handed back the uniform and equipment at the next band meeting. No-one seemed too concerned."

Anto lit a cigarette. He smiled mischievously.

"Pity... for a minute there I thought you might be someone I could learn to hate."

Ruairí wasn't letting up, however.

"No, Eban's not worthy of that Anto – are you, Eban? See, Eban doesn't know what he is: he's nothing, so there's nothing to hate... isn't that right Eban?"

Eban was stung.

"You know nothing about me," he shot back.

Both young men looked at each other, smiling, and simultaneously made a mocking 'Ooooooooooooooooooo' sound, in pretend, scornful fear and awe.

Anto smirked and stood up. "International man of mystery."

Ruairí joined him, standing at his side.

"Oh, *I* know you alright; know your type... think you can come in here and clock up a few hours' community service in the hope that it will put your mind at rest about slappin' your kids around or cheating on your wife. Or maybe you feel bad that you don't visit your old mother anymore... is that it?"

Eban was crushed by this bitterness that seemed to have come from nowhere.

He looked crestfallen.

"You go to college, Eban?" spat Ruairí.

"Yes."

"Course you did... do you think anyone else in this room did?"

Eban was becoming increasingly agitated. "I don't know. Look—"

"Anto; me; Sinéad? No-one here's ever finished school. D'ya thinks that makes us stupid, Eban?"

"You could go further if you wanted to... you're smart."

Ruairí suddenly sprang across the room.

In an instant his face was close to Eban's face. His finger aggressively stabbing him in the chest.

"Too fuckin' right I am, mate... and don't you forget it. I'm your equal in everything but opportunity."

Anto's blood was rising. He hovered over Eban menacingly. "Spot on mate."

Eban wilted pathetically. "My father... was a labourer."

Ruairí wouldn't relent. "Oh yeah – ye hear that, Anto? That's referred to as the 'labour aristocracy' – the ship-building jobs; the aircraft makers... yez kept all those jobs for yourselves."

Forced to defend himself in such a manner and with no obvious justification for the wrongs visited on those less fortunate than himself, Eban Barnard was hoist upon the politically correct, liberal petard of his own making.

The foundation on which he had justified his entire homecoming, and the community relations sense of purpose that had provided him with a personal and professional momentum, collapsed around him like a flimsy house of cards.

He was becoming emotional.

His voice wavered.

"You've got me all wrong... I *do* want to help... because you don't know... you *can't* know..."

Perhaps it was the weariness.

Or the harrowing nature of earlier events, but in the blink of an eye Eban Winston Barnard had lost it completely.

He buried his face in his hands and began to sob quietly.

Ruairí stood over him, deriding him, scorning him.

Then like flicking a switch, he broke off the attack and turned away, dismissive, as if the game was no longer worth the effort.

"Where do they get these people?" he wondered aloud to himself. "You're *such* a drama queen Mr Barnard."

Sinéad, who had returned from making tea, stopped at the sight of Eban in disarray.

Colour flooded into her pale cheeks and she banged down the tray, sending mugs falling onto the floor.

"I swear to God, I can't leave yez for two minutes!"

Ruairí looked at her. "Whadaya takin' *his* side for?"

She mustered a convincing, authoritative maturity in her putdown. "Fuckin' grow up will ya?!"

Ruairí couldn't let her away with it. "What's it to you?"

"One more word out of you and I'm going, Ruairí... I swear to God I am."

She crossed to where Eban sat.

"Don't let these scumbags get to ye Eban... here,,, let me get you a cup of tea."

She fetched the one remaining half-filled mug on the tray.

Eban was staring at the floor now. Too embarrassed to make eye contact with her.

Unbeknown to any of them –perhaps even himself – something had broken inside him.

Simply given way.

Some line had been crossed.

At that moment he could not tell who he hated more. Ruairí or himself.

Suddenly, unexpectedly, his mind began to race.

Drying his eyes on the back of his sleeve, he reached into his trouser pocket and produced a handkerchief. Blowing his nose, he was well aware how he must appear to these hard, young jackals: old, stupid, irrelevant. An object to be used and teased and ultimately derided for being stupid enough to offer them his time and his concern, for having deluded himself that he might have something to contribute here.

But when you reach rock bottom you come up again.

And to do this it was necessary to jettison something.

So Eban Barnard resolved that he wanted to speak.

He had a story to tell.

And he wanted them to listen to it.

That was his price.

His one demand.

For the unwanted intimacy, the humiliation, the rejection… they would have to listen.

And when it was over, they would know who he was.

Who he *really* was.

And maybe they would understand.

Maybe not… it didn't matter.

He pulled himself together, and composing himself, turned to face them.

"Sinéad, have you ever heard the saying that for evil to prosper, it just takes good men to do nothing?"

She raised her pencil-thin eyebrows in surprise. "No, but Ruairí will have."

"Well I did nothing and every day I wake up, and every night I go to sleep, I know… in here" – he pointed to his chest – "I know I did nothing."

Ruairí sensed the change in the atmosphere and it felt uncomfortable.

Barnard looked different somehow.

More composed.

Fatalistic perhaps.

A man resigned in some way.

Ruairí crossed the room, sat down and began to play solitaire. Superficially indifferent, but all the while listening.

Sinéad sat down at the table and placed her hand on Eban's.

She too sensed a shifting of the tide. "You go ahead Eban… if you want to, luv… get it off yer chest," she offered encouragingly.

Eban turned to face both her and Anto, whilst effectively turning his back on Ruairí.

"Do you have a brother, Anto?"

Anto was wary, and fearing that this would be a tactic to divide them replied, "Ruairí's my brother… the only brother I need… isn't that right mate?"

Ruairí Connolly never looked up. He just kept slapping card down on top of card.

Sinéad, still angry with her partner, chipped in spitefully, "Frankie was Ruairí's brother. He could never stand up to him… still can't stand up to the memory of him."

Eban quickly became animated at this. "YES! YES, that's exactly right. You hear that Anto… it's not that easy. You don't get to choose… blood's blood!"

Without warning, Ruairí Connolly exploded.

Throwing over the card table, he flew across the room to where the others sat. He grabbed Eban by the throat and pushed him down.

"OKAY, BARNARD… WHO ARE YOU? WHY THE FUCK ARE YOU IN HERE?"

Sinéad screamed and pushed herself between the men. "RUAIRÍ… NO!

Anto, excited, clapped his hands together like a clockwork monkey. "Now we're cookin' on gas!"

Eban had a wide grin on his face. He made no attempt to protect himself. Rather, he let himself fall lifeless. He was being shaken around like a rag doll, smiling like an imbecile.

"That's okay… that's good… if that's what it takes," he said.

Ruairí, confused by this reaction, was disturbed.

He let Eban go and he fell back into his seat.

All three looked at the older man, instinctively waiting for him to explain his behaviour.

Eban waited an eternity.

Dawn was sending early shafts of sunlight into the room.

When he spoke, it was in a whisper.

"What I'm going to tell you… I've only ever told this to the woman I believed I loved, and I regretted it the minute it was out of my mouth… regretted it ever since, saying the words; hearing myself say them. I thought it would help… but that's why I came back… from England… why I'm here…"

He looked at Ruairí directly. "I've always been here… no matter where I go, I can never leave. You'll find that, Ruairí… if you run…"

Ruairí, to his surprise, found that he could not hold the man's gaze.

Anto fell back on machismo. "Who's running?"

Sinéad maintained a hold of his hand. "Take your time… I'll not judge you," she whispered.

Eban was talking to the others, but never broke his gaze from Ruairí.

"Ruairí and me, we're more alike than he knows… I've a big brother too, Ruairí."

Ruairí found that he still couldn't look at the man. "So what?" he said, failing to sound nonchalant.

"When I was a little boy, I used to mitch off from school by hiding in an old burnt-out pub… McGrew's pub and wine lodge, that was it. If I stood on tiptoes I could see the corrugated iron roof. In the centre of it" – he smiled at the memory – "there was a skylight…"

45

SHANKILL ROAD,
BELFAST, NORTHERN IRELAND
MAY 1970

Unfamiliar, raised voices and the low-velocity crack of small-arms fire woke him abruptly.

He ran to the barricaded window. It was after dusk outside.

The interior of the pub was darker than that again.

Darker than at any other time he had been there before.

Curiously, what he noted first was the absence of the milk bottles from the doorsteps.

Could it be tomorrow already? Had he slept throughout the night? Surely not!

His da would kill him.

Then he saw why.

Saw the young men struggle and falter under the weight of crates and crates of bottles.

Bottles filled with petrol, washing up liquid and stuffed with rags.

A makeshift barrier of wooden planks, upturned bins and rubber tyres was thrown across Snugville Street.

Men, their faces covered with scarves and handkerchiefs, ran back and forward in panic.

"They're comin' up from the Falls... they're comin' to burn us out!"

Eban had often heard Alex say, "There's no way the Taigs will ever get up this far... not our street... no way."

People listened when Alex spoke.

Alex had had a trial for Linfield FC.

People liked Alex.

But the scene unfolding below him suggested that his brother was wrong.

Small pockets of young men swayed back and forth, back and forth.

Advancing, then repulsed.

Yelling and screaming.

Summoning up false courage in their bellowing and shrieking.

Bottles, bricks and petrol bombs flew back and forth through the midsummer night.

Plumes of smoke filled the air, along with oaths and cries.

Some men had been separated from the main melee and lay on the ground, trying to cover up. Their heads being kicked and stamped on.

Abruptly, there was a heavy crash.

The sound of a fallen crateful of bottles.

A sudden slash of brightness and heat that lit up the room all around him.

Looking down, Eban saw a man lit up like a blowtorch.

He wriggled and thrashed on the ground like a maniac.

The flames and sparks from him all fanned out and spread upward in crazy eddies and currents. Twisting like flaming. grasping fingers.

Incredibly, the man did not scream.

He made no noise save for his desperate rolling and thrashing.

Eban was transfixed.

Rooted to the spot.

Unseen. He craned his neck.

At the other end of the street the smoke was thick.

Opaque with a low, orange-red glow behind it.

The tinted smoke itself was mesmerising.

Hypnotic.

It would all of a sudden stir itself, whirl up and around then check one way or the other.

It would dart and slant and settle, then jump up and swirl again.

Coming right at Eban.

Finding ways into the building, through the holes and gaps.

Stinging and watering his eyes.

The glow and the smoke and the sound of the crowd…

High-pitched screams and that low rumbling noise of the crowd.

A *big* crowd. A *huge* crowd.

Activity seemed to be coming from everywhere.

From what seemed the entire city.

A man's voice, clear above the pandemonium.

"Clear the street… clear the street… open up… let 'er go, Billy!"

All at once the confusion below took on a unified sense of purpose.

Men ran for cover, scattering off the main thoroughfare in all directions.

Rifle shots exploded loud.

Eban stood fixed at his vantage point, staring through a hole in the metal screen.

Red tracer bullets streaked up and out of sight overhead.

He knew Alex and his father would be out looking for him.

His mother moaning and wailing and clutching at her breast and sure her youngest was dead or dying.

He had been unaware of his breath rising and falling until it froze in him.

There was a desperate banging and clawing outside in the back alley where he entered and exited.

At the very back door of McGrew's Pub.

The door had been nailed shut and reinforced, but it seemed to Eban like someone was coming, clawing straight through it.

Thin, whining noises, weak and vulnerable and pathetic, seemed to juxtapose the explosive, violent sound of heavy blows and splintering wood.

Eban knew at once that whoever was on the other side of the door was *very* afraid, and singularly focused on escape.

He pushed back further into the shadows.

Voices…

Shouts…

Running feet echoing, the sound beating back and forth off the walls of the back alley.

A young man crying… praying… and with a confusion of dawning recognition… dread expectation… pitiful resignation… the frenzied assault on the door ceased.

Silence.

Then he heard a scuffling noise and his attention was drawn to the top of the wall.

Over the wall that he had earlier climbed, appeared a leg.

Drainpipe denims.

A black Chelsea boot.

Torn and bloody from the jagged glass atop.

The young man, astride the wall now, pulled himself unsteadily erect.

His hands cut and bleeding.

He looked about nineteen, long frizzy copper hair and sideburns. He wore a denim jacket.

Teetering, his hands a gory mess as he pushed down on the unyielding broken bottle necks for balance.

Eban hardly breathed.

He silently prayed to the God of DC Comics for invisibility, and bit his bottom lip hard.

The man was making a different noise now.

He was crying like a child.

"*No mister... mister... please... NO!*"

Suddenly the back door heaved and gave way, swinging wildly on one hinge only and falling forward into McGrew's back yard.

"*It wasn't me mister... I never done nothing... mister... don't... PLEASE! DON'T!*"

Eban pushed himself tight back against the wall.

He could see two silhouettes framed in the doorway.

Did that mean they could see him?

Both men were laughing and jeering.

Drunk with the adrenaline pump of pursuit and relishing the spoils of the hunt.

One had scrambled over the fallen door and into the yard, grabbing and pulling down on the hanging leg above.

The ginger-haired man – caught now behind enemy lines – let out a plaintive cry of such pain and anguish that Eban considered making a run for it.

Some deeper reason borne from fear and his complete concealment kept him still and unseen.

"*Grab his other fuckin' leg Fish... grab the bastard!*"

"*I can't, he's kicking me. Yer dead, Taig... yer fuckin' dead wee lad!*"

Eban knew then.

Could see what was coming.

He closed his eyes tight but the young man's screams stabbed right on through.

Painting his unconscious with the images of the castration as vividly as if he'd watched it all wide-eyed.

"*Yoohooo! Ride 'em cowboy... yoohoo!*"

"*Yeeehaw! Yeeehaw!*"

The two men ran up and down...

... back and forward...

… pulling and tugging on a leg…

… each side of the wall.

The glass ripped and tore again and again as the flailing scarecrow, helpless, bounced and bumped along.

His screams burned into Eban's very soul.

The men were laughing, excited, out of breath.

The screams stopped.

There was a slipping, sliding noise and a dull thud.

"That's one Fenian won't be breeding like no rat!"

"Leave him, Fish; I'm away… let's get the fuck out of here!"

Eban Winston Barnard opened his eyes just in time to see his brother Alex kick the ragged heap that had fallen from the top of the wall and now lay close at his feet.

They walked off, laughing.

He could still hear them snigger and joke as he cautiously stepped over the body which lay between him and the only way out of this nightmare.

A low moan, pitiful, rose from the prone shape.

A faintly steaming pink-and-red mess seeped from the torn fabric and flesh between his legs.

Blood pooled beneath him.

The man's head turned slowly and he looked up.

Eban could see pink bubbles of saliva rise and fall in his mouth and nostrils.

He looked directly at the boy standing above him.

"H-e-e-l-l-l-p-p-p m-e-e-e…"

The man's eyes rolled back in his head.

Eban ran.

And whilst running, gagged and swallowed hard and often.

And pushed the horror, down, down, into the pit of his stomach.

No-one knew he was there.

No-one ever would.

He ran. And ran.

Through the crossing of the white church.
Under the shadow of the Black Mountain.
Back amongst the little fortresses of common love.

46

INSIDE THE CATHEDRAL VESTRY
6.54AM

"You bastard. How can you live with yourself?" It was Ruairí who reacted first.

Sinéad looked genuinely shocked but reached for perspective. "Ruairí, Eban was eleven years old, for Christ sake."

"So what's stopping him now then?"

Anto too looked shaken. "He's right… you've got to give him up."

Eban looked ashen and empty.

It was done.

"He's a policeman now – really high up… a senior one."

Ruairí was incredulous. "He's *what*?!"

"Oh man… you have *soooo got* to give him up," said Anto.

"You think I don't know it? It's never just as easy as that."

"Why not?" Ruairí demanded

"He has – or had – a family. His life's a mess… his wife left him… took the kids… he lives alone in a little village, Markethill it's called; big white house on the outskirts, stone lions in the driveway. You couldn't miss it…."

As he spoke, Eban, incredibly, could hear himself sound almost apologetic on Alex's behalf.

As if his big brother was not here to defend himself.

It seemed a puzzling paradox.

Most of his life he had hated his brother for what he had done.

Now, in the first time of telling, he struggled as these strangers passed judgement on Alex.

It felt like someone else were speaking and he was merely listening.

"He's done really well for himself, you know, but he drinks – drinks heavily… maybe to forget for all I know. Despite everything I worry about him… what he might do all alone up there, with his police-issue revolver… all that regret… all that denial."

Ruairí was fuming.

"You said you've never talked about it. How do you know he regrets anything? He's an RUC man isn't he? Those bastards have hardened their hearts. How do you know he regrets any of it?"

"I know he's a deeply unhappy man."

"Fuck him!"

Anto agreed, marshalling righteous indignation.

"What about that young guy… what about the life he never had?"

Eban eyed him sceptically. "You want them to lock him up, you mean… get him put away?"

"Maybe that's what *he* wants, in his heart… save him from himself; set him and yourself free," suggested Sinéad, curling a lock of hair around her finger.

Eban's voice faltered. His eyes were red and sore.

"We all know that's not the way it works. I couldn't do it… all these years I couldn't do it, and I still can't do it now."

Sinéad stood up and crossed to the window. Looking out on the new day, she placed a hand on her unborn child and spoke back over her shoulder.

"Eban, I'm not a religious person – how could you be after all we've been through? – but Ruairí's mother has a saying: 'Act as if ye had faith, and faith will be given unto ye.'"

Ruairí, hearing the mention of his name, felt compelled to respond.

To fire off something about religion being the opium of the masses.

Or insisting that his mother be left out of it.

But he somehow realised that he had nothing left.

Barnard's story had shocked him.

And like Eban's, his tank was empty.

His passion was spent.

He felt like he hadn't slept for centuries.

His anger had been replaced by great waves of gloom sweeping over him at the prospect of another day in this fuck-awful room… in this fuck-awful world.

It had sneaked up on him from nowhere.

Anger was energy, but at this moment he felt that all his energy had been dissipated.

Barnard would move on.

His brother would remain unaccountable for his crime.

But they would stay and nothing would change.

Or they would go and everything would change.

The world pressed hard down upon him.

All he could manage was to intone the weary mantra that had sustained them since taking up residence in this cathedral a hundred lifetimes ago.

"Sinéad… stay away from the window."

The girl looked at him and caught something of his despondency. She moved toward him with concern in her eyes, "You alright darlin'?"

"Just tired."

"Well come on and we'll grab forty winks before your ma arrives."

She took his hand tenderly and led him into the antechamber, pulling the curtain behind them.

For the first time in his shift in the cathedral, Eban felt like he was intruding.

His thoughts turned to the life he would soon return to.

He considered telling someone — anyone — about Alex,

But there was simply no-one he felt he could confide in.

No close friend.

No lover.

No confidante.

Some kind of judgement on the life he had chosen for himself, he supposed.

Even if there was someone he could talk to, just like these young people, they would doubtless insist that he act on the information.

That young man was dead, as best he knew.

Murdered in the most horrendous manner.

And Alex and his friend Fish were responsible.

The fallout from such a revelation would be shattering for all concerned.

RUC Chief Superintendent accused of sectarian murder... key witness and accuser is his younger brother.

He had visualised it a million times.

And a million times pushed it away, back into the dark, back into the shadows of the past.

Out of the corner of his eye he noticed Anto cross to the sacristy curtain and listen for a moment. When he was sure they were asleep, he returned and began to collect together his belongings, putting them in a rucksack.

Eban smiled. He tried to change the mood. "Is that the dirty washing bag? Does Mrs Connolly take those away and bring them back clean then?"

Anto did not look up as he spoke. Just continued to place his items in the rucksack, occasionally sniffing a pair of socks or underpants and discarding them.

"Sit down there Eban, I want to have a wee chat with you."

Eban did as he was asked and Anto pulled up a chair beside him.

Smiling, he said, "What the fuck are we doing here Eban? You and me I mean… have you asked yourself that?"

"Oh… only about every five minutes."

"You and I know, right: the people in this town, they don't care what happens to me, Ruairí and Sinéad… I mean… the three of us… we're just scum to them."

Eban nodded his head. "A whole town frozen and useless in the face of brute force… it's hard to believe."

"Yeah… sure, some of them are frightened, but most just don't *care*. Do you follow me?"

Eban disagreed. "I still believe most people are fundamentally good. They're just scared."

Anto sighed patronisingly, or as you might do when trying to explain something to a child.

"Ah, Eban, Eban… maybe you're right… maybe you're right. Now take Ruairí – they say Frankie was a prince, but it's Ruairí; I mean he's smart like Frankie was, but more so… ye follow me? Sure, he's an arrogant ball-breaker, but he's always managed to stay above it all, you know? Even at school, in sports, he would only ever wear a Liverpool shirt cuz they played in red. He said red was the colour of the blood of the workers or something, and how all the great working class teams and soviet teams played in red."

Anto laughed as he spoke, and shook his head at his friend's eccentric principles.

"Nobody knew what the fuck he was going on about! He wore a James Connolly badge; used to joke it was his Uncle James on account of the name and that… joined the Workers' Party when he was fifteen… he was different. Sledger hated him for that."

Eban was surprised. "You knew Sledger at school?"

"Oh sure, we knew all those guys."

"So what's your point?"

Anto stood up and threw the rucksack over his shoulder.

"Look mate, make no mistake: we did it – *did it all*... everything they said and more – and it was mostly Ruairí's idea; like, always... but like he says, who the fuck are *they* to sit in judgement of us? I'm no fuckin' good... I can admit it... never have been. Reform school... probation... suspended sentences, but whatever they do to me, *they* don't get to say that... they don't get to judge me."

Eban began to realise what was happening. Panic began to rise.

"You can't be serious. Sledger; Molloy...they'll eat you alive out there."

Anto moved toward the door.

"It's Ruairí they really want. Maybe the both of them can get away to England. Maybe they'll settle for me."

Eban felt a surge of responsibility. He remembered why he was there in the first place.

He made a move to block Anto off.

The young man was having none of it.

"I'm doing this so all scores can be settled by me... through me."

Anto saw the astonishment in Eban's face.

"Look mate, I'm nineteen and I feel like I've been running away all my life. Sometimes you can get tired of running. Sometimes you've got to just stand still. You should think about that Eban... time to stop running."

Eban felt shamed and dumbstruck.

Anthony Gattuso was handing out lessons for life.

There was a pause when Anto placed his hand on the door bolt.

He took a deep breath. "Aren't you gonna say something inspiring?"

Eban was momentarily speechless.

The young man seemed surprisingly upbeat, considering his certain fate. How could he have misjudged this character so prejudicially? He felt such a sense of respect for what appeared to him to be a courageous act of self-sacrifice.

"I can only thank God it's you and not me," was all he could manage.

"Tut-tut Eban… must try harder."

"Thank you."

"Thank *me*. For what?"

"For doing the right thing. For Ruairí's sake… for Sinéad's…" He felt like he might break down, and swallowed back the rising swell. "…For *mine*."

The young man turned on his heel and walked back to where Eban stood.

He looked deeply into his eyes. "For *you*… what did I do for *you*?"

"Maybe gave me the courage… to act on what I saw – back then, I mean."

Anto smiled. There was something about his smirk that didn't seem quite right.

"Oh, don't thank me… thank your brother."

If this was some joke, Eban didn't get it. "What… what do you mean?"

The young man pushed his face close to Eban's. His breath stank of nicotine, his clothes of sweat. "The first thing I do when I get out there is to tell those animals about your cop brother."

He was still smiling.

"Who he is… what he does… what he *did*… where he lives…"

Affecting a whiny tone, Gattuso mimicked Eban's earlier confession in the cruellest of imitations.

"*'All alone in a little village, Markethilll it's called; big white house on the outskirts, stone lions in the driveway. Sure, you couldn't miss it.'*"

Eban winced like he had been punched in the stomach. His mouth fell open.

"They're always interested in that kind of thing. Sure, you never know… they might be so pleased that they take it easy on me."

Anto crossed to the door again, pulled up his rucksack on his shoulders and turned one last time.

"So no thanks necessary. Wish me luck."

Eban watched him go as the consequences of what he had shared with these strangers sank in.

He had unburdened himself at last, but at what cost?

He moved slowly to the window.

Below, but out of his vision, Eban could hear shouts and scuffles as Anthony Gattuso sought to broker safe passage for himself.

Car doors slammed as he was swept up and away by the South Armagh Brigade of the IRA.

47

INTERVIEW ROOM 1,
THE HISTORICAL ENQUIRIES OFFICES,
POLICE SERVICE OF NORTHERN IRELAND, BELFAST
2014

The mood in the small interview room strained the containment capabilities of its four grey walls.

As did the information just imparted.

In silence, Watson looked at Coulter.

Both men immediately knowing what the other was thinking.

If Eban Barnard's story were true, then – as a purely police matter – Chief Superintendent Alex Barnard's assassination would have to be reopened and reinvestigated in the light of new evidence.

Similarly, the serious assault on Joseph Breslin.

And there was no way of doing this without redress to Eban Barnard, his story and the subsequent besmirching of their colleague's hard-won reputation and proud legacy.

Alex and his as yet unidentified accomplice would warrant a charge of attempted murder.

Even posthumously, it was a disaster of epic proportions.

At the time, Alex Barnard's murder had been a major coup for the Provos.

And a major security fuck-up for their own people.

In post-conflict Northern Ireland, Sinn Féin would have a field day.

Accusations of cover-ups and collusion would rain down upon their collective heads and the matter would be used as a political stick to beat the Unionists into submission on the establishment of a 'Truth Commission'.

Then the whole Pandora's box of state-sanctioned Loyalist murder gangs might be flung open.

Heads would have to roll.

Senior people would have to fall on their swords for the sake of the collective good.

Christ, the Chief Constable would eviscerate the both of them in a heartbeat.

And there was Joe Breslin.

Eban Barnard was unaware of it, but both officers knew that he was still alive.

Knew of his whereabouts.

Where he lived and worked.

Had already written to him as standard procedure since Barnard had requested his case be reinvestigated.

It was now a matter of record.

The poor cunt was between a rock and a hard place through no fault of his own.

How could he possibly know that one of his assailants would go on to become one of the most senior officers in the Royal Ulster Constabulary?

They would have to bring him in.

Question him on the incident.

Open it all up again for the guy in an attempt to clarify Eban's story and possibly bring Alex's accomplice to trial.

The two policemen's minds were racing.

All the while, Watson was trying to read Coulter's expression.

They had worked together for some sixteen years and had established what he believed to be a solid professional relationship.

But this was beyond the pale. Virgin territory.

Trying now to assess the man's character in the face of these unique circumstances, Dan Watson realised he knew little or nothing about which way Sam Coulter might jump.

Nothing could be taken for granted.

If only he hadn't invited him to stay in the room.

Perhaps he could have fixed all this himself.

Nobody would ever need to know.

Lean on Eban Barnard.

Find something to bring pressure to bear.

Let sleeping dogs lie.

Bury it.

In their silence, Eban could feel tangible vindication.

He could smell their fear and confusion as they wrestled with the potentialities of what he had told them. He could read the men's thought processes. Could ascertain the wheels and cogs whizzing around behind their eyes as they considered their options.

The harsh strip lighting in the room seemed to glare even brighter.

It was as if all three had been caught in the dazzling burn of a camera's flashbulb and held there.

Eban massaged the throbbing in his left upper arm, and smiling wryly, broke the silence.

He couldn't resist it.

"Well Inspector Watson... *got your attention now?*"

There was no reply.

"Still want me to talk to a shrink?"

"Why didn't you warn him?" It was Coulter.

Eban had forgotten that the other man was in the room.

"What?"

"Why didn't you warn your brother? You might have saved his life."

Watson thought he could read his colleague's play.

Guilt.

He figured that Coulter was on board with a damage limitation brief that he himself favoured. That the sergeant was about to concoct some nonsense about withholding evidence leading to a murder. That Eban Barnard was, de facto, an accomplice in his brother's assassination.

Brilliant!

But when Dan Watson looked into Coulter's face, he wasn't so sure.

What he saw there was someone genuinely trying to understand.

Someone who was functioning on an emotional level, not a professional one.

"Why didn't you warn him?" the sergeant asked once again.

"They shot him within two days of Gatusso leaving," said Eban. "Look at the dates."

"You could have warned him."

"Oh really, sergeant?" said Eban defensively. "And say what? 'I know what you did, I saw you all those years ago… and now I've told the Provos about it!'"

He wanted to laugh dismissively but nothing would come.

"You could have used the confidential telephone line and—"

"ENOUGH!" screamed Eban. "If you want to arrest me on some bullshit charge, then do it… that's why I came in here in the first place, remember? But we all know that's not going to make it go away… right, Inspector Watson?"

Now that it was out and he had no further use for his reluctant confessor, he wanted to see the detective squirm.

Watson was staring intently at a coffee stain on the thin grey carpet at Eban's feet, still considering all the angles. He opened one of the folders on his desk and stared at it for a long time.

Finally he spoke. "What I'm asking you now, I'm asking you as a favour… for the force… for the men who looked up to him. Don't take this any further. What good can it possibly do?"

Eban replied caustically, "We'll let the family of his victim be the judge of that, will we?"

He rose as if to leave and extended his hand toward the folder Watson had been reading.

"I'll be on my way… or are you going to charge me with aiding and abetting a terrorist organisation in the murder of your colleague?"

Watson was marshalling his temper. He had decided on an appeal to the man's reason.

"Don't be so bloody stupid! From here it looks like a bloody mess from start to finish. Leave it alone… Christ, look what it's done to you, man; carrying this around with you for so long!"

"Maybe I might borrow some of your professional detachment, detective," replied Eban sarcastically.

Watson shook his head. "Alex was a young man—"

"So was I," said Eban bitterly.

"I'm not seeking to justify what he did… but times were different then…"

"Yeah… right… is this the new beginning we've been promised: turning a blind eye to sectarian murder?"

"Joseph Breslin didn't die. He survived the attack…"

Eban Barnard was dumbstruck. Elated.

"Joseph Breslin? His name was Joseph Breslin?"

"That's right."

"*Not dead?*"

"He lives with his mother and sister. I have the address."

"How do I know you're telling me the truth?"

"Why would I lie?" He closed the file and handed it to him.

"Keep it. If there's a message in all of this, it's to let it go... get on with the rest of your life. That's what Joe Breslin has done... why can't you?"

Eban's head was reeling with the news that the man he had seen tortured and left for dead was still alive. He could finally look again into this man's eyes and tell him why he had run.

Why he didn't help him.

Ask his forgiveness.

If he had the courage.

After all these years.

He pointed at the tape recorder on the table.

"I want all of what's recorded. I want it transcribed... I want it all written down somewhere as a matter of record!"

Coulter came from behind him, placing a hand on his arm.

"For Alex's reputation... He was your only brother, for Christ sake... there must have been something between you?"

"Something between us? Aye... about ten years in age and a whole miserable fucking lifetime ever since."

48

"And how does that make you feel?" asked Dr Amanda McCabe, fingers linked, hands below her chin, eyebrows raised in benevolent inquiry.

Emily twisted her tear-stained handkerchief a few more times around her fingers and tried hard for something to say.

"Sad, I suppose."

She had been meeting with her psychotherapist every week for the last month and frankly was beginning to question the validity of this increase in visits and expenditure.

"And your mother… how does she feel about all of this?"

"She says I can go back and stay with her at any time; just to say the word."

There was a long silence.

Dr Amanda McCabe was thinking about attending little Audrey Thompson's birthday party. She was wondering whether enough time had passed since her own daughter Katie and her two friends had terrorised young Audrey in a cyber-bullying incident on social media.

"I mean, I haven't decided definitely or anything…" prompted Emily.

Dr Amanda McCabe looked directly at her with blank eyes and nodded in vacant affirmation.

"I have been looking at Tuesday's education supplement in the *Guardian*. There's a job in Dudley, in a primary school there, that would suit me."

Another long silence.

Emily felt awkward and attempted some humour.

"Although, if you know the Dudley accent, well, it's like learning a foreign language…"

Dr Amanda McCabe beat out a little rhythmic tattoo with a pencil on her front teeth.

She was thinking about her husband Gary's new secretary and whether she should be worried about their lunchtime squash games together.

"I have been working on my children's book – you know,*The Witch; Rag-Nag-Hag-Bag* – Rosemary says she may know an illustrator…"

Another long silence.

"I know that you don't think she presents a strong role model for young girls, but – the witch, I mean… not Rosemary…" Emily trailed off.

Dr Amanda McCabe reached for her pad and pen and wrote something down.

Emily was encouraged.

"I don't know if I should tell Eban how seriously I'm thinking about moving back to England. After all, we've talked before about how I'm not responsible for anyone else's life… or their behaviour…"

Emily bit her bottom lip.

"I know no-one can *make* me feel how I sometimes do; I know you said I *choose* to feel that way."

Dr Amanda McCabe looked directly at her once again with blank eyes, and nodded in vacant affirmation.

"It's just, I'm not sure I can go on with this level… this lack of commitment…" She was tearing up again.

"My mother keeps going on about me not getting any younger…"

Emily blew her nose and looked at Dr Amanda McCabe, desperate for validation.

Another long silence.

Eventually the therapist leaned forward, proffering a box of Kleenex. Emily's stomach tightened.

Please don't ask, 'and how does that make me feel?' Please don't ask, 'and how does that make me feel?' Please don't ask, 'and how does that make me feel?'...

"*And how does that make you feel?*" asked Dr Amanda McCabe, sitting back into her chair, fingers linked, hands below her chin, eyebrows raised in benevolent inquiry.

49

Unbeknownst to Emily Atkins, across town in the Royal Victoria Hospital Cardiology Unit, Eban Winston Barnard was having to face up to more hard truths.

Mr Ashook Khan had travelled from the interior-landscaped gardens and Japanese fountains of his private clinic in Malone Road and was slumming it for two of his scheduled days a week with the NHS proletariat.

"You seem a little agitated Mr Barnard... are you under any stress at the moment?"

Eban had to stop himself from laughing out loud.

'Stress' wouldn't begin to approach; couldn't begin to describe how he had been feeling.

But he'd had enough professions of his circumstances and his angst to do him a lifetime and he wasn't about to engage this balding, dapper, rotund consultant with any more of it.

"You mean other than from having to attend here this morning?" he quipped.

"Quite so... quite so..."

The doctor's mobile phone buzzed on vibrate. He looked at it quickly. "Excuse me, I have to take this."

Mr Khan proceeded to speak Gujarati in an animated fashion whilst Eban looked around the room and wondered why the senior physicians always called themselves 'Mr' instead of 'Dr', like they had nothing to prove.

Mr Khan ended the call, smiled and reassumed what he imagined constituted his bedside manner.

"Can you slip off your jacket, please, and I will take your blood pressure."

He did so and sighed. "160 over 85... that is not good for someone like you."

"Someone like *me*?"

"Do you smoke Mr Barnard?"

"No..." said Eban, lying through his stained teeth. "Well, I did... but I gave up."

"And when you were smoking... how many a day?" asked Mr Khan, wrinkling his nose at the smell of cigarette smoke permeating Eban's clothes.

"About twenty a day."

"I see... I see," he said, flipping through a file in front of him. "I have here the results of your stress test... not very good I'm afraid."

"Well, yeah... I'm a little out of condition."

"Oh dear me, no... that's not what this is about I'm afraid."

Eban thought to himself, *Here it comes. The moment that every middle-aged man with no health history to speak of dreads.*

"I've never had a stay in hospital overnight in my life!" he blurted out, realising how foolish and irrelevant that sounded.

"Unfortunately that is about to change," said Mr Khan. "I am reading that you suffer from angina. Your left arm, the left side of your face... no?"

"Maybe... sometimes," said Eban unsure, defensive.

The door opened behind him and a porter stood there with a wheelchair.

"I have arranged as a matter of some urgency for you to undergo an angiogram. This is a short, non-invasive procedure that will determine the extent of the narrowing of your arteries and how advanced your heart disease has become."

Mr Khan was inviting Eban to climb into the wheelchair.

"The nurse will bring you back here afterwards and we can discuss the results and how we shall proceed."

Eban weakly complied.

As he was pushed down corridors full of men, women and children sat atop trolleys and gurneys awaiting attention, he struggled to take in what Mr Khan had said, and the speed of events unfolding.

"Just keep your feet on the footrests," was all the porter said as he weaved his way in and out of a semi-bedlam.

Through A&E, with the wails of people in pain and shock, and the whiff of diarrhoea.

Through X-ray, where broken individuals hobbled and hopped around on crutches and in slings. Down to theatre, with its *Do Not Enter* red-lit admonishments, swinging double doors and irrefutable, antiseptic, clinical finality.

Here he was given a relaxant, told to get undressed and to put on the gown provided.

Then to lie down on the trolley and wait.

Everyone was very nice.

The surgeon on duty – speaking from behind his green surgical mask – explained what was going to happen in some unnerving detail.

"An area of skin in the right groin will be cleaned and shaved. This is to allow access to the arteries through which we will access your heart arteries. We've given you a local anaesthetic to numb the skin over this blood vessel. After that you will feel very little discomfort. A tube is placed into the blood vessel of the groin. It carries the dye directly to the blood vessels of your heart, which we can see on the X-ray screen. You can choose to look at the pictures if you wish. At different times you may be asked to take a deep breath and to hold it for a few seconds while the camera moves around you. At the end of the test it's quite normal to feel warm and flushed when some dye is pumped in by machine. This lasts about five or ten seconds and may be associated with the feeling that you are emptying your bladder... please try not to do that though."

Eban heard himself laugh, a little manically.

As he could only see the man's eyes, he was unsure if it was meant to be a joke.

The procedure itself was over with quite quickly, and after a short wait to ensure the wound had closed to the nurse's satisfaction, a porter arrived, and worryingly quipped, "I hope you've brought your pyjamas."

Eban was returned forthwith to Mr Khan.

"That wasn't so bad... was it?" The physician had changed from his dark suit into a white medical coat. Eban was unsure whether this signified anything.

"Well... not for you maybe..."

Mr Khan didn't laugh.

Eban reflected on his penchant for making impromptu quips at inappropriate times.

A number of X-rays of Eban's heart were pinned to an illuminated wall screen.

He had looked once at the pumping organ during the procedure but couldn't maintain his gaze.

It was just too unsettling to see your own beating heart up there on the screen, pulsing and pushing dye and blood around the tributaries, deltas and inlets of the muscle.

He had thought about the stripped-bare tree in the back garden below his window, with its delicate ecosystem of branches that would grow new leaves in the spring.

He had thought about aerial maps he has seen of the Mississippi Delta and the Florida Everglades. How the streams and rivulets of water somehow found their way unerringly into the Gulf of Mexico. The Ganges. The Amazon. The Nile. They all found their way home.

And he wondered about his own circulatory system.

How he had ignored it, fucked with it, disrespected it. And how life had countered in this most severe of natural disasters.

"Not good I'm afraid,"' intoned Mr Khan. "Not a laughing matter at all in fact."

"I didn't mean to seem—"

"This is how things will proceed." Mr Khan had adopted a more officious and formal manner now.

"Under certain circumstances we could try an angioplasty technique. This inflates a small balloon to open the artery. The procedure is much like the one you just went through... but with more risk. We might also have looked at inserting a stent... this is a wire mesh tube which remains in the vessel, keeping the plaque pushed outwards."

Eban nodded to convey measured and considered understanding of the information being imparted, but beads of sweat were popping out like orbs on his forehead.

"However," continued Mr Khan, "in your case I don't believe that we have the luxury of these approaches..."

"Luxury?" said Eban. It seemed a strange choice of word.

"Indeed no... we are looking here at advanced disease affecting three of your vessels, and so I am recommending an immediate cabbage." Mr Khan looked at him gravely.

Eban was unsure he had heard properly. "You want me to eat cabbage?" he asked, incredulous.

Mr Khan sat on the side of his desk and laughed.

His belly wobbled somewhat over the top of his waistband.

Eban didn't see the funny side.

He wondered about the man's appetite for food cooked in ghee, and felt like asking him if he'd taken his own fucking examination.

"Oh dear me... no... no," he chuckled. "If only it were that easy..."

"You did say 'cabbage'?"

"Yes... forgive me: Coronary Artery Bypass Grafting; CABG – in your case triple bypass surgery. We are going to take a saphenous vein from your thigh and lower leg and—"

"Whoa, whoa… you mean open heart surgery!" blurted Eban.

"Quite. Given your profile I am recommending that this take place as soon as possible. The sooner the better in fact. Could you go home and collect some toiletries, pyjamas and a dressing gown and return here?"

Eban was horrified. "What?! No, no… don't I get time to think about all of this?"

Mr Khan seemed bemused. "There is usually a waiting list. Up to six months, but if it's life-threatening we make an exception for—"

"Back up! Back up a minute!"

"Alright then… I can probably have you booked in for this weekend. In the meantime you should be careful not to exert yourself and avoid stressful situations."

He took out his prescription pad. "I am writing you a prescription for blood thinners, blood pressure tablets and cholesterol-lowering statins. You should have this filled and begin the course immediately."

Eban was in shock. "You're kidding."

"Unfortunately no. Please check at admissions on your way out and they will inform you of protocols and take details of your next of kin."

"But I don't have—"

"The operation is routine but a major one and you will require a prolonged recovery period, so I suggest that you make arrangements to be absent from work and for post-surgery care."

"*This* weekend?"

"That's correct."

"Four days from now?"

Mr Khan was sensing denial. "You are in a high-risk category Mr Barnard. You should not be walking around. Talk it over with your wife."

Mr Khan's mobile phone buzzed on vibrate again. "Excuse me, I have to take this."

Eban watched the man become engaged in a fairly heated conversation with someone on the other end.

Whilst he could not understand what the cardiologist was saying, he was sure he registered the terms 'Audi' and 'A5 Series'.

The man's head moved in the manner common amongst those from his subcontinent of origin. It tilted from side to side in little arcs and seemed to wobble like some toy dogs Eban had seen in the back of cars.

Eban felt that he needed to get outside, get away from the hospital if he was to begin to percolate the information just imparted to him.

In fact, what he needed more than anything else was a cigarette.

He rose unsteadily to his feet and found the door.

Mr Khan continued his phone conversation, but on noticing Eban make to leave the room, held up a hand in an attempt to have him stay.

Eban ignored him and left.

The last words he recognised in English were *"bloody bluetooth!"*

He passed the busy admissions area, ignoring the instruction to register his intention to return as an inpatient later in the week.

He felt lightheaded and strangely elated, but with an undertow of awful dread just below this that was somehow being kept in check for the moment.

Then a sadness welled up in him and his eyes filled with tears.

It was not the awfulness of the news that he had just received, or the prospect of his chest cavity being split open and his heart artificially stopped.

It was in the reminder of his isolation.

That he must face this ordeal alone.

Brother Alex… Joe Breslin… those awful memories… they had been his constant companions for so long it seemed.

Where were they now when he needed them?

Next of kin? Post-surgery care? Talk it over with your wife? That's a laugh!

In the short walk into the open air, he had become intimately apprised of his heart's behaviour in a way he'd never previously experienced.

Of its every beat.

Its frequency and rhythm.

He was painstakingly watchful, listening for any indication that each beat would be his last. Anticipating the seizure that would strike him down.

He would rather it happened here with all these people around.

If he died alone…

…in some stairwell…

…or public toilet….

…how sad was that?

If a tree falls in the forest… he thought.

The sky seemed darker than it had been for the time of day.

Something about the clocks going back… or forward. He could never remember.

The rain drifted in fine sheets. Donegal rain. Down from the north-west. Mizzle. The kind that somehow penetrated your outer garments and seeped in, leaving what seemed like a marrow-deep residue.

He was half-considering the idea of abandoning himself to the fates.

Walking away.

Pretending like all of this had never happened.

Just keep on keeping on… waiting for the big one.

Should I make a will? he thought, and then laughed aloud at the thought.

His Ulster Bank account held the princely sum of £635.

His books, DVDs, records… who would want them?

One thought pushed itself to the front of his mind.

It had been there more or less constantly since his session with the HET.

I have to speak with Joe Breslin.

He was sure of it. To explain? To apologise? He didn't know.

Justice for Joe.

It had a ring to it that any self-respecting human rights campaigner would have loved.

A man's wasted life summed up in a slogan.

He thought briefly of proposing to Emily, and noticed that he was grinning widely to himself.

It occurred to him that his reason had temporarily been misplaced.

Mild hysteria might not be far behind.

It's in the lap of the gods, he thought to himself, and immediately began to hum some song of the same name. "*Whoa, whoa, la, la, la… whoa!*"

He heard it escape his lips.

He sang it aloud.

He saw an elderly man in a dressing gown and slippers – on a Zimmer frame, supported by a relative – draw level with him.

Some smokers standing outside the hospital's sliding doors.

An ambulance crew unloading a patient.

All gave Eban a curious look.

He sniggered to himself and sang louder.

"*It's in the lap of the gods… Whoa, whoa, la, la, la… whoa!*"

50

By 9.24pm, Joe accepted that Molly McArdle was not coming to tea.

Anne had chided him for using the term 'stood up' but that's what it was.

Yes, she was correct in saying that any number of things might have caused the delay or cancellation of a cross-town journey for a blind woman and her guide dog.

"Probably some perfectly good reason," said his mother.

Why not ring her mobile? He was not to fret.

But following the conversation he'd had the previous day with Molly, Joe had already surmised that there was a problem.

It had happened before with Delores, why wouldn't it happen again?

During their sharing of his packed lunch – in what had become a regular ritual over these last few months – Joe had felt the time was right to open up to her.

To explain about his past and what this would mean for his – *their* – future together.

She had let him kiss her twice and had rested her hand on his inner thigh both times when assured that they were alone and the kids were preoccupied with their music practice in the main hall of the community centre.

Joe was surprised by how passionate she was. Kissing him hard and long.

Molly was younger than him.

She deserved to know.

"What... *nothing at all?*" she'd asked disbelievingly, when he'd explained.

"That's right, just smooth… just scar tissue. Everything was lost… or has gone up inside."

"But how do you… you know… pass water?"

"There's a… hole; a gap… like a woman. I use a tube thing when I need to go."

"That's… *terrible*. Just… *terrible*," she said, but he knew by the expression on her face that he'd lost her in that moment.

"I can't have kids… if that matters, I mean…"

It had mattered to Delores.

It was why, soon after he'd left hospital, she'd finished with him.

He wondered whether blind people – not being able to see their own reflections in the mirror – were less able to hide the emotions on their faces.

Still, he might be wrong.

Molly's own disability might in some way alleviate her revulsion and she might rise above it.

It was secretly what he had been hoping for from the day and hour they first met.

He liked to make up outcomes up in his head.

Elaborate pictures of how things would be just so.

But he couldn't stop himself from seeing the flip side as well.

The detailed stage set in his mind, where his apprehensions and fears were also played out in clear aspect.

He believed that the two scenarios warred with one another for preeminence, and whatever image prevailed, then that would make it so.

So he had to think hard… *really* hard.

Standing at his bedroom window looking down into the street below him, he envisioned again the special taxi pulling up.

The driver jumping out ahead, sliding back the door.

Keano the golden Labrador bounding out before her.

285

And Molly being taken by the hand and then orientating herself with the dog and harness. Patting her hair and smoothing down her clothes in anticipation of meeting the family he had spoken so much to her about.

Now, try as he might to make this much-anticipated image become flesh and blood, only a solitary junk mail jockey in a baseball cap came through the rain to the threshold of 22 Rosapenna Street that evening.

Downstairs, he knew Anne and his mother would be sitting in silence. Neither acknowledging their worst fears.

He'd had to work hard on keeping up appearances.

To hide his feelings.

Had to scrub the recliner with disinfectant before they got home, telling the women he'd spilled a mug of tea there.

By now they would have set the table for their guest. Sandwiches; egg salad; cheese and ham; tuna. Fresh cream pastries.

A bowl of water for Keano as instructed.

He couldn't face his family.

Didn't know what to say.

Some 'man of the house' he was.

The day had started badly.

Three policemen were waiting in a car outside the house when he'd arrived home early from work to prepare for Molly's visit.

They explained to him that it was about the investigation into his assault all those years ago.

They didn't wear uniforms.

Joe made it clear that he did not want to talk about all of that.

That he saw no point any more.

But they had insisted, and he had brought them into the house at their adamant prompting.

His mother had gone out for the buns and such and Anne was at work, so he did what he thought was best and let them in.

Two of the officers sat with him talking and making notes, while the third excused himself to go to the toilet but didn't return right away.

Joe could hear the boards creaking above them in his room as the hefty man moved around up there.

He complained that they should come back when his sister was there. She dealt with all the official stuff.

Eventually the man returned.

Joe noticed how big he was… like a giant. And how angry-looking.

Just staring at him all the while. Scowling at him.

He sat on their couch making it look tiny, red in the face, saying nothing whilst the others questioned Joe.

Did he remember anything from that night?

What had he been doing on the Shankill Road?

Could he identify his attackers?

Could he recall any names being mentioned?

Joe said he remembered nothing.

That it was all a very long time ago.

The ogre arose slowly and went to stand behind Joe's chair.

His entire body went limp and he dared not look behind him.

He felt sure that the big man's hand was hovering claw-like above his head.

About to rip the very scalp from his skull.

The rest of the men got up to leave. They were laughing.

He thought he heard someone say, *"Fuckin' eunuch."*

They seemed to defer to the big man.

"Have you heard enough, Fish?"

Joe did not see them out when they left.

Instead he poured all his concentration into registering nothing at all.

No fear or recognition or shock.

Showing no emotion.

Nothing.

Focused on staring dead ahead.

Just sitting there in his mother's recliner in abject terror as the hot piss pooled underneath him.

51

To say that Emily was surprised at Eban's unexpected request that the two should journey together to Portstewart and Portrush was an understatement.

The urgency and enthusiasm that he'd shown for the trip away was unlike anything else she'd ever witnessed in all the time she'd known him.

It completely countered her initial reservations concerning taking time off work at such short notice, but did not undermine entirely the feeling that – despite occasional couplings – they had been growing apart from one another to the point of becoming little more than casual acquaintances.

'Fuck buddies' was apparently the term younger people used.

She didn't like it, or the validation of the principle in general.

To this end she insisted that she would feel better if the B&B they stayed in together provided single beds.

Eban appeared taken aback by this, even a little hurt, but he assured her that separate sleeping arrangements would be the understanding if she so wished.

Rosemary Payne seemed disgruntled when she heard the news, believing any rapprochement between her two fellow housemates represented a dire backward step for Emily and an opportunistic snatch at carnal satisfaction for Eban Barnard.

Pascal Loncle wished them *bon voyage* in what seemed a genuine enough felicitude, but was particularly exercised in securing assurances from both – on more than one occasion – that they would be back by Sunday evening, when he expected them in attendance at a significant 'bash' to be thrown in his room.

Intrigued, as they had never been deemed suitable guest material before, they assured him that they would both be in attendance.

On Eban's request, Emily hired a small Nissan Micra car for the trip.

Determined not to be taken advantage of in any sense, she made a point of telling Eban how much his side of the tab came to. To her surprise he produced the cash immediately and paid her for the full amount despite her protestations.

"My idea, my trip, my treat," was his response.

On their short passage to the coast she listened while he talked about how much he loved that part of the world and how we all should do more with our time when we had the chance.

She ascertained that there was clearly something preoccupying him, for despite an outward air of breezy good humour, he had used the terms, *'The clock is ticking'*, *'It's later than you think'* and *'You only live once'* a number of times.

The coastal town of Portstewart had grown exponentially since Eban had first visited as a boy.

The result of the University of Ulster locating in nearby Coleraine and the upsurge in avaricious property developers overreaching themselves with holiday home provision.

Out of season the town maintained a busy enough frisson, thanks in large amount to the off-campus student body and faculty members who had located there.

At this time of year, the sea thundering in from the North Atlantic could be breathtakingly awe-inspiring and sat in dramatic juxtaposition to the quaint, well-tended shop fronts and civic gardens.

Almost annually there were drownings.

Reports of drunken students – habitually male – exiting from a session at the Sea Splash Hotel (aptly named) and venturing out onto the rocks for a better view of the colossal waves which hammered down, throwing spray and suds out over the roads and footpaths.

The currents and tows were pitiless.

When a body was eventually recovered, it invariably was weeks – sometimes months – later, and likely it washed up bloated in Donegal Bay or some other coastal inlet miles away in the Republic.

The holiday town of Portrush was some three miles further on down a windy, twisting stretch of coast road used for the yearly Motorcycle 200 races.

Established for many years as a popular destination for 'townies' from Belfast to vacation, Portrush maintained something of the 'kiss-me-quick', 'dodgems and big dipper' ambiance that had made it so popular in its heyday.

But out of season, the town felt old and tired.

Sea salt eroded metal fairground attractions and scarred and pockmarked the garish signs offering fish and chips and free shots with every pint.

Wind and rain whipped through the empty rides, rattling chains and clanking metal seats against their housings.

The drive into the town was flanked on both sides by some of the most impressive golfing real estate in the country.

Emily was taking the demanding hairpin corners carefully.

She was a conscientious driver and studiously observed the obligatory 'hands at ten and two o'clock' and 'mirror, signal, manoeuvre' protocols.

It was when pulling out to overtake a learner driver that she noticed again the silver BMW 6 Series in her rear view mirror.

She remembered the same or a similar car pulling out

behind them when they had first left Belfast. She vaguely noted that the front-seat passenger wore a bright red sweatshirt, as it had caught her eye.

Now here was the same make of vehicle and the same brightly-clad front-seat passenger a little distance behind them on the North Antrim coast.

Emily never gave this a second thought.

It was perfectly feasible that there were a half-dozen or more cars with red-shirted passengers on the roads that day. Even within the realms of coincidence that these travellers had left from their very own street on exactly the same journey as themselves.

She had no inclination to mention this to Eban, who was going on somewhat in an entirely atypical manner about not leaving goals, dreams or ambitions unfulfilled.

Most unlike him, she thought.

Besides, he would only chide her that she was paranoid and that living in Belfast for too long can do that to you.

Eban directed her to the White Rocks Beach, a long, pristine stretch of sandy strand.

The wind was whipping in at a pace and although the sky looked ominous, the rain had all but ceased. It was virtually deserted now but for a few hardy surfers in wetsuits and a pensioner throwing a tennis ball for his dog.

They had come prepared, each donning a heavy outdoor coat, scarf and hat.

"Do you remember the last time we were here?" he asked. He moved to link her arm and pull her closer but she lightly resisted this and walked a few paces in front of him.

She said something he couldn't hear, the wind taking her words and carrying them by him.

"What?" he yelled.

She turned around to face him. "That was then…" she yelled above the breakers.

And this is now, he finished the sentence in his mind.

Something had changed about Emily, he thought.

This wasn't about playing hard to get.

She was being standoffish.

But more than that.

She was *resolved*, he considered.

She had crossed some rubicon or other and she did not intend to come back from it again.

Although both carried on walking in silence, their thoughts did indeed return to the first time they had visited here together.

It was in summer, in the early weeks of what passed for a courtship between them.

Eban was enjoying his role as unofficial tour guide, showing this English girl the sights. Choosing only those that held an emotional resonance for him personally, and sharing these with her in a more intimate fashion than both were perhaps aware of.

Bonding in a way that he was not prepared to admit to himself.

They had just slept with each other for the first time the night before, and whilst rendered a little awkward through a lack of adequate foreplay, it had undoubtedly brought them closer together.

Caught up in what might have been the first flowerings of a relationship, Eban went a little over the top that day.

She had lost a leather pump shoe in the sand and retrieving it, he pretended to throw it into the waves, dropping it deliberately at the arc of his swing.

Then in a completely unexpected action, he scooped her up in his arms and carried her into the surf, wading in fully clothed, up to his knees.

She screamed with laughter and mock alarm as he

threatened to put her down in the surf, but carried her back to safety on the sand.

They had kissed then and there, his hands buried in her streaming hair, holding each other close and tight as two young boys passed by eating ice cream cones and giggling.

If there had ever *definitively* been a moment when Emily felt that she might be falling in love with Eban Barnard, then that was it.

But today they walked in silence and apart from each other.

He throwing small stones into the breakers, she occasionally pocketing a colourful shell here and there.

Both quietly reflecting on the mixed messages that day in summer had given them.

They had clung together so fiercely, kissed so passionately because of their fear, their loneliness, their longing, their disappointment.

Here today, it was achingly, irrefutably clear that neither had been able to stop the other's suffering.

Eventually it began to rain.

"Are you ready to go back?" she asked. As if impartially, coldly inquiring as to whether he had satisfied whatever notion had brought the two of them out here in the first place.

He knew the moment had come when he would have to find the courage to love her. If it was not already too late to do so.

Both his mother and father had been sentimentalists and throughout his youth he had unconsciously modelled himself emotionally on them.

His father with tears in his eyes, singing to his mother some Jim Reeves or Slim Whitman song – *"If I had my life to live over... I would still fall in love with you..."*

His mother, outwardly less demonstrative, but a devotee of romantic novels and enamoured of Christmases, family and self-sacrificing dignity in the face of tragedy.

It never seemed that it took much to get them going and as he grew older, Eban began to harbour suspicions that this easy emotionalism was being deliberately cultivated as a controlling mechanism. Something resembling a passive-aggressive manipulation of his own feelings.

Histrionics and operatic levels of worry and grief were not uncommon, but all provoked by selfless love and concern of course.

This rendered him suspicious of the maudlin, but left him open both to emotional manipulation by others and capable of it himself.

Therefore, as he looked at Emily now, solitary and vulnerable, her hair being whipped around her face by the wind; the waves crashing on the beach behind her and then being pulled back out to sea, he could not answer her.

Could not tell her he was ready to go back.

Rather, he just turned around in the direction of the car and began walking.

They drove back in silence to their Bed and Breakfast accommodation in Portstewart.

On reaching the edges of town, Emily – distracted somewhat by the growing distance between them and the prospect of the coming evening – took a wrong turn at one of the many roundabouts on the outskirts.

This led her to exit prematurely and drive the wrong way up a one-way street and into oncoming traffic. With horns blaring and headlights flashing all around her, Emily panicked. She slammed the brakes on hard, almost catapulting Eban through the windscreen. He was jerked back violently by his seat belt.

She threw the car into reverse gear and quickly checked that the path was clear in her rear-view mirror.

She was surprised to see the same silver BMW reversing away from them at speed.

She could clearly make out the driver, front and back-seat passengers looking over their shoulders and behind them as their car hurtled backward and away from Emily.

This time there could be no mistake.

The man in the front wore the red hooded sweatshirt she had noticed both times before.

They must have been following Emily and Eban closely to have made the same mistake and travelled some distance along this one-way system.

A lapse in concentration on their part, perhaps, but their cover was blown.

When she had righted the vehicle Emily pulled over to the side of the road.

She was shaking and close to tears. Irate drivers slowed down to glare in and to shake fists as they pulled level.

"Are you okay?" asked Eban, rubbing at his collarbone where the belt had bitten.

"Yes... yes... I'm alright. Eban, listen – this is going to sound crazy, but..."

Emily explained all about their perceived trackers, about the man in the red top and about the unlikely coincidence of it all. She was half-surprised when Eban did not routinely dismiss all this out of hand as nonsense.

"It's been a strange week for me." he said. "I have some information that some people may want kept quiet."

Emily looked at him as if he was joking. When she could tell that he was not, she was deeply perturbed.

"What? What are you talking about?"

When he looked away out of the car window and remained silent, she pleaded with him.

"Eban, you're scaring me."

It was getting dark now.

On the remaining drive back to Portstewart her mind was in turmoil.

Who was this man beside her?

What did she really know about him after all?

What might he be involved in?

Perhaps Rosemary Payne had been correct all along.

For a man of his age, he seemed to be without ties, family, friends… it just didn't seem right.

They pulled into a small public parking facility some yards away from their accommodation and unloaded their overnight bags from the boot.

Walking toward the guest house, Emily suddenly grabbed his arm.

She whispered out of the side of her mouth. "Don't turn around… *there it is again!*"

The silver BMW car sat parked in shadow at the side of the road, some short distance from where they had alighted.

"Keep walking and let's get checked in," said Eban and steered her onto the footpath and toward the guest house.

They walked up the path and rang the bell.

An elderly woman shuffled toward them, smiling. She opened the inner double-glazed doors and motioned them to come in.

Both did so, but all at once Eban turned on his heel and walked back down the path to the street. Emily turned around, puzzled, and stood in the doorway.

He looked back down toward where they had parked their car and saw two men walk around it, shining a pocket torch through the windows and crouching low to peer inside.

"Stay there!" he ordered Emily and made his way toward them, walking purposefully and at pace down the centre of the road.

On seeing this, both men quickly ran to their car and jumped inside.

The powerful engine roared into life.

The headlamps flashed onto full beam.

The car pulled out violently and screeched at speed toward Eban.

He stood stock still in the middle of the road with his arm extended and hand raised like some mythic custodian.

Blinded by the lights, awaiting the impact.

Welcoming it.

The car shrieked to a halt three feet in front of him.

Eban was shaking violently.

He walked around the side and leaned lower.

The electric window on the driver's side droned down.

"Can I help you, officers?" said Eban as calmly and as acidly as he could muster.

"Don't know what you mean, mate," said the driver. He had an English accent.

The other man in the front seat laughed a little to himself and looked straight ahead.

"Don't they teach you anything about surveillance, you wankers? Tell your friend there if he wants to stalk somebody then better not to do it in a bright red jumper!"

"Don't know what you mean, mate," said the driver again.

"Look, if you want me to come back to the station then just ask, okay... there's no need for all of this..."

The big man who had been taking up most of the back seat leaned forward into the semi-light. He was well dressed in a sports jacket, shirt and tie.

Eban could see the moles and warts on his face.

His bulbous nose, red with broken vessels.

His hair thinning and combed over.

His scalp flaking.

"You're the boy who can't keep his trap shut."

"And you are...?"

"You'll know soon enough, Barnard... you'll know soon enough," was all he said.

He sank back into the shadows again. "Go!" he barked.

The car took off at high speed.

It swept by Emily, who had followed him and now stood some steps behind.

She had heard it all.

The veiled threat. The implied menace.

She had seen that ogre of a man.

He had looked straight into her eyes as the car passed by.

Later, she refused to get undressed.

He had kept his word and reserved single beds.

But she refused to go to bed.

She sat up all night long.

Wrapped in a shawl and drinking tea made with the small kettle in the room.

Wondering if they would come back in the night?

If they were at 15 Donnybrook Avenue right now?

Going through Eban's belongings?

Through her own?

Her eyes closing. Jerking awake when a car door slammed outside, or another guest walked down the corridor.

Eban offered nothing by way of explanation.

Nothing that might help her understand, or allay her fears.

Instead he just complained vaguely of some pains, gulped down some pills from an unfamiliar prescription bottle, turned to the wall and went to sleep.

If she had previously been in any doubt, then all that had now changed.

Her flight to Heathrow was already booked.

She would be attending for interview at Dudley Primary School at 4pm on Monday afternoon.

52

Dan Watson couldn't focus on the task at hand.

A rudimentary review of his section workload allocations.

These tiers of middle-management bureaucracy seemed more multifarious and byzantine than back in the good old, bad old days.

Endless self-evaluations to be completed online.

Time and motion studies by any other name.

Usually a prerequisite to cuts and redundancies.

Now they wanted you to justify your usefulness by itemising your working day down to the last minute. Then to produce pie charts and graphs at the push of a button, generated from software he couldn't understand.

He felt ancient.

He could see the age profile of the force change in front of his very eyes.

He would have liked to consider his pension options but knew he would miss the overtime benefits.

Besides, although the kids had grown up and moved away, that didn't seem to reduce overdraft payments from the 'Bank of Dad'.

And the wife still expected her three foreign holidays a year. It had somehow become part of their unspoken contract.

So things ground on relentlessly through the same old, same old.

Because it was just easier that way.

This business with Helen Totton had unsettled him, no question.

It had made him believe for a short while that he might have a second act in him.

Before he was past it and put out to pasture.

That he could reinvent himself in some way that might allow him to start again.

A second bite of the cherry.

Plenty of people had done it at his age. Or so he'd heard.

But Officer Helen Totton now seemed to be disavowing him of that particular pipe dream in no uncertain terms.

Why hadn't she returned his texts or calls?

It was like she was ignoring him.

Like nothing had ever happened between them.

Overnight it seemed like she had vanished from off his radar entirely.

No more 'chance' meetings in the records hall.

No more impromptu, unannounced visits to his office.

No more after-work drinks.

It had got so that he couldn't settle, couldn't concentrate.

Thinking every internal phone call, every ping of his mobile phone, every footfall approaching his door was her.

Christ, he couldn't believe it! He was acting like a lovelorn kid!

If something had changed he wanted to know why.

If things were to be wound up between them, dismissed as a fling, fun while it lasted, then he wanted to be the one pulling the plug.

Surely it was his prerogative.

He'd always imagined it would be that way.

Now he was hearing on the grapevine that she and Constable Charlie Maxwell, a divorced father of two from County Tyrone, were a hot ticket.

Seeing a lot of each other apparently, and for some time now by all accounts.

His pride hurt like a teenager's. He felt silly and stupid but he couldn't help it.

And now this!

One of the secretaries had come to him with a sheet of paper she'd found left behind accidently on the photocopier glass.

It was the last sheet of their file on the Eban Barnard interview and it contained his signature as interviewing officer.

The secretary had brought it to him, believing that he may have inadvertently left it there.

He instantly knew he hadn't.

Such sloppiness wouldn't have been like him.

The file was classified confidential, and given the information it contained he would never have copied it, let alone left it behind in a public area.

So who had?

He exited his office and went straight to the records room, requesting the sign-out book.

Flipping through the last two days' entries, he located the Barnard file code and sliding his finger across to the corresponding signature on the opposite page, his heart froze.

Signed out by Const. Helen Totton; 5.25pm. Signed in by Const. Helen Totton; 5.47pm.

What the fuck is going on? he asked himself.

Dan Watson tried again to reach her now, with a considerable degree more urgency and no little anger.

He did so adopting the most officious tone he could take, and whilst not wanting to go into any details in the email, felt that he left her in no doubt as to the necessity of contacting him urgently. He even used the term *'insubordination'*, and signed the communication with his formal title.

At the back of his mind though, he wondered whether he didn't quite enjoy the opportunity to pull rank under the circumstances of their estrangement.

He might yet have the final word, the last laugh, regain some semblance of control.

Recoup his hard-pressed dignity in the matter.

But none of that explained her behaviour with the Barnard file, and that matter was beginning to push his bruised ego into the ha'penny place.

When she didn't reply, he quickly followed up with an SMS message to her iPhone.

His tone was softer, more of an appeal than an order, but he did mention the distinct possibility of disciplinary action, should an outstanding matter of protocol breach not be addressed.

His phone pinged almost immediately with a response from her.

Try it… and see what happens.

Attached to the communication was a grainy photograph of his face screwed into a gurning mask as he ejaculated over her tits.

53

22 Rosapenna Street looked virtually identical to the row and rows of new-builds that surrounded it.

Fixtures and fittings were modern and utilitarian, but residents sought to bring their own sense of place with the addition of white balustrades in gardens, hanging plants, carriage wall lamps and overly ornate wrought iron gates.

A few gable walls had *Free Dan O'Neill* and *Happy 21st Bridget* spray-painted on them as if performing the role of a municipal message board.

The private lives of every resident seemed to play out behind vertical blinds, the modern alternative to old-fashioned net curtains. They flickered like inverse cinema screens with flashing images projected from gargantuan LED TVs.

Satellite dishes popped out of house fronts like toadstools.

A people pacified through hash and bread and circuses.

"They don't build slums you know… they make them," Archie Adams was fond of saying back at the office.

The Housing Executive seemed to acknowledge that tenants invariably looked after their properties more conscientiously if they resembled modern versions of the redbrick back-to-backs they had grown up in.

A little bit of garden front and back. And a decent spend on heating and insulation.

Social housing allocation had long been identified as the single issue that had galvanised the civil rights movement in the 60s, and by extension resulted in the onslaught of the Troubles themselves.

A succession of poor decisions reflecting UK housing policy in the 60s and 70s further exacerbated the problem, with large impersonal estates of tower blocks and maisonettes just aching to become 'no-go' areas from which guerrilla campaigns could be fermented and expedited.

The city fathers had learned a hard lesson, and now it was rumoured housing estates were planned with security force consultation in regard to exit and entry routes, with containment in mind.

Nowadays, even here in the Republican heartland of 'The Bone', some families still bought into post-Thatcherite aspirations of home ownership, purchasing their property from the authority and therefore, it was imagined, the civil responsibilities that went along with this.

The Breslin household differed from most of their neighbours in one significant respect.

A large square electrical transformer box sat squat in the space next to their house.

It was surrounded by rusting metal railings about four feet high, and contained a yellow warning stencil featuring a black triangle and a squiggly line supposed to denote a lightning bolt.

Danger. Electrical Current.

But this did not deter the local kids from scaling the fence and covering the box with graffiti and sometimes fly posters.

Just because it was there.

Just to show they could.

Anne Breslin worried that it would give all at number 22 terminal cancer.

Its insidious hum secreting invisible tumours into their bodies as they slept.

'*The Bone.*' The Marrowbone, or Macháire Botháin.

It was still a Republican stronghold, but the second coming

of this area was a far cry from the brooding warren of streets that Eban Barnard remembered as a boy.

Looking across the dark, empty playing fields and down onto the valley of brick back-to-backs, notorious for their self-declared autonomy.

He remembered murky nights in those playing fields, huddled around the dilapidated shell of the sports changing rooms, drinking illicit home brew with the other underage boys.

Then, it had all appeared to him as a dimly lit, moon-glow vista.

Smoulder rising from the chimney stacks in a grey pall and hanging low over the roofs. Cloaking the area ethereally in a translucent moon-mist, backlit by orange street lamp glow. Like burnished copper fire chasing silver smoke.

Now, as he stood outside the Breslins' front door, the memory of this caused him to recall a trip to the cinema. Something about simply walking into Mordor…Orcs and all.

Eban had simply walked into Greater Ardoyne.

He looked quickly around him.

It was past dusk, and properly dark.

Perhaps he should come back in the morning.

But since he had obtained Joe Breslin's name and address from Watson he could think of little else.

Joe Breslin was the last part of the jigsaw.

Could he really go another night without meeting with the man who had haunted his waking and sleeping hours for all of his adult life?

The fact that he had survived.

Was alive.

Flesh and blood.

Telling Joe Breslin that he had been there when it happened. *Actually been there!*

That he'd seen it all and knew who had done this terrible thing to him.

And that he'd run away and left him to die.

What might be achieved by such a reunion?

Repentance?

Forgiveness?

Since his diagnosis it had all seemed more urgent, if that were even possible.

All these thoughts tripped through his mind as he stood there summoning up the courage to knock on the front door of 22 Rosapenna Street.

Before he could move toward it however, he heard the sound of a chain being loosened and a bolt snapping back.

A thin, prim woman stood in the doorway.

She was too busy buttoning up her coat and rooting in her bag to notice him at first.

She had turned to pull the door closed behind her when he spoke.

"Oh… hello," said Eban rather timidly.

Anne Breslin jerked around suddenly, startled.

"God bless us and save us!"

"Sorry… sorry if I scared you there. Would Joe be in?"

She stared at him suspiciously, not responding.

"Joe? Joe Breslin? Am I at the right house?"

"Who's asking? Are you the police?"

"No, no… nothing like that." Eban realised that he hadn't thought this through.

Who indeed *was* he?

He saw from Watson's file that Joe lived with his mother and sister.

"Are you Joe's sister?"

Anne was angry now. "Look, the police were here earlier – you've no right to be harassing my brother like this!"

Eban was perturbed that the PSNI had apparently been here before him. He wondered what they'd said about him to Joe, if anything.

"I'm not police; I'm…" He paused, wondering what to say.

How to explain, standing here alone in the street. Trying to reach a man who he thought he'd seen murdered by his brother some forty-odd years ago.

It had begun to rain.

"I'm a journalist," he lied. "I'm an investigative journalist doing a programme on unsolved crimes. *Spotlight* – you've heard of BBC *Spotlight*, right?"

Anne looked at the stranger standing before her and was unconvinced.

The man seemed a little wild-eyed and a tad too desperate.

Not like someone with a professional detachment, there to do a job.

"My brother isn't seeing anyone," she stated firmly. "He's not interested and doesn't want all this brought up again."

She tugged the door handle toward her once to make sure the lock had engaged and turned to go.

"Please…" said Eban pathetically. He put out his hand to touch her arm but withdrew it before doing so.

Something in his tone made her pause and look back. The man had tears in his eyes. He looked like he was on the verge of breaking down.

To her complete surprise, it somehow touched her.

"What did you say your name was?"

"Barnard. Eban Barnard."

"Well Mr Barnard," she said with a little more empathy, "Joe has had a hell of a day with the police and all; he's not come out of his room. Maybe tomorrow—"

"I was there." He heard himself blurt it out… for better or worse.

"Excuse me?"

"The night it happened. *I was there.*"

Anne felt her insides tighten and freeze up. She took a few steps backward, clasping her hand to her chest.

"Who the hell are you... what do you want with us?"

She thought about making a run for Tommy Sweeney's house next door, but saw that the lights were off and he was out. She could make a grab for her mobile phone at the bottom of her bag... but call who?

"Look, mister... if I was you I'd get out of here while you still can; before I call somebody and—"

"I was eleven," pleaded Eban. "I was only a boy..."

Anne calmed down a little.

"Well, why did you wait until now to come forward?"

"I thought he was dead... I thought your Joe was dead..."

The rain beat down harder. Anne was overwhelmed and struggling to know how to react to all of this.

"Why don't you tell the police?"

"I did... but I don't trust them."

She looked again, hard, into his face. She liked to believe that she was good at reading people. Good at looking beyond the obvious.

"Why did you lie? Why did you tell me you were a journalist?"

"I don't know... what *could* I have said? I shouldn't have... " Eban looked away from her gaze and down at the ground.

She took a chance.

"I can't let you in the house; I can't let you talk to him. He's... delicate. Easily upset... you can imagine. Then there's my mother..."

"Then *you* listen to *me* and tell *him*... tell him... *for me*... *please*... *please*..."

Big tears rolled down Eban's face, obvious even in the rain that was hammering down.

Anne Breslin fished into her bag and found an umbrella. Opening it, she crossed closer to him.

"Well, don't stand there in the rain like an ejit! Get under this!"

He moved tentatively closer to her, pulling in his neck, scrunching up his shoulders, leaning in but careful not to touch her.

"We can go down to Henry Joy's for a coffee. It's just down the road," she said.

Eban smiled in gratitude and relief. He would have prostrated himself on the wet pavement in front of her if required to do so.

"I feel safe there," she said, reminding him of boundaries.

Making clear that this was her area.

Her domain.

Anne moved off with Eban trying to keep up, leaning in under the umbrella whilst clutching his collar at the throat.

54

Henry Joy's was a typical working class Belfast pub, and as such shared many of the facets of similar establishments in the North of England.

A large screen showing sports events, pool tables, gaming machines, dart board – it was set up for live Irish traditional music and karaoke later that evening.

The only significant differences from other hostelries were the framed declaration of Irish independence, the portraits of The United Irishmen and the Glasgow Celtic flags that adorned the walls.

As with most bars and clubs in the northern and western suburbs of segregated Belfast, it never took long to ascertain which side of the fence you found yourself on.

The pub was relatively quiet when they entered.

Just two or three men dotted around the place, variously sipping pints of porter or lager and studying the racing form.

The barman acknowledged Anne right away.

"Hi Patsy," she called. "Two coffees please."

Eban could see Patsy and a couple of the customers clock him.

Anne noticed this too and flushed a little.

She had never been in here before with any man other than her brother.

If only they knew what brought her here now with this unkempt, dishevelled-looking stranger. She steered her way through the tables to the back of the bar where it was dark and quiet, save for the rain beating down on the flat roof over their heads.

Patsy arrived at the table with the coffees.

"Do you think I could get a whiskey?" asked Eban "A Bushmills?"

"We've Powers and we've Jameson's," announced Patsy gruffly.

Eban, realising his faux pas, bit his lip. "Anything's fine, thanks."

He looked at Anne. "You don't mind, do you? It's been a hell of a few days."

He could see that she was studying him again. "Look, Mr Barnard… this isn't a social occasion," she chided. "Say what you came to say and I'll be on my way."

Eban Barnard proceeded to recount the whole story from start to finish, omitting only those details surrounding the incident with Joe that he felt were too much for his sister to hear.

At no time did Anne Breslin interrupt or request clarification.

She simply sat there listening, the only indication of emotion being when her eyes grew wider here and there at some detail or other. But she kept any strong feelings she might have had held firmly in check.

Eban related the incidents in a completely different manner to how he had done with Detective Inspector Watson.

After holding on to his secret for so many years, he had now recounted it to two strangers in almost as many days.

When he spoke to Anne he did so cognisant of the fact that he was speaking to Joe Breslin's sister.

To a proxy for Joe himself.

He found that it came out easier.

He found that for once, this was not about him.

When he had finished they sat in silence for a long while. Both simply staring at the table in front of them whilst the slot machines whirred and bleeped quietly across the bar.

When she eventually spoke he was surprised by what she said.

"And what happened to Sinéad and Ruairí?"

It had not been the reaction he'd expected, and it threw him somewhat.

He had just told this woman that he had witnessed her brother's terrible assault, that his own brother had been responsible, that his own carelessness led directly to that brother's murder and that the police might even now be colluding in covering the whole thing up.

And yet she had inquired only about the well-being of others.

Strangers she had never met.

This woman's compassion was heartening.

She had come here with him – a man unknown to her – to hear his story and without judgement. Now she seemed to show understanding for the blighted lives of these two young outsiders.

"It doesn't end well," Eban sighed.

"That's been my experience," she said wearily and with a half-smile.

He saw how it instantly changed her face.

"When I tried telling Ruairí what had happened – about Anto leaving I mean – he was adamant we keep it from Sinéad.

'I'm going out after him… it's me they want,' he said.

"I grabbed his arm. 'What would that achieve? You can't… Anto made me promise not to let you go.'"

"Ruairí just said that he didn't believe me; said it wasn't Anto's style.

"I asked him not to go, for Sinéad's sake… for the sake of the child. He laughed at that.

'I believe, Mr Barnard, the polite terminology is *cuckold*. Although around here we just say, *cheating wee whore*,' he explained.

"Some things made more sense to me after that of course, but in case I didn't get it, he added, 'Well, when you're buying your girl chocolates and your best mate's fucking her it kinda puts a different perspective on things…'"

Anne Breslin looked uncomfortable with the language Eban was using, but he didn't seem to notice. "Why did he go along with it?" she asked.

"That's what I said," cried Eban. "'If you knew, why were you going through with the wedding; why were you all playing out this… this… *charade*?'

'Less people get hurt that way,' he said. 'Things can stay the way they were.'

'And the baby…?' I asked him.

'It's Anto's of course… we never mentioned it, but I'm sure he knew that I knew. Anyway, that's why he's out there now… some fucked-up *mea culpa*…'

'No… it's more than that – he… loves you… like a brother," I told him.

"Ruairí laughed at me. 'Ha! Like the older brother I never had. Except I did of course… didn't I, Eban?' He told me he remembered the first time he noticed – *really* noticed – it was a Halloween party. 'The big ejit went in a white sheet with Brussels sprouts stuck all over it…'

Eban smiled. "I remember Ruairí was laughing now as he was telling me.

'He went as a snotty handkerchief of course. She went as a little devil… even had horns and a tail. God… she looked like sex on legs… stunning, ya know? As usual… at the centre of everything… she can't help that, it's just her way; she drinks in the attention, but she uses it to manipulate people… In a way I don't blame her – don't blame Anthony either; he just can't keep it zipped up... never could. They were dancing together... more than usual... something between them – of course, the more he drank, the louder he got.*What are you doing with him? You should be with me* – innocent enough really, but there was something more in it... he's such a fucking competitor where women are concerned, you know? She never meant anything to me; *he* means more to me than any of that... he's my mate. He's worth ten of her.'

"I told him that Anto wanted them both to make a go of it across the water, with the kid... I think he saw it as the best end to all of this," said Eban.

"Sinéad came back in about then... she'd been sleeping. 'God, I went out like a light and still feel exhausted... where is everybody? Where's the Italian scallion?' she asked.

"Ruairí gave me a look. 'He's gone,' he said.

"She got a bit alarmed. 'Gone? How can he be gone... gone where?'

"Ruairí gave me that look again. 'Sly bastard,' he told her. 'Made arrangements with Conor McVey and Eban here to slip out with a few of the FAIT ones, to... where, Eban... Scotland?'

"I picked up the thread of course. 'Scotland, yes...' – Ayr, I think I said. All set up... best to do it this way... easier to go unnoticed.

"She was clearly hurt. 'But he never said anything... never said goodbye...'

'You know what he's like, Sinéad: does what he wants, when he wants,' Ruairí told her.

'Just need to get you, Ruairí and the baby out the same way,' I added.

"He glared at me. 'That's still to be agreed.'

'Then let's get it agreed,' she said. 'We can always send for Anto when we get settled, isn't that right Eban...?'

'I don't see why not,' I told her. Well, what could I say?

315

"She seemed pleased at this. Like it was over at last. 'D'ya hear that Ruairí: Eban agrees. Look, they've won, Ruairí… they always win. Leave it be… let it go… nobody cares. They've won.'

"Ruairí wasn't having any of it. '*I* care,' he said. 'There's a dishonourable tradition of Connollys taking the boat, for as far back as you want to go. Frankie went there; he was just about my age… he was gonna be somethin'. Losing yourself in the drink and the songs… we're all monsters to them anyway; you know about that, right Eban?'

"I felt like I was being pulled back and forward between them. Each wanted me on their side."

Eban took a drink from his glass and swished around the remainder in the bottom.

"Sineád wasn't listening to either of us. She'd gone to the window and pulled back the blind. She seemed to be smiling… talking to herself. 'Anto, you cute hoor… I might have guessed…'

"We'd all said it so many times by then that it just came out automatically.

'Sineád, come away from the window.'

'It's getting light,' she said. 'The moon is hiding… the stars are hiding too…'

"All Ruairí said was, 'Jesus… I could go a pint.'

"I remember she looked straight at him. 'You never see the sky anymore, Ruairí – you've always got your baseball cap pulled down—'

"It happened so quickly after that. Suddenly, high and to her right, there was the crash of broken glass and a thud. I looked down and saw the red snooker ball roll across the floor in a little arc and come to rest against her foot. She bent down to pick it up and held it up to show us. She tilted her head in curiosity… the way a child might do…"

Eban could see from Anne Breslin's face that she knew what was coming.

316

"We both screamed at her: 'GET AWAY FROM THE WINDOW!' but it was too late. Just as she realised the danger, the window exploded all around her, showering her with broken glass and snooker balls. I'll never forget the image of her raising her hands to protect herself and the baby... never."

"Merciful Jesus," whimpered Anne.

"'Anthony!' she screamed. '*Anthony!*'"

Eban shook his head at the memory. "I never told any of that to the police, you know... it's nobody's business but their own."

As he drained his third whiskey, Anne Breslin could see that this man was suffering.

Would probably suffer for the rest of his life.

The bar was filling up with evening punters, many of whom could not resist a look in the couple's direction, eager to see Anne Breslin's new man.

"I need to get back to my mother and our Joe," said Anne.

"And will you tell him you met me... that we talked?"

"Look Mr Barnard, I can't promise you anything. He's been in a terrible state since them policemen called... keeps going on about somebody called 'Fish'."

At first it didn't register with Eban.

He was crestfallen that despite everything, Joe Breslin's sister might still yet not seek absolution on his behalf.

Then it hit him. "What... *what did you just say?*"

"That I can't promise you—"

"No, not that – that name: *Fish*."

"What about it?"

"I've only ever heard it used once before: on the night that they... hurt your brother."

Anne Breslin went ashen. "You can't mean... you don't believe he was here today...with our Joe... oh my God!" She put her hand up to her mouth in alarm.

317

"Do you know anyone of that name?"

She wasn't listening. Her mind was in turmoil. "Is he a policeman as well, like your brother?"

"I don't know... it could be nothing. Maybe just a coincidence."

She stood up, knocking against the table, making it squeal across the floor as she pushed her seat back. "I have to get back to him. Oh my God, poor Joe!"

Eban was concerned that he had distressed her. "I want to help if I can."

"Haven't you done enough, bringing all this back to our door?"

Eban had been trawling the dark recesses of his memory for things deliberately abandoned there.

Compartmentalised.

Ignored, because to do otherwise was to return to *that* night.

To the pub.

In the dark.

Listening to Joe Breslin's screams.

He thought of Alex's many friends.

A braying, cart horse of a young man with bad skin and wild yellow hair.

Anne turned to go, then stopped abruptly and raised a hand as if divining something from the atmosphere around her.

"Wait... I work in the City Hall; there's a Councillor Henning... Hemingway... something thing like that. I think I've heard people call him—"

"Herringshaw," Eban said. "His name is Cecil Herringshaw. People call him Fish."

55

Pascal Loncle was in his element.

It had taken the last evening and most of today, but it was worth it.

Mackerel on toast with salted cucumber and horseradish for starters.

This to be followed by Moroccan fish stew.

Then to conclude, chocolate mousse with fiery ginger shortbread and candied orange peel.

Arabic coffee and amaretti biscuits for afters.

As a Frenchman he felt a certain obligation where the wines were concerned.

And in truth, his trepidation regarding the paint stripper that his guests might pitch up with reinforced his belief in the necessity for total control of proceedings.

He had chosen a perfectly respectable 2010 Chateau Ste. Michelle dry Riesling, and pushed the boat out a little on a showy 2011 Pinot Blanc d'Alsace.

He was on a tight budget. The reds had proved more problematic.

The Terres Dorées Beaujolais l'Ancien Vieilles Vignes was good with both meat and fish.

But he had gone to the New World for a Californian Pinot Noir, and now worried about the wisdom of his choice.

Fortunately, he had always kept a well-stocked drinks cabinet in his room.

It was one of the things that gave him that debonair, continental *joie de vivre* that so impressed Emily and Rosemary.

He had a German Eiswein and a Vin Santo from Tuscany for dessert wines.

One of his own concoctions, an Earl Grey martini, would get the evening kicked off splendidly. Then later, and at the appropriate time, a Lini Labrusca Rosso Lambrusco in lieu of champagne.

After all, he reasoned, his 'coming out' announcement was something that merited a toast.

Pascal moved around the place settings that he had arranged, straightening cutlery and re-folding napkins.

The large kitchen table had been dragged into his room and placed alongside his work desk, making an admirable dining space when covered by his quality linen table throw. But it would be a tight enough squeeze, elbow to elbow.

A pewter candelabra that had been in his family for years made a splendid centrepiece.

As he stood in the glow from the candles he could not escape the notion that it would all ultimately prove to be pearls before swine. He could have enjoyed the dinner party so much more had he invited Andreas and Luis from college.

But Pascal had always been fastidious in keeping his private life and home life separate and he was not about to change that now.

Save for his emancipatory declaration of course.

Now, on the threshold of his announcement and subsequent departure for a new life far from the parochial prudery and small-mindedness of Northern Ireland, his spirits dipped a little.

In a way he felt sorry for them.

Rosemary would never move on beyond the narrow parameters of library, church and parlour that defined her existence.

Emily was just too indecisive for her own good and would continue to fret about the road not taken until all roads ended in a single impasse.

And Eban Barnard seemed like an angry, sad man who could just as easily slip between the cracks and find himself on the streets, homeless and friendless.

It would be his treat.

His parting gift to them.

His '*Babette's Feast*'. A celebratory, revelatory farewell.

He assumed that a primarily fish-based meal was the safest option.

To listen to Rosemary Payne, it was clear that she liked to think of herself as quite the *bon viveur* in matters of cuisine.

Although Pascal had observed no evidence of this, based on the stodgy lentil-and-pasta concoctions she cooked and consigned to the freezer compartment.

Emily had claimed repeatedly that she was in fact vegetarian.

But Pascal had observed her eating bacon butties and chicken salads on a number of occasions.

Her concept of what actually constituted 'meat' appeared highly selective.

Eban Barnard, it seemed, would eat anything put down in front of him and appeared to have a particular penchant for kebabs, pizzas and Indian takeaways.

Pearls before swine indeed!

He stirred at his fish stew, simmering away in the large ceramic casserole dish, and took off the kitchen apron that was protecting his evening wear.

A broad navy pinstripe with open-neck shirt and scarlet cravat.

A quick check of his watch confirmed that his guests were due within the next half-hour.

He plated up the mackerel on toast and delicately arranged the garnishes of salted cucumber and horseradish in the most decoratively appealing style.

It had been an overcast, barren kind of Sunday.

The kind that Belfast seemed to do so well.

The prayers and doleful hymns of the German Lutheran congregation below permeated the house, the wind-driven organ whining away as air was forced across its reeds.

The day would have dragged like so many other Sundays had he not been so busy in the kitchen.

The others had kept to their rooms, save for Rosemary, who had left to attend a church service with the local Anglican congregation; something she did periodically throughout the year. Pascal suspected that it helped her maintain a sense of her Home Counties Englishness, despite her protestations to the contrary.

Eban had left and returned early with the Sunday papers, as was his wont.

Emily moved back and forward in her room above, as if singularly engaged in a task that involved moving items from one location to another.

Perhaps from wardrobe to suitcase?

Inevitably it was Rosemary who arrived first, and ahead of time.

Her cheeks were flushed, either with excitement, an afternoon sherry or too much make-up.

"Ooooo Pascal," she enthused wafting air up to her face in a demonstrative and theatrical manner, "the smells… *the smells!*"

"Ahh, Rosemary… you are most welcome… let me take that from you…"

He gestured to the tartan Irish tweed wrap that she was wearing around her shoulders and she struggled to release the gold pin brooch that fastened it at her neck.

Eventually doing so, she produced a bottle from its depths and handed both to Pascal.

"It's from my best ever batch… I've been saving it for a special occasion."

She handed over a bottle of her elderflower wine, lovingly cultivated earlier that summer in the small shed at the bottom of the garden.

It had been decanted into an old Black Tower Liebfraumilch bottle, and she had tied a red ribbon around the neck.

Pascal took it from her gingerly, all the while feigning reverence and gratitude. "*So* kind... *so* kind."

While she busied herself flagrantly looking around his room, he slipped it surreptitiously behind the fire screen.

"My word, what a great pleasure it is to at last be invited into the *sanctum sanctorum* of Dr Pascal Loncle!"

"Not quite Doctor yet Rosemary... I have my *viva voce* in a few weeks and—"

"Oh, you'll fly through that, darling," she admonished, placing a hand on his arm and letting it stay there. "I just know you will."

"Perhaps you'd like to try an aperitif before dinner?" he asked, moving to the drinks cabinet.

When he crossed back with her martini, he noted that Rosemary had changed the handwritten place settings around so as to be sitting opposite him.

Pascal pretended not to notice, but died a little inside.

He had intended an altogether less demanding evening's social intercourse, conversing face to face with Emily Atkins.

Rosemary Payne took a sip of her cocktail and her features tightened into a delighted smile, rendering her appearance comparable to that of a podgy Chinese peasant boy.

"Mmmmm... this tastes divinely depraved. You must be wary of inebriated ladies in your rooms after dark, Dr Loncle." Her grin became ever more rictus. Her eyes disappearing entirely behind slits.

There was a knock on the door. *Thank God*, thought Pascal, and moved to open it.

He was well aware that his fellow housemates planned their movements around the place based on auditory information.

Like human bats they acted on what they heard from above, below or next door.

The toilet flushing and bathroom door closing might – following a decent pause for etiquette's sake – automatically solicit a flurry of activity from elsewhere in the house.

Footfalls on the stairs and the front door slamming would convey perhaps that the kitchen was now free.

So he fully expected to see Emily Atkins standing in his doorway, having for decorum purposes judged sufficient time to have passed since hearing Rosemary enter his room.

Instead he found Eban Barnard swaying a little and clearly just the right side of inebriation.

Eban stepped forward without saying a word and thrust out a hand in a rather formal manner. Pascal took it and the other man pumped enthusiastically whilst handing the host a bottle of Châteauneuf-du-Pape that he'd purchased in Tesco along with the *Sunday Times*.

"Pascal… good of you to have me," he said and stepped by him into the room.

"Come in, please…" Pascal said rather belatedly.

All of this rather perturbed the host.

In the first place, he had been unsure whether Eban Barnard would attend his party at all.

And as he had been working in the kitchen most of the day, he was fairly sure that Eban had not left since returning earlier with the newspapers.

Therefore, he would have had to be in his room, drinking alone all day.

Like a startled cat, Rosemary Payne stiffened immediately on seeing Eban.

She too had been expecting Emily.

"Oh... good evening Eban," she half-heartedly greeted him, and turned her back on him immediately, ostensibly to consult Pascal's bookcase.

"Good evening Mizzzz Payne," replied Eban, hoping that some reference to her marital status or a pun on her surname might further convey his barely concealed dislike of the woman.

Pascal sensed this immediately, and practised host that he was, sought to lighten proceedings.

"I do hope that you have brought good appetites with you?"

Eban crossed the room to where the man was standing. "I could eat a horse and chase the jockey!" he said, smiling and slapped Pascal heartily on the back.

Pascal laughed good-humouredly, hiding his surprise.

He had never seen Eban act like this before.

The alcohol seemed to have freed up some inhibitions in him and Pascal noted that he spoke now with a much more identifiable working class Belfast twang.

Rosemary rolled her eyes to the ceiling, hoping that Pascal would see this and so she would be vindicated in everything she had previously told him regarding the obvious shortcomings and thinly concealed vulgarity of their housemate.

"Eban, can I get you a drink?"

Pascal was about to move the party on by saying something witty about how he should really patent his famous Earl Grey martini when Eban spoke over him.

"Would you mind very much if I had a whiskey instead?"

Pascal followed Eban's gaze and saw that it was fixed on his slowly depleting bottle of Laphroaig ten-year-old single malt.

He silently cursed himself for failing to conceal this before his guests had arrived, and enthusiastically assured Eban that it would be no problem.

No problem at all.

They stood around facing each other in a small arc, variously looking into the bottom of their glasses or at their shoes.

The short silence seemed interminable.

Even though they had been housemates for a considerable period and had interacted with each other on any number of occasions on a variety of domestic issues, the incongruity of this social context seemed to render them momentarily incapable of social mores.

Each feared that they should be left alone with one of the others.

After a moment both Pascal and Rosemary spoke at the same time, both inquiring after Emily and her overdue arrival.

A little yelp of delight escaped Eban and he swirled the amber scotch in the bottom of his tumbler, a smile playing about his lips.

Pascal Loncle had the distinct impression that his guest was perversely enjoying these moments of self-conscious discomfort.

They all jumped a little when Emily knocked at the door.

As she entered and reached the table, clutching a pretty box of chocolates as a gift for Pascal and panting a little due to her lateness, the candlelight seemed to be caught and held by her skin, which appeared flawless and brilliantly translucent.

Immediately, all of her fellow diners were taken aback, as if seeing something in her for the first time.

The fatigue and worry of the last week had drained her so that she appeared delicately fragile and otherworldly in the trembling shadow and flame from the candles.

For a moment it seemed as if she might have sat for one of the Dutch Masters three centuries before.

Emily noticed that they were staring at her and self-consciously pushed back a lock of hair that had been pinned high but had fallen delicately across her face.

"Dear Emily... we were getting worried about you," clucked Rosemary and stepped closer to her, reaching up and tucking the offending lock behind her ear like a mother hen.

Emily stepped backward, just managing to resist an urge to raise an arm in protest. "Sorry everyone, I was busy... with *things*..." She tailed off.

"Might I suggest a little music?" offered Pascal, and hit the *play* button on his iPad.

A high clarinet refrain pierced the air as Benny Goodman and his big band joined the supper troupe.

"Oh, excellent choice as always Pascal," purred Rosemary as she sashayed a little on her toes, eyes closed, making the others feel uncomfortable. "We should pass a law that this is the only music to be played in the building!"

She looked directly at Eban when she said this, and he knew that she was referring to the evening some months back when – following a stand-up row with Rosemary over emptying bins or replacing toilet paper or some such – he had returned to his room and blasted the entire *Space Ritual* album by Hawkwind at full tilt.

Sure it was childish, but at the time it felt somehow like taking back control.

"I'm not sure that our Lutheran landlords would agree with that Rosemary... they were in good voice this morning."

It was Emily, who was also aware of that incident and had spotted the potential slight intended for Eban. She was good at that sort of thing. Reading the situation and saying the right thing at the right time.

"Shall we be seated?" suggested Pascal and all three took their places as he returned from the kitchen with the first course.

There was much oooing and ahhhing and general praise from the ladies.

"Does anyone feel like they're in an episode of *Come Dine*

With Me?" joked Eban, and took a healthy pull on his wine glass.

"I can't think what you mean," shot back Rosemary dismissively.

"Oh come on Rosemary, it's that TV show... you know... we've often talked about it," said Emily.

Rosemary glared askance at the younger woman and said with a steely tone, "No Emily... you must be mistaken."

The music paused before the next track began.

In the silence, in the moment, something passed between the diners.

For Pascal it signalled that his last-minute reticence toward having this event in the first place may not have been misplaced.

For Emily it was a reminder that there was clearly an alpha female in the room and it was most assuredly not her. Rosemary's matriarchal dominance was not going to be challenged in front of these men.

Only Eban did not feel cowed or apprehensive.

Given all that had gone before this week and all that was still to come, he no longer felt that he had anything to lose by failing to humour this harridan.

And although he did not take the bait at this precise moment in deference to Pascal and his hospitality, part of him seethed inside as he thought to himself, *bring it on, bitch!*

The Moroccan stew was delicious and was served with bowls of steaming hot, fluffy white rice and couscous.

Eban marvelled at his host's skill in seamlessly keeping the wine glasses charged and somehow disappearing to the kitchen to replenish the table with side dishes and breads, then reappearing effortlessly to add some quip or *bon mot* to the dinner conversation.

By the time the company were imbibing their dessert wine,

all of the awkward silences of the earlier evening had been eradicated, washed away on a fair tide of liquid conviviality.

As the four had few mutual friends, most of the conversation revolved around people in the news, the arts and current affairs.

By coffee, Rosemary was holding forth on the former evils of the Apartheid regime, and what lessons the South African peace process might have for Northern Ireland.

Pascal chided her gently that – this being Belfast – as a rule, he did not allow politics to be brought to the dinner table.

But Rosemary, who did not have a good head for alcohol, was in full swing. She then turned her attention to the topic of cultural identity.

"Now take *your* crowd…" she said, slightly slurring her words and pointing somewhat aggressively at Eban with a teaspoon.

"*My* crowd?" asked Eban, keen to hear what was coming next.

"Yes: the Orangemen… what's all this nonsense about turning the Twelfth of July into a carnival?" she snorted. "Orangefest or some such nonsense… really…"

She looked to Pascal and Emily, eyebrows raised. "Have you heard about this?"

"*My* crowd?" Eban repeated. This time with a hint of incredulity in his voice.

"All these protests… this flag-waving nonsense… the truth is, you have no culture of your own." She made it sound like a personal attack on Eban.

Pascal interrupted. "Has anyone been to see the new play at the Lyric?" He eyed the Lambrusco edgily. It was around now that he had hoped to make his grand revelation.

His efforts were in vain.

Rosemary was warming to her topic and it was clearly one she had exercised at another time, in other company.

"There does not exist – neither could there *ever* exist – any legitimate or worthwhile expression of a valid or meaningful cultural contribution emerging from the Ulster Unionist or Loyalist community."

Emily could sense where this was going and why.

"Come on now Rosemary, that's not very... *nice*." She winced on hearing herself use the term.

Rosemary did not extend her the courtesy of a reply.

Instead she turned her petition toward Pascal, a student of Art History and a learned man in her estimation. She cited as her logic for this pronouncement that – unlike, say, the great Protestant poets, playwrights and novelists who embellish the literary history of the Republic of Ireland – no repressive, sectarian or reactionary state could ever produce art or cultural expression of worthwhile or lasting merit.

As if by way of empirical evidence, a quick inventory was offered.

An entire pantheon of outstandingly successful musicians, writers and actors were presented, all of them first or second generation Catholic Irish and many of them drawing their very inspiration from the muse of Celtic mysticism, Catholicism, dispossession and suffering.

To further support this, she asked the company to consider if any enduring and influential artists had emerged from Apartheid Afrikaans society, the Zionist Israeli state or indeed Nazi Germany for that matter?

"No," she insisted, "great art in general, and edgy, subversive popular culture in particular, remain exclusively the unimpeachable birthright of the dispossessed, the revolutionary and the freedom fighter."

Eban had suffered this kind of liberal fascism many times before when living in London.

But to have to listen to it here, now, from this self-righteous, stuck-up cow...

It was just too much.

He knew from experience that any spirited defence on the matter would render him a bellicose Paisleyite and monarchist lickspittle... once he had left the room, naturally.

Instead, he forced a smile through gritted teeth.

He had some years ago reached the conclusion that he was to be forever held prisoner in the netherworld of the socially mobile.

Never being able to entirely return to his 'own'.

But never being fully accepted by people like those who now sat around the table.

When Eban eventually spoke, he surprised himself with the measured and calm tone that he managed to marshal. He held his hands aloft in mock surrender.

"Okay... you got me... I'm a member of the least fashionable community in Western Europe."

He turned toward Pascal and Emily, addressing them directly, hoping the insult was not lost on Rosemary.

Eban closed his eyes for a moment to gather his thoughts and then began falteringly.

"It is true that certain expressions of my – of our... of Protestant cultural identity could be taken as offensive... by the other side, I mean, and yes, Stormont was built on sectarian abuses of the Catholics, but there's another side to all of this... the collapse of heavy industry... the breakdown of working class neighbourhoods... the IRA terror campaign waged against them... not to mention their *own* organisations on their backs..."

The words just seemed to tumble out of him.

He could see they were impressed. They were listening to him now. A side he hadn't shown them before. It encouraged him to continue.

"... and in direct rule; in laws dumped on them over the last thirty years by – dear ladies – *the English.*"

He paused for effect. "Present company excepted of course."

"Go on," said Pascal, pulling the cheese board toward him. "Trying to explain this... this..."

He reached for the term, eyes closed in concentration.

"... this *experience* has proved a disaster. The 'flags' protests – just another example: legitimate concerns about a threat to political and cultural identity down the drain with the first bottle thrown at the police lines."

Christ, it was like an out of body experience. He heard himself speak but could barely believe it. He sounded like a bloody politician!

It was then he realised what had happened.

That he had somehow managed to mash together everything he'd been reading in the papers, watching on television news and listening to on the radio for the past number of weeks.

He seemed to have effortlessly and unconsciously consumed and now regurgitated them.

But with a clarity of thought and expression previously untroubled and now a revelation to his companions and indeed to himself.

And he was doing so in this perfectly cohesive and credible manner.

This was a talent previously unrecognised in him, and he was revelling in it.

For it was both the incongruity of his entreaty, plus the plausibility that he had brought to his delivery, that had rendered his dinner companions transfixed.

It just seemed to flow out of him.

It felt like a cocaine rush.

Rosemary Payne was having none of it.

"*No culture can live if it attempts to be exclusive. Mahatma Gandhi said that!*"

She spat this at him like it was some kind of deal-clincher.

That it somehow invalidated everything that he had said before.

He looked at her and grinned.

Despite all he had drank, his mouth felt as dry as sand.

He noticed for the first time that his shirt was sticking to his back with cold sweat.

He saw the smug conceit of her cosy certainties and comfortable allegiances, and in that moment decided to consciously and wilfully devalue all the rational capital he had just accrued.

It would be, after all, much in the manner of the community that he was even now seeking to defend, and what he imagined his dinner companions had *really* expected from him all along.

His people.

His tribe.

Council house loser.

Street-corner-boy scum.

Let's join the rush to the bottom.

Let's give them what they want.

"*And what the fuck would you know about it… you fat, dried-up, Fenian-loving cunt?*"

Boom!

Self-detonation.

With extreme prejudice.

Everyone's jaws hit the ground.

"And I'll tell you something else: all your pious, pointless research never saved one nigger!"

"My God, EB… how could you?!" cried Emily, horrified at this deliberate transgression of manners.

"Eban… Rosemary… *no…*" was all that Pascal could manage as he looked back and forth between the two, open-mouthed.

Rosemary was dumbstruck.

Eban noticed that his lungs felt like they were made of lead, and they protested angrily for lack of air by producing a lacerating pain across his shoulder blades.

But adrenaline was flooding his body.

He had allowed himself to be pulled back into the vortex.

Back down into the ancient enmities he had sought for years to rise above.

His left upper arm throbbed like a bad toothache.

Undeterred, he turned his fire on Emily.

"You don't belong here either... you haven't got a fucking clue."

Emily looked a little frightened, and very betrayed. "I know you've been having a difficult time Eban, but—"

Eban turned to Pascal, clammy, his shirt darkened with perspiration. White flecks of spit around the corners of his mouth.

"Did you know when Emily first arrived in Belfast, her very first day here – ecologically sound as ever, in that English-*Guardian*-liberal-guilt kinda way – she telephoned the Solid Fuel Advisory Board to complain about the air quality? *First fuckin' day...* and she was told yes, there was indeed a policy to promote smokeless zones in the greater Belfast area, and no, they had no immediate plans to take the culprits to task."

Emily pleaded. "Eban, don't..."

He had wanted to laugh in her face.

How could she know that this was just another one of those infuriating inconsistencies of civil society in Northern Ireland?

"She was livid, weren't you pet? 'He couldn't give me *one* good reason why no-one had been prosecuted'... that's what she told me – *Christ, three thousand dead and this is what she comes up with on her first day here!*"

Sweat was running into his eyes now and the salt burned and stung them.

He rubbed at them with his shirt cuffs.

He saw that Pascal was looking at him strangely.

Rosemary was gathering her things together in outraged mortification.

Eban stood unsteadily.

"Fuck, did she have a wakeup call coming... she still stiffens at the sight of an armed policeman, for Christ's sake. Where I came from no-one was prosecuted for filling the air with coal smoke and sulphur dioxide or for failing to pay a television licence, or car tax, or their fucking rates. Or for axing the neighbour's dog to death if it barked through the fucking night!"

"I'll show myself out," announced Rosemary, stung that her host had neither moved to her assistance nor defended her honour more robustly.

Eban ignored her, still speaking to the others. "Coal fires mucking up the environment? What would a couple of blazing cars and a bus do to it, then? What about the eleventh night bonfires – have you see the size of *those* fuckers?!"

"My God... I am *so* sorry for you... you are such a prisoner of the past," whispered Pascal.

Eban ignored him.

"I can see why you lot might think Belfast was just like any other big British city. Boots the chemist, Marks and Spencer's, HMV... but it's not, my friends... oh no... *it's not!*"

He reached for an open bottle of wine, sloshed the contents into his glass and onto the table, then gulped it back.

"I have an announcement to make," murmured Emily.

Pascal looked at her in puzzlement. "Actually, so do I..."

"I am leaving for home tomorrow morning for a job interview, and I intend to stay there until I get one – a job I mean. My rent is paid up to the end of the month."

Eban had been feeling nauseous.

Now the room was spinning.

Why hadn't she said something?

He wanted to talk with her alone.

He reached out a hand toward her and almost lurched into the drinks cabinet.

Bottles clinked and rattled and he swayed backward.

"Pascal… thank you for everything." Emily moved toward the door.

Again Eban tried to move toward her, tried to speak to her, but this time it felt like some unseen force was pushing him hard in the chest, backward, downward.

His back pressed against the far wall and he slid down it slowly, leaving a broad ribbon of wet sweat-mark the length of it.

Until he sat, wretched and rasping on the ground, gulping in air, his face the colour of gravel.

The others gaped at him.

"Can someone call me an ambulance please?"

"You're an ambulance," said Rosemary Payne, summoning up all the disdain and indifference she could muster, before turning and leaving the room.

As they strapped him onto the stretcher, the chirpy paramedic assured Eban that it was his lucky day.

"Had this been an ordinary ambulance call-out, mate, you'd be a goner. Lucky there was a rapid response cardio-crash team in the area. You can thank your French mate over there for that."

Pascal and Emily stood in the doorway of the house, washed by the flashing blue lights.

She, her arms folded tightly across her chest and shivering.

He still nursing a glass of cognac in his hands.

Despite the commotion of carrying Eban downstairs, the oxygen mask, the drip, the staccato barking of the men's walkie-talkies, Rosemary had resolutely remained in her room with the door closed.

No-one had felt it necessary or wise to consult her.

As he waited to be lifted into the ambulance, the paramedics had asked for next of kin.

Asked who would accompany Mr Barnard to the hospital?

No-one had stepped forward.

Pascal just looked awkward, whilst Emily muttered something about an early flight.

It might have cut him to the quick.

Or shook him hard.

But in truth, he felt relieved.

He could expect no more from them.

And in that moment he realised that he was, at last, truly and utterly alone.

And after all, hadn't he somehow been working his way toward this point for all of his life?

Emily returned briefly to the kitchen to retrieve her bag before leaving for her room.

Neither she nor Pascal quite knew what to say to one another, so they remained silent.

On the landing she paused and looked back to where she had left him.

To her surprise he seemed to be wrestling with the neck of a bottle which popped loudly, sending foam and spray into the air in a bubbling spout.

Pascal poured some into a flute and raised it in her direction.

"*I am gay!*" he proclaimed. "*Salut!*"

56

If you didn't know a man after thirty-five years of marriage to him... well... when would you ever know him?

Elaine Watson felt that she could read her husband like an open book.

She knew when he was worried about something. When he was bringing his work home with him and fretting about things that he could neither affect nor change.

When he was off-colour with an unspecified ailment but was keeping it to himself.

When he quietly beamed with pride at the accomplishments of their son and daughter, whilst in actuality wanting to proclaim it to all who would listen.

And when he was hiding something important from her.

Even though he had been largely left to attend to his own physical needs within the marriage for some time now (through, she assumed, pornography and Kleenex tissues), she had always believed that they had successfully navigated the uncertain waters of mid-life adultery.

Besides, she liked to feel that she was 'grown up' enough to overlook a minor misdemeanour if one arose. That an isolated fall from grace was best left uninvestigated for all concerned.

That said however, she was well aware of the self-delusion and self-serving fantasies that middle-aged men were capable of.

And that casual sex was one thing.

A passionate affair quite another.

So when Dan Watson began to arrive home most nights, smelling freshly showered and enveloped in deodorant, she was silently sceptical regarding his explanation that he'd been attending the police gym.

Of course she knew that her seeming indifference to his changing routine and behaviour would only encourage him to believe that he was getting away with it.

And thus become cocky.

And that's exactly how things transpired.

Clearly over-confident or indifferent, or simply rushed for time, he had arrived home some weeks ago reeking of the whore.

Dan had been passing by her in the kitchen on the way to his office-cum-den when she caught a whiff of it.

Unmistakeable.

She grabbed his arm and pulled him toward her.

"New shampoo?" she inquired with as much nonchalance as she could muster.

He reddened immediately, but secretly trusted that Elaine would not make an issue of it, believing that there was too much at stake to call his bluff.

He silently vowed to himself to be more conscientious in these matters.

It was only fair to her.

Not to flaunt Helen Totton in her face that way.

He would be the first to agree that she didn't deserve that. Good old Elaine.

Happy with her bridge and book clubs.

Her gardening, afternoon nap and G&T before dinner.

As Elaine Watson stood naked before the full length mirror in her steamy bathroom, she grabbed handfuls and lifted the drooping sachets of fat that hung down each side of her torso like saddlebags.

Turning full frontal, her ample breasts also swung low and

she cupped them and pushed them upward in defiance of age and gravity.

She noted the small pink crescent scar on her left breast, and was briefly reminded of the crisis some five years past when a tumour had been detected and removed.

Dan hadn't been very good about all of that.

For a resourceful man, able in a crisis, he was useless when it came to illness.

It was as if his way of dealing with these things was to ignore them completely.

And that had hurt her.

Hurt her deeply.

For it reinforced her fear that – despite the years given to him and to the family – she was destined to face life's catastrophes alone.

And so it was proving.

Elaine Watson believed that she had earned more than that from him.

That she had paid her dues.

She sat down on the edge of the bed and hid her face in her hands.

But no tears came.

She found it hard to remember what she had loved about her husband.

For so long now they had simply been little more than business partners in mortgages and life insurance policies of a done deal.

A marriage of convenience.

A pact for companionship into old age.

Or so she thought.

And now this.

Some younger woman no doubt, stroking his dick and his ego.

Men were such bastards!

Such stupid, infantile idiots and bastards.

It's the small things that matter, she thought. *They just don't get it.*

Elaine slipped her wedding and engagement rings back on over swollen, arthritic knuckles and smiled a little to herself, remembering her earliest reservations regarding her choice of life partner.

It had been only a matter of days after their wedding.

On honeymoon in Santorini.

They were young and in love and enjoying their first foreign holiday together.

He sat outside their apartment on the blindingly bright whitewashed steps, in the full glare of the Greek afternoon sun, waiting for her to join him.

His gaze was drawn away from the perfect azure sea to some movement down between his feet.

A beetle, attempting to scale the step, had fallen back and was struggling now, baking in the sun, trying to turn itself over.

By the time Elaine had joined him, he was gazing down, watching this life-or-death struggle dispassionately.

Elbows on knees, hands propping up his head.

The beetle was struggling more urgently now.

A thin line of ants had become aware of its predicament and were making their way toward the stricken insect.

Try as it might, it could not right itself.

"Oh Dan, help the poor thing... flip it over," she implored.

He smiled strangely. "I can't play God... what would happen if we weren't here?"

It had somehow upset Elaine. She thought he seemed to be enjoying it.

Like a schoolboy with a magnifying glass.

Dan stood up and walked away down a few steps.

He trailed a hand behind him, expecting her to take it.

She bent down and flipped the beetle over.

It scurried urgently for the shadows.

It had continued to bother Elaine all through dinner that evening but she never broached the matter with him again.

Yet it hinted at something about him previously unnoticed.

And it was a characteristic that would return many times in their married life.

When her mother died.

When Harvey, the family Retriever, had to be put down.

She had recognised it again, clearly, in his attitude to her cancer scare.

This cold fatalism that he could show at times when she expected compassion, understanding, empathy.

The desensitisation.

An occupational hazard?

Perhaps it was what made him a good policeman?

And her silence, her continuing compliance with this remoteness.

This indifference.

Did that make her a good policeman's wife?

Was that how she saw herself?

What she wanted to be?

Her sister and her family had been happily settled in Chipping Norton this forty-something years.

Got out early.

Pleaded with her, Dan and the family to join them.

She loved the Oxfordshire countryside and had gained a glimpse of how things might have been whilst on holiday there with the kids.

The ringing telephone roused her from her torpor.

Some magpies clacked noisily outside the open bathroom window.

Elaine could not shake the notion that something had run its course and was most assuredly coming to an end.

57

Helen Totton pulled on her white towelling dressing gown, pinned up her hair and returned from the ensuite bathroom to sit on the edge of her bed.

The muted TV was showing seemingly endless ads.

Her Twitter and Facebook accounts demanded attention, prompting her as they did with a number of notifications to address.

She ignored them.

She took a sip from her glass of white wine, lit a cigarette and pulled hard on it until the tip glowed orange.

Her request for leave had been approved. Herringshaw had greased the wheels…or at least that's what he'd told her.

A week of quality time alone, getting out of her head on prescription drugs and Chardonnay.

The spray tan she'd had done some weeks ago was fading now. Soiled white towels with brown streaks from when she'd first returned from the tanning parlour still lay balled on the bathroom floor.

Loosening the dressing gown belt and pulling back the flap, she crossed and uncrossed her long legs, inspecting them.

Her nail varnish was fading.

She needed a pedicure.

She sipped again at her glass of wine – this time tossing back two antidepressants with the swallow – and puffed again a few times on her cigarette.

Pulling the front of the dressing gown further open, she took a deep breath then pushed the orange tip slowly into her inner thigh and rotated it back and forth there.

Turning it steadily one way then the other, for greater effect.

The pain was immediate and welcome.

Her eyes watered and she closed them tightly, forcing the tears in tracks down her face.

The tip turned to grey ash almost immediately as the intensity of the burn faded into a secondary sting.

She closed her eyes again and let the blackened butt fall to the floor, before herself falling backward, spreadeagled onto the bed.

On the dressing table, on top of a hand mirror, sat a newly unwrapped box-cutter blade.

The soft, pale skin of her inner arm ached in anticipation of the cut.

It seemed so long ago since she had been able to revisit her cherished self-harming.

The thing that she owned.

That no-one else could take away.

Her thing.

The dull, faded scars from old cuts – dating as far back as her school days – had almost disappeared.

Or had been creatively concealed with make-up.

A routine that was second nature to her by now.

And all through this Dan Watson business.

And all through her dealings with Cecil Herringshaw.

She knew that there would be *this* payoff at the end.

This reward.

The longed-for depersonalisation.

The high of the dissociative state.

The cold, sharp caress of the blade and the deep burn waiting to make her reacquaintance like long-lost friends.

Helen remembered her first time cutting.

As a little girl of twelve years old.

An early bloomer.

Following the sometimes visits to her room by her father.

How he cried after he'd touched her.

Wondering how she'd displeased him?

The rows from downstairs. The screaming matches.

And afterward, how her mother had looked at her.

The blame and accusation in her eyes.

She had to be punished somehow.

For the way she made men behave toward her.

All through these last few months she'd had to settle for snapping hard a rubber band worn around her wrist.

Couldn't let Dan Watson see any scarring on her naked flesh.

Couldn't reveal to Cecil Herringshaw any show of weakness.

Trying to please older men… again and again.

She'd met Jamie Herringshaw at the hockey club. Rugby jocks often hung around there.

He was more her own age. It had been whirlwind.

The Herringshaws had seemed keen to welcome her into the fold.

What with her father dead and her mother in residential care with Alzheimers, it felt like a family again. Well, for a short while anyhow.

Jamie was a prick. She had no respect for him because he had no respect for himself.

Christ… she thought, *I'm a great one to be lecturing anybody about self-respect!*

Cecil had been good to her. Stood by her in many regards.

Set her up in this apartment. Helped with the PSNI job by 'disappearing' some embarrassing social services records.

He was a bad man. She knew that. She'd heard all the stories.

But you take people as you find them, don't you, as she was fond of saying.

Now Cecil had instructed that she was required to meet with him and Watson.

Since all of this business with Alex Barnard had finally come into play, it was time to 'reel him in', he'd said.

Dan Watson had arranged the meet.

In that awful dump of a semi in Stranmillis where they'd fucked a couple of times.

It would be hard but she was glad.

Relieved.

Surely to God this would be an end to it now.

No pretences this time.

No more lovey-dovey.

Fucking bastards… both of them.

She reached for the blade and slowly slipped the cutting edge out of its plastic sheath.

The long sleeves and trousers would suffice for this rendezvous.

The next spray tan and pedicure might yet be a long time coming.

58

Number 172 Stranmillis Parade, Belfast 9.

Dan Watson read again the crumpled paper tag, the words written in blue ballpoint pen.

The tag attached to the door key with matted, fraying yellow cord.

Number 172 Stranmillis Parade, Belfast 9.

It was an address that the police had used since way back in the day.

A safe house for on-the-run informants and sometimes British Army Special Ops.

From the outside it was deliberately anonymous.

Just another red brick semi, dirty lace curtains behind a high privet hedge.

Paintwork peeling, windows grimy, rusting wrought iron double gate, like the majority of student rentals that surrounded it.

The area had once been a desirable family destination for young professionals, academics and those with a bohemian inclination. But as more and more of these had moved to the suburbs, a proliferation of *For Sale* and *For Let* signs had mushroomed.

The main street had seen an explosion of fast food joints and express mini-supermarkets.

Watson ruminated on whether the entire street had anyone over the age of forty left living in it.

Number 172 Stranmillis Parade, Belfast 9.

He went outside and as had been agreed, left the key under the rotting, mottled carcass of large potted plant by the door.

What a bizarre and pathetic place to end it all.

But wasn't that what he himself had become? What his conduct, his existence had become?

Bizarre.

Pathetic.

He had used the house twice for trysts with Helen Totton.

It was straightforward enough for him to get the key.

Just walked into the duty office, opened the filing cabinet and pulled out the folder marked *Residential/Capital Assets*. In it was a clipboard to which a number of keys for properties in the area were attached, all with identifying address labels.

Their first time there, the sheets on the bed felt damp and smelled musty.

There was black spongy mould in the far corner of the room and a chill in the air.

All of this hadn't really mattered until afterward. As they lay together naked, sweating, smoking a cigarette, with little to say to each other except office talk.

He knew *now*, of course, why she had been so interested in the Barnard case.

Knew that bastard Cecil Herringshaw had been pulling the strings all along.

The second time they used the house, Helen Totton had brought cosmetics, a toothbrush, a sleeping bag, some air freshener and a flask of coffee.

At the time he'd preferred to believe that this suggested an attempt by her to make things more 'homey'.

More permanent.

More personal.

That blind, urgent, angry sex was turning into something more, perhaps.

Would they look back and laugh at the clandestine nature of all of this?

A wry smile broke from his tight lips.

In fact, she has been just making herself as comfortable as possible before putting in another shift on her back.

Number 172 Stranmillis Parade, Belfast 9.

Watson extended his big hand in front of him, sweating palm upward. It was shaking.

He brought the other hand level.

The blue-black Glock 17 standard issue semi-automatic pistol lay flat across his palm.

It felt like a toy, its lightweight plastic casing hardly suggesting the full seventeen rounds that it held in the clip.

The fabric armchair he sat in seemed to cling to the chill and damp from a house that was only occasionally occupied.

He again looked at the brass cartridge present in the chamber, a tactile metal edge protruding slightly out, immediately behind the ejection port on the right side of the slide.

The weapon was loaded and ready for use.

He pushed it down in the narrow gap between his thigh and the rough cloth of the chair where it could be easily and quickly located.

He rested his hand there.

Let it go limp.

The furnishings in the house were a mish-mash of 80s tat and Ikea self-assembly.

It made for an incongruous mix which could not rise above the overriding impression of the squalid and the seedy.

The whole property stank of cigarette smoke and dampness.

The wooden hearth surrounding the barren fireplace had

been burned and scarred black by a number of cigarette butts that had been carelessly left there by some earlier occupant.

A crushed Coke can and some biscuit wrappers lay abandoned in its mouth.

Its edges were sooty and blackened.

On the dining table sat a vase with some plastic lilies.

A beer mat had been peeled back so that someone might use it to write on.

High above him, the water tank in the loft groaned.

He had left the tap running in the bathroom following several unsuccessful attempts to throw up in there.

The fluorescent strip lighting in the kitchen hummed loudly. A moth trapped inside the translucent cover beat in vain against the plastic.

Little or no natural light seemed to permeate the living areas of Number 172 Stranmillis Parade, Belfast 9.

He had asked both Helen Totton and Cecil Herringshaw to meet with him here at 3.30pm.

He told them that he had a proposal that would take care of any continued meddling from Eban Barnard, whilst protecting the identities of both Herringshaw and Alex Barnard from any reopening of the Joseph Breslin case.

Watson was particularly keen to emphasis the results of his deliberations, which placed Councillor Herringshaw at the scene of that assault all those years ago.

It wasn't just pride in his own police work – he needed to be sure Herringshaw would attend.

Needed to hook him and bring him to a place like this, for reasons Herringshaw could not reveal to others.

As for her, well… it was nothing more than revenge.

He could live – and die – with that.

The bitch had strung him along and played him for the fool he undoubtedly was.

How could he have let it all slide away so quickly?

He was weak.

A weak, wretched man and Helen Totton had seen that somehow and used it against him.

No resolution of this debacle would be complete without her inclusion.

And he told himself that it was for Elaine.

Long-suffering, compliant Elaine.

Her natural generosity of spirit and capacity for forgiveness would not have extended to Helen Totton selling her story to the Sundays.

He felt sick again at the thought of the mess he was dumping in her lap.

And the children's of course.

But he could in conscience find no better solution to the impasse facing him.

Blackmail, professional ruin, lonely, solitary, humiliation, an old age waiting, wishing for it all to end.

It was better – much better – this way.

Watson's eyes stung with the tears now welling up in them.

He shook them free to clear his head and wiping his nose with his sleeve, steeled himself again for what he must do.

He was aware that almost as many people had died from suicide in Northern Ireland since the signing of the Good Friday Agreement as were killed during the entire Troubles.

A significant number of these were police officers who had used their own legally held firearms.

He knew this because he had recently attended the biannual seminar arranged by Human Resources for officers of sergeant's rank and above.

They had subcontracted the mental health of the force out to a high profile psychotherapy practice.

Earnest, well-meaning, touch-feely members of the caring

professions, who nodded soberly whilst taking notes on paper emblazoned with their distinctive logo.

"Please don't allow the stresses of the job to imperil your mental well-being."

Please don't blow your own brains out more like!

Add to that the recent high profile cases of love triangles resulting in murder-suicides and it all fell into place.

The press would have a field day of course.

But that hardly seemed to matter now.

What was important was that there had to be enough uncertainty around whether Watson had taken his own life or was in fact a victim of one of the other two.

In this way, Elaine's police pension could be protected and his own character perhaps redeemed, if only partially.

Suddenly Watson stiffened.

His mind had been wandering.

To the day of his passing-out parade.

To Elaine's laugh… or the way it used to be.

To a model aircraft he'd made when he was a boy.

To a song his father used to sing when coming home from the pub.

There was the noise of voices outside.

A key in the lock.

They had arrived together.

So much the better.

Probably cleaner that way.

Do them both at once.

One shot.

Him in the temple, up close.

Her in the heart.

Then…

He tensed, sat up straight and allowed his right hand to drop and rest again in the narrow space between his leg and the chair.

A colleague who had survived a terrorist shooting had once confided in him his fear that an abrupt, violent act resulting in his murder would leave his spirit suddenly dispossessed and exiled forever, in the very place that the attack had happened and at the moment of his death.

He had gathered up a stack of junk mail and bills when he'd first arrived and left them on the kitchen table in front of him.

He glanced at the transparent windows of the brown envelopes, spilled across the Formica surface like a beaten hand of cards.

Number 172 Stranmillis Parade, Belfast 9.

59

He often stayed in his room for long periods of time with the door locked.

Mother and daughter had always felt it important that he should have his own space.

His privacy.

He kept a kettle, a radio, a portable TV in there.

Sometimes the only way you could be sure of his presence at all was when he crossed the landing to use the bathroom.

"Sure he's no trouble to nobody," was how Mrs Breslin described him.

Anne knew he would go to ground following the visit by Herringshaw and the crushing disappointment regarding Molly McArdle.

It was only natural.

She didn't want to worry their mother when she'd asked after him. Asked why he hadn't gone into work. Anne reassured Mrs Breslin that he was just a little bit down in himself.

But she had been to Joe's door three times now and he had refused to answer her.

That was unlike him.

She couldn't sleep.

She was rendered distraught beyond belief at the thought of the animal who had destroyed her brother's life, only yesterday sitting below in the parlour of their own home.

She prayed to God and the Virgin that Joe did not comprehend who his callers had been.

It was bitter wound inflicted upon bitter wound.

She had heard the noise of the radio carry on all through the night.

But Joe had made no visits to the bathroom.

Anne was desperate to speak with him.

To learn what they had said to him.

If they had threatened him.

And to tell him that there was someone for everyone in this world and he was not to fret over Molly McArdle.

But if that were true, then where was *her* shoulder to cry on?

Anne did what she always did when confronted with the prospect of a solitary, loveless existence and buried her own disappointments deep down beneath selfless anxieties for her brother and mother.

Now, as she stood outside Joe's bedroom door knocking and calling once again, she wondered why the volume and the station playing had not varied for close to eighteen hours or so.

She felt icy dread rise from the well of her guts, but pushed it back down again.

Crouching, she peered through the keyhole but her view was blocked by the key in the lock on the other side.

Taking a pair of scissors, she pushed through the aperture until it fell to the floor.

What she then saw caused her to cry out in a plaintive wail that she stifled as quickly as it had escaped her.

Joe's lower body was visible. Inanimate.

He lay on the floor in an unnatural position, one arm trapped beneath his leg.

Anne's first instinct was to scream for help.

To hammer on the door and to screech his name.

But there was no-one there to help her.

Her mother's voice came from downstairs. "Anne... did you call me?"

She closed her eyes and gathered herself.

"No Mammy... I just took a fit of sneezing."

"Oh. Will you ask Joe if he wants tea?"

"I will."

"Do you want a drop yourself?"

"No Mammy… thanks…"

Her mind was racing.

A fall? A stroke?

Her brother might be dead or dying.

It took all of her composure to collect herself and enter the kitchen where Mrs Breslin was pulling on the lid of the biscuit tin as the kettle boiled.

Anne took a deep breath. "Mammy, Joe says he'll take a drop of tea but he's dying for one of them snowball buns he loves."

"Sure I've nothing in… you know I don't do my grocery shopping 'til tomorrow."

"Sure put your coat on and nip down to the wee home bakery."

"Their stuff is very dear. He's a bandit, that one," she complained.

Anne was opening her purse and pressing a ten-pound note into her mother's hand.

She tried hard to stop her own hands from shaking.

Tried hard to push away the image of her brother upstairs, slowly choking to death on his own vomit.

"That's far too much!" scolded the old woman.

"Get a few fresh creams and a bap… I'd go myself but I'm waiting for an important phone call from work."

Mrs Breslin pulled on her coat and searched for her shopping bag. "You say Joe wants snowballs?"

"Aye."

"See if you can get him to come down for his tea… I'll not be long." She paused at the door. "They're slave drivers in thon place of yours!"

"I know Mammy, I know. I'll get a pot of tea made."

Anne waited for the garden gate to close, the metallic clang and click.

It seemed like forever.

She stood fighting tears, pushing her nails into the palms of her hands in an act of sheer willpower.

When she was sure her mother was gone, Anne flung open the front door and flew as fast as her feet would carry her to Sweeney's house next door.

Tommy answered her urgent knocking.

"It's Anne Breslin," she heard him say to his wife Rita as he turned the deadbolt.

"Tommy, it's our Joe… can you come?"

Seeing Anne's face, the man followed her in next door and bounded the stairs two at a time, apprising himself of the situation instantly.

"I can get my tools and take the hinges off, but…"

Anne's expression answered his question.

"Stand back then."

He aimed a kick at the base of the handle and it splintered but held.

A second broke the door handle off completely.

A third and the door opened a small way, pushing against Joe's prone body.

Tommy placed his shoulder in the gap and levered it wide enough to slip though.

He immediately dropped to his knees and placing his ear close to Joe's mouth, looked for a pulse.

Anne peered in through the opening.

On top of Joe's bed were a number of paper chemist bags and a small pile of brown pill bottles.

He must have been stockpiling his medications, she thought, and mentally ran through what he might have taken.

Rita Sweeney now arrived on the landing.

"Antidepressants," said Anne, aloud but to herself.

"Will one of the two of youse phone an ambulance… he's still breathing!" shouted Tommy from inside the room.

"I'll do it," said Anne. "Rita, will you keep an eye out for my mammy when she comes back and take her into your house?"

The operator asked her for the nature of the emergency.

Anne heard herself say, "My brother took an overdose."

It came out of her sounding almost matter-of-fact.

"Just bear with me while I take a few details."

She remembered Joe building her a doll's house, carrying her on his shoulders down Royal Avenue, sitting up nights, caring for a sick dog he'd brought home.

"Do you know what he might have taken?"

She felt anger swell up inside her.

Resented these 'by the numbers' protocols.

Felt that her brother was being judged somehow.

How could they know what he'd been through?

What he'd had to endure?

The daily prolongation of a body and soul in torment, representing some kind of pitiful existence.

And they couldn't even leave him that.

"He's taken just about all that he could take," she said and began to cry quietly.

60

When the smiling anaesthetist leaned over Eban's scrubbed and prepped body, he asked him to count backwards from ten.

Despite the adrenaline and dread rising up in him, such was the potency of the general anaesthetic being administered that it was unlikely that he would make it to seven before oblivion overtook him.

Not such a bad thing perhaps.

The anaesthetist looked at Eban like he was some kind of simpleton when – being pushed on a gurney into theatre – Eban had asked him, rather matter-of-factly, if he was familiar with the phenomenon of anaesthesia awareness; of being awake during surgery.

Of the awful prospect of being *compos mentis* whilst undergoing a major operation?

If he knew the percentage figures for this… and if he was taking steps to avoid it?

The prospect of this locked-in syndrome – of some Edgar Allan Poe-like premature burial vibe – had been fucking with his sensibilities from more or less the time when the orderly had been around to shave off all superfluous body hair so that tape and tubes might affix more easily.

This was exacerbated when he learned that Mr Khan would be performing the procedure.

And that his heart muscle had sustained considerable trauma during the incident.

It was explained to him solemnly that irrespective of the success of his operation, this damage could not be reversed.

Only hours earlier, before they'd arrived to take him down to pre-op, Eban had looked around the ward as a man might look upon death row.

The black second hand on the functional Roman numeral clock seemed to judder noisily around the face, thudding out every second.

Every tick. Every tock.

6.17am and 32 seconds and counting.

The pre-op ward, despite attempts to remodel it as a modern, cutting-edge facility, could not seem to completely shake off the aura of some 19th century institutional workhouse.

Or so it seemed to him.

It was quiet and dark.

Few words were spoken and only then in whispers.

Three elderly men in the ward stirred occasionally.

His fellows on the scaffold in striped pyjamas; they had all arrived just that day. Mercifully, no time for pleasantries or discussions on the things to come.

Sighs and coughs and farts and the pulling up of blankets to throats, as if to ward off the coming of the blade and the chest-splitter.

That inevitable first incision.

Their families had been in of course.

Quiet prayers whispered up in entreaty.

Soft crying and the repeated exhortation of the need to be strong.

Seeing him alone and cowed, one elderly woman took pity on Eban. "You're so young for something like this," she said.

He thought that strange.

How he hadn't felt young for the longest time.

Had he ever?

If so, he couldn't recall it now.

All he felt was alone.

Utterly alone.

I have no-one to blame but myself, he thought.

He had consciously rejected belonging.

Fought against it.

Ran from it.

And it had led him here.

To the sovereignty of self.

The sovereignty of one.

They had asked him to sign the form acknowledging the possibility of a fatality should there be 'complications', and asked him again about his next of kin.

Eban misunderstood and told them about the family grave, where his father and mother were buried.

But now Alex was buried there as well, and with his ex-wife and kids having gone to live in Australia after their divorce.

He thought again about his brother, the policeman.

Thought now, in this moment, of the reasons that had so driven him in his quest to expose and discredit Alex.

Blood will have blood.

Abel had risen from the dead and killed Cain.

It was an unacceptable sacrifice unto the Lord.

And it was without honour.

Alex had always loved his garden; loved to tend his roses.

They were the last thing he saw as his blood soaked the ground and mixed with the soil that they grew in.

The soil he had fought for.

The soil he now lay in.

Eban had always thought that he would be interred alongside them.

But the council had passed an edict some years ago reducing the number of corpses in any one family plot from four to three.

Whatever happened.

Now or in the future.

He would be interred alone.

The pre-surgery relaxant they had given him to lessen anxiety was making him woozy and morbidly pessimistic about his prospects.

Eban wished that he had written down somewhere the words he would like on his gravestone.

He remembered again the text from Psalm 91 that he had first learned in Sunday school with John Parkes.

In the white mission hall under the dark silhouette of the Black Mountain.

He that dwelleth in the shelter of the most high shall abide in the shadow of the almighty.

His eyes felt heavy but underneath the enveloping chemical blanket he could discern the adrenaline coursing through his body in expectation of the coming ordeal.

Abruptly he was aware of two figures standing by his bed.

When his failing focus revealed to him that they were not in medical uniforms, he squinted hard to make out their appearance in the half-light.

Anne Breslin and her mother moved uncertainly closer to his bedside.

"We saw you when they brought you in… through A&E," said Anne. "They said you didn't have anybody with you, so me and Mammy… well…"

She hesitated, seemingly uncertain as to whether this intrusion was appropriate.

"Do you need anything?"

Eban was momentarily speechless.

He coughed, clearing his throat, and pulled the bedclothes up around him a little.

He reached over for the glass of water on the bedside table, but Anne, seeing this, reached for it first and handed it to him.

Eban drank, then spoke. "But that was hours ago… have you been here all this time?"

Anne exchanged a glance with her mother and then said, "We're here with Joe…. he's… very bad…"

Anne reached across, and taking her mother's hand, held it to her.

"Would you not go back up to the café, Mammy… order us both a cup of tea? I'll be up in a wee minute."

Mrs Breslin turned to leave, but before she did she turned back again and reaching into her handbag, produced a small crucifix.

Leaning over Eban, she pressed it to his lips whispering, "Pray to the blessed Mother for grace and deliverance."

He felt it would be churlish not to comply, but her action had only served to further alert him to the gravity of the situation.

Mrs Breslin shuffled out, dabbing at her eyes with a hanky.

"No atheists in foxholes," said Eban, feeling awkward and reaching for some gallows humour.

Anne didn't respond.

"What happened to Joe?" Eban suddenly became animated. "Was it that bastard Herringshaw?"

"In a way…" she said.

Eban understood her ambiguity immediately. "Ahh, God no… he didn't…"

Anne shook her head. "You never got to know him… if you had, you'd realise what a softy he was… how easily hurt he could be…"

"I've let him down," said Eban, and he bit down on his lip. "*Again…*"

"No… no…" she protested. "He never would have blamed you… probably wouldn't even blame your brother if truth be told."

"I don't understand."

"Joe lived his life one day at a time, and he tried never – ever – to look back…"

She started to cry. "My God… I'm talking about him like he's already gone."

"How is he?"

"He took a whole stash of meds – antidepressants… blood pressure… painkillers – he has a fifty-fifty fighting chance, they say. It's just… *I don't think he wants to fight anymore.*"

363

She pushed her dark hair back from her face and despite the worry and sorrow in her eyes Eban saw a grace and poise in her that he'd glimpsed before, on the night she had taken pity on him for the first time.

"Mammy doesn't know about you... I just explained that you're somebody who knew Joe a long time ago."

"Thank you."

"He was never the same... what they did to him... he couldn't have weans of his own, you know, and his girlfriend Delores... well, you couldn't expect her to... the way he was. And then Molly, and seeing Herringshaw again... it's just a pity, that's all."

"And he wasn't bitter?" asked Eban, disbelievingly.

"Our Joe" – she smiled with affection – "didn't have a bitter bone in his body."

"Did he ever... talk about it... what happened... *that night*, I mean?"

"Never – well, not to me anyway. But Mammy said he wasn't himself, you know... after it, I mean. It must have been hard – he was so young; his whole young life... his manhood taken away..."

Anne could see that Eban was deeply affected by what she was saying, and quickly regretted saying it.

But having no-one herself to confide in, to articulate her feelings, a great wave of sorrow rose up in her and she could not help herself.

"It's just... I just think he wanted to give up, you know? He was just tired, God love him, and now... now I'm frightened that they're going to ask me to decide whether to switch off his machine or not..." She looked distraught. "I shouldn't have to decide something like that..."

Anne looked like she might collapse under the weight of it and lose herself in a torrent of anguish. She gulped back tears twice with deep inhalations of breath, then somehow she pulled herself back from the brink.

Eban reached out and took her hand.

It seemed the right thing to do.

It felt delicate, soft and cool.

She did not pull away.

"Your mother… do you think she'd want to know? Would she want them caught and punished?"

Anne seemed to think about this for a moment. "So much suffering… so much death… no, no, it's in the past. It won't change anything, or give him back the years he lost. I know she forgives."

"But how can you be sure? Why would she do that… why would Joe… *why would any of us?*"

Anne looked at him, and furrowing her brow, allowed herself a weak smile.

"Sure, to keep Jesus in his glory and the saints rejoicing."

She pressed his hand between both of her own, laid it gently back on his chest, before turning from him and walking slowly from the ward.

Eban was overwhelmed by the strength of emotion, the unexpected surge of affection he felt toward her.

When they arrived to take him to theatre sometime after that, he was ready.

One of the porters wheeling his trolley spoke of the breaking news story on morning radio.

Of how the Attorney General was talking complete amnesty for all past crimes.

A move that would render Alex and Fish, Tootsie and Sledger, Anto and all those involved in terrorist and sectarian crime over all the years exempt from prosecution.

The porter told the nurse it was all about 'making peace with the past'.

But where would *he* find his peace? He had carried around his guilt and his frustration for a lifetime, and for what?

No-one cares about the victims, the families, the dead and those left behind them, he thought. *Their heartbreak, their long, slow, lonely creep toward the end… without their loved ones…*

They were made to feel like the ghosts at the peace.

Expected to keep quiet for the sake of the next generation.

For the sake of a future they could not share in.

An awkward, tragic postscript that belonged to the newsreels and libraries.

To be consigned there and forgotten save for empty platitudes and memorial Sundays in draughty churches.

When the smiling anaesthetist leaned over Eban's scrubbed and prepped body, he asked him to count backwards from ten. The anaesthetic pressed down upon him in what felt like a relentless wave of shimmering chemical subjugation.

A calm voice in his head told him that he was about to die for some short while.

But unlike Elvis, he would never leave the building.

Momentarily, a brief eddy of recent and long passed memories bled together.

But no corridor of light.

No celestial waiting room for him.

Just the clunk and hiss of pumps and tubes.

Pushing thin red lines down drip, up catheter.

Nothingness.

Not fear.

Nor regret.

Nor suffering.

Nor loss

Just void.

Until returning, dulled and sore, perhaps to touch her hand and see her face again.

10

9

8

7